# Chakra Kong
## part 2:
## Sex
## or
## Busier Than a Three-Legged Cat Trying to Squeeze Blood from the Tip of an Iceberg

## By
## S.T. Gulik

The following prophesy takes place far in the future. Nothing/no entity referred to in these texts will exist for well over one-hundred years from the date published (except for the immortal/eternal ones who are not litigious). This is exactly how shit goes down as revealed by extradimensional beings.

# SEX

Words with a * next to them indicate that more information can be found in the Appendix. Everything you need to understand this world is in the main text, but it's there if you want to delve a little deeper into the history. A lot has happened between now and when this story takes place, and I didn't want to bog the story down with trivia.

Thanks for giving my book a shot. -S.T.

# SPIES WITHOUT A FACE

Adhra pointed her sonic keychain at the lock on the morgue's side entrance and jiggled the handle. A few seconds later there was a crunch as it came off in her hand.

She moved aside and let Kaden nudge the door with his shoulder. It popped open with a little squeak, like someone had stepped on a mouse. It was lunchtime, so she expected that everyone to be out, but her team went in first, just in case.

When Paco signaled the room was clear, Adhra followed Kaden through an office and into a large rectangular room and cringed as the formaldehyde hit her sinuses. Harsh fluorescent lights reflected off pale green tiles giving everything a sickly seafoam cast. The five plastic autopsy tables and their rolling steel counterparts stood empty. It was all methodically tidy, sterile. It reminded her of her mother.

Adhra gazed into the empty waste basket. Something about empty garbage bags had always given her the willies. As soon as they were unfolded and flicked into being, they took on an especially desolate and unnatural quality. She saw a dead swollen mouth gaping hungrily, unable to feed itself.

Kaden followed her gaze. "Slow day."

She nodded and gave the signal to move ahead. Her men threw open the door to the basement and surged down the steps. She pictured a janitor just finishing up, a good man who worked hard and had the respect of his coworkers despite his position in life. She imagined the shock on his face, the stricken expression as he dropped his mop and raised his hands, sputtering questions as to why a squadron of Iiites* was tramping dirt across his sparkling floor, then exploding, spattering his life's work with his life essence, sizzling.

Adhra wasn't a sadist. This was what her brain did when there was something scary coming she didn't want to think about. Having just betrayed her government and killed her boss, she wasn't looking forward to her meeting with his smarter, crazier brother. Even if he believed her story, she'd still have to answer for her failure. Whose brain wouldn't tiptoe off to frolic in some menial distraction?

Paco gave the all-clear.

She was glad. It was best for everyone if they could pass through unnoticed. She was a spy, after all. Like Jacob said, "If people can tell you were there, you're doing it wrong."

She closed the door and followed Kaden down to the room where people were stored like bowling shoes. Three rows of ten square metal doors lined the walls. Most of her men were gathered around the mop sink next to the stairs. The access grate that would take them home was wired to a bomb, but it looked simple enough she didn't feel it necessary to leave the room while Kaden disarmed it. On the other side of the stairs was another enclave housing a dusty Crap Cooker* that had been used for cremation before the NAADP* made it illegal to destroy pre-animated corpses.

Adhra opened the nearest door and found the compartment empty. She moved to the next and found it empty as well, so she finished out the row. "It really is a slow day. Now that the war's over, the hospitals might go out of business."

She closed the last door and stared at her reflection in the haze of brushed steel. There was something very Zen about being blurry, the eroticism of merging with cold metal. She was a living ghost. No artist could create a more apt representation of her life.

Thirty seconds later she was bored. She put her back to the doors and watched Kaden fiddle with the bomb. He took his time, which she supposed was a good thing when disarming an explosive, but the delay grated on her nerves. She also had a tendency to make puns when she got bored.

Her sinuses weren't helping her mood. It felt like angry puffer fish were fighting behind her nose. It was probably a lack of Victory* making her antsy.

I guess it's time to feed the beast. She glanced at the clock on the wall. Twenty-seven minutes. God, I really need a treatment.

Adhra turned so the troops couldn't see, pulled the vial out of her purse and tapped the last of it into her fingernail. She sniffed it up, slid the vial back into her bra, and flipped around in one smooth motion.

That's better.

She took a deep breath and exhaled all the tension from her body. Now that her head was clear, she noticed Kaden looking nervous.

"How's it coming?"

"Got it." A gentle, sewery aroma seeped into the basement air as he pried away the cover.

Adhra half-smiled and cleared her throat. "Home, sweet home."

He smiled too, but weakly and with worried eyes. "Not for long."

She narrowed her eyes to remind him the M.I.L.F could be listening.

Eyes to the ground, he set the grate aside and returned to heel.

Kaden wasn't the brightest, but then soldiers didn't have to be bright. They had to be big, and size he had in spades. He was six-foot-nine and built like a gladiator. More importantly, he was in love with her, making him loyal to a fault. She wouldn't have minded taking a test drive, but she couldn't risk losing that level of devotion. Men were so much easier to control before they got what they wanted. Hence rule number three; never sleep with your subordinates.

She lifted the hem of her little black dress a few inches higher than necessary and climbed down the ladder to the carpeted hall. The stink brought back a flood of memories from her childhood, but both faded long before the last of her men had joined her. The slow passage between worlds had always been a problem. Luckily there were enough buildings with sewer access that they rarely had to migrate in plain view.

One by one, the troops planted their boots on the moldy carpet of Corridor 32, one of the long, segmented passages that served as a pedestrian highway connecting densely populated areas. There had been a proposal to put in People Movers, but Adhra had made sure that didn't happen. She liked the posh hotel look. Like many areas damaged by the war, the 32 had been shut down and most of the areas it serviced evacuated. The stillness of a once bustling place had the same sucking emptiness as an empty garbage bag or a dead grandmother. But there was something else. Something felt wrong.

For one thing, Jacob should have been waiting for them. He was always going on about the virtues of punctuality, poise and patience.

That prissy little fuck better not have turned on me.

His tardiness was definitely a bad sign, but that wasn't it either.

"I have a bad feeling," Adhra said, glancing around. "This area wasn't hit until a few weeks ago, but look at the mold on that painting. It's months overdue for a change." She crouched to inspect the little bronze trash can. "This garbage bag has dust on it."

Areas like this were constantly being booby-trapped by both sides. The Nrrds'* bomb on the manhole cover was obvious, but the Fist would have had time to hide theirs more thoroughly.

Kaden nodded. "This area's probably rigged. We should wait here for somebody to respond to the sensors. There are cameras everywhere. They must know it's us."

"You're assuming someone's watching the cameras. If this area's as abandoned as it looks, we could be waiting a long time."

Kaden barked to his men. "Moe, sweep north. Paco, sweep south. Everybody else stay close."

The designated soldiers made off in opposite directions, searching for anything out of the ordinary. Moe was headed towards the M.I.L.F., so all eyes were on him as he approached the door. After a thorough inspection, he opened it slowly and scanned the other side.

Glancing back hopefully, he stepped through and exploded. The walls and ceiling tumbled onto him, sealing the path.

"Motherfucker!" Kaden put his fist through the wall.

Adhra brushed the dust off her dress. "Somebody's bound to have heard that."

"Paco," Kaden screamed, "come back." He dropped his satchel and plopped into one of the decorative chairs, releasing a fine green mist of spores. He jumped up coughing and slapping at his clothes. The rage and embarrassment were too much for him to process at once, so his brain reset. "How long do you think it'll take?"

Adhra shook the debris out of her short black hair. "It depends on whether or not they've moved." She picked a bit of stucco out from between her breasts and dropped it in the trash. "From what I hear, Xavier has been pretty paranoid lately. Anything could have happened after he cut off communications."

Kaden glanced angrily at the chair. "Well, we could go back to the morgue. At least there we can sit without having to worry about booby-traps or bronchial infections."

Adhra wrote a short note on the wall with her lipstick. 'Went topside. You owe me a lipstick. Addy.' She dropped the tube in the waste basket. Glossy Bordeaux was too dark for her complexion, anyway.

Kaden gave the order and the troops climbed the ladder one by one. Just as the last soldier was pulling himself out of the sink, the knob on the basement door began to turn. The guards sprang into action. One flung it open while the other yanked the interloper down the steps. Jacob landed at the bottom, yelping as his left shoulder popped from its socket.

Kaden rushed over and snapped it back into place. Adhra chuckled and walked over slowly.

She noticed his shoes. Even in the worst of times Jacob managed to look crisp as a million-dollar-bill. His penny loafers were freshly shined, his khakis perfectly creased, the long-sleeve baby-blue button-up shirt hung on him as neatly as it would on a department store dummy. Even his hair was immaculate, and all this after a tumble down the stairs. Even she couldn't look good that effortlessly. What did he do, sacrifice children to Paul Poiret? It was disgusting.

Adhra smiled. "How was your trip?"

Jacob sniffed the snot back into his head and glared at her.

"I was only trying to cheer you up. You know, ha, ha, levity."

One of the soldiers helped him to his feet.

"I am not in the mood. You wouldn't believe what I had to put up with today. Xavier wanted to greet you with a court-martial. I managed to talk him out of it, but he's so paranoid these days I can't guarantee what sort of reception you'll get. It was a miracle I was able to come at all."

"I take it things have deteriorated?"

"Oh god, don't get me started. You know how bad it was before. Well, it turns out the Mittons are psychically linked. He knows his brother died a long painful death and he suspects betrayal. He's already killed a quarter of his guards because he thought they were double agents. The M.I.L.F. is crumbling like a big stale cookie, and Xavier's the retard that's eating it."

Adhra's eyes went wide with shock.

"Oh, don't worry. They can't hear us. I'm the one in charge of bugging everything, remember?"

Adhra cocked an eyebrow. *He'd better be right.* "Yeah, so you don't think it's a good idea for me to go see him?"

"On the contrary, I need you to use your special talents to cool him down long enough for me to get this mess cleaned up. Of course, there's also a possibility he'll have you executed on sight. Best to get your story straight before you talk to him."

"It's straight. Let's get this over with. We have a schedule to keep."

Jacob gestured towards the steps then grimaced and grabbed his shoulder.

"Why can't we take the sewers?"

"There are booby traps everywhere. All the manholes are welded shut. I had to have one cut out just to get to the surface. Xavier's so paranoid that he's painted himself into a corner. All Max would have to do to take us all out would be to repeat the stunt he pulled on his first raid. He wouldn't even have to come down this time."

"He can't do that, though. If he kills us all, there won't be anyone to fill the power vacuum. I can hardly see him stepping up to take the reins of the world on his own."

They shared a chuckle at the thought of Max trying to solve the world's problems.

"Too right. Well, shall we go?" Jacob gestured towards the stairs again, this time with his good arm.

✱✱✱✱✱

Meanwhile, back at the penthouse.

"Prost!" Max slammed his shot glass on the bar and slid it in line with its brethren.

Hawk attempted to do the same, but instead slid out of his chair and consciousness altogether.

"Ha, ha, I am victorious." Max's exuberant fist jerk almost landed him on top of his friend. "You, comrade, must learn to hold your fire-water without being burned."

He braced himself and bobbled his head around the room looking for Adhra, but all he saw was a bunch of Nrrds and blood-crusted velvet furniture.

Oh yeah, she left.

The way dusk was rubbing against the decimated skyline made him miss her even more.

Thousands of feet below, rescue crews were still trying to figure out where to start digging. Six skyscrapers made a lot of rubble. He wanted to crawl out a window, climb down the wreckage and run to her, but that would seem clingy.

Probably get my drunk ass killed in the process. At least I wouldn't have to smell Felix anymore.

He cleared his throat and leaned against the bar. The whistling of the window Hawk had shot out was driving him crazy. The smell stayed the same, but now it was always fucking cold.

"Goddamn I hate this place."

Felix grew riper by the minute. The acrid black-blood stench was rapidly being overtaken by the richer, more bombastic reek of rotten flesh. Those with weaker constitutions had retreated to the lower floors with the body, but Hedorah, Pope, Magog, Blister, and Wormwood had laid the organs out on various tables and were picking through them like it was a buffet at Herschell Gordon Lewis's house.

Max ran his fingers through his scraggly mountain-man beard, smearing the greasy fibrous mess in search of his lips. "Hurry it up, guys. He's not gettin' any fresher."

Pope looked up from the sickly, purple meat. "Neither are you."

Hedorah added, "Yeah, you smell like a gas-station bathroom."

The others ignored them and continued working. Apparently, all they needed to get back to normal was a good old-fashioned vivisection. Max was happy to see them in a good mood, but he couldn't help being a little disturbed.

He glanced back at the wall of booze behind the bar and thought about trying the brown stuff he'd never heard of on the top shelf. He tried to climb over the bar, but his lack of motor function made it more trouble than it was worth. He plopped back onto his stool and turned around.

Cheeky was curled up in the center of a big red chair with a look of irritation on his face. He was having trouble getting comfortable because of the helmet Magog had made for him out of an Iiite skull. It was twice as big as his head and had to be held on with a strap, but damn if it wasn't the cutest thing Max had ever seen. The need to feel the patchwork of fleshy mounds on his cheeks and the gentle kneading of suckers yanked Max off his barstool and drew him forward.

As he wobbled forth, a little voice in the back of his head asked how long it would take for the Nrrd's curiosity to get the better of them once the war was over. The image of Cakey staring up at him from the floor at Bio-Corp punched him in the stomach. It was all he could do to keep from soaking the carpet with the previous round.

He held his breath and tried to focus on one spot on the carpet. The little fibers swam in and out of focus in kaleidoscopic waves of nausea. He hadn't meant to drink this much, but it had been forever since he'd been able to cut loose. If bringing down the Iiite's military branch didn't earn him the right to get good and palsied, nothing did.

He was stumbling toward a divan for a nap when Emma appeared in front of him.

He screamed and stumbled backward, tripping over Hawk and bashing his head against the bar. Luckily the booze had wrapped him in a few inches of invisible cotton.

"Dammit, I told you to stop doing that," he slurred.

"Sorry, I had to be sure I wasn't followed. Please tell me you aren't as drunk as you look."

"You couldn't have decloaked in the elevator? I could have died." Max attempted to climb his bar-stool, slipped and banged his front teeth against the rungs.

Emma examined the back of his head. "You'll be fine. Let's get some coffee in you. Come on." She took his hand and attempted to pull him to his feet. He didn't make it. She grabbed his other hand and dragged him toward a couch.

Max whined through a mouthful of carpet. "Leave me alone. I'm fine."

Emma groaned and let him go. His arms hit the floor like dead fish. The carpet was so comfortable he immediately fell asleep.

✳✳✳✳✳

Emma stared down in disbelief. "God! How much did you drink? Can somebody give me a hand, please?"

When no one else acknowledged her, Hedorah stomped over, helped her drag him onto the couch then returned to his work.

She set Max up straight and held his eyes open. "Hmm, nobody home."

Cheeky squirmed over, looking a little concerned and a lot disgusted. He crawled up Max's chest to sniff his breath. Looking genuinely worried, he planted two suckers on each cheek and gave him a good shake. Receiving no response, he repositioned himself on the back of the couch and took on an expression of deep thought.

Emma grabbed a fistful of Max's hair and slapped him as hard as she could. Still no response, so she turned her attention to Pope. "I need you to give Max a message when he sobers up."

Pope continued working. "Write it down. Can't you see I'm busy?"

"Stop pretending to know what you're looking at and listen to me." She grabbed Felix's digestive tract and flung it behind the bar. "Xavier's gone crazy. He's not talking to anybody. From what I could piece together from his muttering he knows Adhra betrayed him and that Max is still alive. You'll all be walking into a trap tomorrow."

Pope frowned. "For a girl whose specialty is stealth, you are remarkably proficient at obstreperous behavior."

Emma's cheeks were shaking with rage. "I spent the better part of a year trapped underground, trying to get into Xavier's big freaky head. I almost died three times trying to find my way back. The least you can do is listen to what I have to say."

Pope looked at her like she was a bratty little sister who just wanted attention.

"What is the point of spying if nobody will listen to what I find out?"

Pope let out an exasperated sigh. "So we're up against a powerful madman who may know we're coming for him. Well, snafu to you too. Can I have my digestive tract back?"

Emma growled. "It's more than that. He has toys you don't know about, powerful stuff that mixes quantum physics with the occult. I didn't even know what I was looking at half the time.

"The only way we're going to win is to nuke that section of the city. On the up-side, Xavier's so paranoid he's gotten himself trapped in a remote area with only one exit. I stole plans for a device that can teleport an atom wherever we want. We can entangle some plutonium then teleport one to their base and smash the other at the power plant. Instant victory."

Pope looked amused. "As much as I would love to try that, Max isn't going to appreciate you nuking his girlfriend."

Emma knitted her brow. "Girlfriend?"

"You're not a very good spy, are you? Girlfriend. You know, significant other. He and Adhra have apparently been rutting like cockroaches on Spanish fly this whole time. It's how he managed to get this far. I suspect it's also the explanation for the see-saw anomaly."

"What's the see-saw anomaly?"

Pope stood and walked behind the bar to retrieve his project. "It's our term for the problem we were having during the main part of the war where we were taking turns winning with the Iiites. We won every other battle, so neither side ever got ahead. It seemed deliberate, but nobody considered the possibility our leader was taking orders from a third party. In retrospect, given that everything he said from the moment he returned was a lie, we would probably do well to toss him off the roof before he sobers up. Unfortunately, it's a bit late in the day to be changing management."

"Well, that would explain a lot. I only knew she was supplying information. It makes sense she'd be getting something in return, but can you prove Max killed his own troops?"

Pope laid the organs out on the bar and inspected them for damage. "No, it's just a hypothesis. It doesn't really matter. We won."

Emma thought her head might explode. "What is wrong with you?"

"Is that a rhetorical question?"

"Have I ever mentioned that I hate you?"

Pope looked startled and hurt. "Why would you hate me?"

Emma went back to Max, grabbed his hair and gave him a good shake. "Wake up you worthless lush!"

She let him go. His head slid down the couch, and sprayed the right cushion with eighteen-year-old bourbon. The combination of smells and liquid trickling through his matted beard made her gag.

"We're fucked. We are absolutely fucked."

Hedorah threw a small blue organ at her. "Will you please shut the fuck up?! I'm trying to work."

"All right, that's it." Emma grabbed a plasma-cannon and scrambled onto the bar. "The Iiites that are on our side have probably been killed. The most powerful man in the world is playing with weapons of mass-destruction while suffering a mental breakdown. Our leaders are passed out drunk, and nobody seems to care. So, I'm sorry if I'm disturbing you, but somebody needs to pay me some goddamn attention right fucking now or I'm going to kill you all myself!" She punctuated her tirade by blowing several holes in the ceiling.

Everyone stopped and stared at the darkening clouds above.

"Look, if we can't nuke them, I need to get back now. I'm missing some very important stuff. I came to warn you that you're all going to die if you go down there. Does anyone have anything to say about that?"

Wormwood cracked a wry smile. "Looks like it's going to rain."

# THE CLOSET OF LOST SOULS

Jacob led them through the city and down a manhole behind the restrooms at the Igor Stanislavski Commemorative Park*. Adhra stepped off the ladder and turned to find Cornelius and a gaggle of Fisties standing at the intersection of the narrow passage and the main hall. It would be a stretch to call them soldiers. They were shell-shocked puppies waiting for their chains to be jerked.

The flickering of the sparse yellow light made Cornelius look even more ghoulish than usual. IIis cracked, pockmarked skin bore little resemblance to flesh. It was too white, too powdery and stretched too tight by cut rate surgeons. Adhra had always wondered how a man this rich and powerful could look like that after having work done. It suited him, though. She wouldn't have been surprised if he'd gone to the best and requested the undertaker special. She wanted to swipe her nails across his cheek just to see if they would come away clotted with blood or wax.

She forced a smile. "Corny, fancy seeing you here."

Cornelius's lip curled into a tremulous sneer. He seemed happy to see her, which was a very bad sign. She'd been trying to get him kicked off the high council for years, and he knew it.

Cornelius was the political equivalent of a raven. He was the grand marshal of the parade of death and misery. Worse, he was an out-of-the-closet pedophile with the body of an undertaker and the personality of a pointed stick. The thought of his taxidermy eyes with their hot-pink wetly sagging lids towering over a shivering child, that grey little tongue sliding across thin bloodless lips in anticipation...

Still, in a way she had to respect him. It couldn't have been easy for a man like that to get into a position of power. Rumor was that he had something on everybody, and it had to be some pretty interesting shit to give him power over a bunch of shameless hedonists like the M.I.L.F.

Cornelius's rancid wormlike lips twisted into a bow. "So good to see you."

"I bet."

"I've been asked to accompany you to—" He made the secret gesture for the area so secure it didn't have a name.

She'd heard rumors about this place, pillow-talk mostly, but she'd never been able to learn anything specific.

"Why?" She asked simply to annoy him.

"You should know because of the very nature of the place that I can't answer that."

"My men are tired. Can they at least freshen up?"

"They can do as they please. You alone have been summoned."

"I don't suppose I could freshen up."

Cornelius's smile grew twistier.

Jacob raised his brow apologetically. "Well then, I guess we'll be off."

Jacob and her men followed the Fisties down the northeast corridor.

"Lead the way." Nervousness was an alien emotion to her, but it was there now, squirming in her mind like bot fly larvae.

Cornelius led her down a long, ruined hallway, deep into the old Fist training facility. It was one of the sectors destroyed by the war. The caved-in areas forced them to snake through a seemingly endless series of rooms that were only in marginally better shape. More than one had holes in the ceiling large enough she caught glimpses of buildings on the street above. She was grateful for the added light, but less for the small showers of grit that blew into her face whenever a car passed.

"Isn't there a safer way to get to this place? I can hear the asphalt cracking."

"It is safe enough. We have sensors measuring the structural integrity."

"Assuming they still work. It doesn't look like anybody's been here in months."

The next door opened into a hallway that was in slightly better condition. The supports, walls and ceilings had all been patched up, but the rest lay in ruins. The carpet was rotted to bits and the figures in the portraits stood in a green fog of mold. The shiny new surveillance equipment was only sign the hallway was still in use.

It was a brilliant hiding place. Even if she had cross referenced the maintenance plans with destroyed areas she wouldn't have seen anything unusual. Max would never think to look here on his own. She hoped she could send a messenger before Xavier did away with her.

Cornelius stopped by a door marked "supplies" and cracked a poisonous smile. "Here we are. Ladies first." He stooped to reach the handle, twisted the knob and walked backward, releasing a gust of musty purple air like gas escaping a dead Muppet.

Adhra shivered as the wind tainted her flesh. What she saw was impossible. They were underground. There was no way a door could open into a forest. She wanted to run, but something drew her forward.

She'd been playing chicken with life ever since she was a kid. Nothing had killed her yet, so she gathered her wits and stepped in — or out. She wasn't sure.

"Enjoy your stay," Cornelius hissed as he closed the door.

"Hey, wait. Where am I? Where the hell am I supposed to go?"

The door creaked open and Cornelius stooped to peer inside. "You know exactly where you are. Follow the path. Xavier is waiting for you." The door closed and disappeared into the murk.

Death ran his finger up her spine. She could feel the darkness seeping through her clothes, as if the oxygen itself was malevolent. The wind was the bloody breath of a predator.

Bent trees lined a long, narrow forest trail, pulsing with a sound like distress signals ground out by metal insects dying in the maw of something worse. If not for the barely perceptible purple light, she wouldn't have been able to see at all. She stumbled forward with only a vague sense of her surroundings, drawn forward as if by some alien will she was powerless to oppose.

The darkness began to curdle. A smell like burning copper flashed across her palate as the darkness bubbled, burst and shrank away. Xavier stood in a field next to a huge pulsing machine the color of dirty bubblegum. It was alive, shivering off waves of pain, but how?

"Please, join me." Xavier showed his teeth in that raw, indecipherable rictus grin he used instead of a smile. It stretched across his giant palm like a torn valance. The small arm between his legs waved for her to come closer.

He'd always been the creepier of the two. Strange how twins could be so dissimilar. Felix had been concrete, concise, even simple at times, but in a brilliant way. She had gotten past his appearance and occasionally even enjoyed him, but Xavier made everything feel like rape: not just the sex, but the conversations, the looks. Xavier could rape you from a photograph.

She strapped on the smile she'd come up with just for him and ran into his arms. He embraced her with all five of them, the smallest passing between her legs to caress the small of her back.

She searched his eyes, but he was as unreadable as ever. He hadn't killed her, so she kissed him like she'd been lost in the desert and his spit was the first moisture she'd seen in days. Something writhed in her peripheral vision. She broke away and saw everything moving as if the fabric of reality was alive and intent on untangling itself.

The questions stuck in her throat, but Xavier answered her anyway.

"This place is complicated. The rules here are different, but you are in no danger. Suffice it to say that I have tamed it." His fake

English accent usually made him seem less ominous, even laughable. Today, not so much.

"Why did you want me to meet you here?" And what did Jacob say to talk you out of the court martial? Why didn't I ask? God, I'm off today.

"I thought that you deserved a reward. You won the war, didn't you? Consider this a promotion."

"Does this have something to do with the secret weapon?"

Xavier laughed. "It's so much more than that. This is the means and the end of everything, the nexus of power itself."

Practiced though she was, her face betrayed her fear. She'd broken her first and most important rule: Never let the bastards know what you're thinking.

"Don't worry. Despite what everyone is saying, I haven't snapped. I'm having too much fun to contradict them." His voice was giddy. He blushed, looking for a moment like an embarrassed child. "Tell me, do you believe in God?"

This was not the sort of question she had been preparing for.

"Doesn't everyone? He lives in Bryant Park."

He laughed again. "Not him. He's a pretender. In the grand scheme, he is hardly more powerful than a human. I mean, do you believe in a real God? Something more powerful than the human mind can conceive. A force beyond nature. A will that creates realities with every idle thought."

"I don't know. I never really thought about it. If there are beings that powerful, I hope they don't believe in me."

"Good point, but the fact is anything that powerful would have so much to watch, experience, know, etcetera, that it couldn't possibly care about any one tiny planet, let alone one person in all time and space. In any case, God exists, and this machine can harness its energy field to turn my will into reality. I'm like a metaphysical tick suckling at the vein of infinity. Watch."

He pointed to a path in the woods, and the machine began to whine. The twisted grey flora untwisted and blossomed into a lush garden filled with flowers of every shape and color. From where the path wormed out of sight, a white unicorn galloped into view. It slowed as it approached then stopped and licked her hand.

"Where did you find a unicorn?"

"I didn't find him. I made him. In fact, I made him just now, for you. Please don't tell me that you are the one girl who doesn't have a thing for horses."

"I wouldn't say I have a thing, but I like them okay."

"All right then, I'll make him a bit more interesting."

The unicorn sprouted wings, galloped around them once and then took flight.

"Okay, that's impressive." I'm going to have to rethink my strategy. If Max comes after him now, we're both dead.

"That is nothing. Watch."

The animal went around them one more time, then, with a whinny that bowed the trees it began to change. It turned black and snorted fire. Its neck grew long and snakelike while barbed tentacles burst out the other end. Four more legs appeared, and its hooves were replaced with long, twisted claws. Pincers grew from the base of its neck. It erupted all over with long needle-like spines. It was about thirty feet long, belching fire out both ends and making noises that would have Satan on his knees praying for deliverance.

When Xavier got tired of showing off, the creature flew straight up and disappeared.

"Cool, isn't it? I'm putting on a special show for the council tomorrow. Attendance is mandatory. I suppose that, since you are on the council now, you'll have to sit through this again. But don't worry. I'll keep it interesting. Tomorrow's show will make this one look like a petty card trick."

"You're putting me on the council?" Adhra beamed, forgetting everything but her victory.

"Yes, it will be nice to have someone I can trust."

The creature slammed to the ground bigger than ever, crushing the garden path and billowing fire fifty feet in the air. Its massive head came down within an inch of her. Its breath blew her hair back as it looked into her eyes.

"Put out your hands, make a bowl," Xavier said, his grin more rictused than ever.

She did as she was told. The monster made a noise like it was clearing its throat, then wharfed a white, winged uni-kitten into her hands and evaporated.

Xavier reached around her and scratched the kitten's chin. "This is more practical than a unicorn, don't you think? I don't know what I was thinking before. A unicorn in the sewer, that's just silly."

Adhra giggled nervously, unsure what to make of any of this. Was he toying with her? Testing her? Had he snapped or did he know she'd betrayed him? Was this adorable little monster a gift or a threat? Maybe it was meant to spy on her. What did it matter, though? Xavier had won. Game over. Maybe that was his point. It was time to switch sides again.

"The best part is that I will grow exponentially more powerful the more I use it. Eventually the machine and I will merge and I will become a God. Let those nincompoops call me crazy then."

Adhra looked into his big crazy eyes, smiled, and took two of his hands. "Crazy or not, I'm glad I'm on your side."

# THE ABOMINABLE DOCTOR MITTON'S CARNIVAL OF SOULS

Max hated the sewer. The air was slimy and stank like a women's restroom, all baby powder and filth. The Iiites did their best to spruce it up; baking soda and silica insulation, stylish furniture, accent lighting. Still, walking down these halls always gave Max a sickly feeling, like he was petting a slug. It wasn't helping that he was leading his last few men into the most fucked up situation to date. At least this time they were invisible.

After Emma's debriefing, it was all Max could do to keep his troops from running away. He thought he had done a good job with that, but the Fnordian necklaces* made it hard to tell.

Max rubbed his whiskers and checked the GPS. The green dot signifying him and his troops was closing in on the tracker Emma had planted. The target, a door to some freak-tastic alternate reality, lay just ahead.

They heard voices approaching from the rear. "What do you suppose Xavier wants?"

Max hugged the wall as two well-dressed Iiites hurried towards him. One was squat and twelve-ish. The other was a few years older, thin and bore an aristocratic moustache.

The elder straightened his tie. "More paranoid gibbering, no doubt."

The younger one nodded. "These meetings are tedious. I don't see why we put up with him. Everyone on the council wants him gone."

"All I care is that it's over in time for me to make my six o'clock reservation at La Panache. With a little luck, I'm finally going to bed the Smithwick girl."

"Smithwick?"

"You know the one. The ginger they brought in to revitalize our robotics program."

The kids walked by, oblivious to the Nrrds' presence. Max let them get a few steps ahead and then followed at half their pace.

"But I had heard she's a lesbian."

The elder laughed. "Don't be daft. There's no such thing."

"You dog." The younger didn't try to hide his admiration. "You have to order her the Osso Buco! You can cut it with a stiff glance.

And the risotto..." He made a yummy noise. "You also have the subliminal innuendo of putting a large bone in her face."

"Stop talking."

The Iiites opened a door twenty feet ahead, then jumped back like they had just walked in on their parents having sex. Max couldn't hear the details of their whispered argument, but the elder seemed to win. They walked stiffly through and closed the door.

Max crept forward and waited for the Iiites to go a safe distance before going in. This was the moment of truth, the boss in the video game his life had become. At least the on-again off-again with Adhra was over. Now she would either kill him or give him a happy ending.

He opened the door as quietly as possible and saw a long dirt path through the forest. He kept an eye on the dot as he stepped through, but lost his signal as soon as he crossed the threshold.

Figures.

He put his phone away and stared into the darkness. Nausea squirmed in his bowels. Emma's description sounded like Witches'R'Us, but this was way creepier. Even with his retinal implants, he could tell the darkness was much more potent. It throbbed like a headache in his soul. Could it have gotten this much worse since his last visit, or was this another world altogether? And where was that faint hint of caramel coming from?

A strange hum wound through the familiar grinding noise, which now sounded more distressed than menacing. It was as if the darkness infecting Witches'R'Us had been swallowed by an even bigger, darker darkness.

The Nrrds held hands like a kindergarten class and carefully followed the council members. They took a right down a small path that led to a lighted clearing. The odd metallic whine grew louder as they approached, but the source remained hidden. A single set of aluminum bleachers was set up against the forest wall to his right. It squeaked and shook as the kids took sat on a vacant spot in the center of the third bench. It looked like the whole council was in attendance, and none of them were happy about it.

If I didn't know better, I'd think Xavier was putting on a mandatory one man show.

Adhra was in the front row wearing a beautiful red gown and an easy expression. Strange. Seems like she would want to be as far from the target as possible. She'd better not be about to screw me. What the fuck is that on her shoulder? Did she get a cat?

Jacob was next to her, looking nervous but characteristically crisp. Max had never known anyone else who could pull off a blue and yellow argyle sweater vest over a yellow, collared, long-sleeved shirt with pleated white slacks and penny loafers, let alone anyone who would want to. Max had to respect anyone so hell-bent on doing their own thing. He was a metrosexual G.G. Allin among a crowd of business-suited bureaucrats wearing fat ties and expressions of haughty irritation.

He located Emma with his heat scanner, and quietly wrote orders on his little note pad. Setting it on the ground, he positioned Hawk where he would see it, and stepped away. One by one he could feel them taking their positions. He had to close his eyes to keep from getting carsick.

This was the first time Fnordian Necklaces had been used by a whole attack squad. The problems had been easy enough to anticipate: how to communicate when you can't speak or look at each other, how to get around in a group quietly when you can't look in front of you, etc. Disconnection from the network made it that much harder. They had a good plan, but it would have been nice if they could have tested the procedures before putting them into practice.

Where is Xavier? Isn't this his thing?

From the sound of the council's grumbling, they knew less than Max.

He wrote, "We're in position" in his second notepad and walked over to Emma and slowly searched the air with his hands. When he made contact, she jerked so hard he nearly fell. He'd have to be more careful. One little scream or crunching twig could get them all killed.

She took the pad, scribbled a response and handed it back. "No new intel. No sign of Xavier. I have a bad feeling."

The machine sounds were drowned out by loud game-show muzik. Max looked around frantically for the source and noticed everything was going squirbley. The woods behind him withered away to reveal a large wooden stage cloaked in a green velvet curtain with the M.I.L.F. crest embroidered in the center. The curtain lifted, revealing Xavier, dressed in a snazzy pinstriped suit, standing next to a big, pulsing, bio-mechanoid lump that looked like the offspring of some Lovecraftian monster and a cotton candy machine. Applause tore through the forest. The council took the hint, clapping and cheering as if their lives depended on it.

Max had tried to imagine how much freakier Felix had been before he degenerated into a drooling lab-rat, but he hadn't come close to the horrible reality that confronted him now. Those eyes. It was as if they could see everything at once.

Max couldn't explain it, but he suddenly felt violated.

The machine was as much an abomination as Xavier. It's repulsive slimy mass, pulsed with pink light like the entrails of a flashlight-rape victim. Looking at it was the ocular equivalent of licking your grandmother's naughty bits. What sort of perverse science could create such a thing?

Xavier gave them the signal to quiet down. "Hello and welcome," he said, his voice amplified by an unseen sound system, "to the future of the Iiite empire." He raised his hands and the canned applause returned. The council joined in while he grinned and facetiously pantomimed shyness.

He motioned again and the applause died down. "I am sure you are all wondering why you were summoned here and where here is, exactly. I'll get to that, but first I'd like to welcome some special guests. First off, I'd like to welcome to the stage the latest addition to the council, my favorite spy and co-host, Adhra Duke. Won't you join me, Adhra?"

Adhra looked pleased. She should be terrified. Something was terribly wrong.

She stepped onto the stage and into the role as easily as she might a shower. "Thank you, Xavier. I'm honored to be here."

Her voice was amplified as well. Was she mic'ed?

Max didn't give a fuck how Xavier had made the stage appear. It was time to end this. He raised his plasma cannon and crept toward the stage.

"And I'm ecstatic to have you here. Next, I'd like to welcome, all the way from the surface, Maxwell Quick and the last of the Riot Nrrds!"

Max's necklace turned into hamsters, which scurried down his body armor and ran away. He pulled the trigger, launching a little foam plug over the lip of the stage. His plasma cannon had become a toy. Several more plugs arced over his head and bounced off the stage lights.

Shit.

"Retreat!" He tried to run, but thorny vines wound around his ankles, snaggling their teeth into his thighs. He tripped as a mass of serrated tendrils rose to greet him, twisting around his arms and flipping him onto his back.

The air was gritty with the tortured screams of his friends, and he couldn't even turn his head.

Adhra looked on in horror but did nothing.

Max pleaded with his eyes.

She looked away.

"Max, I'm so glad that you could join us on today's program. Shall we begin? All right, first question. Which hurts more, the thorns piercing your flesh, or having been betrayed by your lover?"

Adhra turned to run, but the stage sprung a board to trip her. The cat-bird flew from her shoulder and perched on top of the stage.

Adhra tried to scramble away, but with a gesture of his hand Xavier raised her in the air, limp as a kitten.

A blind old blues-man appeared on stage strumming his guitar dramatically.

"Yes, ladies and gentlemen, that's right. My co-host here has been fucking the competition, playing both sides against one another in an attempt to steal my job."

"Oh yeeaaahhhh!" crooned the blues-man. He disappeared.

"A lesser man might find himself crushed under the weight of this betrayal. I, on the other hand, am going to turn the other cheek."

A flutter of protests rose in the peanut gallery.

"Quiet down, everyone. Let me finish. There is a small problem, though. I have only one cheek to turn." He gestured to his mount of Venus, and the council forced another laugh.

Cheeky.

"Max was sucked into this situation quite against his will. Despite his initial lack of interest in our struggle he rose to the occasion admirably, becoming a fierce and dangerous opponent. I respect that. And that is why I'm going to give him a chance to get out of here alive. Max, all you have to do to return to civilian life is cut out her cheating heart."

One look at Adhra's eyes and Max knew she had been faking it from the start. There wasn't a doubt in her mind he would take the deal. Why shouldn't he? He was being offered the very thing he'd wanted from the beginning.

*That bitch! She was using me this whole fucking time. I'm so fucking stupid.*

"Cool, sounds good. You got a knife or should I just reach in through her gaping lady-hole?"

The vines withdrew their fangs, allowing him to shimmy free.

Xavier let out a bountiful belly laugh. "I always thought I'd like you. If only we had met under more ideal circumstances."

Max climbed onto the stage and a huge ceremonial knife appeared at his feet. He picked it up and admired its long bifurcated blade. Its dual points would be perfect for snapping her dainty ribs. He walked over and tore the top of her gown, introducing her perfect lust-dumplings to the crowd. From the expression on their faces, the majority of council members were already acquainted.

"Wait just a second, Max, there's something I'd like to show you first."

Max lowered the blade.

"I was going to wait, but you were so willing to abandon your mission I think you deserve a reward. Look over there." Xavier pointed to the bleachers, which melted into a giant metallic squid. It wrapped the council in its long, silver tentacles and held them aloft like a child showing off a new toy. They begged to be released, but got a mouthful of writhing metal instead.

Jacob, dangling from one foot, pulled out a tiny gun and plinked most of his clip into the metallic beast. When he saw it had no effect he aimed at Xavier, but the bullet burned up like a meteor before it could reach him. He used the last one on himself. The bullet passed through his mouth and out the back of his head, somehow without disturbing his hair.

"You see, as head of the M.I.L.F., I see quite a lot of betrayal, but it's usually me that's being betrayed. These *were* the least treacherous, but in recent months they have been conspiring against me as well. They think I've gone crazy, that my paranoia has so consumed me that I am no longer capable of doing my job! Well, how crazy is this? I have become a god!"

Xavier moved his hand like he was squeezing an invisible scrotum, and a pale green mist seeped from the council members' eyes, surging toward the machine-like smoke being sucked into a fan.

"You will all be much more useful to me in the afterlife."

Holy fuck, I have to kill this guy.

Max braced the cumbrous cutlery on his left arm, and used every muscle in his body to plunge it through Xavier's back. The mist continued to flow as Xavier turned. He looked genuinely hurt, feeling-wise. He didn't bother to remove the blade.

"That was very stupid. Did you miss the part where I explained that I am a god?" He placed a hand at the base of his head-fingers. "I mean; I'm feeding souls to this machine for god's sake. Excuse me, for my sake."

The machine went crazy. Lightning crackled all around them. In the blink of an eye the dead children and the squid collapsed into a throne. Max was lifted off the ground, and the Nrrds were dragged into a sitting position in front of the stage.

"It looks as though I do have another cheek to turn. Adhra, my offer is now extended to you. Kill Max. If his death amuses me, I will allow you to live as my pet. Make it messy. I shall be very disappointed if I don't get any blood on me."

Hawk looked more terrified than Max had ever seen him. He struggled against the vines, tearing his flesh and screaming, "I'll wear your eyelids for a cock ring! I will chop you into pieces and sew you back together in the shape of a man!"

The vines swarmed into his mouth, muffling his insults but not stopping them.

They lowered Max and held him still while Adhra transformed into a twenty-foot, hulked-out chicken with four legs and chainsaws for wings. Only her eyes stayed the same.

Max was dropped onto the stage. He tried to run, but the wooden boards had become a thick muck sucking at his feet. "Adhra, honey, you know I wasn't really going to kill you, right?"

"Buw-kawk!" Adhra roared as she stomped toward him.

"Adhra, come on now, why don't you let me climb on your back, and we'll fly out of here?"

The chicken-monster shot him a, 'what an idiot' look and picked him up with one of its feet.

Xavier frowned. "I'd expected you to die with *some* dignity."

Adhra tossed Max into the air, and swung one of her chainsaws at him. The blade zipped past his head, close enough to rip out a chunk of hair. He hit the muck winded and writhing like an ant in a glob of hand-soap.

She picked him up, repositioned herself center stage and threw him into the air again. Max kicked at the chain-bar and got lucky. The blade glanced off the sole of his shoe and buzzed away as he face-planted into the gook.

Xavier crossed his arms and yelled, "I know the body is new, but I haven't got all day."

She picked him up again, reared back with her mighty buzzing wing, tossed him in the air and plunged her chainsaw directly into the center of the machine. Before Xavier could react, Adhra was quadruple-fisting the source of his power. A multitude of gaseous green forms rolled out to circle the clearing as fleshy robo-chunks rained from the sky. A swirly blue vortex opened up in its center. Max's vision cleared just as she was sucked inside. The oozing pink mess swallowed her whole. The blue light faded as the machine melted into a gooey, pink puddle.

Max felt a sinking feeling in his stomach.

... She saved me?

Before he could go into emotional shock, he was distracted by an agonized gasp. Xavier's shirt blushed. He coughed blood and fell into the center of his enemies.

Laughter worked Max's midsection like a professional boxer. "Damn, you can't even trust your own chicken-monster." He crawled to the foot of the stage, slipped and tumbled into a pile of brambles. Still, he laughed.

Xavier tried to retort, but all that came out of his mouth was blood.

One of the vines holding Hawk snapped, freeing his right arm. One by one the Nrrds freed themselves from their rapidly deteriorating confines.

Max stumbled out of the brush. "Not immortal now, are ya, fucker?"

Max turned his attention to his troops. "Would one of you please fucking kill him before he pulls something out of his ass?"

Pope and Wormwood held him down while Hawk jerked the blade out of Xavier's back and swiftly separated his bits from his pieces.

While Hawk was busy redefining overkill, Wormwood picked up Xavier's head by its middle finger. He cracked a sly grin, and as the last traces of life trickled from Xavier's eyes, he said. "See ya in three days, asshole."

The arms Magog was holding weren't attached anymore, so he stood and tossed them aside. "Too bad Nietzsche's not here; he'd have loved this."

There was a rustling in the trees. Strange, since there was no wind. It stopped for a moment and then grew louder, closer. Remembering the squiddish tree that had tried to eat Guido, Max scanned the tree-line for movement. "Hmm, is it just me or is this clearing getting smaller?"

Pope nodded in agreement. "It seems to be getting darker as well. It may be in our best interests to save the festivities for later and make like the proverbial banana."

Max glanced at the stage. The woods were growing in around it, tilting it forward. The pink mess that had swallowed his lover was oozing down stage to take a bow. There was nary a feather to mark her passing.

Max would need a lot of time and therapy to wrap his head around what had just happened. Riptides of confused emotions pulled his mind in all directions. He'd won, but lost the woman he loved. But she'd betrayed him. It had all been a lie, or had it? Would she have saved him if Xavier hadn't turned her into a monster?

The kitten provided a much-needed distraction. It was walking behind the pink mass as it slid, sniffing at it and taking an occasional taste. Was it expecting Adhra to emerge, or was it simply hungry?

"Poor thing, we can't leave it here."

Magog nodded. "Certainly not. It is a previously unrecorded specimen."

"Magog down, bad Magog. I called it first. Nobody's going to be looking under its hood without my permission, which you are not going to get."

Max made his way over cautiously, trying not to spook it. He held out his fingers. The kitten stared at them skeptically for a moment then cautiously approached for a sniff. The stage was melting like caramel in a microwave, but the kitten slinked across its surface without disturbing it.

The pink mess finally slopped off the edge and landed with a slippery plop at Max's feet. The kitten launched into the air and circled about ten feet above Max's head. Its fur caught the infinitesimal smidgen of available light, making it look like a bright fish deep underwater.

Hawk cleared his throat. "We should really get going."

Max silenced him with two angry fingers and waited.

A minute later, Wormwood, who normally only opened his mouth when he had a cheesy one-liner, added, "The cat will be fine. It is a weird animal, which is likely indigenous. Furthermore, it can fly, which we cannot; therefore, since it is more suited to survival here than we are, and there are more of us than it, it is silly and irrational to for us to risk our lives by remaining here one moment longer."

Max hated to admit it, but the verbose twat had a point. The kitten showed no signs it would be coming down any time soon, and the path to the main McRoad* had all but closed up. He flexed his jaw and glanced at it one last time. "Okay, fuck it. Let's get the hell out of here."

Pope raised his fist and screamed, "To the egress!"

They ran, but the path was gone before they were halfway there. The trees crept ever closer, their worm-like roots dragging them through the dry, black earth. The trunks were black, purple, and brown striped strands of shining flesh that rippled, expanded and contracted as they pressed ever closer.

Hawk slashed at the wriggling roots with his machete, but it was like trying to mow the lawn with a cheese knife. The trees recoiled, but returned moments later—or in the best cases, one was replaced by another. The Nrrds were forced apart, playing leapfrog with the roots, dodging the swipe of sinewy branches, and occasionally cringing at the schlorping screams of their comrades.

Max pulled out his little red hammer and landed a few ineffectual blows, then jump-kicked an encroaching trunk, lost his balance and barely avoided stumbling into the mouth of the enemy. "This sucks! Anybody have any ideas?"

Hawk responded from somewhere nearby. "Fraid not, unless anybody's got a plasma cannon I don't know about."

Then it came to him like a sex-punch. "Fuck, my sonic screwdriver!"

He ripped his keys from his pocket and located the little black fob they designed to melt the locks out of doors.

Any laser in an ambush.

Max pointed it at the nearest tree, pushed the button, and giggled as the cloying purple roots caught fire.

"Fuck yeah! Everybody make your way towards my voice. I got this." He shot his little ray fore and aft, screaming, "Pew, pew!" and giggling maniacally. His men dodged the thrashing limbs of desperate foliage, and made their way towards the flickering carnivorous flora.

Max zapped out a path. "This way."

He took stock of his last nine men. Luckily, the flagitious forest had only pruned the sicklier branches of his family tree. He was sad to lose so many, but at least his inner circle was still there.

Hawk slapped him on the back as they ran. "Good thinkin'."

The keys slipped out of his hand. He heard a crunch and spun around in time to see Pope slam into Magog and step on them again.

Max clenched his fists. "Why the fuck would you hit me at a time like this?"

"Sorry."

The trees slowed their retreat, and cautiously rotated in place.

"Oh, well that makes it all better then, doesn't it?"

Pope picked up the keys and examined the wreckage. "He's dead, Jim." He threw them at Max's feet.

Max scooped them up and saw the circuit board had snapped in half. He stuffed them back in his pocket then patted himself down to see if he had anything else that might be useful.

The trees crept closer, but cautiously, as though they thought it might be a trick.

A familiar groan rustled the leaves where the keys had hit the ground. Looking closer, Max noticed a nose and a bit of chin. Everyone jumped back except Hawk, who rushed forward to introduce this newest threat to his size 12 boot. Max jumped in front of him and ordered him to stand down.

"Carla?" Max reached down and carefully checked beneath the leaves. "You're remarkably accident prone for someone who never moves."

Even with the added husk of sleep, her voice was hollow. "Max? I was just having a nap. What happened? The earth feels... itchy."

"You tell me. This place has gotten a lot more dangerous since the last time I was here."

"Oh yes, The Darkness has grown ever more powerful."

Max picked up a rock and hurled it at the closest enemy. "You don't say. We're being attacked by a bunch of trees. Can you help me out? Ask them to stop?"

"I could ask, but it would not work. Like everything else, they are being controlled by The Darkness."

"Why aren't you affected?"

"No offense, but you wouldn't understand. It's all very complicated."

The trees were only five feet away. Max was about to bolt. "Gee, thanks. So there's nothing you can do?"

Carla grinned. "I didn't say that."

There was a deafening rasp as the earth belched up its entire insect collection. The sky set loose a storm of beating wings as swarms of surrogate soldiers engulfed the enemy, mulching the militant mammoths with a million moldering mandibles. Within seconds there was nothing left but stinking puddles of sap.

Max stared in disbelief at the clearing she had made. "Wow. Just wow. How... uh... thanks?"

"No need to thank me. We are friends, after all."

"Uh, yeah. So is everything here going to try to kill us?"

"Yes."

Can you make us a nice friendly path back to our world? Better yet, can you open up a door right here and spare us the hike?"

Carla's smile, juxtaposed with her stitched-up nose and eyes, was the most unsettling thing he'd seen all day. "I'm afraid that is beyond my capability. You see, I am a conduit between the world and the creatures which inhabit it. The Darkness is similar, like a conduit between matter and the spectrum of negative energy. Doorways between worlds would fall under his power, and he is not letting anyone in or out at the moment. That mutant's ham-fisted attempt at domination has put him in a foul and defensive mood. You may not make it home for quite some time."

"Wait, *his*? The Darkness has a gender?"

Carla shot him a wow-what-an-idiot look, an impressive feat for someone whose eyes were sewn shut. "You really are out of your depth here."

Max could feel himself blush. At the risk of making himself look even dumber, he had to ask, "Why is that a stupid question?"

Max glanced around. Everyone was looking at him as though he had just asked for an explanation of toast.

Carla feigned annoyance, but he could tell she was happy to have someone to talk to. "All things exist within a quantum spectrum. Each thing consists of many facets which define it. For intelligent creatures who use a semantic system, to understand a thing is to define it by identifying as many of those facets as possible and putting them into the best words so that identity can be stored in the brain and communicated to others. It is not so much that The Darkness has a gender as it is that its characteristics fall on the masculine side of the spectrum. Positive energy has always been associated with light, females and creation. Negative energy has always been associated with darkness, males, and destruction."

"As a man, I have to say that's kind of offensive."

Carla smiled. "That is because you perceive destruction as bad. Everything must eventually be destroyed so that new creations can come into being. Destruction is as important to nature as your fear of it is to you. Your ego defines things that can destroy you as bad to help you preserve your current form. It is impossible to see things as they truly are while looking through the eyes of the ego."

"I guess that makes sense, but..."

"The aim of religion is to help the practitioner see more clearly, but most people are too lazy to pursue the esoteric foundations for their beliefs. Luckily, the nature of true witchcraft leads most people to at least partially transcend the self, long before they discover this place. A witch with an ego is as dangerous as a blind man driving a bus. That is what brought The Darkness here to begin with. Xavier was not the first to try to harness the power of the Creator."

"Is what he was trying to do even possible?"

"Honestly, I do not know. I doubt it. If it is possible it would most likely upset the balance of creation and destruction, and lead to the obliteration of all things. You did well to kill him."

Bearing an expression of extreme befuddlement, Hawk took a knee beside Max. "You mean we're stuck in this demonic shithole until evil itself decides to let us go?"

Max elbowed him in the ribs. "Learn some manners."

Carla was obviously offended, but she replied politely. "That is all right. This realm is not everyone's cup of tea.

"There are many beings capable of opening a doorway. You simply need to locate one of them and convince them to help you. Your best bet lies at the top of Castration Mountain on the Island of Ultimate Doom. If you are lucky, "Bob" will be at home. He has a nice little chalet on the eastern face: number 456. He will most likely open up a doorway in exchange for copious amounts of money or souls. If you have the time, or if you are lacking in money or souls, you may want to make a detour to the Caverns of Relentless Suffering to retrieve the Santorum diamond. "Bob" has an open offer of one free wish to anyone brave enough to retrieve it."

Hawk groaned. "I hate fantasy."

"Can I talk to Marvin?"

"As I said, I cannot open a door to another dimension against the will of The Darkness."

"What about the twins?"

"They are visiting their cousins in Boca."

Night turned to day. Everyone instinctively looked up and saw a figure descending from the heavens. It was a man in an inflated, white, jewel-encrusted jumpsuit. A memory flitted across Max's mind; he was at a fair, his father giving him a stuffed clown that smelled like packing peanuts.

The man's descent was slow and unthreatening. His arms were outstretched, like he wanted a hug. On his shoulders sat a big white helmet that looked like a cross between an old computer monitor and a Neo-Catholistic* church. The series of golden T's on top reminded Max of an old antenna. Adhra's kitten fluttered around his head like a furry cherub.

Carla sounded afraid. "Max, I advise you to run away now. Go to "Bob" before it is too late. That man is..." Her sentence tapered into a snore.

Max was about to run when a velvety southern drawl spread like butter through his mind. "Don't mind her. There's no reason to fear little ol' me." The weird churchy being landed in front of him, raised his arms in a Y and continued. "My name's Ernie. I have come to set you free."

The kitten landed on his helmet and curled up like it was going to take a nap. Inside, there flickered a big expensive face, hovering neckless against a backdrop of muted praying forms. A voiceless choir was reflected in the glass, but Max was not. Whoever this guy was, he obviously didn't care much for the laws of physics.

*Better proceed with caution. Carla did recommend a guy who collects souls over him.*

Ernie let out a hearty laugh and slapped Max on the shoulders. "Ol' Carla there's had a bee in her bonnet the size of an airplane ever since I told her I don't have all day to sit around yakkin'. You know how she is. That yapper flaps dawn to dusk. I reckon she's trying to compensate for her eyes and nose bein' sewn shut." His teeth sparkled in 3-D, somehow more real than the rest of his face.

Under normal circumstances Max would want to get away from him as fast as possible, but Carla's plan sounded like a lot of trouble. Max forced a big reciprocal smile and a friendly laugh. "Yep, that's Carla all right. So you know a way out of here?"

"Yessiree, I sure do. But that's not all. I come to tell you a secret. You may not realize it yet, but just as I am your personal savior right now, so must you be the personal savior of the world."

*That's worrisome.* "Uh, you're a little late. Been there, done that. The world's saved. It's time to go get drunk."

Ernie guffawed. "That's just precious—but no. See, you just killed all the people who kept things running. All that's left is a bunch of greedy underlings with no sense of morality—or any other kind of sense, for that matter. Somebody's got to fill that vacuum, and *you're the guy.*

"See, you have two choices."

Max groaned. "No, seriously, no, do not start in on that two choices shit. I saved the fucking world. What happens now is up to it. I will not go on wiping the world's ass indefinitely."

After more guffawing, Ernie slapped him on the back and continued. "Max, you are nothing but a hoot. Let me tell ya boy, you are more fun than a barrel of crabs. Seriously though, you have two choices. You can let those brain-dead sycophants take over and cock everything up worse than it was before, or you can tell the world what you did and seize your destiny.

"I'm not stuck in linear time, so I already know what you do when you get back. I just popped in to lend a hand so your life don't turn into some silly fantasy story. You got more important things to do than run around playin' with heavy metal clichés. Plus, your soul's got real potential. I can't very well let you trade it off to that capitalistic som'bitch for something silly as a ride home."

Pope tapped their savior on the shoulder. "Excuse me, did you say that you are unstuck in time? If so, I'd like to ask you a few questions about a theory I've been working on."

Ernie ignored him. Pope cleared his throat, tried again, and, with a waft of caramelized sausage, disappeared.

Hawk picked up a big stick. "Hey, what'd you do to him? Bring him back 'fore I..." He disappeared as well, then the others.

Max's brow could have knitted a sweater. "What did you do to them?"

"Don't you worry your little head. I just sent 'em on home. Their destiny ain't as impressive as yours, but I got nothin' against 'em.

"Now, I can't tell ya the particulars, but here's a few things to look out for. Remember: purple pillow, stamped bird, squidgy willow, black dirt. Can you remember all that?"

"No."

"Sure ya can."

Something about those words seemed familiar. "Say, do you happen to know anything about the night noodles?"

"You go get 'em, Tiger."

Max blinked. He was standing in a crowd in front of a shopping mall. Bright white light seared the back of his eyes, but his implants were quick to adjust.

Everyone was staring into a hole in the parking lot while a reporter plugged the K Co insurance program. Max pushed his way to the front, keeping an eye out for his men. It looked like the parking lot had partially caved in on an Iiite shopping district. Hundreds of Iiites stared up in befuddlement.

He heard someone near him say, "Hey, isn't that the leader of that terrorist sect?"

Another voice, "Yeah, I think so. He probably did this."

Someone else, "Hey man, you owe me a fucking car!"

The Iiites below recognized him as well. One of them pulled a hammer out of his shopping bag and threw it at him. The cameras turned on him just as he was catching it.

The reporter's eyes bugged out. She rushed over to shove the mic in his face. "Maxwell Quick, do you have a statement for the press? Do you claim responsibility for this attack? Why a shopping mall?"

With a heavy sigh Max grabbed the microphone and stepped towards the camera. "Sure, I have a statement. First off, I didn't do this. At least not directly.

"Secondly, good news. The war's over. We won. And I don't mean 'we the normals'. 'We the people' won. This war was never about race or culture. It was about freedom from manipulation and making the world a safer place for your kids.

"Iiites are people too. As a people, they have every right to be mad about what was done to them. The problem was that some of them, the ones in charge, were taking revenge by poisoning our children and creating catastrophes. Now, they've been brought to justice."

He pointed into the hole.

"Those people down there are just like you. They have jobs, friends and families. They just want to be safe and happy. We have to forgive each other for the circumstances that shaped our lives. Nobody chooses whether to be born normal or Iiite. It's a stupid thing to hold against somebody, and we have to let it go.

"For a long time there has been a twisted upper class playing games with your lives. The Iiites couldn't have accomplished anything without the help of corrupt normals. What matters now is that it's over. No sanctions, no reparations, no grudges. We forgive each other and move on.

"By the way, let me take this chance to apologize on behalf of normals everywhere for the way your ancestors were treated. That was fucked up. I'm also sorry for all the trouble this war has caused. That goes for normals too. Believe me, I didn't want to do any of this.

"Now the world has two choices. We can make the same mistakes we've made over and over in the past, or we can take responsibility for our lives and forge a new path. A lot of people are going to try to rush in and set up a new government. They'll come all happy faced, promising you the moon, but don't listen to them. They are not necessary. Ask yourself, what has the ruling class ever done for you? What is their purpose? They don't keep you safe. They don't look out for your interests. They don't give a shit about you or your family. They don't feed you or house you or get you laid. They're worthless. We don't need them. What we need is to step up and take responsibility for our own lives. We need to act like adults for the first time in the history of man, and use logic and compassion to find ways to do things that benefit everyone.

"I did my part. Now I'm done. The rest is up to you. All you have to do to protect what I've given you is not listen to their bullshit when they come to take it away. Don't join them when they offer to organize a better world. Everybody do your own thing, but be considerate. Work to help others instead of yourselves. Above all else, think for yourselves, because if you don't, if you let the fuckheads take it all over again, you deserve what you get. And what you'll get is a big shit-sandwich; oppression, hunger, war, rioting, every flavor of misery.

"Sorry if I'm not as eloquent as normal. I've had a really crazy day. I'd appreciate it if you would all just leave me alone."

He dropped the microphone and turned to leave, but what he saw stopped him dead. Why were they all crying? The Iiites were crying too. People were hugging each other. Had they actually listened?

He heard flapping above his head. The kitten was back. It landed on his shoulder, held out a paw and meowed.

Someone said, "Maybe he really can save the world."

"He's come to fix everything!"

"It's the messiah!"

Shit.

# I DIDN'T COME HERE TO SPY

The last thing Max needed after the mall debacle was a drag-queen in mamma-mode, but he had nowhere else to go. His apartment had been blown up, he didn't have any friends or family, and he couldn't go outside without being mobbed by fans. So he ended up in the kitchen behind Rusty Nails, waiting for Hawk and Pope to save him from this plush, lilac-scented hell.

Rusty was somewhere behind that thick beaded curtain, shooing away the last of his customers. Each one thought the others should go, but that they were somehow special. They made turkey noises and flapped their arms in rage as Rusty spoke in cool even tones and prodded them toward the door with a curling iron.

Max was slumped over the kitchen table, staring sideways at himself on the little TV mounted above the sink. His speech was getting more coverage than the latest flu pandemic.

The urge to stick his head in the oven was growing stronger by the second.

The Media©-swine had turned his attempt to get the world off his back into a trough of juicy memes. His name dripped from their lips half-digested as they gorged themselves on his words. The verdict was in. He was the second coming, and it was all the goddamn cat's fault.

He glanced over to where his new pet flopped innocently on the checkered tiles, at war with its own tail. "Why did you do that? Little magic fucker! If you weren't so cute I'd stuff you down the garbage disposal."

He flipped the channel, and saw the video of the kitten landing on his shoulder.

Of course they think I'm the messiah. I probably would too if I didn't know me.

Rusty poked his head through the beads. "How's my little holy one holding up?"

Stupid world.

"The only part of me that's holy is telling me it's time for fellowship with the porcelain god."

"TMI, you're making me feel religious. Be right baaack." His head disappeared.

"Mm."

Cheeky was under the table, twisted up in a cocoon of blankets. He'd been glaring at the kitten ever since they were introduced.

He'll come around. She's too cute to hate.

Wait. Do animals have a concept of cute? They seem to know when they're being cute. Maybe I should say something.

Max poked him with his foot. "Cheeky?"

The worm turned, his expression changing from hate to hurt.

"The kitten isn't competition."

Cheeky huffed and puffed as if to say, "Damn right she's not."

"She's not even mine. I brought it home because I thought you might like a pet of your own; something to keep you company while I'm off getting shot at."

Cheeky puffed again with eyes even more expressive than normal. "Why can't you just take me with you?"

"Sometimes I have to leave you home. Sorry. I can't have you getting hurt. Don't blame her. Be cool and you two will be best friends in no time."

Cheeky's eyes said, "Condescending asshole."

"What would have happened if that bulbous freak had zapped you somewhere? You can't exactly borrow a cell phone. I mean, I don't know, it wouldn't surprise me to find out you have some kind of magic homing capability, but I don't want to take the chance. Accept the gift. Think of a name for her, or eat her. I don't care. I have too much going on right now to deal with your jealousy issues. Think about what you want to call her."

Cheeky puffed and went back to glaring at the kitten, but with twenty percent less hate.

"All right. We'll call her Puff. That's actually pretty good."

Puff continued to flop, oblivious to all but the twitching of her tail.

Max addressed the kitten, "Don't mistake my trying to keep Cheeky from eating you for us being cool."

Max glanced at the naked-guy wall-clock. Each click of its pendulous genitals brought him one second closer to Rusty's return. Max snuck upstairs for a poo. He locked the door quietly, dropped trow and plunked down on the heated toilet seat. The toilet sang him the Green Meanies' Crunchypoofs theme.

Rusty's been on eBid again.

He put his face in his hands and relaxed his sphincter. It was nice. He wished he could hide in there forever.

It had all gotten to be too much. He was at a point beyond emotion, beyond reason.

How's a guy supposed to feel when he finds out he was just a pawn in his lover's power grab; that she was going to kill him, but then she turns into a chainsaw-handed chicken-monster and saves his life. Next a magic man appears and teleports him into a situation where the whole world thinks he's the goddamn messiah. The human brain is simply not equipped to process this sort of shit. A normal person would snap under that sort of pressure. Good thing I'm a sociopath.

What does that mean, anyway, sociopath? Society defines it in negative terms, as someone who is antisocial and has no moral responsibility or social conscience. In short I'm missing something everybody else has. But that thing, that need for the approval of others, always seemed silly to me. The games people play with their greeting cards and their, 'How are you today?' 'I'm great. How are you.' 'I'm excellent, thanks for asking.' It's all bullshit. Neither of them is doing great, and neither wants to know about the other's problems. You say what you're supposed to when you're supposed to. Failure to lie makes you an asshole. Failure to understand why makes you a monster.

His brain was a blender. Years of judgment, rage, and disgust shredded, mixed, liquefied, and congealed into a putrid smoothie of pain. All those voices asking, "Do you even have a soul?"

Quite unexpectedly, he began to cry. Goddammit, I do feel. I feel a lot. It's fucking hard, and I want to stop.

It didn't take long for his brain to get defensive.

Maybe sociopaths aren't monsters. Maybe we're the next phase in evolution. We're more conscious. More focused. We care more about fewer things.

Maybe if we weren't labeled as monsters we wouldn't become them. Maybe if we weren't made to feel like we don't feel properly we wouldn't withdraw. Maybe if we weren't always being told we were broken we wouldn't fall apart.

He was shaking and staring angrily at his feet when something weird bubbled up in the back of his mind. Something he'd never thought about before. He'd been a happy kid. Where had all this hate and rage come from? Wasn't it a direct result of how fucked the world was; learning about politics, war, rape, censorship, watching the world make the same mistakes over and over, getting dumber and more violent every day? Wasn't it that feeling of powerlessness that created the rage that made him that person diagnosed as a narcissist and a sociopath? Wasn't it those labels that had made him completely withdraw from the world and degenerate into a cynical alcoholic?

Wasn't he now in a position to make the world a better place?

Hadn't he already?

What if I am the messiah? I mean, how many people have to tell me this shit before I believe it? The Media©, the people, and that freaky house all seem to see something in me. Why can't I see it too?

Better question: why the fuck do I keep letting people tell me who I am? I'm a sociopath Goddammit. I'm not supposed to care what they think. I don't know if I was misdiagnosed, or if their definition is just wrong. Hell, maybe I got better?

Nah, that's not it. I'm going to go with 'psychiatrists don't understand sociopaths'. How could they? By definition, their brains work differently. How arrogant do you have to be to think you can define the way another person thinks, let alone condemn them for it?

A long string of farts derailed his train of thought. A great blockage was removed from his mind and bowels simultaneously. When they had gone, he felt like a new man.

I suppose the question I should be asking is; what do I want?

That life I've been trying to get back to is boring. I know, when this is all over, I'm going to drink too much, watch too much TV, and waste the rest of my time trying to get laid. That's what people do. Do I really want that for myself? I mean, I won a war. I brought down a fucking government. I don't see TV and video games doing it for me anymore.

Rusty tapped on the door with his fingernails. "Max, you have a visitor."

"I'll be out in a second."

There came a banging at the door, then Hawk's sarcastic drawl. "Wise and all-knowing master, won't you please climb off that mountain of shit, and let me feast my eyes on a genuine messiah. Regale me with your wisdom and plans to save the world that my eyes will be opened to the glory of your..."

"Fuck off, I'm wiping."

He could hear Hawk's chuckles trailing down the stairs.

So much for peace and quiet.

Max washed his hands and stared at himself in the mirror. His eyes were still a little glassy, but not too bad. He took a deep breath, tried to clear his head and made his way downstairs.

"Prepare to have your minds blown in eleven minutes." Rusty stuck a pan of cookies in the oven and closed the door with his foot. He'd changed again. Fifteen minutes ago, he was dolled up like a line-dancing cenobite. Now, he wore a shiny black suit with a purple shirt, and a porn-print bowtie.

When did he have time to make cookies?

Hawk sat at the kitchen table, still giggling. He raised his arms and bowed facetiously. "Well, if it ain't Mohammed his self. Whatever did I do to earn this great honor?"

"Drop it."

"Hold on now, don't talk so fast. I gotta get this down in stone. Can't misquote the messiah."

Max sat, and shot him a look that bitch-slapped the giggles right out of his mouth.

Hawk ran his fingers through the thinning, black mess on top of his head. "Well, excuse me. I was only playing."

Rusty squeezed Max's shoulder. "I'm going to go put some fresh sheets on your bed."

Max nodded appreciatively and sat across from Hawk. "So where did you get zapped?"

"Zapped? Oh, yeah." He tipped his chair back and chuckled again. "Believe it or not, the fucker put me in the VIP room of a strip club called The Burning Man. It was nice until I got tossed out. I'll tell you what, though. Them boys sure was surprised when I turned out to be the one teaching manners. Yessiree, I bet them boys are filling out job applications as we speak."

Max pursed his lips. "So, you kicked their asses for doing their job?"

"I didn't hurt 'em bad or nothing. I more just broke their spirits. Tamed 'em down real good. Drained all that macho, Johnny-confidence shit right out onto the pavement. They were... they were really rude. Don't judge me."

It was Max's turn to laugh. "Anyway, where's everybody else?"

"I sent out a text, said we'd meet 'em later at the penthouse."

"You really want to go back there? I smelled it enough."

"Hairspray don't smell much better. At least I'm used to the smell of death. You want to find a new base; you won't get no arguments from me. I just said the penthouse, cause we ain't got nowhere else. Meetin' up ain't that urgent, anyway. War's over." Looking sad and worried, Hawk set his chair back on all fours. "Shit. War's over. What're you gonna do now?"

Max threw up his hands. "I don't know. It's not up to me. The universe has the rest of my fucking life planned out. That's more or less what Ernie said. He knows everything that happens, and apparently I get to keep saving the world, or else."

"Yeah, I was there for that part. What'd he say *after* I got zapped?"

Max went to the fridge and grabbed them each a beer. "Not much. Whoever he is, he likes being cryptic. I asked him about the Night Noodles, and he zapped me off to my press conference. It is absolutely amazing to me how, no matter what I do, I have no control over my life. Nobody will let me relax. Everybody wants something from me. It's like they think I'm magic, like every time I piss the toilet turns into a unicorn."

Max plopped back down, and shook his head. "Free will is such bullshit."

Puff jumped into Max's lap and kneaded his thigh with her claws. He twisted the tops off the beers and handed one to Hawk. Max was halfway through his first sip when Puff jabbed him in the side with her horn.

"Ow!" Max grabbed her gently by the face to keep her from doing it again, but scratched her chin with his other hand.

Hawk nodded. "You can say that again."

"I've been thinking. It might actually be less work to give the people what they want."

Hawk's eyes bugged out and he leaned forward. "Who are you, and what have you done to Max?"

"If you think about it, this is totally in character. I mean, for as long as I can remember I've been going with the flow, like a dead fish. I've done my share of bitching, and kind of fought it, but not really. I didn't have to fight this war. If I'm being honest with myself, I did it because I was less scared of dying than I was of having to figure out a better plan.

"Fuck, I'm lame."

Hawk stared at the tabletop in awkward silence.

Max propped his head on his hand and continued. "Anyway, the war made me face my fears, and I didn't just survive, I *lived*. As surreal as it is, saving the world, and having the position of messiah foisted upon me kind of kick-started the introspective faculties I haven't used since high school.

"Believe it or not, I was a smart kid. In second grade, I was obsessed with Greek mythology. I started reading philosophy in fifth. Six through eight, I was soaking up epic poetry, reading everything by Goethe, Dante, Milton, Shakespeare. A Season in Hell was my favorite.

"Anyway, something happened in high school. A lot of crazy shit was going on in the world. I didn't see any hope for the future. I started smoking copious amounts of pot, dropping a lot of acid, and drinking. I got bored with pot, and the acid dried up, but I kept drinking. I guess I got sick of learning. I started reading a lot of new fiction. Next thing I knew I was shitting my way through genre fiction."

Hawk feigned falling asleep.

Max kicked him under the table. "I guess you could say I've had an epiphany. I've been wondering how I got to be so pathetic, and I realized the war saved me from myself.

Max heard sobbing coming from the direction of the stairs, and turned to see Rusty dabbing his eyes with tissue.

Oh God. What have I done?

Rusty rushed over, and wrapped Max in his big mallowy arms.

Max tried to squirm away. "Uh, Rusty? You okay?"

"That was the most beautiful thing I've ever seen. It was like the Doctor Al show right in my kitchen."

Cheeky ran up Max's leg, and rubbed his face on both of them, bringing Rusty's emotional assault to an end.

"Aw, look who's jealous." Rusty came around the side of the chair, and stuck his face in Cheeky's neck flubber. While Rusty was distracted with baby-talk and Eskimo kisses, Max mouthed "Thank you."

Cheeky's eyes said, "See, I'm useful."

Max's response would have to wait. He wasn't sure how to communicate wordlessly that Cheeky's taking bullets for him was exactly what he was afraid of. He shouldn't still be thinking in those terms. His enemies were all dead. His days of raiding secret bases were over. Still, seven months of guerilla warfare changes a man. He didn't know if he would ever go back to the way he was before, or if he even wanted to.

The doorbell rang, and Rusty rushed off to answer it.

Max nodded at the steps. "Hey, you want to go somewhere more private?"

"I guess we could, but I got a hankerin' for them cookies I'm smelling."

Rusty came in, followed by a haggard Pope, who sniffed the air and perked up. "Do I smell cockies?"

Max grimaced. "Cockies?"

"That's right. It's a special recipe I've been working on for nearly a decade: oatmeal cinnamon with white chocolate chips, made from scratch."

Pope and Max both raised an eyebrow.

Rusty added, "By Billy."

Max cracked a wry smile. "Oh, okay, I was about to say. Last I checked you didn't know how to cook a frozen pizza."

"Oh, come now, I'm not quite that bad."

"You didn't know you had to take the cardboard off the bottom."

"There's no cardboard on cookie dough. Fine, if you're going to be that way, you can't have any. I was trying to do something nice to welcome you home." Rusty looked as though he might cry.

Max had forgotten how easy it was to hurt Rusty's feelings. "I'm sorry. I was just kidding. I'd love a—cocky."

Rusty's face went from brooding to bawdy. "Oh Max, why does everything you say sound like a come-on?"

"Careful, you're going to make me *toss* my cockies."

Rusty grinned. "Can I watch?"

The timer went off. Hawk, being closest, pulled the cookies out of the oven. Whoever made them, they smelled amazing. Less surprisingly, Rusty had shaped them all to resemble male genitalia and put extra chocolate chips at the tip.

Rusty carefully picked one up, and blew on it. "Well, what are you waiting for? Grab a cockie. Put it in our mouth. I like to suck the tip while the chocolate's still all melty."

He demonstrated.

Pope picked one up and nibbled the balls.

Hawk selected a smaller one and crammed the whole thing in his mouth. His eyes bulged with pain as his garbled swears escaped in bursts of steam. "Goddamn, this thing's hotter than a virgin's tits."

Max grabbed a big one, held it up for Rusty to see and then snapped it in half.

"Ouch. Message received."

When the steam died down, Max took a bite and nodded. "Not bad for someone who finds the preparation of boxed mac and cheese daunting." He took another bite and turned to Pope. "So, whadda ya know about running a planet?"

# THE SPIDER AND THE GUY

Max parked his car between the large circular fountain and the front door of Greystoke's castle. He stepped out and handed his keys to a large Iiite valet who smelled like baby powder. The castle stretched into the trees as far as he could see to his left and right, making it hard to gauge its actual size. The Count was obviously compensating for something.

I can't believe I'm doing this.

IIe walked up the steps, knocked three times and waited. Greystoke opened the door, his goatee a salt-and-pepper heart of greedy delight. Gold doubloons might as well have been falling from his eye sockets. He couldn't have been more animated if the gargoyles perched atop his gothic cathedral were singing a chipper theme-song.

"Nice digs," Max said, forcing a smile.

"I had it flown in from France. Napoleon used to keep his alchemists here. Won't you come in?"

At least Mephisto wasn't so desperate.

Max followed him through the vestibule, down the hall, and into a drawing room, which would have made Anton LaVey cream his robe and keel over, having envied himself into a state of Satanic Zen. The room was an apartment-sized museum full of occult memorabilia, large taxidermy, and dark wooden bookshelves lined with enough books to blind an army of fourteenth-century scholars. The air smelled of sandalwood and oiled leather.

Man, Rusty would love this place. I've never seen so much silly shit in one room.

Greystoke poured him a Cognac, and invited him to sit on one of the huge leather chairs by the fireplace.

Max was so nervous he tripped over the bearskin rug. "Sorry."

The Count smiled but his eyes were perplexed. "No worries. He didn't feel a thing."

Max accepted the booze and downed it in one gulp. "Thanks."

Greystoke poured another.

Max wondered how many it would take to make this seem like a good idea. He kept reminding himself that the Order of the Owl* were professionals, and no matter how silly or pretentious they might be, they had the connections he would need to get the job done. He downed the second, and held his snifter out for a third.

Greystoke's smile was strained as he poured. "I am not sure that you have noticed, but this is Henri IV Dudognon. It *is* meant to be savored."

"Oh, sorry. It's good stuff." Max sat in the chair next to the stuffed panther and took a little sip. He had meant to be facetious, but the Count had a point. "Henry IV, huh? I'm going to have to get me a bottle."

Greystoke guffawed. "Max, I do appreciate your ambition; however, it will likely be some time before you can buy a five-million-dollar bottle of liquor."

Max choked on Greystoke's words, taking a few grand into his sinuses. It was oddly pleasant. He laughed. "You're probably right about that."

The Count set the bottle on the side-table, and settled daintily into the other chair. "What say we get down to business?"

"Yeah, you said you had some ideas about how I can use my celebrity to do some good. Shoot."

Greystoke smiled slyly. "Well now, I have no interest in defining good or bad. I am simply a publicist. Tell me what you hope to achieve, and I will make it happen."

Max's head was already getting fuzzy. "I'll get to that. First, the Media©, which is controlled by you, has decided I'm the new messiah. Why?"

"It was only logical after the performance you gave on live TV. That was the single most impressive publicity stunt I have ever witnessed. You must tell me how you got the inspiration, and the flying feline, and how did you train it? I've always found cats extremely difficult to work with."

Max grimaced, and set the snifter on the arm of his chair. "That's the thing. I didn't train it, and that wasn't a stunt. I was just trying to inform people the powers oppressing them are gone, and they're free to... you know, live."

The Count frowned. "We are really going to have to work on that. It was your passion that sold the speech. We can't have people realizing that, for all your efforts, nothing has changed, and nothing will make them realize faster than putting *that* tone and expression on a television screen."

"Things did change. They had a secret society poisoning them, dumbing them down, manipulating them, and keeping them in constant fear of terrorist attacks. Now they don't."

Greystoke raised his eyebrows smugly, as if Max was a child talking about his adventure with the Easter Bunny. "But if they did not notice the harm, do you honestly believe they will notice the improvement?"

Max took another sip and stared at the deflated bear beneath his feet.

Greystoke continued. "It doesn't matter how many people are out to get you, how dangerous the world is, or what you have. Happiness is simply a matter of perception. As long as people feel safe, and occasionally get things they want, they are happy. The Iiites knew that, which is what made them able to rule so efficiently. You have already made life better for these people by *telling* them you have. The better you sell yourself, the more good you do, and selling is my specialty."

Max shook his head. "No, I made life better by killing the people who have been blowing up kids and putting carcinogenic mood stabilizers in the water. I intend to build on that by continuing to attack the big problems. I want to do away with all the poison they've been feeding us, literally and metaphorically."

"All right, I see where you are going with this. I like a long-term strategy. If you play this right you will be the most beloved man in the world, and the beauty is that you can save them from things indefinitely."

Max scratched the base of his neck. "The way you said that makes me think we're not on the same page."

"Oh, I'm sure we are. We come out with a huge Media© blitz focusing on a few of the more obvious Iiite schemes, which will no longer be in action. Then you publicly uncover and thwart another every few months or so. We can make a reality TV show about your research. For the most impact, we should make people think there's something wrong with them, then thwart what is causing it."

"Nope, definitely not on the same page. I want to help people. I want to get rid of the culture of fear, not perpetuate it."

The Count set his snifter on the side table and leaned forward. "But what I propose is the opposite of a culture of fear. It will create a culture where people are sure everything will be okay because you are watching over them. You will be more than a big brother, more than a super hero. The people will worship you as a god."

"That's not what I want, and to be honest, I hate that way of thinking. I'm allergic to bullshit. I will not be a part of manipulation for personal gain."

The Count smiled. "That's the fire that made you a star. I never said you couldn't fix problems. I only outlined the way to make people best understand and appreciate what you have done for them.

"Max, you probably didn't know this, but you had horrible cancer before I cured you just now. Are you relieved? No. You are probably confused, though. On the other hand, if I told you that you had melanoma and made you believe you had a sixty percent chance of dying, then gave you a few months to obsess over every little wart, zit and mole, before telling you I cured it, you would be elated and in my debt forever. In either case, the point is not whether you ever had cancer or whether I healed you. The point is that in one scenario you are merely confused, and in the other you are happy. You feel alive and appreciative for what I have done. It's not what you do that makes life better, it's how you sell it."

The Count leaned back and crossed his legs. "Now, if I understand you correctly, you believe that the world can and should be made safer, more enjoyable, people should be smarter, strife should be eliminated, etcetera. You want to achieve these goals by filling the vacuum left by the Iiites. So you must also believe that your single, surface-educated brain can manage the world better than all the genetically modified, hyper-educated strategists who have been running things since before you were born. That's the kind of ego I like to work with. I honestly believe that if you can drop the altruistic pipe-dream and the self-doubt, and come up with a specific set of goals, we will be able to achieve them. However, you will have to let me do my job. Do you want to be Mother Theresa or Sister Mary nobody-gives-a-fuck who did the same things in the same places, but did not inspire millions of humans to be slightly less shitty to each other?"

Max groaned, squeezed his eyes shut, and flopped backwards. "I don't care about fame and I don't want to rule the world. That's always been the problem with government. Anybody who wants power shouldn't have it. I basically just want to fill that vacuum so some other asshole can't come in and fuck things up again.

"I figure, if the world has to have a leader, it might as well have one who wants to make it better for everybody instead of just himself." Max hiccupped. *Maybe I shouldn't have shot all that liquor on an empty stomach.*

Looking amused, the Count leaned forward, made a pyramid out of his fingers, and rested his nose at its peak. "Tell me, what *is* the first thing that comes to mind when you think of the world's problems?"

"People are selfish shits. They always want to get ahead by trampling each other. Among other things, I want people to realize that:

Most things aren't important enough to get worked up about.

The important stuff, like how to make the world more efficient, safer, and more pleasant, are basically universal. We like having enough to eat, clean water, plenty of oxygen, safe shelter, abundant sex, a few toys. We don't like being sick. We don't like being oppressed or taken advantage of. The necessities are all taken care of. That alone should make us happy, but we get tripped up by our primitive instincts. Basically, we aren't evolved enough to be happy. We're in an evolutionary awkward phase..."

Greystoke cleared his throat loudly. "All right, that's a good enough place to start. Your best bet is to start a new religion. We can do that. The Neo-Catholistics, Metists, Jengists*, Baptastics*, Atheists, and other religions are all going to come after you like a pack of rabid dogs, but I'll take care of that. Would you prefer to create a deity from scratch, or would you rather refurbish one of the dead ones?"

"Why would I want to start a religion?"

"A religion is nothing more than a map of reality, a system of beliefs which makes sense of the way things work. If you want to make people adhere to your belief system, you have to motivate them, hence the all-powerful, vengeful deity. I suppose you could write a book of philosophy, but, aside from a few college students stupid enough to waste money on a worthless degree, no one is going to read it. Also, you would be throwing away your messiah status, which is a huge step backwards."

"Yeah, but why can't I just do the world leader thing? You know, give impassioned speeches, set up organizations, advise people. That sort of thing."

"We can do that, but it's going to be significantly more difficult to sell the public on a form of government given that they didn't have one before and you just fought a war to "free" them. You aren't going to become another Fidel Castro, are you? I'm afraid that is what people are going to think if you come out in favor of government."

Max hung his head. "I'm not in favor of government. I'm in favor of electing a head of cabbage president, putting it in a room with lots of guards, and making one law that says no new laws can be made without the president's consent."

"What happens when the cabbage rots?"

"Well, you'd obviously have to have the guards change the head out on a weekly basis without telling anyone. I mean, people would know it was symbolic."

"And who would pay for the guards and cabbages? Would you levy taxes?"

"I don't know. I mean, I obviously wouldn't do that for real. That would be silly. I was just trying to state my political views metaphorically. Truth is, I have no idea how to make the world stop sucking. We could kill the richest one percent and redistribute their wealth evenly to the rest of the world."

The Count looked like Max had just skull-fucked his grandmother.

Max explained. "Sure it's simplistic and cruel, but it would give everyone left an equal chance to do something significant. Stuff would get invented. Poor people could start their own businesses. The money would all be in the pockets of the new one percent by the end of the year, but it would shake things up a bit."

Greystoke was so mad he momentarily lost his accent. "Never let anyone hear you say that. I mean it. If anything that stupid passes your lips again... I shall have you out on the street immediately.

He regained his composure and continued. "For the good of our partnership, I will assume you are simply drunk, and do not really want to kill my family and redistribute my assets. Surely you understand that in order to accomplish anything on a large scale you must make friends of those who are in a position to help you.

"Someone will always have the most money and power. The best thing the poor can do to improve their position is to ingratiate themselves to the rich. Look at the microcosm of family politics. You haven't earned the money for a car of your own yet, so you have to borrow theirs. You are proposing we slit their throats and take the car instead of complimenting them, asking nicely, and getting the full benefits of their resources."

God, I must be drunk if this pompous ass can make me feel stupid. I know he's wrong. Why can't I think of anything to say?

Max stood, and tried to clear his head by pacing in front of the fire. "I wasn't really proposing that, but I could argue that good parents don't try to keep their kids from succeeding in life. They know everybody benefits if the kid has his own car. If dad can't afford to buy another car, he at least wants to see his kid earn enough to buy one of his own. In your metaphor, you're defending shitty parents, and, yes, if your parents are abusive it probably is best to slit their throats."

The Count sighed, his anger fading into boredom. "The smash-the-system stance is great for rock'n'roll or cinema, but completely worthless in the real world. The system has been improving itself ever since man first traded a stick for a rock. It *is* flawed. There *are* those who take advantage, but starting from scratch is not so much "throwing the baby out with the bathwater" as it is dynamiting the bathroom.

He poured himself another drink and continued. "You have a lot of ballyhoo right now, but don't think for a moment that you are bulletproof. I could end your celebrity with one phone call, and I'm far from the top of the social totem. The first key to success is to know when to destroy and when to befriend."

"Look, stop right there. I'm not selling my soul, or crawling into bed with a bunch of assholes. You think I'm naïve or altruistic or whatever because I want to do something for others. You might be right, but I'm not naïve enough to think I'm going to make a difference by doing things the same way they've always been done. That would be like trying to steer a boulder while it's rolling down a mountain by pushing it along. It's too big to steer. What you need is a big wall, or another boulder, something to get in front of it."

Greystoke looked as though he might bite at any moment. "The metaphors have gotten a bit out of hand. Let's put this into literal terms. I have an infrastructure of manipulation which can help you achieve the level of power that you desire. Once you are there, you can do as you please, but to get there you will have to work within the system. I will help you as long as it benefits me, but it does not benefit me to throw myself in front of rolling boulders, metaphorical or otherwise. Please tell me in plain English, can we work together, or not."

I was right all along. There's no way this is going to work. If I'm going to do this, I'm going to do it my way. What do I need them for anyway? They already coached me on making public appearances.

Max finished his drink and set the snifter on the table. "To be honest, I think our goals might be too different. I'm going to try to come up with a game plan, something specific. When I have something more concrete we can talk again and see whether or not you can help me."

God, I hope I'm not standing over a trap-door.

Greystoke frowned. "You disappoint me, Max. I thought you were ready to face your destiny. We will speak again, but if you waste one more second of my time I will ghost you so thoroughly that your headstone will be blank." He pushed a button on the side-table, and two Iiite butlers appeared in the doorway.

"Please show Mister Quick the door."

"No need for that. I know the way." Max offered his hand. "It's been interesting."

The Count sneered and gave it a weak squeeze.

Max smiled. "I don't think this was a waste of time at all."

"Yes, well, I'll send you a bill for the Cognac."

Max laughed as the goons locked arms with him and dragged him towards the door. *I guess the 007 stuff's not over after all.*

# TEENAGE PUNK ROCK ACTION MUTANTS

"Goddammit! Munchkin god hates me."

Max gritted his teeth as Hawk slid the "...of the ancient gods" modifier card into place. All Max had in play was a pair of shitty ghouloshes. Pope was doing pretty good, but Hawk had half the deck laid out in front of him. He won every game they played, and it was getting old.

*Fucking Munchkin.* Max drew a door card. "For fuck-sake, Cowthulu? Really?!"

Hawk grinned, and let out a little snort of approval. "Golly Max, you think there's a high-level monster you haven't lost to yet?"

Pope was smiling as well. "I'll help you—for four treasures."

"I'll get more treasures if I die."

"True, but you won't get any levels. You win by getting levels."

Max didn't care anymore. This was the twelfth losing game in a row, and it was starting to get to him. He hadn't been outside in days. He'd have already gnawed through his wrists if not for the contact-high he was getting from the beauty fumes that wafted through the beaded curtain from Rusty Nails.

Max tossed his cards in the middle of the table. "Do whatever you want. I'm done. If I don't get some fresh air soon, I'm going to eat my own face."

Hawk looked deeply concerned. "You don't want to finish the game?"

"Don't worry. You win, like always."

Pope's voice went up an octave. "No he doesn't. We're both at level eight."

"Whatever, you both win."

Pope lay his cards down and began to condescend. "There cannot be two winners. Two winners negate competition, the very foundation on which all games are based."

Hawk lay his cards down too. "Tired of Munchkin? We could play Illuminati again."

"Nope, can't take it anymore." Max stood and stretched. "I'm going to go get something to eat. Anyone care to join me?"

"You know you're gonna get mobbed, maybe killed, right?"

"This game is not over until someone wins! Accept my offer, or roll to run away."

Max ignored Pope's outburst. "You think it's going to get any better after tomorrow? This might be the last chance I have to go out without a full security detail."

Hawk nodded. "I guess you got a point. We're gonna hafta get used to bein' famous some time. Might as well get some practice in."

Pope picked up the dice and rolled for Max. "You die. Draw eight cards."

"Sorry man, we're going out. You can come if you want."

"This game will be finished if I have to play all the roles myself." He drew eight cards, laid out Max's new spread, and kicked open a door. "Boomp! Level four, the Geek Ones, minus-two against females. My sex was changed to female, I have plus thirteen, and my level is eight."

"You beat it. You win. Game over."

"I most certainly do not. Even if neither of you interfere, I still have to kill one more monster to reach the winning level."

Max and Hawk shared a look of exasperation. "Cheeky! We're going out."

They heard a rash of crashes and squeals followed by effeminate curses as Cheeky burst through the beads. He looked at Max as though to ask if he was serious.

"Yes, we're going out. You want to come?"

Cheeky did a backflip, then rushed up Max's leg to snuggle around his shoulders. Max scooped a pair of Rusty's sunglasses off the counter, and slid them on. "What do you think? Good disguise?"

"Nothing says inconspicuous like a big pair of pink, rhinestone-crusted sunglasses."

"I'm glad you approve."

Pope was still reciting Hawk's bonuses as they left.

Max spotted several zombies shuffling around outside. He wondered if one of them might have a message from Adhra, then remembered she was dead and the war was over—and had been over for almost a week. Why couldn't he get that through his head? Why didn't that make him happy?

It was a nice day; maybe a few degrees cooler than Max would have liked without having a coat on, but much better than the stifling seventy-two degrees Rusty insisted on. The sky was lemon yellow, the color for no suspected terrorist activity. Max was a little surprised there weren't more people out, but their absence made the day all the nicer.

Hawk looked at the sky and snorted. "I don't know if I'll ever get used to that."

"Yeah. No terrorists to have alerts about. It seems unnatural."

"Buck up." He slapped Max on the back. "Somebody'll get a hair up their ass soon enough, 'specially now you've gone all holy."

"Eat a crate of dicks."

Hawk smiled big and toothy. He wasn't going to let go any time soon.

"Dude, I tried to share credit. I wish I could make the Media© recognize you, but I can't. Stop taking their dickishness out on me."

"No need to get all bent out of shape. I's just ribbin' ya. I'm just glad you smartened up about that dick-pimple in a top hat before it was too late. Still can't believe you were gonna work with that guy."

"That dick-pimple still has all the resources. We might need him down the McRoad."

Hawk's lip twitched. He stared straight ahead like he wanted to punch a hole in the world. "What do you want to eat?"

Max knew there was no getting through to him once something triggered his mental warzone. One of these days, his hatred of Greystoke was going to cause major problems. Greystoke was like a new cat that wouldn't stop pushing the old dog's buttons. All Max could do was keep them apart until they got used to each other.

"I don't care. I guess we need to go somewhere with a patio, somewhere cheekworm* friendly. Let's just walk until we see something."

Cheeky drooped around his shoulders staring upside-down through the windows of the businesses they passed. To their left, McKanics were pulling the engine out of a Super Car. Some sort of Mass was going on at the McChurch, but Max couldn't tell what religion. They all used bacon incense now.

A woman with three Chihuahuas on leashes came around the corner and walked their way. She stopped a few feet away so two of her dogs could claim the ex-cheerleader whose neck was chained to the fence around the parking lot. The third dog looked around frantically as if he was only interested in free-range zombies.

The woman noticed them looking at her and turned her back to them. She was pretty in a TV sitcom kind of way, but obviously a shitty person. Max couldn't resist fucking with her.

"You know, she's probably somebody's daughter. They're not going to be happy she smells like piss."

The woman jerked the leashes and walked away without looking back.

"You have a nice day, now." The wind shifted, blowing pissed-on zombie funk straight up Max's nose. She was not as fresh as she looked.

Hawk coughed and pulled his shirt over his nose. "Phooee, goddamn dog piss is an improvement. Folks need to learn to let go."

She seemed to be wearing fresh makeup. Max held his nose and lifted her skirt with the toe of his shoe to confirm his suspicions. "Eww, why do people always have to be gross and pathetic?" He hurried away from the stench.

"Huh?" Hawk jogged up next to him, and they continued ahead at a normal pace.

"No panties. She's somebody's loved one, but they ain't family."

A second later Hawk understood. "Eww. You think she's somebody's fuck toy?"

"Zombies don't shit, and parents usually want their daughters to wear underwear beneath their skirts. She's dressed as a cheerleader. Do the math."

"Damn, I've heard of people doing that, but I figured it was an urban myth. It can't be safe. Gives new meaning to the term crotch rot." Hawk shook the nasty thoughts out of his head. He noticed a Mega-K down the street the lady had come. "Could go to the FÜD Kourt".

"I don't really want FÜD, and I don't know their policy on animals."

"We're headed for an S-district*, so there won't be nothing nice enough to have a patio for a while. Let's take a right by the Kreamery. I think there's an I-district a few miles up."

Max shook his head. "I don't want to deal with I-district right now."

"Neither do I. Those I-Force fuckers'll shake ya down for wearing the wrong shoes. But the closer we get, the more chance there is of finding a patio."

"Good point."

Cheeky perked up at the mention of the Kreamery. "Yummmm!"

Max scratched the back of Cheeky's head to calm him. "Maybe on the way back. I need some real food first. It's been ages since I've eaten anything that didn't come out of the freezer."

He heard two pops, and the taste of blood filled his sinuses.

He was on the ground. His ears were ringing.

"What the fuck?"

His vision cleared as a zip-tie pulled tight around his wrists. Hawk was on the ground beside him. Cheeky was oozing yellow goo from a hole in his side, while two K-squad pigs nudged him into a garbage bag with the barrels of their guns.

Three other pigs held Max down and breathed chipotle in his face while the fourth stood proudly above him. "Thought we forgot about ya, huh? Semper fi, motherfucker!" His boot crashed into Max's ribs.

His buddies grabbed Max by the hair and dragged him into an alley. Two others took Hawk by the feet. His face ground against the pavement as they followed close behind.

If I survive this, I'm going to get some security.

When they were out of view of the shops, Hawk and Cheeky were tossed into a dumpster. Max was thrown face down in the center of the alley, and all six commenced stomping on his legs.

"Can I do something for you gentlemen?" Max asked through gritted teeth.

One of the pigs punched him in the face. "Nobody kills my men and lives happily ever after."

"Not sure what you mean, man, but I'm sure we can get to the bottom of this if you'd just stop beating the shit out of me."

The pig, Max assumed the leader, picked him up by the hair, and slammed his head against the pavement. "That ring any bells, fuckwad?"

His ears were ringing, but his memory wasn't picking up.

The alpha pig motioned for his men to stop. "You really don't remember, do ya? Well let me jog your memory. First, your little freak killed five of my men who were responding to an Iiite attack. Then—"

"Actually that was a different..."

The alpha pig's boot butted in. "Don't you fucking interrupt me. Then, you bust into Bio-Corp and kill two more of my men to get the little freak back. Yeah, we figured it out. You must think we're the dumbest bunch of cunts in the fucking world. On top of everything else, you killed my sister and her douchebag boyfriend."

Oh yeah. That happened.

"I don't give a shit what the Media© says. You're a lobster lover and a homicidal fucking maniac."

Fuck.

The pig stuck the barrel of his pistol in Max's mouth. "Any last words?"

Max mumbled around the barrel. "I'm sorry for your loss?"

"Smartass piece of shit!"

The pig drew his leg back then flew into the wall so hard his cranium exploded. An Iiite with an ambiguous smirk and purple elf-locks stood in his place. Two other Iiites launched themselves at the pigs and proceeded to toss them around like water balloons. Max kept his eyes on the leader. It was over before the pigs could get a shot off.

The first Iiite cocked his head in recognition. "You *are* the guy."

Well, double fuck.

Max wriggled into a sitting position, scooched over to the wall and tried to smile innocently. "What guy might that be?"

"Don't worry. We like you. A lot of us wanted to do something about the Mittons for a while, but we didn't know how." He cut Max's hands free and offered to help him up.

"Thanks, but I think I'll sit here for a minute." Max rubbed his legs, but he could barely feel it through the white-hot agony of displaced cells. "Would you mind checking on my friends? They're in that dumpster."

They opened the lid. Profanity and the stench of rotting Tex-Mex flooded the alley. Hawk was still snarling as they set him on his feet. "What the fuck just happened?"

"Pigs are assholes. What'cha gonna do?" An Iiite with a green mullet cut his hands free.

Max's voice was high and desperate. "Please tell me Cheeky's okay. It looked like they shot him."

Hawk retrieved the bag, and handed it to Max without opening it. Max poured his little friend onto his lap. "Shit, they did."

Cheeky was barely moving. His eyes were full of pain and fear, but not the fear of a dying animal. The hole in his side had already stopped oozing. He licked his wound, made an ick face and sneezed. It was one of the cutest and saddest things Max had ever seen.

"Are you gonna be okay, little guy?

Cheeky sighed and nodded yes. His eyes returned the question.

Max laughed. "I've had worse hangovers." He put his thumb in one of the suckers. "Go ahead. At least one of us can get back to normal.

Cheeky took hold and Max felt his life-force draining into his little friend. A few seconds later Cheeky was good as new.

Hawk huffed. "I'm fine too, thanks for askin'."

The right side of his face was dripping blood, but there was no permanent damage. Max raised an eyebrow to warn Hawk he was sliding into whiny bitch territory.

Hawk let out a little growl, and tried to look manly. "You sure you're all right? You look like you just got done filmin' a German porno."

Max smiled, setting off his busted lip. "These guys pooped the party before the pigs could get my pants off." Hawk offered him a hand, but Max waved it away. He could feel himself healing. The pain had already decreased by half, but he wasn't in a dancing mood either.

Hawk glanced around at the punks, picked elf locks as the alpha and slapped him on the shoulder. "Thanks for the help, boys. Could have used you during the war."

The Iiite shook his head. "No, you couldn't have."

The mulleted one came forward aggressively. "War is fucking stupid."

The alpha reined him in by his hair. "Down, boy. What my feisty comrade is trying to say is we don't believe in solving problems with violence."

Hawk broke into one of his big-as-Texas smiles. "Coulda fooled me."

"We're not idealists, we're not pussies and we're not stupid. I could pontificate on our ideology for the next week, but I'm guessing you don't really give a shit.

"Fair enough."

The pain in Max's legs was reaching manageable levels. "How are things down below?"

"A little better. Getting around is a bitch, so a lot of us are coming up to the surface more. Good thing for you."

"So people down there are generally okay with me?"

The Iiites all laughed.

"Hell, no!" Elf Locks plopped down beside him. "They're better off, for the most part, but you did blow up their stuff and kill their loved ones. You know how petty the little people can be."

Mullet shot Hawk a dirty look. "But I'm sure they'll get over it in no time."

"Some of the shops you destroyed are using their insurance money to relocate to the surface. You're finally going to have access to good music again."

Max offered a crumpled smile. "Well then, I guess it was all worth it."

Mullet guy crouched and looked Max in the eye. "You really serious about all that brotherhood stuff?"

"Yeah, why wouldn't I be?"

"A lot of people think the speech you gave was a stunt, or you were just trying to keep the Iiites from killin' ya. A lot of other people think you're some kind of messiah. Not sure which one worries me more."

"None of the above. I'm just an unfortunate jackass who's being toyed with by beings from another dimension."

Everybody laughed like he was joking.

Elf Locks punched him on the shoulder gently, sending a sharp pain down his spine. "You're all right, man. I kinda expected you to be a douchebag, but you're all right. The name's Paul, by the way."

"Pleased to make your acquaintance. I'm Max. That's Hawk. This little guy's Cheeky.

Mullet guy nodded. "Skeeter."

The third Iiite, a quiet guy sporting numerous tattoos and an impressive goatee shoved his hands in his pockets. "Charlie."

Paul threw his arm around Charlie's shoulder and dragged him over to Max. "Charlie's a big fan of yours."

Charlie turned beet red, and elbowed Paul in the ribs.

"He was the one that talked us into following you."

"Well, thanks, Charlie. Maybe I can return the favor sometime."

Charlie couldn't take his eyes off his shoes. "Dude, you got rid of the Fist and the M.I.L.F. Least I could do."

"We were just on the way to get some food. I'm buying, if you guys know a good restaurant."

"We just ate, but I got nothin' better to do." Paul glanced at his friends, who shrugged in agreement. "There's a burger place around the corner with a patio."

"Works for me." Max draped Cheeky around his shoulders, and put out his hands. "Help me out?"

Hawk and Paul helped him to his feet and around the corner to Hole in the Wall burgers. They made their way through all the hipsters to a picnic-table in the back. The walls were covered with reproductions of classic rock posters; toothpaste and gum mostly, with a few vodkas here and there. He'd always hated places like this. Scenesters flocked by the millions to feel cool eating the same burger they would get at McDougle's for half the price. He smiled, knowing they would soon have to spend millions redecorating with non-commercial art.

Paul gave him a funny look. "What's with the grin? This place isn't that good."

"Nothing, just picturing what'll happen to this place when people stop paying to be brainwashed."

"My dad owns a memorabilia company. He's already gearing up to flood the surface with concert posters from the 1960s."

"Why does he think everybody's going to go hippie?"

"Normals are just as gullible as they were a month ago. They'll buy what's available."

Max smirked. "So you're okay with your dad profiteering on the stupidity the M.I.L.F. cultivated."

"Not really, but it's a lot easier to get people to take you seriously if you've never hit them up for change. What's that look for? You think he should refuse to sell them stuff until they pass a college level music appreciation exam?"

Max smiled. He liked this kid, but he wasn't done giving him shit. "So, you'll use the money your father dupes them out of to try to spread the message of freedom?"

"Duping them? Seriously? Even if you classify selling people relatively interesting concert posters as duping them, that ranks pretty low on the list of social atrocities. I'm a realist. People are gonna do what they're gonna do. All I can do is try to set a good example. I try to do no harm. I try to get others to think for themselves, but in the end everybody's responsible for their own happiness, and their own mistakes."

"I didn't think there was such a thing as a moderate punk."

Paul laughed. The other two turned red. "Yeah, well..."

A cute, bald girl walked over and pulled a pad of paper out of her apron. "You guys want something?"

They ordered three Black Flag burgers and a bucket of sweet potato fries, and the girl moped to the kitchen.

After a few moments of uncomfortable silence, Skeeter and Hawk went to the restroom. Charlie was staring nervously at his hands.

"So, Charlie, what do you do when you're not rescuing damsels in distress?"

Charlie jumped at the sound of his name.

Paul answered for him. "Charlie's the lead singer for Chemical Compound, he's a Tantra instructor at the Youth Enrichment Service, and he does a lot with the Niites."

"Yeah? I heard about them. It's like a civilian Peace Corps, or something."

Charlie sputtered. "I... uh... yeah, we... we do stuff to try to cure the insanity living underground has caused. Like, we're really disconnected from nature, so we would take the next generation of M.I.LF. on field trips to the woods, and feed them mushrooms." He scratched the top of his head nervously. "When they got home, they'd go right back to being little assholes, but at least for a minute they knew what it was like to be an animal instead of a super-genius overlord."

Max raised his eyebrows and nodded, unsure what to say. It made sense in a goofy antiquated sort of way, but he'd expected something more original.

"Interesting, I never would have thought to try that."

Charlie took it as a compliment. He smiled real big, turned bright red and was about to respond when a big, bear-looking fucker butted in.

"Hey, you that Max guy from the news?"

"Yeah, I guess I am."

"You killed my father!"

The blade of a Swiss Army knife flashed in front of his face. If the blade had been a little longer—or the bear a little less spastic—it would have sliced him right across the eyes. Charlie jumped up, thrusting his shoulder into the guy's side. Vengeance Bear lost his balance and tumbled forward. His nose exploded on the next table over, and he hit the ground rapid-firing puffs of red mist into the floorboards.

He slowly raised his head. "This ain't about you, lobster! I suggest you go back home and eat some shit."

Charlie brought his boot down on the man's head three times before he stopped growling racial slurs and settled down for a nap.

Hawk pushed through the crowd, saw the man, and groaned. "I can't leave you alone for a second."

Max stood and growled. "I'm sick of this shit." He locked eyes with the waitress. "Can I get that order to go?"

Looking a little scared and a little horny, she disappeared into the crowd.

Max walked around to where Charlie stood over their attacker. "Thanks *again*."

"No problem, though you might want to hire some real security. It looks like you got yourself some enemies."

"No shit. Sorry I'm going to have to cut this short. Let me give you my number and we can get together sometime. Maybe I can figure out a way to repay you."

Charlie stared at the napkin Max handed him like it had the meaning of life written on it.

Paul shook his hand. "It's been fun."

Charlie pulled a crumpled sticker out of his pocket and handed it to Max. "My number's on the back. Call me for, you know, whatever."

The sticker showed two arms in the process of fist-bumping, a variant of the M.I.L.F.s symbol, which was two arms locked at the hand as if shaking.

"Cute. Is this your activist group, your band?"

"Both."

"Ah."

The waitress returned with their bag. Max handed her twenty-five dollars and said, "Keep the change."

He and Hawk nodded to their new friends and made for the door.

Skeeter called behind them. "You two be careful now. Good luck not getting killed."

# BEYOND THE GREEN ROOM DOOR

The Dick Chompsky Show's green-room was less impressive than Max had expected. It wasn't even green, more of a grayish blue, and the chairs were little more than a metal frame with itchy black cotton stretched over eighth-inch padding. The finger-sandwiches were dry, and the fruit tray was so old the flies were dying of liver failure.

Max jerked open the mini-fridge. "Hey, Juicetastic! Oh, it's all Peachberri."

Hawk chuckled. "Pass me one. Still don't understand why you hate peaches."

Max shrugged and tossed him a bottle. "I don't know. They taste fuzzy, like there's an animal juiced in with it."

Hawk cracked it open and took a swig. "Probably are a few critters in there, but no more than the other flavors."

"Still." he shut the door and glanced at the fruit tray one more time. He couldn't help but think how much more comfortable he would have been if Greystoke had been involved. He probably wouldn't have him on Chompsky at all. Unlike most news shows, Dick had a vague idea of what was going on in the world and occasionally seemed to care.

Max sat next to Cheeky and lovingly squished the fatty lumps on his head. A live feed of the show played on the old TV by the door. Dick was funny, as always. Max liked him despite his occasional pandering to the lowest common denominator. All pundits did it, but Dick was good enough that people would watch him even if he opted for a little bit of class. He hadn't whipped a dildo out so far today, so that was a good sign.

Dick's first guest, The Han, was being stupid enough for the both of them. All his responses were in burp form, and he'd already given the audience the red eye twice.

Why did I have to be scheduled the same day as that douche-y, no-jetpack-sharing little shit?

The Han dropped his pants a third time.

Next time I'm going to have to ask who else is on the show.

Hawk gave Max a long look. "Nervous?"

"Actually, I'm not. I should be. People are going to be paying attention, picking me apart, sizing me up. I guess once you've been shot at, blown up, and attacked by a giant chicken-monster, public speaking isn't that daunting. I mean, what's the worst that can happen? If I flop, I get to fade into obscurity.

"The worst that could happen is some vindictive asshole slipped past security with a gun."

He was still pissed because I-Force wouldn't let him help with security.

"I'll be fine. Those guys know their shit." Hawk needed to be needed, so he added, "Besides I feel safer when you're here with me."

Hawk smiled and puffed up.

A girl with an ePad appeared in the doorway. "You're on in two minutes."

Max kissed Cheeky on the forehead. "You be good."

Hawk walked with him to the door, but the woman blocked him with her arm. "I'm sorry, who are you?"

"Private security. Please step aside."

"I'm sorry. Only Guests and crew are allowed on set."

"I'll stay in the wings, then."

She shook her head. "We have strict rules. You can watch the show from here."

"How am I supposed to guard his body if I can't be near it?"

"Stay in the room or we will remove you from the building." She glanced at her tablet then at Max. "We now have one minute."

Hawk looked like he was about to break her toy over her head, so Max got between them. "It's okay. Just keep an eye on Cheeky. I'll be back in a minute."

"It's not fucking okay. I can't have your back from another room."

The woman jabbed her tablet into Hawk's ribs. Max heard the clicking of electricity as Hawk seized up and fell over.

"Fuck. That wasn't necessary."

"Forty-five seconds."

Cheeky growled at her. Max hummed a few bars to calm him, then said, "Cheeky, stay here and behave. I'm okay. He's okay. Don't get in trouble."

"Thirty seconds." She pointed her tablet at Max.

"Okay, shit."

He dragged Hawk into the hall and closed the door to keep Cheeky out of trouble, then followed her to his mark. The Han was wrapping up his pointless pandering by thanking the voters for all their 'dope' support, and for voting him the new CEO of Allbright Records.

The stage was bigger than it looked on TV, presumably to make the massive ex-front lineman seem less like a meathead. It was all done in black and orange—his old team colors—making it look like a big Halloween diorama. But at three-hundred-and-fifty pounds of muscle and attitude, Dick wasn't the type of guy you wanted to criticize. He could decorate with dead babies and macaroni art, and nobody would say a word.

When the Han finally shut up, Dick played a clip from Max's speech. "Don't join them when they offer to organize a better world. Everybody do your own thing, but be considerate. Work to help others instead of yourselves. Above all else, think for yourselves, because if you don't, if you let the f—heads take it all over again, you deserve what you get. And what you'll get is a big s—sandwich; oppression, hunger, war, rioting, every flavor of misery."

Hmm, I'm going to have to be careful to not contradict myself.

The clip ended. Dick and the Han stood, clapping as the announcer screamed, "Maxwell Quiiiik."

Max ran out, screaming and jumping around like he'd just made a touchdown. He hated this part, but it was more important than ever that he display energy and self-confidence.

The Owls might be a bunch of corrupt douche-bags, but they'd taught him well. The audience was going crazy. The guys were screaming so hard they barely noticed the girls had all lifted their shirts.

Max did one more lap around Dick's desk and then took a seat between him and the Han.

Dick's handshake was so firm Max felt something crack.

"Welcome to the show."

Max smiled through the pain. "I'm honored to be here."

The Han offered his fist for a bump. "My ninja."

Max nodded, and offered his fist for further abuse.

Dick tapped his pen on the desk. "There's been a lot of buzz about you lately; pundits, sit-coms, artists, etc... all because of a speech you gave, impromptu, as I understand, about how you saved the world from an unseen menace. You ended saying you just want to be left alone. So, I guess my first question has to be, what the fuck are you doing here?"

Max laughed along with everyone else, and tried not to sputter. "Yeah, that's a good question. Uh, I don't really know. I guess it's so I can hopefully put an end to this Max-o-mania stuff that's been consuming the Media©. I mean, it's crazy, every time I go outside somebody tries to kill me, worship me or both."

The audience laughed.

"I'm not the messiah, by the way. I'm not even a hero. I got caught up in a crazy power struggle, and I didn't die. Whoop-di-doo."

Applause.

"But you did more than just not die, you won. You took down an epic, evil organization. In the last few days, a veritable tsunami of witnesses have come forward to back up your claims. The stuff they were doin' to our food, our water, our air, our kids, it was nothin' short of diabolical. It seems like every five minutes somebody else comes forward with new info about how the M.I.L.F. was wrecking our world. You put a stop to that."

Applause.

The Han raised his fist. "Freedom be, yo."

God, I hate that guy.

"I really can't stress this enough; I didn't mean to say that *I* saved the world. I was just one of many who collectively brought the M.I.L.F. down. Thousands of the world's greatest minds gave their lives for this, every one of them braver, smarter, and more deserving of life than me. A wise man once told me it's the cowards that get the medals and give the speeches about bravery. Everybody else is dead."

Everyone shared an uncomfortable laugh. Max realized he was killing the mood, and decided to change the subject. Before he could, Dick continued. "That *is* a good point. Still, millions of Quickians are hoping, and even expecting that you're going to somehow bring about a new eon of blissful prosperity. There's even rumors the Catholistics're afraid you're gonna go full-blown religious, and take all their parishioners. The world is your oyster. What are you gonna do now?"

Max crossed his legs and tried to look cool. "We've been talking about that a lot. The Riot Nrrds want to get back to their areas of study, but the consensus is that would be selfish. The Riot Nrrds have always been about helping people, helping society. Now, we have the opportunity to do something significant. Right now, we're leaning towards a foundation to keep an eye on big business, a place for people to go when they know something bad is being done, but they can't stop it on their own."

The Han cocked an eyebrow. There was no applause.

"But I thought you were done saving the world. What was it you said?"

They rolled the clip of Max saying, "I did my part. Now I'm done. The rest is up to you. All you have to do to protect what I've given you is not listen to their bullshit when they come to take it away. Don't join them when they offer to organize a better world."

Dick tapped his pen on the desk again. "Isn't that what you're proposing to do, organize a better world?"

"That's whack, yo."

Max uncrossed his legs. "No, not really. I don't want to start a government, but the way things are now, it would be easy for some megalomaniac to sneak in and take things over."

"That's true, but I am curious. What happened that made you lose your faith in humanity?"

"Nothing. We just want people to know we have their back."

Smiling slyly, Dick leaned back in his chair. "But isn't that how every government in history has justified their existence? In some twisted way, don't you think that's what the Iiites thought they were doing?"

Max shook his head. "The M.I.L.F just wanted to make things better for the M.I.L.F. and maybe the Iiites. But to be clear, I am not proposing a government. This would just be an organization that watches out for corruption, and informs the people when they find it. We wouldn't be governing anything or putting anybody in jail.

"The problem with government is that it attracts people who are hungry for power. The people who should run things never do, because they have no interest in controlling other people. The old system of government collapsed because anyone who got into a position of power owed too many favors to do any good. Well, that and M.I.L.F. manipulation."

Max took a sip of water from the cup with his name on it. "Governors always devolve into bloated, self-indulgent monsters. The world doesn't need a government. It needs a superhero; someone to inspire them to do the right thing, and protect them from those that won't."

Dick took off his glasses and leaned forward. "But who decides what's right? This ideological juggernaut of yours would need to be more than human. Are you proposing we make God get off his ass and guide us, or are you talking about yourself? Are you the superhero the world needs?"

"No. I'm just a guy who's always been annoyed with all the evil and stupidity in the world. I don't want to feel helpless again. I grew up that way, like most people. If there's something I can do to keep helplessness from being a common experience again, I feel obligated to do it. The war taught me a lot about living, and personal responsibility. I learned to take action instead of bitching. I hope I can inspire others to do the same. Nonviolently, of course. If everybody started waging war on everything they don't like, we'd all be dead by the end of the week."

Applause.

"I'm surprised to hear you say that. My people did some digging, and painted a very different picture of you."

"Huh?"

Dick put his glasses on, and looked at a stack of papers on his desk. "Were you not diagnosed as a classic narcissistic sociopath?"

"Well, if you want to discuss psychiatry, it's important to consider that most psychiatrists were drawn to the study of the human mind because they wanted to figure out what's wrong with *themselves*. Also, you have to have a massive ego to think you can talk to somebody for a couple hours a week, and then define them using a small set of disorders that were all discovered by other psychiatrists. Not to say there's nothing valid in psychiatry, but you have to take what they say with a grain of salt."

Dick laughed, but the crowd remained silent. "I'm going to take that as a yes."

"Yes, technically, when I was sixteen, but my psychiatrist had just gone through a messy divorce. At that point she was diagnosing all her male patients as narcissistic sociopaths. Also, I challenge you to find a teenager who doesn't think the sun rises and sets in their ass. You can't do it. It's a natural developmental stage."

Dick looked like he'd have Max in checkmate in three movies. "I can see you've given this a lot of thought, and I do see your point. But not every teenager is connected to a string of accidents and disappearances the way you are." Dick stared at the papers as though he was reading them, but his eyes weren't moving. "Less than a year ago a woman named Heather Rickett disappeared shortly after she started seeing you. What ever happened to her?"

What the fuck is he doing? I thought this was supposed to be a puff-piece.

"I don't remember a Heather. Just before I got mixed up with the Iiites I was going out a lot, meeting a lot of people. I guess it's possible one of them was her, but I don't know anything about a disappearance."

"She also went by the name Scarlet."

Max could feel himself looking guilty. "Oh, Scarlet. Yeah, she was one of the many casualties of this war. She got mixed up in it the same way I did, wrong place, wrong time. I hate that. She was a sweet girl. She stuck by me when nobody else would."

"But you didn't know her name."

"Well, she was kind of obsessed with her image. I guess she didn't want me to know her last name was Rickett. Isn't that a disease, or something?"

"What about your parents?"

"They died in a car crash, but what does that have to do with anything?"

Dick was looking at him like a hungry dog. "Sally Miles, Lisa Duboise, Sam Turner, Rick Shay..."

The Han scooted his chair a few inches away from Max.

*Are those lights getting brighter?* "Yeah, like everyone, I've known people who've died. Where are you going with this?"

"I'm sorry, it's just that, after looking at your history, your medical records, the contradictions in what you've said, it's hard not to consider the possibility this has all been a charade. It seems the M.I.L.F. did exist, and you did have a hand in their downfall, but it's hard for a thinking man not to consider the similarity between you and, say, Fidel Castro or Adolf Hitler."

"What the fuck, man? I've been watching this show for years, and I've never seen you attack anybody like this."

Damn, it's hot.

Dick cocked his head and purred, "You're the first guest I've been afraid might take over the world."

The image of the Han holding his arms while Dick pummeled him on live TV was all that stopped Max from jumping up. "Have you listened to a word I said? I don't want to take over the world. I want to sit on my ass and watch TV. I want to eat poison-free junk food, play good video games—you know, normal stuff. All I said was that we thought it might be a good idea to try to keep the Hitlers and the Castros from taking advantage of the power vacuum we've left. I'd feel really bad if I overthrew The Iiites just to see something worse take their place."

"As would I." Dick's performance was more convincing than Max's honesty.

Size and history were mattering less and less. If he keeps this up I might have to punch that smug grin right down his throat.

"Look, I know you think you're doing the right thing, but I can't help wondering if a vindictive little birdie might have guided your thought process."

The audience booed.

Dick looked genuinely shocked. "You come on my show and accuse me of conspiring with the forces of evil? You just strengthened my resolve, sir. That is exactly what a manipulative sociopathic narcissist would do when confronted with the truth. But I assure you, sir, my viewers are not gonna buy it. Did you really think they wouldn't notice all your doublespeak? They're too smart to fall for your flim-flam."

Applause.

This is bad.

They rolled the montage Max had been dreading. "A lot of people are going to try to rush in and set up a new government. They'll come all happy faced, promising you the moon, but don't listen to them. The thing we're leaning towards right now is a foundation to keep an eye on big business. I did my part. Now I'm done. The rest is up to you. We're in a position to do a lot of good. What we need is to step up and take responsibility for our own lives. The people need somebody watching out for them. That's all we want to do. Don't join them when they offer to organize a better world. Everybody do your own thing. Think for yourselves, because if you don't, if you let the f— heads take it all over again, you deserve what you get."

The Owls are making a point. Everything I say is going to be twisted into something bad. Should I walk off, or would that make things worse? How much longer can this interview last? There has to be a commercial coming any second.

"Now, you're new to public speaking, and, to be fair, it's easy to get all twisted up in your own words. People make thoughtless statements all the time. They change their mind, make mistakes. We're running out of time, and I'd hate to think I didn't give you a fair shake. So how about you stick around, and I'll give you a chance to explain yourself. We'll put it up on the web, and straighten things out once and for all."

Fuck! Fuck! Fuck! Bastard! He won't even let me slink off in defeat! What should I do? Fuck!

Max forced a smile. "Thanks, *Dick*. That's mighty *big* of you. I'd be happy to explain myself."

"All right then. Check the website, bigdickchompsky.net, for more on Maxwell Quick: Messiah or Menace. That's our show. Everybody have a good night."

Applause. After the fanfare, the audience was ushered out of the building.

Dick turned to him and laughed. "You know, Max, I actually like you. Sorry about all that sociopath stuff."

Max worked his jaw like a rabid donkey. "Huh?"

"Look, we all answer to somebody. And my boss wanted me to take you down a peg. They gave me all this information, and you have to admit it makes you look kinda fishy. You don't strike me as evil. You're not charismatic enough. You come across as honest even when you're being attacked. That's really rare."

Max looked at the empty seats. "Is this the interview? I'm confused."

"I thought it'd be nice to take a break and explain. I don't think this interview's gonna hurt you much. You held up really well. It won't be hard to turn it around in the second part. I'll let you talk a lot. Just admit you changed your mind, talk a little more about how much work it was bringing the M.I.L.F. down and how guilty you'd feel if something terrible replaced them."

"Greystoke isn't going to let me do this on my own, is he?"

"No ass is wiped without the Owl's consent. One more allusion to them on live TV and your career is over."

"But they're as bad as the fucking M.I.L.F. Hell, they were one of their biggest tools. I don't want to have to have anything to do with them."

Dick shook his head. "Goddamn, and I thought idealism was dead. You think I wouldn't like to leave the whoopee-cushions and the dildos in the drawer? I'd love to be the next Ed Murrow, but that can't happen with the world the way it is. I'm doing what I can from inside the system to change it for the better."

"Yeah, cause that always works."

"It's hard and it's slow, but it does."

"The war used up most of my patience."

Dick laughed, looking confused. "Well, according to my sources, you were getting inside info from your girlfriend and feeding her bad info that led the Iiites into traps. There're also allegations you might have intentionally led the Nrrds into some traps. If that's the case, I'm sure you had your reasons. Point is, you were taking them down from the inside."

Dick's right. The Owls have to go. You can't make a utopia without breaking a few nefarious organizations.

Max relaxed. Finally, he knew what he had to do. Eventually he'd figure out a way to build something good in the world, or at least inspire others to, but in the meantime, he could stick to what he was good at. He would crush the Owls with their own arrogance and make way for a new renaissance. Then he'd find another bunch of assholes and take them down. Lather, rinse, repeat.

"How the fuck do you know all this?"

"I got people. You know, detectives and stuff. I don't know where they get their info, but they're never wrong."

"Yeah, no such thing as privacy anymore."

"You ready to do this? I got a date I need to get ready for."

Max nodded and put on his game face.

Dick straightened up, looked sternly at the camera and began. "Maxwell Quick: Messiah or Menace part two.

"Max was just about to explain how he went from retired general to wannabe superhero."

Max smiled and shook his head. "I did no such thing. The Media© keeps trying to paint me as more than I am. I'm not Jesus or Superman. If anything, I'm a late-blooming Harry Belafonte."

Canned laughter.

Max stopped his eyebrow from cocking and continued. "When I gave that speech, I'd just gotten out of a crazy battle with the head of the M.I.L.F. I was tired, full of adrenaline and all I wanted was to sit down and have a beer. I didn't set up a press conference. It was just like, boom, you're on live TV. I wanted to give people the good news and be done with it. Later, when my head was clearer, I started thinking about what would happen next. I started thinking about how much work we'd put into saving the world, and how much it would suck to see somebody screw it up again. It was talking to the Nrrds that convinced me to try to do something good. Before that, I had just wanted to get back to my normal life.

"I can see how it would look strange and contradictory, but, like you said, I'm new to all this. I changed my mind. I'm human. Humans learn and grow over time. Lack of contradiction would either mean I was born omniscient or my mind was stagnant. Neither of which is the case."

Dick leaned back in his chair. "Fair enough. So what exactly are your politics? What is this better world you want to work toward?"

"Politics is stupid, but human nature makes anarchy unsustainable. Anarchy only works as long as everybody wholeheartedly embraces mutual respect. Unfortunately, all you need to turn anarchy into a dictatorship is a small group of people who disregard that balance in favor of their own agenda. I don't know if you've noticed, but that's sort of mankind's jam. We just want individuals to be able to decide what they want, and pursue that ideal without some asshole ruining it for them."

Max took a sip of water and continued. "Freedom's complicated, and I freely admit I have no idea how to balance individual will and collective will. I mean, obviously if an individual's definition of a better world is one where they can run around raping children all day, that's not going to mesh with another person's desire for a safe family environment. Luckily, most people don't want to rape kids. So pedos are oppressed by the majority, and the kids are safe. When a pedo steps out of line, he's punished. That's society in a nutshell.

Dick cracked his biggest smile. "I'll be damned, you're a superhero after all. Captain Obvious, everybody."

Canned laughter and applause.

"Very funny."

Dick sat forward and put on his serious face. "All right, how about you define what you think of as actionable. At what point should a person or group take action to fix a problem?"

Max saw his serious face and raised him a thoughtful look. "One person's rights end where another's begin. If someone is hurting you, you have the right to do something about it. And I'm not talking about things that make you uncomfortable. If I have an opinion you don't like, you don't have to listen to me talk. If you think drinking is bad, don't drink, and avoid alcoholics. But if you start to make people sick, or attack them physically, something like that would be actionable. Anything you can walk away from, you should."

Applause.

"So your idea of utopia is just everybody acting like mature adults?"

"Basically. I'd like to see people working together, overlooking each other's differences, focusing on the good things, loving each other in spite of who we are.

Dick took off his glasses. "Do you think that's possible?"

Max laughed. "Hell, no. That's never going to happen. I wouldn't even know what to do in a world like that. I'd shit myself with joy if people would just stop picking each other's lives apart and focus on their own. *Maybe* after a few hundred years of *that* we might be able to start accepting and loving one another, but probably not."

Canned laughter.

"Well, Max, after talking to you I'm inclined to believe your psychiatrist was full of shit. You don't seem like a narcissist or a sociopath, so either you're a damn good liar, or you are every bit the hero you're not enough of a narcissist to see you are. Thanks for coming on the show and being so forthcoming. I know it can't be easy to talk about that part of your life."

"That's all right. Thanks for giving me the opportunity to explain everything."

Applause.

They stood and shook hands for about twenty seconds. It was agonizing. A few more handshakes like that and he'd have arthritis.

Dick reached under the desk and flipped off the applause.

"Is that it?"

"That's it. We'll get this up on the web, and people will go back to thinking you're the messiah. In a week, nobody'll even remember this happened. Assuming your PR guys put the proper spin on it. I imagine they set this up so you could get your dirty laundry out of the way while showing you how smart they are, and flexing their muscles."

"Assholes."

"Yeah, well, assholes get shit done."

"I guess you're right. If you can't beat 'em, join 'em."

Dick offered a weak shameful smile and slapped him on the shoulder. "Don't worry, you'll get used to it."

Max nodded then returned to the green room, scooped Cheeky up and carried him to the back exit where he figured I-Force had tossed Hawk out of the building. He opened the door to screaming and arcing projectiles, but slammed it shut before any of them hit.

Cheeky jumped to the floor, hissed and looked back and forth between Max and the door as if to ask what was going on.

"It's nothing to worry about. Just a hiccup."

The metal door rattled under the fists of his disillusioned fans.

Cheeky didn't believe him.

Well that's just great. Fucking live TV! How am I going to get to the car?

Max whipped out his phone. He had six missed calls from Hawk. He hit the call button, and Hawk picked up immediately.

"Whatever you do, don't come out. There's an angry mob surrounding the building."

"You don't say."

"I woke up in the alley, hearing people talking about what a shit you are. Can't say I disagree."

"What was I supposed to do, attack her? She was just doing her job."

"That bitch electrocuted me."

"Yeah, because you were menacing her. We're not at war anymore. You can't just kill everybody that gets in your way."

"Sure I can."

"Where are you?"

"They were working themselves into a lather, talkin' 'bout beating your ass. I pulled back to the coffee shop around the corner and called for reinforcements. Everybody said no. Said I-Force had plenty of security, and they weren't gonna go shoot a bunch of civilians. Pussies. What happened in there?"

"Fucking Owls happened. This is a message for me to fall in line."

"I told you that ass-grape was trouble." He could hear Hawk smiling.

"Noted."

"There's a droid on the way. Should be on the roof in the next couple minutes."

Max laughed. "That old nugget. I guess that works."

"I'll pick you up on Fifth. Just try not to draw any attention along the way."

"I promise I'll dangle from the tiny helicopter as inconspicuously as possible."

"You know what I mean."

"See you in a minute." Max climbed the four flights of steps to the roof. The droid was waiting, but he couldn't resist peeking at the enraged idiots below.

Damn, I thought I'd left this kind of crap behind. There must be five-hundred people down there. Is that guy selling projectiles?

He looked at Cheeky. "At least it's not zombies this time."

He stepped back and made for the droid. Cheeky lingered at the edge staring in bewilderment.

"Come on. Time to go."

Cheeky turned. His eyes were black holes of worry.

"I told you, it's just a hiccup. Now come on!" Max put his foot through the loop.

Cheeky tore across the gravel and clung to his leg.

"It's going to be okay, really. This'll all be fixed by tonight, and believe me, we'll get 'em back."

The Owls aren't the only ones who know how to keep things interesting. If they won't let me do this without them, fine. I'll use their resources to drown them in their own hubris.

He grabbed the rope and let the droid lift them away. All the way home his mind was filled with images of steaming owls, their asses stuffed with cornbread, juices trickling from their flesh as meat and bone parted ways. It might take a while to prepare, but this victory was going to be delicious.

# KISS OF THE SPIDER BABY

Greystoke's cigar filled the study with a stench like smoldering compost. The air hung in grey layers, giving the impression that the cryptozoological specimens were wearing cartoon prison uniforms. The aesthetic had seemed silly before, but now Max detected a hint of desperation.

The Count's just a big kid pretending to be a Bond villain. I mean, where do you even buy a smoking jacket? Is there, like, a catalogue for villains where you can order ascots and egg chairs with retractable spikes? He can afford the toys. So what? In the end, it's always the bad guy drowning in sharks.

His host got an A for effort, though. He was grinning like a child who had just blown up his first frog. Firelight played in the smug, bristly crevices of his conceit. His lips twisted around his cigar in a way that would make the devil clench his anus. That was fine. Let those lips enjoy the time they had left. This time next year they'd be tattered and teasing turds for quarters. Max could put up with a lot of shit, but there was a line beyond which lurked a wrath so pure it'd make you shit swords.

Still, Max would have given just about anything for the fucker to say something. He didn't know how much longer he could sit there looking weak. It was driving him crazy. Those eyes, that leer, that smoke... It was taking one-hundred-and-ten-percent of Max's willpower not to run over and kick that putrid dog-turd down his throat.

The Count pulled the stinking thing from his lips and looked at it as though it had disappointed him. "I take it, by your presence here, that you have deemed my services useful?"

Max did his best to sputter. "I... I never doubted the usefulness of your service. I just needed to figure out what I wanted to do. I didn't want to waste your time." The leather cushions made farting noises as he sat forward.

The Count's leer twisted into a sneer. "Yes, but I could have sworn you found my views distasteful."

"No, no, not at all. I was just concerned that you, uh, didn't want the same things as me. Trust me, I'm a lot less idealistic when I'm sober."

Greystoke took this as a cue to raise his tumbler to his lips and pour a generous quantity of whatever he hadn't offered Max down his throat. He held up the glass and stared lovingly through the sparkling crystal, or diamond, or whatever it was. "Yes, one thing you must learn if you ever hope to achieve your goals is to sin exquisitely. Liquor is not happy-funtime-party-juice. It is a vicious demon whose will must be bent to fit the contours of your own. Never allow it to gain the upper hand."

"I totally agree. I hate making an ass of myself."

The Count laughed. "And yet you are so proficient."

I should let Cheeky kill this asshat.

Max's furrowed brow earned him a look of warning. He forced a laugh. "Yeah, well, practice makes perfect."

"Indeed, and that perfection is one of the reasons this conquest of yours will work. The people love a jackass. Honest, respectable people can't get anywhere in this society. The public distrusts them. Smart people are viewed as sneaky. Responsibility makes you a bore. So far, the public sees you as bat shit crazy, dumb as a post, sincere, and well meaning. People look at you and see what they would like to be themselves."

Want to hit him. Want to hit him. Want to hit him.

"It's the ruling class one must watch oneself in front of. We must always display dignity, control and taste."

Don't laugh. Don't laugh. Don't laugh

"Under my tutelage you will learn to be the perfect jackass, no, a holy fool for the masses, while at the same time garnering the respect and jealousy of your peers. Would you like that?"

I'd like to smash all the glass in this room, strip you naked and kick you from one end to the other until there's not enough of you left to lubricate my cock!

Max's hatred made him smile. "I can't wait to get started."

The Count pulled a phone out of his smoking jacket, tapped out a quick message and put it back. "The proverbial ball has begun to roll.

"Now, I have been thinking about your public image. In order to be the total package you will need a girlfriend, someone who is beautiful enough to make everyone jealous and naughty enough to keep you on the front page of the newspaper. Allow me to introduce you to your new partner, *Felicity Ambrosia Greystoke*."

He's loaning me his wife?

The Count pushed a button on the console. The doors opened, and in walked the most spectacular creature Max had ever seen. She was as beautiful as Adhra, but with the eyes of a masochist. Natural auburn hair tumbled in elegant curls onto poreless, glowing flesh. It was like a big, sexy glass of milk had a child with Venus's prettier sister. She had an elegance about her like an old-time movie star, so hot she shimmered. He was powerless against the dark flow of her eyes. He wanted to write her a poem, but his mind reverted to infancy. If he hadn't been paralyzed, he might have reached out his hands and cried for the breasts, which threatened to overwhelm her strapless evening gown.

Greystoke looked on with amusement. "Lesson two, always rise to meet a lady."

Oh, I rose alright.

She waved away his command like a bad smell. "No need. I'm not a pompous cunt like my father. So, *dad,* what do you want, and what's with this dress? I feel like I should be accepting an award for best cum-shot, or something." She mimed accepting an award and then fellating it.

She's perfect!

The Count cast his eyes to the floor. "Must you always be an embarrassment?"

"Yes." She bounced, thrusting her fist up and to the left, and her right breast out of its cup. She looked down at it, laughed, looked at Max, lifted her breast by the nipple, pulled the cup out, let go of her nipple, and let the cup snap back into place, saying, "I'll just put that back where it goes."

Max was in love.

"Honestly, what is *wrong* with you? If it wasn't for your ability to look stunning in absolutely anything I would think your mother had cheated on me with a cartoon character."

*I guess they really are related.* Max discreetly tucked his hard-on under his thigh.

"I like to think she did."

Greystoke groaned and smeared his face around with his hands. "As I was saying, this is my daughter, Felicity. I was going to try to present her in a more favorable light, but as usual, she has made that impossible. Felicity, this is Maxwell Quick. You may know him as the guy from TV."

Felicity ran over and jumped on Max's lap. "Hi, guy from TV. Nice to meet'cha. You can call me Cat. Everybody else does."

Max couldn't keep the grins at bay. "Cat?"

"Yup, short for catfish, on account of my mysophilia." She illustrated her point by dumping the contents of a nearby ashtray into her mouth. "Nom, nom, nom."

Ash cascaded off her chin and into Max's face, choking him and making him sneeze into her cleavage.

"Forward!" She twisted in an exaggerated gesture of distress, accidentally freeing his unwanted guest.

"Ooh." Her eyes bugged out, and she hopped up, rubbing her butt. Careful now, big boy. I don't need any babies."

The Count was horrified. "Oh god, what have I done?"

"Dad, is this another attempt to hook me up with one of your cronies?"

The Count rolled his eyes. "Does it even matter? You are hopeless. Max is *almost* as hopeless. I *had* hoped to save time by grooming you together, but I can see that isn't likely to work. I'm locking you in here for an hour. Consider it an experiment in morbid curiosity. Do try not to bring about the end of days." He flipped a switch on the console, and his chair rose through a hole in the ceiling.

Max heard the clank of heavy locks falling into place. "What the fuck was that all about?"

Cat tossed her hands in the air. "That's just Daddy bein' Daddy."

"What are we supposed to do?"

"He probably wants me to fuck you so I can gain your confidence, spy on you, keep you on a leash, that sort of thing." She raised her voice. "Daddy hasn't figured out yet that I'm not his to pimp."

"That's too bad."

"Which one?"

"Huh?"

"That I'm not his to pimp, or that he hasn't figured it out yet."

"I don't know, both?" Max laughed, hoping she would take it as a joke.

She smiled, came in close and put her hand on his crotch. "Tell you what. I'll fuck your brains out, but only if you help me trash this study somethin' awful."

"Will you marry me?"

She made an ick face. "Marriage is stupid. So?"

Max jumped up and knocked over a display case. It hit another, spreading the floor with a mosaic of glass and bone. She hurled a standing ashtray through a stained-glass window, and clucked like a chicken.

Max tossed *four dogs with their faces sewn together* into the fire. "Tell me a little about yourself."

She pulled down a Bosch painting, propped it against the wall and kicked a hole in it. "Not much to tell. I like dirt. I worship Eris. I'm in PITA-4*. I'm a Bapta-vaga-vegetarian."

"What's that mean?"

"I only eat women, Baptastics and plants." She stripped off her dress, wrapped it around an antique clock, doused it with liquor, lit it on fire, and set it in the chair where they had met.

"Any particular reason?"

"Women taste better than men, vegetables are full of vitamins, and killing Baptastics is hungry work. Say, you're political, aren't you?"

Max stripped down, and left his clothes in a corner where he hoped they would be safe. "No, not really. I'm kind of anti-political."

She pulled a first edition Moby Dick off the shelf and threw it at him. "Lit fight!"

The tome hit the wall beside his head and disintegrated. Before the last page hit the floor, he reciprocated with a signed War and Peace. It hit her in the stomach and knocked her down. He was rushing over to make sure she was okay when the grapes of her wrath busted his nose. They continued on in that fashion until everything but the winged polar bear had been destroyed. They high-fived and made whoopie on its back. When Cat chewed off one of the bear's ears, Max came so hard he ripped off a wing and tumbled onto the floor.

"Asshole! I wanted you to come in my mouth. What part of mysophiliac don't you understand?"

"Sorry, I wasn't thinking. How about I pee on you in a minute?"

"Aww, you know just what to say to a girl." She lay across the bear's back and sighed, making Max wish he was a painter.

I wonder if she'd freak if I took a picture.

"Hey!" She jerked up and rolled off the animals back. "You wanna do some drugs?"

"Sure. Like what?"

She stood over him stroking her clitoris. "My friend Amanita has some Bliss."

Hearing her say Bliss brought back the repressed memory of being raped by coffee. He would rather do anything else, but staring up at her shimmering labia as they flitted about her fingers like a tickled squid, he knew he could never say no to her. "Ahh, ya got anything else? I've had some bad experiences."

"How could you possibly have a bad experience on Bliss? It's called Bliss, for cripes sake!"

Max noticed the fire creeping toward him and stood. The Oriental rug might as well have been woven out of fuses. He felt like he should put it out, but didn't want Cat to think he was lame. "Well, there are these Night Noodle things that tend to show up every time I do it..."

She stopped masturbating for a second. "You see Night Noodles? Awesome! Now we have to."

"You know about the Night Noodles?"

"Dude, I'm a Discordian. Of course I know about the Night Noodles. I always wanted to fuck one, but they never come for me."

Max laughed. "Well, you're lucky. Night Noodles are fucking annoying. They paralyze you and float you around while making demands in a pictographic language you don't understand. One time they raped me with coffee."

The more he talked the bigger her smile got.

"It sucked."

"In what way?"

"It was just... it...I mean..."

"Eloquent. So, I'm gonna call my friend and we're gonna do this thing. But first, somebody owes me a shower." Still masturbating, she got down on her knees and said, "Ahhh."

Max smiled and blasted her in the face with his morning coffee. She came, yipping like an excited puppy. Oddly, it didn't feel dirty, or even kinky. It was the most innocent thing he'd done in years. He felt like a child again.

After sucking out the last few drops, she slapped his new erection and walked away.

"Hey, where ya going?"

"Gotta find the phone."

"Are you sure you wouldn't rather have another go?"

"Yup. I wants me some drugs."

*Damn, and double damn.* He couldn't help wondering if she'd been disappointed in his performance. She seemed to like the pee more than its packaging. His erection shrank along with his ego.

She dug the phone out from under a splintered display case that used to contain a fortune in early Japanese erotic art. She dialed the number, said, "Amy, bring me drugs" and hung up. Max skulked off to get dressed. He had barely buttoned his pants when his pale and bewildered host returned.

"Oh my!"

He was taking it fairly well, surveying the damage the way one might a child's room after it discovered the contents of its potty could be used as art supplies.

Cat smiled innocently. "Hi, Daddy."

Max pulled on his T-shirt and avoided eye-contact.

The Count sighed. "Well, I *had* been running out of room in storage." He looked at Max and cocked an eyebrow. He seemed to think his experiment had been a success. He looked at the foot of black smoke collecting on the ceiling and sighed again. "Lesson number three; never tempt fate. Both of you come with me."

Three butlers ran into the room with fire extinguishers and went to work on the blaze.

Greystoke left the room with a naked Cat skipping behind him. Max hopped after her, trying to get his shoes on.

When they arrived at a garden, Max and Cat were invited to sit on a marble bench beneath a trellis atwitch and twittering with the activities of countless birds.

Instead of joining Max on the bench, Cat climbed the trellis and stared into the hedge labyrinth as if looking for her pet minotaur. The Count took a seat across from Max and leaned forward in an unusually casual way.

"Max, I cannot have my daughter killed. You, on the other hand... You just destroyed more priceless art than the bombing of Dresden. However, I shall refrain for two reasons. The first is that, were I to have you disappear, you would be unable to repay your debt to me. The second is that Felicity seems to like you."

Greystoke paused for a moment, searching the air above his head for the right words. "She is a very *special* girl. Not retarded, mind you. In fact, she's quite brilliant in her own way. She's just exceptionally weird." He cast his eyes to the ground.

"To be honest, I have been trying to find her a man for ages, but she makes most people uncomfortable."

Max looked to Cat for a reaction, but she continued to stare into the maze as nonchalantly as if they were discussing corn futures.

The Count smiled at Max's concern. "Oh, you don't have to worry about hurt feelings there. She is profoundly self-satisfied, arrogant even. It is the thing I love most about her. In any case, I believe the two of you would make a dazzling couple. What are your feelings on the matter?"

"Uh, *yeah*. At the risk of showing my cards too soon, your daughter is fucking awesome."

Cat tangled her feet in the latticework and hung upside down, facing him. "Aren't I?" She blew him a kiss and smiled.

Max reached up and scratched her head like a cat. She purred and rubbed against his hand.

The Count raised his eyebrows approvingly. "Well then, the two of you shall make your debut tomorrow. There is a club opening in the art district. Dadance, I believe. Some sort of avant-techno monstrosity; dada meets disco. It sounds atrocious, but the Order has an interest in its success. I will have some business cards printed for you. There will be a small army of paparazzi there. I trust you will find a way to draw their attention."

Max looked at her questioningly. She shrugged. "Whatever. I'm bored now. Wanna see my room?"

Max laughed and shook his head. "I'd like that very much."

She flipped down onto his shoulders with the grace of an Olympic gymnast, pointed at the house and said, "Sally forth, great stud."

She directed him through a series of corridors, past countless paintings, mostly of the Count, and into a large red bedroom with airbrushed walls depicting pale drippy men mining mushroom clouds out of a ruby cave. It had the feeling of a sugar-overdose. The rest was surprisingly sparse. There was a Bio-Bed*, a couple of nightstands, a dresser and a desk, all of which were of surprisingly low quality and devoid of decorations.

Weird. I wouldn't have pegged her for a clean freak.

He sat on the bed. "Nice place."

Cat laughed. "You should have seen my last room. Daddy doesn't let me have nice things anymore. Says I don't take care of them." She opened the door to her massive walk-in closet. A spider-monkey dressed as a detective scurried out and ran out the door screaming.

"Mr. Stabby! Come back!"

He didn't.

"Crazy monkey." She disappeared into her closet and came back a moment later wearing a big, floppy white hat. "You wanna hat? Be hat-people with me."

"Uh, sure, why not?"

She went back in and retrieved a purple sombrero with little white mice dancing on the brim. He tried not to cringe as she put it on his head.

"Ooh, who's the fresh meat?" A girl with short black hair and a platypus-skull T-shirt stood in the doorway.

"Amy!" Cat ran over to hug her. "Max, this is Amanita. She has drugs for us."

"Do I now?"

"Well you better. I don't have any."

"You know; you could buy your own stash sometimes. We know the same people."

Cat wrapped her arms around her friend, picked her up and spun around. "Amy brought me drugs! Yay!"

She continued spinning until she got dizzy and they fell over laughing. Amy got up and stumbled over to the bed. She removed her turtle-shell backpack and pulled out three bulbous, green bottles. Cat crawled over and snatched one of them. The other was offered to Max.

He grimaced. "Bliss, right? Do you have anything else? I tried to explain that I have bad luck with this stuff, but..."

"Cat wouldn't listen? She never does, to anything."

Cat poked her in the stomach. "I do too listen. Max gets visits from the Night Noodles when he drinks Bliss. I think the ritual's gonna work this time."

Max's stomach sank. *Ritual?*

"Oh, well in that case you have to partake."

Cat cracked open a bottle, and put it to his lips.

"I'd really rather no..." he choked as the thick green liquid was poured down his throat.

Everything turned to macramé. He traveled through the strands to where they burst into fractals. He surfed the jagged waves of space-time, immersed in the great clock, trying not to get stuck in the gears. Something grabbed him by the back of his neck and forced him down into the body of a woman. It was Mesopotamia around 300 B.C. She was carrying a baby past rows of dirty singers. There was an altar up ahead. The baby belonged to Moloch. It was his day.

Hush child. All things are as they must be.

She shed no tears, but stayed to watch him twist and bubble, screeching his first and final hymn as he was borne to god on wings of flame.

The pressure returned. He was a man again, rioting in protest. He was helping a group of people turn a car on its side. How dare they say he touched those kids? How dare they bring shame to Penn State? They ran a clean game. They always played fair. How could they do this to me?

Again, the pressure. It was all going by so fast. He was writing off his strip club budget as a business expense. He was slashing an ex's tires, crying as the Pope drove by, pinching a child's neck so it wouldn't make a scene. He was punishing his daughter for her perverse body, locking another in a room with a gas can and a book of matches. She shouldn't have spoken to the American.

He was stringing up blacks because the bulge in their pants turned him on. He was bundling sub-prime mortgages. He was mad at his dog for barking. How was he supposed to wake up early and get his presents if Brownie wouldn't let him sleep? He was opening the window, aiming, pulling the trigger.

The pressure was rubbing his nose in his mistakes. But they weren't *his* mistakes. It all made sense at the time. This is your brain on Earth. So much fear. So much suffering. How is anyone supposed to work under these conditions?

Behind it all he could feel a distant but immense sadness coupled with joy. Behind them both was love, infinite and indescribable, light itself exploding and imploding simultaneously. It was himself, but it was them, too, all those wretched little cowards, the weak, hungry monstrosities. They all took their turns as victims. They all had joy. He was all of them, and they were God.

He came out the other side surfing on the back of his head, watching his feet stretch on to infinity. He was taffy, caught in nature's transmission. He was cross-legged, hugging the floor drooling, crying and giggling maniacally.

He was barely back in his body when the acid starburst all around him. Colors blossomed, shifted and pulsed as the room washed over him. His soul looked upwards. He knew all those things had happened, but that they were inconsequential, that perception is a matter of random placement. He could just as easily have been a child eating ice cream, a teenager exploring his girlfriend with his tongue, a kitten running around on piano keys. He could have been anyone doing anything, but he wasn't. He was tripping his balls off, watching Amy and Cat lying stiff and spread eagled on the belly of a giant cat.

Cat locked eyes with him, begging. "I'm a pancake. Flip me over, or I'm going to burn."

He glanced at Amy. Her jaw was clenched so tight it looked like she might break her teeth. The Bliss had transmuted her boyish, ghostly charm into something darker. It was primal, and a little scary, especially with her eyes rolled back like that. "Hurry up, asshole. We're carbonizing."

Max to the rescue. He flipped them over and ran in search of syrup.

The infinite tangle of passageways, stairwells and rooms interlocked and looped back into each other in way that might have confused M.C. Escher. The hallways crowded around him, the walls inching ever closer, nervous but intent on making contact. Maybe they wanted his autograph.

No time for that. I'm on a mission. Stakes are at life. Must stop the screaming of sugar-drenched breadlings!

Ignoring the menagerie of shiny baubles, sparkly knobs, and mysterious minutiae, he focused on the task at hand, trudging through thieve-thick tunnels of tantalizing textures in search of tree-blood, thick and sweet enough to perform the necessary necromancy to save his sumptuous sidekicks from crunchy crepuscularity.

Minutes passed, maybe years.

He had almost lost hope when the old wall-hanging signaled with a pelvic thrust. Max recognized a lot of the imagery from books he read as a child. Alchemic symbols surrounded old men who were hunched over various apparatuses. The scenes were connected by geometric patterns, and snatches of Latin. All this surrounded a circle in a triangle, with a six-pointed star with a baby's face in the center. The baby winked, as if it shared Max's suspicion that the Count had such a poor understanding of alchemy he probably had a room full of lead bricks.

On the other hand, this could be where he keeps his particle accelerator.

He peeked behind the tapestry and found another set of hallways leading in all directions. It was a creepy passage of stone flavored cakes sprinkled with alchemic doodles, and doors.

Somebody watches too much Scooby Doo. Maybe I'll meet a haunted suit of armor I can ask for directions. Must find syrup!

He started checking doors. Most were bedrooms, which was pretty creepy. He could see some innocent houseguest snoring away as the bookcase opened up, and in creeps the Count wearing only a cape and a tri-pronged scrotal-mount. Max's arm-hair shivered at the thought.

Continuing on, he found a study, a bowling alley, a theater, a room of dolls, a small museum, and a larger museum dedicated to the Count. There was even a restroom for when one's creeping led one away from the public facilities. Eventually he came to a dining room with an intricately carved wooden table, which couldn't have been less than thirty feet long.

Aha! The kitchen lurks nearby. I can smell it.

It smelled like lobster bisque being prepared, which smells like boiling bug guts, which it is. Yummy, yummy bug guts. It made him hungry and nauseous at the same time. He ducked back into the hallway, and went around the corner.

What? Dead end? Really?

Max groaned and searched the wall for signs of a third layer of passages. Finding none, he made his way back through the fireplace to the dining room. He tried pressing on each of the dark wooden panels lining the room, but nothing happened. The paintings were all too high to be accessible, and the suits of armor weren't talkative.

"Dammit! Why is this place so stupid?"

A door near the fireplace opened and a tall, pink man wearing a chef's uniform stepped through. "Can I help you?"

*How did I miss that?* "Do you happen to have any maple syrup?"

"Of course. How much do you need?"

"I don't know. A couple bottles."

"Two... bottles?"

"Yup."

The chef went back into the kitchen and came out a minute later with two gallon-jugs of maple syrup. "Two bottles?"

"Syrup!" Max snatched the bottles, turned, and realized he had no idea how to get back. "Say, what's the quickest way to Cat's room from here?"

The chef's brow wrinkled, filling the room with crevices and unhelpfulness. "I just cook the food."

Max nodded politely. "Thanks anyway."

He went back through the fireplace, past the museums, to the big Incan statue where he'd taken a right. Rather than retracing his steps to where he was originally lost, he went straight. Fifteen doors later he found a bedroom with a similar style to Cat's, only everything in this one was burnt to a crisp. He smiled, imagining the sort of hijinks that might have happened here, then noticed the Bio-Bed shaped circle of pristine carpet. A big flaming kitty appeared, flailing helplessly, incapable of even rolling over. His hand moved to his pocket, but he didn't keep Spooky's ear there anymore. Since the war was over it had become an unnecessary downer, and it took up a lot of room.

There was probably something seriously wrong with Cat. She might even be dangerous. He wondered if this was what it was like to be a male black widow.

His smile only widened. *Well, if you have to go…*

He went through to the main hall and called her name. Giggles trickled through from somewhere, but the direction was difficult to determine. Five rooms to the left he couldn't hear it at all, so he tried the other way. He followed the giggling around a corner and saw the open door.

"I got syrup!" he burst in, jugs held high, to find his pancakes had fallen on the floor. The girls were naked, sitting Indian style facing each other with a pile of bras on either side. Cat pulled the under-wires out of the one she was holding, tossed them into the pile between them and the bra onto the stack to her left. She took a bra from the other pile, held it out to Max and asked, "Wanna help? We're removing the infrastructure of oppressive patriarchal society."

"No more pancakes?"

The girls shook their heads and laughed hysterically. "No more pancakes."

Wild goose time has denied me something.

Max dropped the syrup, took the bra, and tried to chew through to the wire. Amy dropped her bra, opened the syrup and poured it over the under-wires. "Take that, rape."

Cat stuck both hands into the sticky mess, kneading it to distribute the syrup. She held her hands out to Max. Little metal semicircles dripped slowly from her digits. "Robot guts."

"Robot guts!" Amy dug into the pile then held her hands out to Cat.

They squished their hands together and cried, "Robot guts!" in unison.

Max was at a loss.

Cat jumped to her feet. "Hey, Max is here. We can do the thing!"

"Yeah, the thing." Amy jumped up, and hit a button on her phone. A strange song began to play. Something Japanese with lots of twirling vocal harmonies drifted like incense into his gaping brain. Cat switched off the main light, grabbed an algebra book, and went around the room building small fires out of its pages.

Max sat on the Bio-Bed, befuddled but loving every second of the show. By the dying light of a dozen little fires Max watched Amy pull a big pack of hotdogs out of her purse. She opened them, stuck one in her mouth, gave one to Cat and tossed Max the rest.

Max stuck out his tongue in protest. "The Iiites made these out of abducted children, pig tumors and actual dogs."

Amy grabbed a fist-full and smashed them in his face. "Eat it!" He managed to deflect the first wave, so she grabbed another handful, sat on his arms and forced them into his mouth.

Max jerked his head back and forth until the gross pink squish was everywhere but his stomach. "I don't want any. Let me u..." He choked on another wad.

"Just eat the meat. It's part of the ritual."

Max coughed them out, screaming, "What fucking ritual? I didn't agree to this."

Amy pulled the last dog out of the bag with the thumb and forefinger of her left hand. Her right hand scooped up a hunk of smooshed up meat and cat fur. "You're gonna eat a wiener. Would you prefer this one," she wiggled the hotdog in her left hand, "or this one?" She shook her meaty fist.

Max grimaced and choked down the hotdog.

Amy smiled. "Hail Eris."

Cat lit another fire. "All hail Discordia."

The girls locked arms and frolicked in a circle. "Gooble gobble. Gooble gobble. Come to us. Come to us."

"Oh, the Night Noodle thing." Max made himself comfortable, secure in the knowledge that the only life form they were going to summon was a North American trouser snake.

They carried on that way for five minutes then made jazz hands at each other, reared back and slammed their skulls together, knocking themselves out cold.

Max felt excluded, so he stripped off his clothes and rolled around in them like a happy dog. Amy's mouth popped open and a big, brown cockroach crawled out onto her chin. Max screeched, and flung a handful of underwires at it. The ones that didn't stick to his hand splatted across Amy's chest.

All the little fires around the room jumped up to three times their size. The roach stood on its hind legs, raised the rest of its appendages and let out a poor voice recording of a woman saying, "Hello. You've reached Eris. I can't come to the phone right now. Please leave a message after the beep."

"Beep," said the cockroach in a deep sexy voice.

Max shrieked again and brought a nearby lamp down on Amy's face. Her jaw tore free from its socket, and snapped back at an awkward angle. She choked and coughed bloody teeth onto the carpet, but didn't wake. The roach flew around Max's head in erratic wave-forms singing, "Nananana booboo." Even the tracers seemed to mock him.

"Fuck off!" Max snatched up a shirt, tossed a shoe inside and swung it like a mace. On his third swing he pulled a muscle.

"Ah, fuck!" He grasped his shoulder and tried to massage the pain away. The roach hovered overhead, laughing deep and velvety.

"What the fuck are you laughin' at, you ugly little shit? Oww!"

The roach grew to the size of a large dog and dropped, pinning him to the ground. It leaned in close like he was going to kiss him with those big bristly mandibles. "Now that you got that out of your system, what'chu want Maxwell?"

Shaking, crying and on the verge of shutting down, Max was a hair beyond verbal response, so the roach communicated telepathically.

The big bug's laughter was oddly soothing. "I take it this wasn't your idea?"

Max was still unable to scrape enough words together to form a coherent sentence.

"I see, not a fan of insects, are ya? Well, you brought this on yourself." It cocked its head, staring him down with one big black eye. "All tryin' to smoosh me and shit. If I let you up, are you gonna drop the bigoty bullshit?"

Max nodded his head violently in the affirmative.

The bug turned into a jolly, naked Hispanic lady, patted him on the chest and took a seat on the bed. Her teddy-bearish heft sank deeper into the feline's belly as she rolled onto her chest. From where he was sitting she looked like she was swimming in fur.

Still shaking, Max crab-walked to the farthest corner, and sat there hugging his knees. The woman ran her fingers through the big kitty's fur and stared at him suggestively. "Rumpy pumpy?"

Enough of Max's wits returned for him to ask, "Eris?"

The woman laughed, rolled onto her back and stared at him upside down. "You sayin' I look like a goddess? That's sweet." Its voice hadn't changed.

It felt like his goose pimples were dosie-do-ing. Maybe they were. "So who the fuck are you then?"

"Me llamo Gulik."

"Okay, what do you want?"

"What do I want? You summoned me! Well, you summoned the goddess, but she's busy. I sometimes function as an answering service."

Max's head was clearing. It occurred to him this chick might be able to provide useful information about his bullshit destiny. "Okay, so, what the fuck does Eris want?"

Gulik chuckled. "What does anybody want? Love, Joy, a shoehorn with teeth..."

"From me! What does she want from me?"

The woman's smile curled around her ears. "Don't you know that authorial intrusion is against the rules? I am Gulik, messenger to the goddess, not some lazy plot device. Anyway, how should I know? I just work here."

"Why is it so hard to get a straight answer out of you fuckers?"

"Why is it so hard for you fuckers to enjoy the ride?"

"What? Fuck you."

"Oh, hell. Why not." She flipped off the bed, and rolled over to him like a big horny tire. Her ass hit his face, wedging him in the crack. It smelled like red curry and sounded like a choir of castrati crying over spilled milk.

He struggled to get away, but she had him pinned. Her feet had sprouted setae for better grinding leverage.

"Please, don't!" His screams were lost in her jiggly spam chasm.

He screwed his face as tightly shut as possible, and tried to pretend he was being groomed by a giant cat. Her orgasm was like a cream pie to the face. It tasted like boysenberry thayir.

Finally, she rolled off him. "Thank you for a wonderful evening."

He scraped the thick white goop out of his eyes in time to watch her spit out a couple of lit cigarettes. He gratefully accepted one and stuck it in his mouth, free of expectations, dead inside.

"Max, I'm gonna tell you something I probably shouldn't. You know how some people bring certain impulses to the surface in others. Some people you automatically like. Others would make Martin Luther King want to throw a brick at them. Well, for whatever reason, we like ya. We ain't trying to make your life hard, but chaos is our thing, dig? The more you buck us, the harder it is to resist fucking with you."

He took a drag. It tasted like smoked ham. "You're doing this because you like me?"

"That's what I said."

The puddle of goop melted and slithered into a puddle a few feet away.

"I'd hate to get on your bad side."

Gulik chuckled, and bit into her cigarette. "It's all perspective, man. It's all polarity. Order and chaos are two necessary elements, forces of nature in constant flux. Their battle for space on your plane is the only thing that makes it interesting."

Maybe it was the drugs, but that made sense. "So who's in charge of order?"

"Lots of people. All just manifestations of the same guy, though."

"What's that supposed to mean?"

"You wouldn't understand."

"Try me."

"No."

"Fine then, what am I supposed to do?"

"Have fun."

Max grunted, and slammed the back of his head against the wall. "Goddammit, I mean specifically. Can you give me any advice about what I should do next?" His head snapped forward, and he locked eyes with the flubbery rapist. "Better question; why does the goddess of chaos want me to save the world?"

"Good question, and on that note..." Gulik turned into a roach and flew over to Amy's mouth.

"Wait! Don't go yet!"

Gulik perched on her nose and turned around. "What?"

"I have more questions."

"Too bad, time's up." He put his four arm-legs together like a diver, and bent his leg-legs.

"Will you at least fix Amy's mouth for me?"

Gulik cocked his head thoughtfully. "I shouldn't. You need to learn a lesson about trying to kill folks that look different."

"It won't happen again."

"On the other hand, she does have a pretty mouth. It'd be a shame to have to wire it shut. I guess I'll help."

Gulik hopped up, and turned into an old, bald guy. Still naked, he picked her up like a ventriloquist's dummy, and put her on his knee. "This won't be pretty." His voice was now a raspy whine. He plunged his arm into her ass. "Alright, where are ya. No. No. That's not it. Ooh, what's this?" He laughed low and dirty. His cock sprang up with a sound like a slinky rolling down the stairs on its side. He squeezed his eyes shut and groaned as something black and chunky oozed from the tip.

Max gagged, but he couldn't look away.

"What was I doin'? Oh yeah." Several grunts and worrisome facial contortions later he said, "Got it."

Amy's jaw dropped all the way to her collar-bone then snapped back up with a meaty click. "Testing. Testing. One, two, three." She said, blank eyes staring in opposite directions. "Beetles are one of the largest orders of insects, with 350,000–400,000 species in four suborders (Adephaga, Archostemata, Myxophaga, and Polyphaga), making up about 40% of all insect species described. Even though classification at the family level is a bit unstable, there are about 500 recognized families and subfamilies. One of the first proposed estimates of the total number of beetle species on the planet is based on field data rather than catalog numbers. The technique used for the original estimate, possibly as many as 12,000,000 species, was criticized, and was later revised, with estimates of 850,000– 4,000,000 species proposed. Some 70–95% of all beetle species, depending on the estimate, remain undescribed."

"Yep works fine. Now, if you'll excuse me, it's time to go lay eggs in her brain." She slid off his arm into a small puddle of blood.

"Is she going to be okay?"

"Dammit Max, I'm a cockroach, not a doctor." He reverted to his previous form and disappeared into her mouth.

"Hey, one more thing," Max pulled her mouth open and called inside, "they wanted to see the Night Noodles. Any chance they could pop in on them some time?"

He waited for a response, but none came.

All the fires went out at once. Max stumbled around until he found the light switch then rushed back, opened her mouth and screamed, "Gulik?"

"Aah!" Amy jerked up, bashing him in the teeth with her forehead. "Ouch! What the fuck, man?"

Max jumped back. "Fuck!" He probed his teeth with his tongue to make sure she hadn't knocked anything loose. "Sorry, you were out cold."

She raised her eyebrows, blinked and noticed the blood. "Why does my ass feel like a bar after a Nero and the Roman Showers concert?

This won't be pretty.

She pulled her legs back behind her head and stared into the twitching cavern Gulik had made. "Asshole!"

"I didn't do that. It was Gulik, I swear."

"Gulik my ass!" Her eyes dropped to his erection. She stopped short, pointed at it and then slowly scanned the room. "Okay, you didn't do it with your pee-pee. That's for sure. I don't see any bowling pins. I think the lamp would have killed me. Did you say Gulik?"

"Yeah."

"You're not Discordian. How do you know about Gulik?"

"He was here. Freaky bastard. Trust me, I got the worst of it."

"Gulik was here, and I missed him?"

"Well, you did knock yourselves out. What did you expect?"

"But he came?"

"Several times, actually. It was... not good."

She crawled over and checked Cat. "She isn't bleeding." She looked at Max questioningly.

"Gulik didn't touch her."

Max had never seen a look of such joy.

"Gulik came and chose me? Me?" She looked at the ceiling and slapped herself in the face. "Oh my goddess! Thank you. I am so honored. He chose *me*! I have to tell... everyone." She squealed, and rushed to her phone to update her social networks.

Max decided not to offer any more details.

Groaning, Cat rolled onto her back. Max checked her for concussion. "You okay? You hit your head pretty hard."

"Damn, you get the number of that forehead?"

Amy cracked a smile. "Five fives bi-yatch. You ain't so soft yourself, ya know. You made me miss St. Gulik. He was here. Oh my goddess! He was here!"

Cat raised her eyebrows at Max.

"Yeah, you were lucky. You missed it. It was even worse than the Night Noodles." His lip twitched. "I hope I never meet Eris. I don't think I'd survive."

Cat looked like she might cry. "No fair. What happened?"

Max glanced guiltily at Amy, unsure what to say.

Amy saved him the trouble. "He fucked me in the ass! See." She stood and bent over slightly to better display her divine gift.

Cat took one look at the trickle of blood running down the back of Amy's thigh and punched Max in the back of the head. "Asshole!"

Amy shook her head. "No, that's what I thought too. Then I had a look at exhibit A dangling between his legs there, and realized he isn't man enough for this degree of destruction. No offense." She clutched her hands to her chest. "I got date-raped by a demi-god."

Max chuckled. "You know, for once I don't mind being average."

Cat spun Amy around and spread her cheeks. "But Gulik's a roach. His whole body couldn't do that."

"You are such a good Discordian. There's a lot more to Gulik than what's in the Principia. He can shapeshift, he had a successful political career, and he even wrote a few novels. They aren't that good, but they're worth a ton on eBid."

"Do you have 'em?"

"Of course, but no, you can't borrow them. They're in mint condition. I've seen how you treat your books."

Cat pouted. "I'd be careful with 'em."

Amy frowned. "No, you wouldn't. You..."

Max cleared his throat. "Is anybody still tripping? We should be. We only dosed about an hour and a half ago, but the, uh, buggering... well, I'm sober now."

Cat scratched under her left boob. "Come to think of it, I'm sober too."

Amy set her phone down and scrunched up her face. "Me too. Maybe Gulik can like, suck the psychedelia out of people."

Thoroughly worn out, Max crawled onto the bed and slid his legs into the warm, fuzzy pouch. "You'd think it'd be the other way around." He tilted his head and rubbed his cheek against its fur eliciting a deep rumbling purr.

Amy ran over and slid in beside him. "You don't understand chaos at all, do you?"

"Apparently not, but I think I'm beginning to. I've been going about this all wrong."

"About what?" Amy dug her chin into his chest, and stared with big purple eyes.

"I don't know. I'm just tired."

Both girls snuggled in close.

Amy whispered, "I bet I know how to wake you up."

I could get used to this.

Cat licked his face like a happy dog. "Where did you get Indian food?

Well, maybe.

# THE SILENCE OF THE JAMS

Beyond the thick tinted glass of the limo's window, the entertainment district posed like a dejected drag queen with a brand-new wig. Everyone was out in their ceremonial Friday night garb performing whatever rituals were necessary to purge themselves of the week's abuses. The alphas strutted. The rich slummed. The poor catered to them both. Zombies shuffled blankly among them like shabby paladins of truth.

Max starcd through them, blind to all but his own reflection. He poked at the swanky helmet the cosmetologists had made of his hair, wiggling it nervously with one finger.

*Why did I let them do this to me?*

He looked like a movie star in his tailored green and black plaid tux. The chest was a little tight with all the business cards they'd given him, but otherwise it was surprisingly comfortable. Greystoke said tailored suits were but one of the many things he could look forward to getting used to, but would he?

*I wonder if this will ever not feel like a costume. No, not a costume, a uniform. I'm a celebrity going to work. First day on the job, and I already hate it. Why did I let him talk me into this? I hate clubs, and I don't dance. This is going to be a disaster.*

Cat was watching TV at the opposite end, singing The Happy Fun Time Super Show theme while Captain Ajax pinned a slime monster to a wall with a flagpole.

*Ahh, the good old days.*

The light flashed three times to let them know they were getting close. Cat didn't seem to notice.

"Hey, we're almost there. You ready for this?"

She looked back with big, fluttery eyes augmented with red and green glitter. She looked like a blossoming snake princess from an old sci-fi show. "Ready for what?"

"Ready to make your appearance, or whatever."

"Appearing is easy. I do it all the time. It's disappearing that's hard."

Max smiled. *Why am I so nervous? All I have to do is get drunk and make an ass of myself. Not my thing, but how bad can it be? People do it all the time. The world isn't going to end because I step outside my comfort zone.*

He downed the last of his bourbon, and glanced at the half-empty bottle. A lesser man would be passed out in a puddle of vomit, but not him. No-sir-ee, he'd been training for this his whole life. He slid his tongue around his teeth, then opened his mouth and exhaled an oaky gust of satisfaction.

Ooh, here we are.

They pulled up to the red carpet in front of a three-story building, the front of which was a ginormous TV flashing red and black patterns at a seizure-inducing rate. A line of scene kids stretched into the distance, gawking in anticipation of the emergence of some higher being. Paparazzi gathered at the door, cameras poised low to catch the best angle of anyone willing to show it.

"Come on, let's show these fuckers a time."

Cat crawled down the aisle, grinned, poked him in the nose, pushed open the door, and crawled out like a cat. The cameramen moved in, catching every angle then crowding behind her as she continued forward. He couldn't blame them. Her green cat-suit was so tight they could count the rings in her labia. Max climbed out, and winced as the pulsing colors raped his eyes.

Somebody's gonna get sued over this.

Cat stood and turned to him. Her eyes sparkled back into her hair. The paparazzi swarmed like angry bees.

"Am I on drugs?"

Her lips expanded into velvety oblivion. "Of course. Come."

He took her hand and pimp-walked up to the bouncer, who opened the door. Binaural beats blasted them in the face. Max glanced back at the jealous jumble, winked and flipped them off.

They stepped through the door, and onto the catwalk.

"Wow. Just, wow."

It was a big, open room, mostly dance floor with a few recessed booths in the back spaced about ten feet apart. Above was two stories worth of ceiling, below a jumble of fumbling famous folk, trying to dance to erratic drones. The only light came from a series of swiveling projectors, which washed the walls with black and white scenes of Amish life and silent era horror. Max noticed several metal monoliths moving among the masses as a barn-raising flitted over the dance floor. He eyed them curiously as he descended the stairs.

"Why does it smell like Christmas?" His voice drowned in a sea of bups and wahs.

At the bottom, they were greeted by a beefy, bison-headed man who was yoked with twelve long, thin glasses full of milky green liquid. There was a fish, maybe a tilapia, dangling from the center of his nipple-clamp chain. An S-hook had been shoved through the base of its tail, and something had been carved into its side. Max pulled it closer.

"Who's afraid of the green menace?"

It flopped out of his hand, and slapped against the bison's navel.

"Bah!" Max jumped back, startling the bison, who nearly lost several of his burdens.

Cat pulled two drinks off the right side of his yoke, which tilted in an uncomfortable looking way. The bison redistributed the glasses for better balance while she took a sip from the long bendy-straw. She smacked her lips, and held the other out to Max. "James Joyce?"

"Huh?" he screamed back.

"Absinthe and Irish cream!"

He took a sip. It tasted like a cough syrup milkshake and kicked like a footballer just diagnosed with leprosy.

Oh well, when in Bedlam.

He took another sip and followed her onto the dance floor. There was a huge headless chicken running across the wall to his right. The left showed a demon with human legs sticking out of its mouth. Every few feet there was a vacant-eyed celebrity posing or attempting to dance.

Max didn't notice Cat stop, and bumped into her. She turned around, poked him hard in the stomach then kissed him.

"Now what?!"

"We dance, silly!" She did the cabbage patch.

"Um, I don't really dance. Even if I did, how do you dance to a drone?!"

"You do it, just like everything else!"

"What?!"

"Dance, fucker!" She got down into the booty dance position and ground her ass on his crotch.

Hmm, fuck it.

He took another sip, tossed his glass aside, and joined in. He gyrated and slapped her ass as best as he knew how. It was almost fun. He was sweating and gritting his teeth. Electricity sparked in his blood. The walls were spinning, black and white dissolving infinitely, absorbing everything. The pulse rose to consume him. Then he fell over.

He looked up and saw one of the big, dildo-looking things moving away from him. The drone that had been messing with his head grew quieter, and he realized that was where the "music" was coming from. *The speakers are robots and the music is drugs. Well, that's—different.*

He stood, and noticed the way everyone was looking at him. *Scorn. Yup, that's definitely scorn. I'd know it anywhere.* Cat was break dancing, but nobody was looking at her.

"What? It bumped into me."

The crowd was smirking. A few were even laughing at him.

"Hey, fuck you. I saved the world. What the fuck have you done lately?"

Cat finished with a tuck and roll, which ended with her on one knee, jazz-handsing with her mouth agape. Max stuck his tongue out at the crowd, took her hand and led her over to a booth. He admired her by the light of the flames spouting from the outside edge of the table. Her chest was heaving. Sweat was dripping out of her cowl. She was so beautiful he wanted to put her whole head in his mouth.

The table spit out a fireball, singeing the hair on the back of his hand.

"Having fun?" she asked between breaths.

He rubbed the ash away with his finger. "I don't know. It's not really my scene."

"But are you having fun?"

"I don't think it's going well. People were laughing at me."

She bared her teeth, grabbed him by the lashes and made his eyelids dance. "But... are... you... having... fun?" She let them snap back into place.

He grinned and scratched her under the chin. "I always have fun when I'm with you."

"Aww," She rubbed her face in his hand then looked up dead serious, "but we're in agreement that this place is stupid?"

Max licked his squirming gums. "Mmm hmm, too many pretentious assholes."

"You want to get out of here?"

His head wobbled. "Don't we have to get noticed more?"

"I'll take care of that." Something about her tone was a little scary.

She pulled her phone out of her cleavage, tapped out a quick text and put it back. "Let's go out the fire exit over there. Hurry." She pushed him out of the booth and shoved him towards it.

He hit the door. The fire alarm went off, but the clubbers only danced harder. Cat was still at the booth. He couldn't tell what she was doing. A moment later, she ran and pushed him out the door.

"Come on, hurry! We're gonna miss it." She grabbed his hand and they ran up the steps to where the limo was waiting.

"Where are we going?" Max asked, not really caring. Cat could make a trip to the dentist fun.

"It's a surprise."

The limo took them just outside the city to a water tower in the hills. Cat rushed him to the top. "I'm cold." She pressed her body into him.

He leaned against a pole and wrapped his arms around her perfect waist. "You know if you wanted to cuddle you just had to ask."

"Shut up, and enjoy the view."

It was a really nice view. The city sparkled like a drag queen in an evening gown. It had a few more sequins than necessary, but whatever. It seemed happy. It wore Dadance like an ugly brooch. He was staring at that brooch, remembering his failure when it blossomed into a big orange flower.

Cat screamed, "Pop goes the weasel!"

Max blinked and stared closer. Black smoke rose from the pit and spread through the neighborhood like a chubby octopus.

His stomach sank. "Is that how you planned to get us noticed?"

"What, you don't think it'll work?"

"No, I'm afraid it will."

"Did I do good?"

Max looked down. "Uh, yeah, sure. What exactly did you do?"

"They shouldn't have put an open gas flame in a place somebody might accidentally sit on it. I burned a hole in my butt." She leaned to the side, revealing a four-inch hole in her cat-suit, and a big white blister on her ass. "Kiss it. Make it better."

He wasn't happy she had just killed a bunch of innocent douchebags, but a girl like that didn't have to ask twice. He stuck his fingers in the hole and unwrapped her like a pack of toilet paper. He undid his pants, but left his clothes on. It was cold.

And so he found himself drunk and on drugs, wearing half a plaid tuxedo, having anal sex with a beautiful woman whose tongue was frozen to the top of a water tower, while suffering from vertigo and expecting at any moment to be arrested for the murder of sixty-some celebrities. He searched for a word to describe what he felt at that moment, but there wasn't one. Supercalifragilisticexpialidocious was the dumpy trailer trash cousin of the word he was looking for. He came, and the clouds parted, drenching them in moonlight.

Max howled for the first time in his life.

He collapsed, panting so hard he could taste the James Joyce trying to claw its way out of his belly. He peered back at the city; tiny people scrambling to put out the blaze, tinier people scrambling to capitalize on the tragedy, the lights playing tetherball with the dust. Then he saw it in the smoke, that huge leering face, at once alien and terrifyingly familiar, still despite the billowing wind. The face of evil looked him in the eye from a mile away and winked.

# TICKED OFF GRANNY WITH GUNS

The limo came to a stop in front of a midsized, ranch-style house in a Sonian neighborhood. The path to the front door was lined with gnomes wearing green and purple softball jerseys. Each was different and, Max assumed, representative of specific players. The flag on the mailbox bore the image of a scrappy looking Jesus with a bat. Max couldn't remember the name of the team, but he was pretty sure they were the ones the fundamentalists formed because they thought the Baptastic Bears were too secular.

Max glanced around at the various cookie cutter domiciles with their pastel shutters and their pert green lawns. "This can't be right."

He rechecked the address. It was right. "Why in holy hell would the Riot Nrrds make *this* their new headquarters? All these birds and bouncing basketballs and barking dogs must be driving them crazy. Magog lost his shit one time because Pope's shoes were squeaky."

Cat launched herself across him and stuck her head out the window, filling her lungs with suburbia. "I like it here. It's purdy."

"It smells like a funeral. Too many flowers and old people."

She reached back with two fingers and shoved his head playfully. "You."

He slapped her hard on the ass and pulled her, giggling, into his lap. She kissed him then grabbed his shoulders, threw him to the floor, and pinned him with his arms crossed under her legs and her ass pressed against his nose and mouth so he couldn't breathe.

Cat grabbed his hair and pulled until he could smell her root chakra. "I call his one the Wet Dreamer."

He couldn't get any leverage, so he stuck out his tongue. Before long, she was leaning forward. Her grinding freed his nose, and he sucked greedily at both the air and her labia. She unzipped him and pulled out his erection, then grabbed his leg and pulled his foot up, so she could suck the toe of his shoe. Max waited for the perfect moment then jerked his leg away, pulling her forward and giving him the leverage he needed to flip her over and plant his flag in her dirt. They came together, bleating like stabbed lambs.

Only then did he notice they had acquired an audience. Children of various ages stared through the open windows, their eyes filled with fascination, confusion and horror. Max grabbed a bottle of liquor to throw at them then thought better of it.

"Get out of here you little perverts!"

Max smiled as they skittered back to their homes.

Cat bit him hard on the shoulder. "Bully."

Max pulled her off and put his cock away before she bit it too. He climbed back into the seat and watched for signs of angry parents. Eventually he relaxed and straightened his clothes. "Well, at least it wasn't crackheads."

He rolled up the windows so the passing joggers wouldn't see Cat. "I still don't understand why your dad wants us to play dead. It makes us look guilty. Seeing as we are guilty, this seems like a stupid idea. Am I wrong?"

Cat shrugged. "Daddy knows what he's doing."

"If you say so."

Max dialed Pope's cell. It rang four times, five, six. Max was about to give up when a nearby explosion rocked the limo. A plume of grey smoke rose from the back yard.

"Yep, this is the place." Max hung up and offered Cat his tuxedo jacket. "You should put this on. If you walk in there naked, those guys'll spontaneously combust."

She put it on, but it only made her sexier. It lifted her breasts and pushed them together so they bulged out the top. The tails partially covered her poo poo platter, but the front left something to be desired.

He was about to offer his pants when she opened the door and pushed past him.

"Come on, I wanna meet your friends," she said, skipping away.

"Wait. You can't go in there like that." He jumped out and tried to catch her, but she was already rounding the house. His phone rang. Pope was calling him back.

Cat was closing in on the small building with smoke billowing from a hole in the roof.

Max answered as he ran. "Don't answer the door."

Pope ignored him. "I was just working on a very important..." Max heard Cat knocking over the phone. "Now who could that be? I told Nana I didn't want to be disturbed."

By the time Max arrived, Pope was already caught in her headlights. He said "Goodness me," and collapsed faster than a piece of Sav-Mart furniture.

"I told you. These guys can't handle seeing a real naked girl." He lifted one of her tails and gave her a spanking. "Don't run off like that."

"Sorry." Cat giggled, and put her hand between her legs.

"That's not any better."

Hedorah appeared, poised to say something snarky, but seeing Cat, he choked on his malformed witticism and dropped his cigarette.

Cat giggled again. "Your friends are funny."

"You're enjoying this way too much." Max stepped inside and helped a stunned Hedorah out of his lab coat. "Really? You're smoking while the building's on fire?"

"It has a filter."

"Here. Put this on before somebody nosebleeds to death." He handed Cat the lab coat, and glanced around at the makeshift base. It was a mid-sized storage building large enough to keep a riding mower and tools out of the rain and still have plenty of storage space. The walls were thin aluminum reinforced with two by fours and empty gun racks. The smooth concrete floors bore the scars of several decades of abuse. A thin sheet of wood had been erected to create a separate room. Judging by the smoke peeking through the jagged door-hole, that was where they performed their experiments.

Emma's voice pierced the smoke. "Guys? We're still on fire in here! The extinguisher's out of— oh." She stopped at the sight of a half-naked woman flapping her too-long sleeves like flaccid wings.

Cat covered herself with one hand and waved with the other. "Hi, I'm Cat." She squeezed her eyes shut and shook her head. "I think the smoke's messing with my eyes."

"No, that's just me." Max could tell by Emma's tone that she was smirking.

Max helped Cat button the coat while he explained. "Emma's specialty is invisibility. Best spy you could ever hope for. Just don't look at her face."

"But I wanna see it. Why can't I see it?" Cat was still trying to blink the haze away.

"I'm sorry. I permanently altered my appearance to make it hard for the human brain to register my features. It makes meeting new people a tad awkward. Just a second." She pulled a ski mask out of her purse and put it on. "How's that?"

Max cocked an eyebrow. "Better. When did you start carrying around a ski mask?"

"Since the operation, but I didn't need it during the war. I'm trying to get back into the habit."

Cat pouted. "Not fair. Can I touch it?"

Emma didn't respond, so Cat ran over, pulled off the mask and commenced smooshing Emma's face around like a kid with pizza dough.

"Neat. You can see the parts up close, kinda." Emma tried to back away, but Cat had her cornered. "Peek-a-boo," she said with a deranged giggle, as she continued molesting her new acquaintance.

She was moving in to explore with her tongue when Max pulled her off. "That's enough. She tastes like everybody else."

Cat looked jealous. "How do you know?"

He walked her over to the desk and sat her in a swiveling chair. "Stay."

Cat crossed her arms and pouted, but did as she was told.

"Sorry about that. She's a little frisky."

Hedorah was still standing in the doorway with a big grin on his face.

"Holy shit, you *can* smile? You learn something new every day."

Hedorah flipped him off, still grinning.

Emma cleared her throat loudly. "Sorry to interrupt this farce, but the building is still on fire, and we still don't have a fire extinguisher."

Max glanced at the doorway. The smoke was getting thicker and darker by the second. "What about that sonic watchamahicky dampener thing. Is that here?"

Emma flipped her hands.

Hedorah ran over to the desk and retrieved a device that looked like a TV remote. When it didn't come on, he flipped it over and opened it up. "Somebody stole the fucking batteries."

"Of course they did. Steal some from something else."

They scoured the room leaving no doohickey unturned, but there were no AA's to be found.

"This is what always gets me about you people. You're smart enough to design gadgets that can do just about anything, but not smart enough to stock up on batteries."

"It's too hot in here." Cat shrugged off both coats and climbed on top of the desk.

"Dammit Cat, if you're hot you can go outside, but put the coat back on."

Hedorah was still groping his way through a pile of old gadgets, but he was no longer looking at what he was doing. Max could hear Emma's teeth grinding beneath her mask.

Cat stuck her tongue out again as she snatched the clock off the wall. She removed the batteries and tossed them to Emma.

"Good girl." Emma stuck the batteries in their slots and ran through the smoky doorway. Moments later the smoke disappeared, and Emma returned.

"You know; you could try to do something with all these inventions. I'm sure Greystoke would set you up a company for a percentage. Then you'd have lackeys to buy batteries for you. You want me to talk to him?"

Hedorah chimed in. "What, and leave all this behind? You must be crazy."

"Yeah, how did you end up *here*, anyway?"

Dishes exploded on the ground behind him. Max turned to see a shocked toad of a grandma standing behind a pile of broken china and cookies. Milk soaked into her slippers as her eyes darted around the room.

"Cookies!" Cat hopped down and attacked the pile like a muppet with an eating disorder.

"Orville!" shrieked the old lady.

Pope jerked awake, eyes wider than the old lady, and commenced sputtering nonsense.

The old lady took a puff from her inhaler-necklace and waddled over to him leaving a trail of large milky footprints.

"I told you no hanky-panky!" She grabbed the front of his shirt and yanked him to his feet. "I said you and your friends could play in my shed, just so long as there's no hanky-panky." She took another puff from the inhaler and pointed at Cat. "Now, you tell me what that is over there eatin' my cookies off the floor? If that ain't hanky-panky, I don't know what is."

Pope stared at the floor. "Sorry, Nana."

"And why's my rider sittin' outside? It's gonna rain. You can't leave a rider out in the rain."

"Sorry, Nana."

"Well, sorry ain't good enough." She reached under her sweater and pulled out a large caliber revolver. "You and your friends get out of my shed."

Max raised his hands. "Ms—uh, ma'am, this isn't Pope's fault."

She fired a warning shot out the hole in the roof. "Take your hanky-panky somewhere else. This here's a Baptastic household. You got five minutes to get your junk and your whore off my property, then I'm callin' the po-lice." She waddled to the door, then turned and stared at Pope through angry tears. "You used to be such a good boy." She shook her head and waddled back to the house.

Tears darkened the cement by Pope's feet as he ripped garbage bags off a roll and tossed them to his colleagues. Max walked over to apologize, but Pope's glare stopped him short.

He looked to Emma and then Hedorah for help, but they were too busy stuffing inventions into their bags.

"So, that's it? We have to get a new base?"

Hedorah stopped long enough to light a cigarette. "That's it."

Pope tossed Max a garbage bag. "Make yourself useful. Anything we leave here's going to the dump."

Max threw the bag onto the desk. "This is ridiculous. I'm going to go explain, apologize, whatever. I'll get this straightened out."

Hedorah laughed so hard he snorted. "You do that. She'll probably answer the door with a shotgun blast."

"She can't possibly be that bad."

"Dude, Pope's grandfather, her husband, once peed with the bathroom door open because he thought she wasn't home. Nana walked by, saw his penis, called the police, and pressed charges. It got thrown out of court, obviously, but that was her husband. The bitch is crazy."

"But how did... I mean, she *is* a grandmother."

"Fuck if I know. Just stuff whatever you can in the bag, and pray we get out before the cops show."

Max shot him an incredulous look, but everyone seemed to think she really would call the police. "Well, all right then." He went into the other room and quickly filled his bag with as many gadgets as it would hold.

# PIERCING TONGUES

Max rubbed his eyes as the limo pulled into the cave.

Of course the Count has an underground lair. Why wouldn't he?

The limo wound through the maze of tunnels with a precision that implied frequent use. Max could barely imagine what sort of hanky-panky would justify the need for such a thing, let alone the regular use of it. He began to wonder if it was possible that, behind the cartoon villain veneer, the Count was someone to take seriously.

Maybe the cheese is a way of throwing people off, like wearing pink to a fight. Anyone with an endless supply of money and power can't be a complete idiot.

It felt like Shub-Niggurath was waking in his bowels. He twisted his bag of complimentary popcorn shut and tossed in on the floor.

At the far end of the limo, Cat was trying to cheer Pope up with a puppet show. Hedorah was pretending to help so he could get a few more glimpses through the openings of her coat. Pope was ignoring them both. He seemed to be applying the same tenacity he would to an invention on the refining and distillation of the perfect pout.

Emma had been staring out the window opposite, but now she scooched in close, her ass squeaking against oily leather. "How much do you know about this Greystoke guy?"

"I'm starting to wonder that myself."

"This tunnel is ancient. See those carvings on the wall?"

Max had been too preoccupied to notice them before. He rolled down the window. The lights were dim, but the black markings on dark grey stone stood out like the contrast was turned up to one hundred. Alien symbols were etched in regular lines, jagged yet somehow precise, nagging, familiar though he knew he had never seen anything like them. "Oh, wow. That's creepy."

Emma nodded. "It's Aklo, an ancient pictographic language that predates Sanskrit."

Max looked closer. Old Shubby was awake now.

"H.P. Lovecraft wrote about it a lot. He thought Arthur Machen made it up, but Machen was deep into the occult, Golden Dawn, Glass Hand, you name it. He used some of the things he learned in his stories, but unlike Crowley, who he hated, he did it in a way that wouldn't piss off the Grand Poobahs, which I think is strange because a bunch of horror writers were all playing off each other's work at the time and Machen's secrets got a lot more exposure..."

"Aklo's a thing. I get it."

She nodded. "No linguist has ever figured out how to read it. It only appears in small amounts in weird places connected to inexplicable disappearances, death cults, and supernatural phenomena. The greatest Aklo discovery so far only had three lines, but this cave goes on for miles. How long have we been in here? At least ten minutes, right?"

He raised his eyebrows in agreement. It *had* been a while. Emma continued talking about how a find like this would be worth billions, it didn't make sense to keep it a secret, blah, blah, blah.

Max couldn't listen anymore. All that mattered were the symbols. Bits of meaning smacked against his mind like it was strapped to the front of a jet in the rain. He felt sick. Couldn't focus. The Night Noodles were bad enough, but this...

Ancient words teemed like maggots in his mind, boiling through his eyes, out his ears, filling the cabin with their phlegmy pops; writhing, slinking slippery syllables, taking root, growing, pressing deeper. His brain was expanding unnaturally. His spinal cord felt bristly. The colors were all wrong.

"Max?"

"Dude, what's wrong with him?"

"Is he choking on something?"

"Max, say something coherent. You're freaking me out."

✳✳✳✳✳

Max woke up to the sound of moaning and shuffling feet. He was lying in a puddle under an overpass. Zombies lumbered all around him, heads cocked, staring, but not in a hungry way. He smelled freshly baked doughnuts

"What the fuck?"

He patted his chest in search of his hammer and noticed he was naked.

...

A familiar voice came from behind him. "Howdy there."

"Shit, I should have known. Why did I say that out loud?"

Ernie laughed, and his face flickered inside his helmet. "Don't you worry. I take no offense. You can't think to yourself 'cause you're inside your head already."

Max sat cross-legged, turned around and put his hands in his lap. The jumpsuit was the same as last time. He wondered if it was Ernie's only outfit, but it didn't seem wise to ask. "And where might my head be?"

"Right where you left it, silly: freakin' out your friends in that glorified taxi-cab."

"Fair enough. You mind telling me why I'm naked?"

"Hell, boy, we're all nekkid in our own mind, and yes, this is all a construct of your subconscious. So don't bother askin' why your happy place is a ditch full'a dead folk."

Max groaned. "Okay, whatever. What do you want?"

Ernie cocked his helmet. "I'm sorry, am I boring you?"

"Sorry, it's nothing personal. It's just that I seem to spend most of my time asking obvious questions and getting snarky cryptic answers. You're obviously here to tell me something. Just say it."

Ernie snorted. "Riddle me this, ya smug little prick; what was happening to your head before you woke up here?"

"Fuck if I know. It felt like it was being torn apart."

"It was. If I hadn't dragged you to your happy zombie ditch that doggie treat you call a brain woulda sprouted tentacles and busted loose from your skull. I saved your fuckin' life. 'Scuse me for being friendly after."

Max felt bad. "I'm sorry. Aside from Cheeky you're the only non-human that hasn't tried to kill me or rape me. You've saved me twice now. I appreciate that. I do wonder why you take such an interest, though."

"We've been over that. You're the chosen one and so forth."

"Chosen for what? I don't see how one more guy giving speeches or setting up watchdog groups is going to do anything significant enough to warrant the attention of somebody like you."

"You know, you're like a feller who just got this big new computer, but he can't enjoy it 'til he knows where it was made, how much it cost and how the damn processor works. You can't understand it all yet, but you will, in time."

Max sighed. "Can you imagine how frustrating it is to constantly be told what to do by people you don't know, who won't explain why?"

Ernie crouched next to him. "Think about it this way: most people live their whole lives without doing anything interesting or significant. You're lucky."

Max didn't feel like debating the virtues of comfort versus passion, so he changed the subject. "What was all that about brain tentacles?"

"Words make reality. Things and concepts are made of words. You learn the words, understand and make new things and concepts. But some languages have more resonance than others."

Ernie made a deep throaty noise, and all the zombies turned into cans of chicken soup. Max felt like somewhere deep in his subconscious he let out a fart he'd been holding in for years.

Ernie beamed a grandfatherly smile and continued. "Aklo's one of a bunch'a old languages that can speak things into existence. Your world is made from words like that. Not them particular words, mind you. Aklo words open doors, poison your world with information it ain't used to. Poisoned a lot of worlds, truth be told. Not to say they're bad, just different. They're bad the same way it's bad to write a computer program using two different languages."

"But it's harmful to read them?"

"Depends on the words, but it ain't good to jumble 'em up like you was doin'."

"But why can't anybody else read it?"

"You read them kind a words with your third eye. Yours opened up a while back. There's no need to hide 'em, cause to most people they ain't nothin' but a bunch of squiggles."

"So was it Aklo the Night Noodles were speaking, or whatever?"

"No, it was somethin' else, but it works the same way."

"Am I going to have brain cancer now?"

"Nah, you'll be fine. Just remember," A string of indescribable noises issued from Ernie's mouth. Max felt like he was being hugged by light, then he woke up on a couch, in a study with Cat sitting on his chest and Cheeky on the arm behind his head sniffing his mouth.

"He's awake!" Cat bounced on his sternum filling his vision with a million tiny sparkles.

He stared through the glitter at his curious companions. The Count had a particularly odd look about him, but there were too many variables to tell what had him so intrigued.

The cacophony of are-you-okays and what-happeneds boxed his ears, but the TV, where people he had never met were talking about him like they were old friends, had his full attention. At the bottom of the screen he saw the ghostly words, "Maxwell Quick, in Memoriam".

"M*aaaaaax*," Cat grabbed him by the hair and shook his head, "speak to me."

Cheeky hissed at her, then crawled between them and shined a tiny flashlight in one eye then the other.

Max wheezed under Cat's weight. "Stop that. I don't have a concussion." He yanked the flashlight out of Cheeky's nubs and tossed it across the room.

Puff was rubbing herself against his other hand. When he didn't respond, she poked him in the wrist with her horn. "Ouch, fuck! Don't do that. I'm serious about filing that thing off."

Hedorah leaned in close. "You look like shit."

The Count cocked an eyebrow. "On the contrary, for someone who died in an explosion Max is in excellent condition."

Despite their efforts, Max's attention lingered on the screen where Hawk had just appeared. "Oh crap, did anybody tell Hawk I'm okay?"

They all looked at each other. The Count smiled guiltily.

"How could nobody call Hawk? You know how emotional he is."

No one answered.

"Stupid narcissistic bunch of...Wait a minute. Cheeky and Puff were with Hawk."

Max shot his pointy eye at the Count. "Holy shit, this whole thing is a publicity stunt, isn't it? You knew we were fine, and you let Hawk believe we were dead to make his performance better. Did you tell Cat to blow the club up?"

The Count's smile was cruel, but his eyes shone with unexpected pride. "Of course not. I lost a lot of talent in that explosion. I will admit to using some directorial license with your friend. One has to when working with amateurs."

"You stupid bastard!" Max tried to sit up, but Cat pretended she was breaking a horse. "Damn it, get off me."

Cheeky issued a warning growl, which grew more ferocious when she shook her head no.

Max stopped struggling and patted Cheeky to let him know he was okay. "Why would you make an enemy of the greatest living military mind? Hawk could have been a big help."

The Count giggled. "*Max*, do give me some credit. As soon as they finished shooting, I swept him up and apologized for the oversight. After all, I can't be expected to know who is on every show we make."

Greystoke bopped his head to the side. "Of course, he didn't take the news as gracefully as one would have preferred. I had to tranquilize him for his own good. He's still sleeping it off, but don't worry. When he sees you, he will be so happy he'll forget the whole thing and likely applaud me for my strategy."

Max sighed shallowly. Breathing was becoming more and more difficult. "You don't know Hawk. Cat, get the fuck down, now."

He grabbed her hair and her left arm and rolled off the couch, so he was on top of her. Framed once again in the sparkles of trauma, she giggled, her eyes shiny with pleasure. Max momentarily forgot what he was doing and kissed her.

Greystoke cleared his throat.

Max looked up to find the Nrrds staring incredulously. The Count's jaw was clenched so tight Max thought he heard a tooth crack.

"Sorry." He pinched Cat on the cheek and said, "You behave."

Emma grabbed Max's hands and pulled him to his feet. "What happened?"

Max scooped Cheeky up, then raised his eyebrows to the Count, daring him to speak. The Count countered with a practiced look of ignorance.

"I'm fine. I must have ingested something I shouldn't have." Max tried for a subtle we'll-talk-later smile, but subtlety was never his strong suit.

Emma looked back and forth between him and the Count. "What's that supposed to mean? You two are obviously hiding something. It's also obvious that Aklo is connected to Max's throat singing and subsequent collapse."

Goddamn geniuses!

The Count did a better job of suppressing his irritation than Max, whose eyes rolled before he could stop them.

Oh, fuck it.

"Yeah, so what's the deal with all the Aklo down there? You in some sort of fish cult?"

The Count's mask of bored arrogance was momentarily shattered. His voice was nervous and rushed. "What, precisely, is Aklo?"

Cigarette clenched firmly in his teeth, Hedorah got in the Count's face. Max could hear the crackle of singeing goatee. "Cut the shit, magic man. We know all about Aklo. Explain those tunnels right now, or we're going for a ride."

Greystoke slapped the cigarette out of Hedorah's mouth and karate chopped his throat as elegantly as he might silence an applauding audience. In a far less sophisticated manner, Hedorah crashed to his knees, choking and clutching his neck. Pope took two steps back while Emma rushed over to massage his trachea.

Greystoke furrowed his brow and glanced around at the rabble. He looked disgusted as he spat out the first few words. "Fine, then. I suppose it was foolish to lie."

He strode over to a wall of books, climbed the ladder and opened a hidden safe, then returned with a ragged old book, the pages of which had the color and smell of a hobo's teeth. He set it on the desk and pressed on its cover with his fingers as if, unrestrained, it might begin cackling and fly around the room shrieking, "Swallow your soul!"

"I must begin this somewhat epic tale with a confession. I was not always the icon of taste and refinement you see before you. I began life as a Savanian, living in a Super House* with my Catholistic parents and six sisters. I was the only one who refused to work for the church and tithe away any hope of a better life in the hope of a better death." He paused, his sneer softened by sentimentality.

"I did all I could to make my sisters happy. It's why I became a magician. We had to entertain ourselves.

"In any case, as a young man, I was consumed by rage and the desire to escape my pitiful surroundings. I pursued money and power, regardless of its source. I recognized the importance of friends at a very young age, joining every society that would have me from the Bloods to the Masons. I won't bore you with the details, but I came to believe the ancient words of power were real and dedicated a great many years of my life to tracking them down. What I found was amazing, in the archaic sense."

He shook his finger at Max. "What you so blithely refer to as a fish cult came very near to destroying the world. Of course, I didn't know that was their aim at first. I only recognized their tremendous power, both magical and political. I was blinded by the honor of being hand-picked to join the most exclusive society unknown to man." He smiled smugly.

"It was interesting at first. Well," he said with a laugh, "it never ceased to be interesting."

He grew sober. "My acquisition of this book," he tapped it twice, "is the sole reason this world still exists. You see, the aforementioned fish cult was dedicated to the opening of the gate, which would supposedly free the elders who would bestow upon us immortality and power beyond comprehension. They taught me just enough to dazzle me into servitude and charged me with locating certain artifacts. I came across quite a few interesting things, but none more so than what you see before you. This, boys and girls, is the secret Grimoire of St. Francis."

Max cocked an eyebrow. "Saint Francis, the bird guy? Why would a Catholic saint have a grimoire?"

Greystoke snorted. "If only there was a way to capitalize on your talent for understatement. Yes, to put it in words even you can understand, this is the book that made the *bird guy* able to communicate with animals. Unfortunately, it is only a transcription of a transcription of his grimoire which was based on the grimoire of John the Baptist. The latter was not actually written by John the Baptist, but rather compiled by the apostles for use by leaders of the budding church. Francis was obsessed with the natural order and didn't think man should have the power of God, so he pared it down to the basics, and shrouded what was left in cryptic poetry."

"So that book is the Rosetta stone of Aklo?" Emma reached for the book, but the Count waved her away.

"Of course not. Don't you know anything about mythology? Jesus was from a place of love and harmony. He spoke the language of Heaven, the one from which the fabric of this reality was woven.

Aklo originated in a foul cesspit of a dimension, one of many planes that make your understanding of hell seem like a children's theme park."

Pope piped in. "Jesus Christ was real?"

"Of course he was, as were most other prophets and deities. They didn't have Social Media© back then. Every meme was passed along by word of mouth. Do you really think the bizarre stories which make up any religious text could be proliferated in that fashion and believed by that many people if they had no basis in fact?"

Pope scrunched up his face and retreated to the couch to ponder.

The Count launched back into storyteller mode. "One might say this is the penultimate tome of nature magic. Francis removed most of the rest, but I was able to use this and Aklo in tandem to receive visions and knowledge beyond even that of the leaders of the cult. The truth left me quivering in terror."

He cast his eyes to the floor. "For weeks on end, I lay naked in my own filth, howling like a wild animal. I saw no point in eating or leaving my room. I used scotch to numb the pain tempered with just enough water to keep hydrated, so I could continue my self-medication."

Max looked to Cat to confirm or dispute her father's story. She made a hell-if-I-know face and shrugged. The Count was too wrapped up in his story to notice.

"In my delirium, I gained insight that can only come from hopelessness." He turned his gaze to Max. "It was not dissimilar to the situation that brought you to me. There were only three options. I could do nothing and wait to be devoured along with the rest of the universe. I could continue working with the cult and live as a demon's pet for all eternity. Or, I could try to stop them and risk dying the old-fashioned way. The choice was not difficult."

He held the book above his head like a Baptastic evangelist and rushed his speech for dramatic tension. "I knew this tome held the key, the only hope for my soul's salvation, as well as that of the world, but there was so little time. Malnourished, sleep deprived, still stinking of my own waste, I summoned up my final scraps of sanity and searched for the words that would foil the cult's diabolical machinations." He brought it down and pretended to search the pages franticly.

"Finally, I found it buried under layers of symbolism, encoded and tucked away where only the greatest mind with the greatest motivation could find it." Hedorah tried to read over his shoulder, but the Count slammed the book shut and smacked him on the head with it without breaking stride.

"I dredged it up from the bottom of the sea of esoterica and rushed to Bohemian Grove. I arrived mere moments before the final ceremony. The Grand Guignol was already warming up his throat. The choir was beginning to moan. The air was already thick with a smell like fish rotting in an unkempt reptile cage. The forest glowed as if under black light, despite the moon being totally obscured by clouds. It was ever so exciting."

Max didn't buy a word of it, but at least he was entertained.

"I went just far enough into the woods not to be heard and called forth the fog. The fools thought it was a good omen. Little did they know my antique canisters of nerve gas were still fully functional. By the time anyone knew something was amiss, they were writhing about on the ground, gasping for air.

"Unfortunately, the gate had already opened. All sorts of slimy, beastly things could be seen slinking beneath the water's surface, but I was prepared. I climbed the steps, stood tall and said the words..." The Count choked up, clutching the book to his chest. "When I said those words, I could feel all the power of the universe flowing through me. A great white light enveloped all that I knew, filling me with love and peace. I knew nothing could stand against me, for I spoke in the voice of God.

"The water boiled with inhuman cries of torment and began to swirl. The creatures struggled against the current, but they were out of their element, powerless in the face of God." He pulled out his kerchief and dabbed the froth from his lips.

"Moments later, I was standing in the middle of the most beautiful and serene bit of nature I have ever experienced. Animals appeared all around me in the forest. They came right up to my feet to thank me. Any other time it would have been quite unsettling, but I was still filled with that wonderful light. I stayed the night there, soaking in the beauty of this world. No man has ever been so humbled."

He climbed the ladder and returned the book to its hiding place. "The next day, I arranged to purchase the Grand Guignol's property, ordered it demolished and had my castle moved to take its place. As long as I live, no one will have access to the Aklo library transcribed in those tunnels, except me, and I have the good sense to stay away from them. I suppose I should have them chiseled away or plastered over, but I haven't had the time."

That was the lump of horse shit that broke the cart. "So you saved the world, purchased and demolished a guy's house the day after he died despite, I'm assuming, nobody knowing he was dead. You replaced it with a historical castle, and it was all just a day in the life, but you want me to believe calling a contractor to get rid of something that could destroy the universe is too much trouble?"

The Count glared angrily for a moment then sighed. "All right, to be honest I can't bring myself to do it. It would be the occult equivalent of the burning of Alexandria. Also, it's the crown jewel of my collection of occult artifacts. In any case, I can hardly see how it is any of your business."

Emma chimed in. "Anything that can suck the whole world into a hell dimension is everybody's business."

"Agree to disagree?" the Count asked with a haughty smile.

Max was about to open a big can of Ranty brand logical whoopass, but Cat slapped him hard on the stomach and changed the subject. "Max here had a few ideas about turning the Riot Nrrds into a business. They have a ton of neat inventions that need to find their way to market."

The Count clasped his hands in front of his chest. "Finally, a productive conversation! What sort of business model to you propose?"

Max glared at Cat. "I haven't had much time to think about it."

The Count cracked a predatory grin, whipped out his phone and tapped a message. It dinged its response before he could get it back into his pocket. "Ah, excellent! We have been invited to a dinner party at Joseph Heller's mansion tomorrow at seven."

"Who's that?"

"Joseph is many things: an entrepreneur, a tactician, a captain of industry so great that only a select few have ever heard of him. He also plays a mean oboe."

"And he's just going to set us up because he's your friend?"

The Count let out a belly laugh. "Don't be silly. He is a hardline objectivist. He has no friends, but a million contacts." He plucked a cigar from the box on the desk and lit it. "The wonderful thing about objectivists is that you always know where you stand with them. He is going to make billions off your success, but he can only do so if you become successful. He does not waste his time on anything that isn't a sure thing. If he is talking to you, it is because he wants something only you can provide. When you lose your value, he will disappear. The trick is to make the most of it while it lasts and retain your value as long as possible. Also, develop a business plan. You don't approach someone for funding until you can prove you will make money. I'll set up a meeting with some of my best draftsmen." He tapped out another message and returned the phone to his pocket.

The cigar smelled like burning cat diarrhea. Max backed away from the imperialist cloud. "Can we trust him?"

"You can trust his motivations. I understand some of your friends are good at calculating probability?"

Max nodded.

"Well then, you're all set. Next order of business?"

"What about me and Cat? At what point do we stop being dead?"

"Tonight, or tomorrow morning if you prefer. I've had people working around the clock. They have created a secret passage between the basement of the restaurant next door and the VIP room of Dadance. It was barely affected by the blast, which is ironic since it was the only empty room in the club. It was never meant to be used by anyone, you see, just was a symbol of unattainable power. If the owners had been using it, snorting drugs off naked sycophants as nature intended, they would still be alive and rolling in insurance money."

He paused to see if the lesson he was trying to convey was soaking in. It wasn't.

"Makeup is standing by, so whenever you are ready you can go down and I will give the order to have you rescued. It should happen before eleven o'clock tomorrow morning, though. Otherwise we risk losing the public's attention."

"How will we get there without being seen?"

The Count cocked an eyebrow. "I was under the impression that sneaking was one of your specialties."

"I guess we could use Fnordian necklaces and drones."

"That's a good lad. All you need to worry about is emerging with poise and grace. Show them your trademark bravery. Console the masses in velvety tones. Tell them you'll never leave them alone again. You will have them eating out of your hand in no time."

He puffed his cigar. "And don't eat anything for a few hours before the rescue. Being buried alive for a day is bound to build up an appetite. I'd like to provide the viewers with lots of images of you eating ravenously shortly thereafter to really sell it."

"Next order of business?"

Max tried to wave the smoke away from his face. "I'd like to get back to the library of the apocalypse discussion."

"As would I. I'm very curious to know how you came to know of such things. Unfortunately, I am running late for an interview on the Ed Shepp VI show. I hope you will excuse me. I *have* just lost my daughter."

"Far be it from me to get in the way of your capitalizing on the death of a loved one."

The Count stepped onto the elevator. "It is such a rare opportunity."

Max sighed as the doors slid shut. How the fuck did it come to this?

Cat gasped and grabbed his arm. "Hey, as long as we're down here, you want to see my Borgia collection?"

"What's that?"

"When I was a kid I got kind of obsessed with the Borgia family's hijinks, so Daddy had them exhumed and made a replica of the Pope's throne room, and he gave it all to me for my birthday. Come see!"

She dragged him down a hall and around a corner then stopped abruptly in front of a pair of tall wooden doors. She flipped a light switch and dragged one of the doors out of the way to reveal a perfect reproduction of St. Peter's at mass, complete with a grinning skeleton in full miter and robes placing a communion wafer on the nonexistent tongue of a cardinal. The air smelled of dust and old incense.

The room was full of the penitent dead, toothless skulls hung in respect of one of mankind's most infamous criminals. It was beautiful. As far as he could tell, the pews and clothing were authentic. Even the light coming through the stained glass seemed real, which wasn't likely since they were inside a mountain. As with everything else involving the Count, it was impossible to differentiate between illusion and Shinola.

She skipped down the aisle dragging him behind her.

"These are the actual bones of Pope Alexander VI and his family?"

"Yup! I started out with just Rodrigo, Caesar, and Lucrezia, but he's given me a couple more every year since, so now I have them all. Every wife, lover, friend, enemy. Well, not *every* enemy, but all the big ones. The guy in the front row center is King Charles VIII."

He examined the crack on the King's burnished brow. "How the fuck did he get all this?"

Cat's cartoonish façade vanished, and for the first time her eyes registered genuine affection and worry. "Max?"

"Yeah. What's wrong?"

"Don't underestimate Daddy, ever. Okay?"

He felt dizzy for a moment. "O...okay?"

Cat snapped back to her usual self. She gasped again. "Want to see a real dragon?

# DEAD PIT BY DAWN

Dawn came as a rabid peacock, spreading its violet feathers along the horizon, as it chased Max across the sky. Buildings whizzed beneath his feet like stupid bugs. He glanced indifferently at the ones he'd stomped during the war. He wanted to count them, but at the moment he was too tired.

It's too hot and too early in the morning to be dangling from a goddamn droid. I feel like a dead mouse on the way to the trash. A dead mouse with herpes.

Back in the good old days, when everybody was simply trying to kill him, he'd been able to set his own schedule. Hawk was his guard dog and alarm clock. He missed Hawk.

Max squirmed in his harness, trying to unbunch his wedgie without falling to his death. Every time he moved, the ropes and padding between his legs twisted tighter around his nethers, chafing and blistering the skin between his balls and legs.

Max scratched his greasy stubble and yawned for the billionth time. Cat had kept him up all night showing off her collections. It had been like spending the night with a hyperactive child, but with sex breaks. He was starting to think he couldn't keep up with her.

This early in the morning I couldn't keep up with a fucking waffle.

A pigeon flew by, so close it brushed his face with its wing. Max flopped his head back and shifted uncomfortably.

I wish I had a waffle.

He squinted into the sunrise. It was weirdly dark for eight in the morning, and something in the air wasn't right. It felt slimy, but that could have been the interplay of humidity with the residue from a dozen sexual encounters. In any case, his tux was sticking to him, clinging in all the wrong places. The legs of his boxers were crawling up his ass. His guts were all twisted up, and the closer they got to Dadance, the worse he felt.

Max shut his eyes and tried to relax. He considered taking a nap, but the droid had already begun its decent. He forced his eyes open and surveyed the destruction.

All that was left of Dadance was a pit full of rocks surrounded by a bunch of idiots with nothing better to do than point their phones at a hole. The handful of vendors on the street looked bored, even from five hundred feet up. He knew it was stupid, but a small part of him

was offended by the light turnout. This hardly qualified as a Media©
Circus.

No Ferris wheel? What the fuck? I thought this was supposed to
be a big deal.

Behind him, on a different droid, Cat was spinning around,
going, "Wheeeee!" at the top of her lungs. She'd been doing it the
whole trip, and it was driving him a little crazy.

Where the fuck does she get her energy?

She seemed to think that since people couldn't see her they
couldn't hear her either. Or maybe she didn't care.

A few gawkers heard Cat and looked up, but the Fnordian
necklaces kept them looking in the wrong direction while the droid
lowered them into the chimney of the pizza place next door.

Max unhooked and quickly climbed down the ladder the Count
had arranged for them. The stink of concentrated grease and ash
made his tummy grumble with both hunger and nausea.

Burnt pizzas crunched under his feet as he dismounted. He
kicked them out of the way and stuck his legs through the oven's
mouth. It was a tighter, grittier squeeze than he had expected. Lately,
his midsection had been puffing itself up, trying to reclaim its role as
alpha body-part.

Now he was stuck.

He sucked in his gut and wriggled until the oven spat him out.
He slipped and landed hard bruising his tailbone on the greasy tiles.

"Fuck you gravity!" Max stood and scanned the restaurant for
signs of life. The power had been knocked out by the explosion, but it
was an open kitchen, and there was enough light streaming through
the decal-covered windows for him to see. The blast hadn't done
much structural damage, but the panicking customers had apparently
had a food fight on the way out. It looked like someone had detonated
a giant calzone full of C4. The summer heat was turning the debris
into a mushy beacon for every bug in the city.

He turned off his necklace and slapped at the ash on his tux. His
hands came away streaked with grease.

"Goddammit." He took off his jacket and looked it over. The
streaks blended in with the plaid well enough, but he'd have to stay
downwind of the reporters or risk having to explain the smell.

He heard Cat's feet hit the tiles, and he had a sudden urge to look
at the dining room.

"You can turn the necklace off now."

"No, I like being invisible." She made ghost noises and moved
around the room picking things up and making them fly. "*Ooooo.*"

Max laughed, then gagged on the smell of sour marinara. "You
really don't understand how the necklaces work, do you?"

"Do you?"

"Not technically, but, I mean, you're not invisible. You're just hard to look at."

He had a sudden impulse to look to the left followed by one of Cat's signature atomic bitch-slaps. The force spun him around and sent him crashing into a prep table. A few pans and knives clattered to the floor, but he caught himself, narrowly avoiding contact with the food that was being prepared when Dadance blew up.

"Dammit, don't do that. I don't want to have to explain how I got smeared with pizza sauce while I was buried underneath a dance club."

Cat giggled and turned off her necklace. She was shiny with sweat, bursting out of her expertly shredded, replacement cat-suit and chewing on her pinky-nail. "We could say we were attacked by Italian mole men. They pelted us with pizza while performing an opera about abusive police officers."

He smiled and ran his fingers through her professionally disheveled hair. "I wish I could live in your head."

She bit him through the hole in his jacket and jerked her head around like she was trying to tear a chunk off. He begged and tried to pry her off, but she didn't stop until he punched her in the stomach. She came away smiling with red teeth.

"Goddamn, you have a jaw like a fucking Doberman."

She made her fake "I'm offended" face and slapped him again. This time he landed face down in a pile of sliced mushrooms.

At least it's not anchovies.

It felt good being horizontal. The earthy squish formed a surprisingly comfortable pillow. His body sank into the floor. He was moments from resigning himself to a nap when the searing pain of Cat standing on his back in her stilettos jerked him awake.

"Give it a fucking rest." He flailed until she fell off and hit her head on a stack of metal pans. Her temple split, leaving a bloody kiss on the tile floor.

Max stood and brushed off as much flour as he could. "You deserve that. Now let's get trapped under some rubble before we both end up dead." He stalked off towards the secret tunnel.

Cat got up and chased after him. "Don't be mad. I was just playing."

"I'm too tired to play right now. And that fucking hurt. I'm not like you. I don't enjoy pain."

She grabbed his arm and made him stop. "Don't be mad!"

He jerked away and left her standing by the booths.

He opened the door to the basement then cringed as Cat began to cry a horrible choking waaaahhhh. It sounded fake. He turned, cruelty welling up inside him, but stopped when he saw her sitting on the floor gouging her thigh with a steak knife.

Before he could say stop, she had sliced her leg open in five places.

"What the fuck are you doing?!" He rushed over and kicked the knife out of her hand.

She looked up with big raccoon eyes and held up a bloody hand. "Is this enough?"

"Enough what? Why the fuck did you do that?"

"I'm sorry. I was just playing. Please don't hate me."

Shit, there is something seriously wrong with this girl.

It hit him that getting involved with the platypus-shit-crazy daughter of one of the richest, most well-connected men in the world might have been a mistake. Until now, he'd been having too much fun to let it cross his mind. A mixture of pity and fear glazed his eyes as he knelt to take her into his arms.

"Of course I don't hate you. I could never hate you." He kissed her on the forehead and tasted iron. "I'm sorry, I'm just grumpy because I'm so tired."

"So you're not mad at me?"

"No. Those heels really hurt, though. Please don't do that again."

"Okay."

She raised her head and kissed him, the flavors of blood and runny nose mingled with thick saliva and neediness. Once again, Max felt like a monster.

He forced a smile and wiped her nose with a fallen napkin. "You ready to do this?"

"I guess."

Max stood and helped her to her feet. "Let's knock 'em dead."

They clicked on their headlamps then walked down the stairs, into the closet and through the hidden door. Max's headlamp flashed across a mosaic of broken mirror. The VIP room was a mess, but surprisingly intact. The speaker-bots were lying on their sides. The ceiling was partially caved in, but the couches were only a little dusty. The Champagne cooler and gourmet beer bar were intact, but the lack of refrigeration had rendered their contents undrinkable. Luckily, the wine rack was untouched.

"Man, these guys must have been serious about their wine. The rack's bolted into the foundation." He pulled two wine glasses off the rack and inspected them. They were the big, super-thin crystal kind like Greystoke used.

Hmm, I could do with a nice Malbec right about now, but it'll probably look better if I'm sober when they rescue us. Then again, if this was all I had to drink, it wouldn't make sense for me to abstain.

He checked the time. *They'll be rescuing us in about five minutes. I might as well. I can't get drunk that fast, anyway.*

He selected one with a screw-cap, so he wouldn't have to waste time looking for a wine key. He rinsed the glass out with wine then poured one for himself and one for Cat.

He looked her over as he sat beside her on the couch. *Nobody would doubt they had been in the explosion. The makeup artists had done an excellent job, but the fresh wounds and mascara-stained breasts were the perfect finishing touch.*

"Damn, you could make cancer look sexy."

She smiled bashfully.

*Well, if she's the train to hell, at least I get to toot the horn.*

Cat ran her fingers through his hair. A mushroom tumbled down his shoulder and onto the dusty cushion. She popped it in her mouth and her eyes burst with excitement. "Hey, you want a blowjob?"

"Well, of course, but we don't have time. We're due to be rescued in like two minutes."

"I can be fast." She dove for his crotch.

Max grabbed her hands. "Well, I can't." She looked disappointed. "You can give me a blowjob in a little while. I promise. Tell you what, I'll even pop it in your pooper first."

"Promise?"

He nodded.

She grinned and backed off.

*I am the luckiest guy ever. Just not sure if it's good or bad.*

He could hear the machines moving closer. The rubble shifted, sprinkling ceiling-dust into his wine.

"Dammit! Stupid ceiling." He tossed his glass into the corner.

Cat stared at him with wide curious eyes. "What'd ja do that for?" Ceiling chunks tinkled like ice cubes as she swirled her wine.

Max half-smiled, but his response was cut short when the claw of an excavator tore through the wall filling the room with blistering, calculous air.

"Holy fuck!" He grabbed Cat's hand and jerked her out of the way as a huge piece of ceiling crushed the couch. Their headlamps fell as they scrambled to the far corner of the room.

Max screamed, "Fucking stop. There are people in here asshole," but his voice was lost in the cacophony of splintering wood, crumbling plaster and heavy machinery.

The operator couldn't see them, and they couldn't get close to the light without risking serious injury, so Max tried throwing bottles of wine at the cage to get his attention. Panic and a sissy technique smashed the first few bottles on the rubble around the machine, but his aim got better with every throw. Bottles exploded on the claw and on the cage, but the driver didn't stop.

Is he drunk, or did the Count decide I'm worth more to him dead?

Seven bottles later he hit the bull's-eye, spiderwebbing the glass in front of the operator's face. The machine ground to a halt. A guy who looked like the offspring of a doughnut hole and a drain clog stuck his fat, stupid face out and screamed.

Max couldn't make out what he was saying, but it didn't seem friendly.

The other workers stopped and stared as Max climbed out of the wreckage wielding a bottle of Merlot in one hand and Cat in the other. The Media© caught wind, and rushed the ledge like a herd of lemmings. Anchors toppled down the melted stairs and over the rail, breaking their bodies on the rocky dance floor. The cameramen split their attention between the survivors of the old tragedy and the victims of the new one.

The workman turned off his machine and climbed down from the cab.

Max resisted the urge to excavate the idiot's skull, and walked past him towards the pile of squirming flesh. Some of the runts from the smaller networks were still coming over the wall, using the flesh of their former colleagues as a landing pad. The ones in heels seemed to be having the most fun, though several lost their footing and added themselves to the wreckage.

Max suppressed a smile. Never before has Dada opened so many minds in such a short time.

The survivors dug through the bodies looking for major-network microphones. Some of the not-quite dead defended themselves with whatever was at hand, further thinning the ambitious herd.

The luckiest began to limp towards him. None of them looked familiar. They shuffled forward screaming questions, desperate to make a good impression on their new bosses.

"Mr. Quick, how does it feel to be freed from the wreckage?"

"Mr. Quick, are there any other survivors?"

"Mr. Quick, are you aware that the world thought you were dead?"

"If you were alive this whole time, why didn't you call and tell someone?"

"Mr. Quick, what do you plan to do now?"

Max no longer gave a shit about the plan. He snatched the closest microphone. "I have a better question. Do you ever lose sleep over the fact that this," he pointed at the pile of broken flesh, "is the only way to get ahead in your line of work? Do you ever think about how that'll be you someday, lying in a ditch bleeding out while some fresh-faced young go-getter walks off with your microphone in their hand and your eyeball stuck on the heel of their fuck-me pump?"

Six were stunned speechless. The seventh, a tall blonde with more plastic in her than a Real Doll, smiled and turned towards the cameras. "Amazing, what a role model. Ten seconds after crawling from the wreckage, Maxwell Quick is already holding a mirror on our society, helping us to think the thoughts that will lead us to a brighter future. Max, I wish we could all be as selfless and brave and insightful as you. And with your help, maybe someday we will be. This is April Meadows for channel," she checked her microphone, "ten news." She put her arm around him and thrust her chest forward, using his body to pull her low-cut blouse even lower to display her talents in classic form.

The other reporters wheeled around and stammered into their microphones. What little wasn't gibberish was a pitiful attempt at an echo.

So this is the new batch of prime-time reporters. Nifty.

Cat picked up a piece of rubble and bashed April in the head. "Hands off my man!"

April fell to the ground unconscious while her colleagues showered Cat with questions. She was obviously enjoying the attention, but Max thought it best to leave them wanting more. He grabbed her elbow and dragged her towards the service ladder. "Sorry everybody, but we have places to be, things to eat. Cat's just suffering from low blood-sugar. We'll have a press conference later. Congratulations on the promotions."

As they approached the ladder the pile of bodies began to stir. Arms and legs clawed the rubble as the pile boiled, rolling forward on a wave of flesh big enough to surf on.

"That's not right." Max stopped and glanced back at the rookie reporters. Three were in shock. Two armed themselves with rocks and one launched into a fresh report.

I guess we have a runner up.

Cat jerked him out of the way as a shovel swished by his head. He turned to find the workman from before muttering unintelligibly, yogurt dripping from his mouth as he reared back drunkenly to take another swing. Max shoved him to the ground, straddled him and bashed his skull in with the wine bottle.

"What the fuck is wrong with you?"

Doughnut boy wasn't the only one with his panties in a bunch. The other three workers were closing in on the reporters. One rammed a pickaxe through the back of Channel 6's head so hard one of her teeth bounced off Max's cheek.

That chick just earned herself a Peabody.

"Uh, Max?" Cat yanked on his sleeve.

He turned to see the wall of slavering dead closing in, teeth gnashing in anticipation of his tender lumplings. Hands were sprouting from the rubble, forgotten celebrities making their comeback.

"Fuck me!"

"Here?"

He took Cat's hand and dragged her to the far corner where the explosion had ripped the fire exit off its hinges. Hand in hand they scaled the pile of rubble, ran up the steps, rounded the block and jumped in the back of the ambulance. The driver was about to shut the door when Max stopped him.

"Fuck! Wait. This is all being recorded. If I leave, I'll look like a pussy." He rubbed his face. His skin felt numb and his eyes were full of hornets. He squeezed Cat's thigh. "You go ahead. I'll deal with this and catch up with you later."

"I'm not lettin' you hog all the fun. Meany." She poked him in the chest. "Let's dingalingadong their dingalonglinglongs."

He laughed, then grabbed her hair and kissed her. "You make everything more fun."

"I'm your rubber duckie!"

Max pointed at the Sav-Cop riot van. "I bet they have some guns in there. Let's go kill some fucking zombies."

"Hoo ha!" She head-butted him then jumped out of the ambulance.

She ran to the van while he surveyed the carnage.

The pissy zombies were bottlenecked at the fire exit, but there was no telling how many got through before the hole clogged. The workmen had killed the reporters and turned on each other. The last man standing was jackhammering the foreman's ribcage.

The cameramen's live feed was drawing a crowd. It looked like everyone within five blocks had come out to gawk, but Max was the only one willing to do anything about it.

Max screamed at the Sav-Cops, who were standing around betting on what would happen next. "This isn't fucking TV, people."

One of the cameramen turned to him. "Yeah, it is."

"Well, I guess since you're here it technically is, but fuck you. Those are rogue fucking zombies down there, and they're going to eat us as soon as they get up here." He wiped the sweat off his face and slung it to the ground.

"Does this not strike you as weird? They came back too fast and way the fuck too mean for this to be normal. Back in the day, journalists would want to get to the bottom of this. Granted, that was way before my time, but I'd like to see a resurgence of ethics and common sense..."

The cameraman stared blankly. He looked like he'd rather be filming dogs screw.

"You know, never mind. You just do your thing. I'll handle it."

Cat ran up with two assault rifles and a bag of clips.

He took one of the guns and said, "Body shots don't count. Head shots are worth twenty points. Full decapitations are fifty. The loser has to buy the winner all the ice cream they can eat."

Cat raised the gun above her head. "It's on, bitch."

They took their positions and went to work.

A fat stupid voice came from behind him. "Hey, you can't shoot those people. They haven't been confirmed as dead yet."

Max glared at the chubby Sav-Cop and considered pushing him into the hole.

Another uniformed kid ran over and slapped his friend on the stomach. "Pay up dude." He turned to Max. "Ignore him. He's just mad he lost the bet."

Max turned the gun on them and they ran away. Meanwhile, Cat was calling out points as she got them. "One-twenty. One-forty. Ooh, one-ninety."

"Damn, where the fuck did you learn to shoot like that?"

"Blacktooth mafia. Gamers represent! Two-ten, futhermucker."

"I should have played more shooters." He lifted his gun and reimagined the foreman's skull. The crowd cheered them on while the Sav-Cops took bets on the winner. The distraction had made Cat an early favorite, but her gun jammed at two-hundred and sixty points, giving Max a chance to catch up. In the end, Max won by ten points. The crowd went crazy, three quarters demanding a recount while the rest hooted and pounded their chests victoriously.

The pudgy Sav-Cop crawled onto the hood of his car and motioned for them all to quiet down. "The verdict is final. Maxwell Quick is the winner with five hundred and ten points." Someone near the back of the crowd hurled a fist-sized chunk of cinderblock and knocked him into the pit.

Next thing Max knew he was in the middle of a full-blown riot with the losers tossing the winners into the hole chanting, "Bonus round."

At least they didn't turn on me.

"Bonus round!" Cat jammed in a fresh clip and took her position.

For fuck sake. What is wrong with everybody?

The funnel cakes were beckoning with their greasy powdered sugar fingers, but he forced himself to deal with this situation first.

He replaced his clip, climbed on top of the farthest wagon and fired three shots in the air. "Everybody chill the fuck out!"

He had their attention. "Look, however much you lost, it's not worth killing people over. Even if it was, you threw the guys holding the money into the pit. You're acting crazy even by angry mob standards."

The crowd fell silent and looked over the edge.

One person called out, "Hey, is anybody alive down there?"

Nobody responded.

"See, you guys just killed all those people, and for what? I'd have happily conceded."

One of the crowd screamed, "Hey, we got movement! You guys zombies?"

A familiar moan rose from the pit.

Cat sat Indian style and put the gun in her lap. "Well? Can I shoot 'em?"

"We don't have a lot of choice now, do we?"

The crowd nodded their agreement.

"Bonus round!" Cat emptied two more clips into the hole. "I win!"

Max noticed a figure coming down the street with a weird gait, but it was moving too fast to be a zombie. He looked through his scope just as it tackled someone at the edge of the crowd and bit into their skull like a ripe apple. Max took its head off and splattered the victim too.

"I think it would be best if everybody went home now. There's something seriously wrong here. The dead are acting weird, everybody's behaving irrationally, and it's pissing me the fuck off!

"And why's it getting darker? Anybody notice that? No clouds, but it looks like twilight at, what, like nine in the fucking morning."

Surprisingly, the crowd complied. Only Cat and the cameramen remained. Max climbed down and joined her at the edge of the pit. It smelled like an open septic tank and looked like a mass grave.

"We should fill it in with cement. Keep whatever's doing this down there."

One more body began to move. Cat raised her gun, but Max slapped her muzzle making her miss. "Hold on. That's the reporter you hit. She might not be dead."

"So? I don't like her." She raised her gun, but Max snatched it away.

"There's been enough pointless killing for one day. If she's gone bad you can shoot her, but let me check first."

April was on her feet, looking around at all the dead people.

"Hey, news chick, you okay?"

She snapped her head up at him. "Hell no, I'm not okay. I missed it. What did I miss?"

"Don't worry, you'll get an exclusive. The competition's all dead. You'll probably get a book deal out of this."

She squinted up at the cameramen. "Hey, what stations are you guys with?"

"Three."

"Six."

"Newspot."

"Where the hell did my guy go?"

Max pointed. "I think that's a bit of him by your foot there."

She grimaced and tried to shake the gore off her shoe, then lost her footing and fell into the guy with a jackhammer sticking out of his chest.

"You might want to get out of there. The zombies are kinda rowdy today."

She squeezed her eyes shut, took a deep breath and stood. "Okay, here's what's going to happen. I'm going to give the report of a lifetime. You three are going to film it, but it is going to be my intellectual property. We'll edit one exclusive out of all the footage and you will all get an equal cut. Do you understand?"

The cameramen agreed, but the Newspot guy looked pissed.

She pointed at Max. "I need a quick interview with you two."

"Fine, and I'll even give you the exclusive rights to my story, but I do have a condition. I need someone in the Media© that's loyal to me. Help me out where you can. Let me know when there's an ill wind blowing my way. Make me look good. That sort of stuff."

She smiled. "Keep the exclusives coming and you have a deal."

While she was climbing the ladder, Max grabbed a couple of pop-up chairs from one of the news vans and set them up by the hole. He munched funnel cake and filled her in while Cat took her frustrations out on the pigeons. Max didn't approve of the senseless murder of animals, but he was afraid of what she might do if he made her stop. At least he didn't have to worry about the mush left by the twelve-millimeter round coming back as a zombie Air Force.

When Cat stalked to the van for another clip April asked, "Is she always like this?"

"Sort of. I think she's jealous."

"Why?"

"Because you've been flirting with me. I'm flattered, by the way, but nothing's going to happen between us."

She laughed and her head jutted forward. "Flirting? What gave you that idea?"

"You did. And her. I'm not crazy. You all but motor-boated me after your ass-kissy response to my questions."

"I most certainly did not. If you are referring to my admittedly lewd pandering to the cameras, that was professionalism."

Max pursed his lips and dared her to say that again with a straight face.

She smiled sadly. "I'm not the bimbo I appear to be. I've always wanted to be a journalist. When I was a kid I read the biographies of all the greats and even the not so greats. Their lives seemed so glamorous, like they were part movie star, part spy. They had fun and lived full lives while making a difference in the world. But you know how it is today. If you want to get into journalism you have to major in elective surgery. I know my response seemed ass-kissy, but I meant what I said. Thanks for that, by the way. My first time in front of a major network camera and you gave me an opportunity to respond to something meaningful."

Might there be a real person underneath all that plastic?

"It's really been a wonderful day."

Nope.

"I've been Vlogging coverage for years, but I got my first real news job last week. I was supposed to start at NudiNews.com tomorrow. Not my dream job, but I would finally be getting paid. After today, it's prime time all the way." She grinned so wide it looked like one of her lip implants might shoot out.

"And I almost didn't come. I didn't see the point in covering a red-carpet pageant of dead celebrities when there was so much else going on, but I had a gut feeling. You know?"

"What could be bigger news than a bunch of dead celebs?"

"All kinds of stuff. There's a weird rash going around that doctors can't identify. Mosquito-borne Ebola has claimed its eighty-third victim in the city. AIDS went airborne, but that was in North Western Sylvania 236, too far away. Then we have the outbreak of violent crime, multiple reports of cannibalism not related to PITA, uh, animal attacks. The last twenty-four hours have been a journalist's wet dream."

"All that happened in the last day?"

She nodded. "It's like somebody spiked the city's water with super-crack."

Max had a bad feeling. "What was the first big story?"

"This was. Dadisaster!" she moved her hands like she was picturing a headline. "It's the best story overall, too. It started as a tragic tabloid piece, but someone survived, so it turned into a great human interest piece. You being the survivor made it real news, but then there was the second 'tragedy,' the violent attacks, super zombies and a riot! Shooting the super zombies could be a great human rights piece, but I'm not going to go there. You're welcome."

"Yeah, thanks. The NAADP isn't going to be happy about this."

"Are you ready to start the interview?"

"Yeah, I guess. Where the hell did Cat go? She hasn't shot anything in a few minutes."

He looked around and saw her crammed under one of the nearby vans, eavesdropping. It was sweet, in a sort of insane way. He was walking to get her when he heard her scream. She slid out of sight and reappeared moments later tangled in the entrails of a wing-covered orb the size of a Pilates ball. Somehow the pigeon mush had fused together to create a flying gut-monster. It was trying to fly away with her, but didn't have the strength to get her off the ground.

Cat struggled against her meaty tethers. "Help me! This is weird."

The thing was apparently semi-intelligent. When it saw Max, it gave up flying and started bouncing along the ground jumping and beating all its wings at once.

"Indeed it is."

Each bounce dragged her about seven feet farther away, which was pretty impressive for a ball of dead pigeon, but not as impressive as his machine gun. Three short bursts and the gut monster looked like the floor of a Chicken Church, minus all the flour.

April and her camera-guys stood behind him gaping at the mess. "You got that, right? Nobody's camera is dead, or out of memory or anything?"

While the guys rewound the footage and showed her it was good, Cat ran towards Max, stripping away the viscera like Silly String. She landed in his arms with a bloody squish, and he kissed her, ignoring the taste of pigeon blood and hoping there were no communicable gut-monster diseases he didn't know about.

When she stopped shivering, laughing and sucking on his face, he asked, "You want to go somewhere else? I'm really starting to hate this part of town."

She pouted and nodded.

"Let's get out of here. I'm hungry." He knocked the giblets out of her hair and led her back to the ambulance.

April called after him. "Where are you going?

"I gotta see a man about a fish cult."

She chased him down. "What about my interviews?"

"Call my guy, he'll set it up."

"Who's your guy?"

Max pulled a bloody business card out of his breast pocket and held it out with two fingers. "You should get out of here too. It's fucking dangerous."

He climbed into the driver's seat and found the keys in the ignition. "Finally some luck."

As they pulled away Cat asked, "Can we use the siren?" She was smiling. Her eyes were bright dazzling things, not the eyes of someone recently accosted by a gut-monster. He knew it was the crazy in her head that made her like that; no remotely normal person could deal with that and be okay, but it made him feel better, nonetheless.

He smiled and pinched her cheek. "Try and stop me."

He felt like this should be an ending, like they should be driving off into the sunset, happily ever after and all that, but it was only nine-thirty in the goddamn morning. He had meetings and press conferences.

God, it's going to be a long day.

# THE GRUDGE

Max turned off the siren as soon as they entered I-District.

Cat looked up from the XL McBeef Nugget she was nibbling on. "What'd you do that for?"

"It was getting annoying."

She nodded thoughtfully. "Yeah, that did get old surprisingly quick."

Max stuffed the last of his triple quarter pounder with cheese into his mouth and crumpled the wrapper. His stomach was gurgling before it hit the floorboard. He'd been so hungry he'd stopped at the first restaurant he saw. The fullness of that mistake was now becoming apparent.

"Oh yeah, *that's* why I don't eat McDougle's. Their FÜD just turns one form of stomach pain into another. Damn you, hungry Max. You never make good decisions."

Cat smiled. "I like it. It makes me poop elephants."

"That it does. Still, we would have been better off eating literally anything else. At least it was fast. We couldn't very well indulge in Greystoke's pancake feast and press release while gut-monsters accost people on the streets. It would look like I was shirking."

Low-hanging maple branches scraped the top of the ambulance as he squeezed it through the gate of Greystoke's main drive.

Cat stared at her deep-fried meat-wad. "That's what this is missing. It's not pancakes."

A hot, wet bubble of carcinogenic gas barged through Max's esophagus as he pulled up in front of Castle Greystoke. Cat sat up, cocked her head and tried to respond in kind, but only mustered a petite ribbit. She looked disappointed and adorable.

"You're so cute when you're competitive."

"I win mad games, yo. Speaking of which, where's my fucking ice cream?"

"Oh yeah, sorry. I'm really tired. We'll go later when the grease trap in my stomach empties."

Max stopped the ambulance, tossed the keys to the valet and ran up the steps before she could respond. He nodded to the doorman and stepped inside.

No matter how many times Max walked through those doors, he always felt like he was entering a museum, or a church—like he shouldn't speak above a whisper. He had a theory that old, expensive objects could soak up so much arrogance they eventually became arrogant themselves. Those objects would slowly emit waves of pretentious energy that became exponentially more powerful the more of them there were in an area. Prolonged exposure to that energy field could alter a person's brainwaves to accentuate selfish impulses that help them claim more tainted objects. Greystoke's house was an intelligent ecosystem where all the parts lived in symbiosis. Or maybe Max was delirious.

Cat screamed, "Daddy, we're home." When the Count failed to present himself, she grabbed a vase from a nearby pedestal and hurled it down the corridor. "Daddy!"

A butler appeared behind them with a broom and dustpan. Max had no idea where he'd come from.

"The master is in the cells." He swept up the mess and disappeared into another door.

"What does that mean?"

Cat's gaze dropped to the floor. "Well, you know how daddy has a kind of villain fetish?"

"Yeah."

"It's where he keeps his heroes."

"What the fuck is—oh. He has a dungeon, doesn't he?"

She nodded. "But that's different. The cells are just cells."

"And that's where he's keeping Hawk, isn't it?"

She nodded again.

Max groaned. "Take me there."

"You owe me penis."

"You'll get all the penis you want later, but first I want to see the cells."

She made an angry face, but took his hand and dragged him to the elevator.

The cells were three floors down, but they could hear Hawk's angry barking as soon as the doors slid open.

"This is going to suck."

They stepped in and Cat hit the button.

She pressed against him and smiled. "We could skip it."

"It's only going to get worse. Why can't your dad leave him alone? If we were on a playground I'd think he had a crush."

Cat smirked, but didn't respond.

The doors opened, revealing a surprisingly shiny series of cells. He'd expected something draconian: twisted, blackened arms jutting between rusty bars, victims wailing and begging to die. This was all quite posh, more sci-fi than period fantasy.

The hall was lined with eight-by-ten rooms, each with a full-size bed, enclosed shower, and toilet. The rooms were minimalistic, but aside from the two-inch Plexiglas doors and lack of a TV, it was nicer than some hotels. It was also reassuring that they were empty.

Hawk's voice ricocheted with such intensity, Max half expected the glass to crack.

Cat led him past the cells to another, much longer hallway lined with more of the same. The Count was at the far-left cell, watching Hawk pound on the glass like a gorilla on crack.

"I'm gonna floss my teeth with your spleen! I'm gonna strangle your kid with your intestines! I'm gonna bind a diary in your skin and fill it with examples of shit I'd do to you if you weren't already dead!"

Max quickened his pace, but Hawk didn't notice him until he was standing right next to the Count.

"Max, thank God. Kill this bastard and get me outta here." He stuck his fingers through the holes and rattled the door so hard it looked like it might come off its track.

Max looked at the Count. "You mind if I talk to him in private?"

"By all means." He turned and walked briskly toward the elevator. "Good luck. Your friend is an animal. I'll be in the study."

"Which one?"

Max could tell he loved having to answer that sort of question. He took an extra moment to come up with something witty. "Downstairs. Come along, Felicity."

Fail.

Cat frowned, but allowed him to lead her away.

"Max, what the fuck? Let me out."

"You have to chill out, man. Greystoke's a cock, but we need him."

"He's a manipulative, derisive, arrogant lump of shit! Fuck him!"

"Seriously, man, chill. I mean, yes, he is all those things, but there's a lot going on I haven't figured out yet. There are forces at work, creepy shit, and Greystoke's the only person I know who can help us deal with it." Max mouthed the words, "Your cell is probably bugged. Really, though, chill."

Hawk took a deep breath and exhaled slowly. "I *really* don't like that guy."

"You don't have to like him. Just put up with him. Okay?"

Hawk grunted.

"I need you to control yourself for both our sakes. Look around you. The guy has a private prison, and this is one of the least worrisome things I've seen here. There's a lot more to him than the comic book façade. Also, his daughter's pretty awesome."

"Please tell me you ain't got yourself pussy-whipped already."

"Are you going to behave, or not?"

Hawk crossed his arms and grunted his assent.

Max looked at the ten colored buttons on the panel to his right. He pushed the green one, and the cell began to fill with green smoke. "That's not right."

Hawk stripped off his shirt and held it over his face like a mask.

Max pushed it again, but nothing happened. He tried the red one next. Hawk hopped around the room and threw himself on the bed.

"Problems?"

"Goddamn electric floors!"

"Oh, sorry. There aren't any labels."

Afraid to try another, Max whipped out his phone and dialed the Count.

"How the fuck do you open this cell? The floor's electrified and it's filling up with gas."

The Count chuckled. "Push green and blue at the same time."

He did and the smoke was all sucked away.

"Now press red and blue at the same time. Then tap blue twice."

The door opened, but Hawk stayed on the bed, gasping for air.

"I take it your friend has seen the light of reason."

"He'll behave himself."

"Excellent."

Hawk's eyes darted between the floor and the open door. "Is it safe to come out?"

"No more zappy floor, right?"

The Count answered. "When the door is open all other systems are disengaged."

"Yeah, come on."

Hawk tested the floor with a gob of spit then ran out the door. He was about to put on his shirt, but saw it had been tinted green by the smoke. He grunted and threw it back in the cell.

"Just out of curiosity, what kind of smoke was that?"

Greystoke giggled. "Just a little something to help him sleep."

"Right. We'll be down in a minute." He hung up.

Hawk stared at him. "Well, don't keep me in suspense."

"Don't worry, it was just sleepy gas. He probably had it tinted green for dramatic effect."

"You sure I can't kill him? I'd really enjoy it."

Max smiled and slapped him on the chest. "Don't worry, man. You'll get to kill something soon."

Max heard Greystoke and Cat arguing in hushed tones as he approached the study. He was so tired it didn't occur to him to listen in. The argument stopped the second he and Hawk entered the room.

Greystoke leaned a little too casually on his desk, and Cat was in her innocent-little-girl pose she always struck when she was up to something.

Dammit, why can't I ever remember to eavesdrop?

"Am I interrupting something?"

Hawk puffed himself up. His eyes asked, *How 'bout now? Can I kill him now?* One look from Max and he fell in line.

Good doggie.

Greystoke smiled unconvincingly. "Felicity was just giving me the details of your little adventure. Quite remarkable, and wonderfully handled. I knew you would take to the Media© like a fish to water."

Max smiled bitterly. "More like a fish to lemon pepper."

Greystoke laughed. "Quite."

"You're the expert in all this metaphysical crap; what's going on?"

"I do have a theory." He was as somber as Edger Allen Poe after a prostate exam. "When the zombies attacked, did you happen to be giving one of your altruistic lectures?"

Max narrowed his eyes and flipped him off.

Greystoke chortled. "How should I know why they attacked?"

"Zombies are magic."

"Not these ones. Necromancy has always been a dark and dangerous corner of the occult. To bring even one body back to life is an almost insurmountable task. Only the desperate or terminally foolish attempt such a thing, and neither of those factors lends itself to successful conjuring. Therefore, in my professional opinion, these common, mindless, uncontrolled creatures must be a scientific anomaly, and as such lie outside the area of my expertise."

"There was nothing common about those fuckers. They were faster and more violent than any I've ever seen. *Furthermore,*" Max mocked the Counts pomposity, "*in my humble opinion* gut-monsters don't make themselves."

Hawk furrowed his brow. "Do what now?"

Max ignored him. "Did she mention the pigeon-guts-creature-thing had reasoning skills beyond those of an ordinary pigeon? I think something was controlling them."

He finally had Greystoke's attention. "Why do you say that?"

"The most profound thought a pigeon can have is, like, 'Hey, I can eat that.' They won't even get out of the way of a car. This thing recognized my gun as a threat and tried to run. Then, when it realized

Cat was too heavy to fly with, it adapted, changed into a kidnappy bouncy-ball."

Hawk cocked his head. "Are you bein' serious right now?"

Max glared at him and continued. "What's freaking me out is that even if all their little pigeon brains were networked together they still should have been limited to pigeony thoughts. So where did the extra IQ come from?"

Max pointed at Cat. "I don't even want to know what it planned to do with her, probably some kind of Urotsukidoji shit."

Cat smiled weirdly and got a far-away look in her eyes. Her response made him horny and ashamed, but only enough to create a pervy feedback-loop.

The Count pursed his lips, trying not to register the obvious. "I sincerely doubt that. Nevertheless, I agree. This is odd. I will look in to it, but right now your focus should be on preparing for your meeting with Mr. Heller, which, incidentally, has been upgraded. We are all due at Heller House tonight at eight o'clock, and believe you me, what happens there is of far greater importance." He shoved off the desk and came closer.

"It is absolutely essential that you make a good impression. Mr. Heller doesn't put up with insolence as well as I do. Only speak when spoken to. Answer his questions from the perspective of an employee, and don't elaborate unnecessarily."

Max butted in. "Yeah, I get it. It's important, but I think the other matter is a tad *more* important. Fucking gut-monsters, man! I'm not making this shit up. Pigeon guts oozed together and formed a creature that tried to drag your daughter away. That really doesn't concern you?"

Anger twisted the Count's brow. "Of course it concerns me, but I have put a lot of work into you, and I cannot let you foul it all up because of one stupid little anomaly."

"Have you been watching the news? The world is going guano. Every five minutes there's another account of somebody eating their grandmother, or themselves, or someone nailing their pet to the wall. People are freaking out, talking about the end of the world."

"Yes, I know, but those cases have all been in Savanian districts."

"What does that have to do with anything?"

"Today is the hottest day in the last hundred years. When extraordinary heat is applied to high-crime areas where the inhabitants are ill equipped to deal with said heat, aberrant behavior is not only likely, it is inevitable."

"Maybe so, but the weather itself is an anomaly. The temperature has risen thirty degrees since we blew up the club. Explain that shit."

Greystoke scoffed. Max had never seen someone scoff before. It was impressive. "Wonderful, you've been a b-list celebrity for five minutes and you already think your actions affect the weather. Either I've made a monster, or you are destined to be a star. However, at the risk of redundancy, this meeting will determine which it will be. You really must prepare."

Hawk was glaring at the Count as if he were a juicy steak that had been used to kill his puppy.

"Why? Why do I even need to be there? It's supposed to be a business meeting about marketing Nrrd inventions. Not exactly my wheelhouse."

The Count looked exasperated. "Must you be told everything in explicit detail?" He snorted. "What am I saying? Of course you do."

He picked up a black walking stick and twirled it in his fingers. "When I contacted Mr. Heller, I expected nothing more than a business lunch. I had no idea he would take such an interest. Rather than granting you all a standard meeting, he has invited you to his annual bacchanal."

"What's that?"

"A soirée, not so much a diner party as a summit. Once a year the upper echelon gathers together to compare notes, test the water for their future plans, and meet the up-and-comers. Once that is done, it tends to deteriorate into a hedonistic free for all. It's how we make it fun." The Count's leer suggested things Max would rather not think about.

"If you really want to change the world, this is where you will make the connections to do so. You and your little friends will meet all the people who make those big killing decisions you want to save us from, and you will have their ear, but only so long as you can provide an easier, more secure or more profitable means of achieving their ends. I have but a few hours to train you all how to behave around People. It will be tremendously unpleasant for you and doubly so for me, but I believe it is possible."

"So, you're suggesting I use flattery to manipulate monsters into being less monstery?"

"This is how civilized people exert their will on the world. Perhaps if you had attended sooner you would have simply talked the Mittons out of all those horrible things they did and saved yourself the trouble of a war."

Hawk growled. "You're tellin' me we're gonna go rub elbows with the fuckers we declared war on?"

"No and no. I was telling Max that, and neither you nor Cheeky are invited, as guests are expected to leave their pets at home."

Hawk started toward him, but Max grabbed his arm. Hawk jerked loose, but stayed where he was.

Greystoke came right up to Hawk, cocked his head and stared fearlessly into his eyes. "Does that bother you?"

Max knew Hawk wouldn't go against his wishes, but he jumped between them anyway. "What the fuck is wrong with you guys?" He put a hand on each of their chests and shoved them apart. "Quit this snake and mongoose bullshit. We're on the same team."

Max was caught in a hurricane of justifications, condemnations and spit that all but spun him in place. He grabbed a vase and smashed it at their feet. "Shut the fuck up!"

They did. Cat clapped.

"Hawk, he's a cunt, but he's sort of right. You make your feelings a little too clear sometimes. It's probably best if you sit this one out."

Hawk's eyelids trembled. It looked like he might cry, or explode.

Max turned to the Count. "And you, stop rattling his fucking cage. He's my friend and a valuable member of my team. You don't have to like him, but if you don't stop fucking with him I'm gonna have to throw him a bone, and it's gonna be one of yours."

Greystoke stifled his retort, but his forehead was a marquee announcing his displeasure.

"Now, if you'll excuse me, I need to take a shit, fuck your daughter, and find my other tux."

Max motioned, and his friends followed him out of the room. He hated having to assert his dominance. All the chest-beating, alpha-male bullshit made him feel like an ass, but sometimes that was the only way to get through to people. It probably wasn't wise to get on the Count's bad side, but for the moment he was too valuable to be in any danger. At least, he hoped he was.

# SIX DEGREES OF FORNICATION

Emma let her head bang against the limo's window. "Why are speed limits in gated communities always so low?" Greystoke's seven-hour crash course on etiquette had maxed out her capacity for boredom.

She was wearing a sheer veil that made her features easier to see. It was the fifth piece of headgear she'd modeled for them, and struck the best visual balance. The stocking had made her easiest to see, but it's impossible to make a good first impression wearing panties on your head.

Pope was equally bored, and looking more like a creepy uncle than usual in his seersucker suit and bolo tie. "Actually, it dates back to the time of feudal townships. Visitors were rare and sieges were common, so it was considered a sign of good will to ride in slowly to your destination. It gave the residents a chance to look them over and see that they weren't violent. Anybody riding in fast was likely to have to dodge a few arrows, even if it was just a friend with urgent news."

He paused for questions. When nobody acknowledged him, he slumped against the door.

"Yay! Almost there!" Cat clapped as the limo turned right through a guarded archway and into a park. They passed the fifth "10 mph strictly enforced" sign as Heller House came into view. The driveway was a mile long, but at least the end was in sight.

The Count finished combing his goatee and nodded to the window. "They call that 'La Foret de Sang'. What, from a distance, appears to be a park is, in fact, a high-security defense system. The trees are motion sensors, the grass a highly conductive filament hiding laser pistols, knock-out darts, et cetera. It was all inspired by Aeon Flux. He has a passion for old-timey two dimensional movies, but don't bring it up unless you want to spend the rest of the night talking films."

Max pressed his face against the glass for a better view of Heller House, a building so tall and bland it was almost camouflaged by the mountains behind it. "It must take forever to get his mail."

The limo stopped in front of a large metal door that could have been on a bank vault. Four guards held assault rifles at attention as they approached. Max expected to be hassled, but they stayed perfectly still as he passed into the long, black marble hallway.

The architecture had the presumption of a bank, the arrogance of a church and the ominous undertone of a ruin. Quality and age echoed in every step. Max could feel eyes on him, but he didn't see any cameras.

Greystoke noticed Max's unease. "Don't be afraid. They know exactly who is supposed to be exactly where, exactly when, and so on."

The only door in sight was an elevator at the far end of the wide, shiny path. Cat skipped toward it, her excitement doing little to soothe his paranoia. She'd be excited to jump into a grain thresher if somebody told her it was fun.

It was weird walking into the enemy's lair through the front door. It reminded him of his substantiation, though he wasn't sure why. He expected a trap to spring any moment. A golden cage would drop, and all the dirty rich would stream out laughing, their lips chapped with wine, slinging caviar like feces.

Pope sneezed.

"As an added bit of security, the air is full of nano-tracers, which cling to your skin and clothes."

Pope screamed, pulled his shirt tail out and tried to blow his nose on it. The walls on either side of him slid open, and he was dragged away by security. "No, wait! I'm very sensitive to dust!"

He was gone before it occurred to anyone to help him.

"He'll be fine." Greystoke put his arm around Max and led him on. "As I was saying, by the time we reach the elevator we will show up on their tracking system in 3D. They will have mapped our genes by the time we get off. In addition, they are lie detectors, mood rings and shock collars, so behave."

The elevator doors slid open as they approached. Cat hiked up the red chiffon of her gown, ran inside and motioned for them to hurry.

Max stopped on the threshold. There was something ominous about that elevator. There was no button to call it. The elevator had been watching, waiting for someone to step into its mouth.

Greystoke continued. "Mr. Heller hates being lied to, but, as you can imagine, he has developed a high tolerance to reality."

"Are you trying to make me nervous?"

Greystoke smiled wickedly. "No, I am simply providing you with information *and* allowing the systems to calibrate themselves to your physiology." He stepped onto the elevator. "There is no need to be nervous. It's all quite standard."

Max glanced at Hedorah and Emma.

"What?" Hedorah asked as he stepped past him into the box.

Emma tilted her veil, shrugged and joined Hedorah and the Count.

"Nobody else feels violated?" Max asked, stepping inside.

Hedorah did his impression of Pope, speaking through his nose and bobbling his head around like a chicken as he explained the obvious. "There hasn't been any real privacy since the dawn of Social Media©. Thousands of programs tracking every click, coupled with incentives to share personal information led to a voluntary big brother state where everyone knew everything about everyone else. Soon after, all informational systems became linked, so anyone with access to those systems could know everything and even predict behavior with greater accuracy than the individual behaving. Nano-trackers are only the next logical step. *Duh.*"

Emma slapped him hard in the stomach. "Stop that. You're even more annoying than him."

The elevator rose slowly. After the fourth floor the black glass turned clear, allowing a view of a snazzy restaurant.

Cat pretended to be an elevator attendant. "Fifth floor, food and potation." She bent to wave at the diners then snapped back to attention. "Sixth floor, music and merriment."

A nineteen-twenties era dance club came into view. Flappers flapped and bunnies were hugged to swing music, while girls in pillbox hats sold cigarettes to men sipping Pimm's. It looked just like in the movies, but with more pubic hair.

Who are all these people?

"Seventh floor, bordello and burlesque."

A sixteenth-century bordello appeared with a WWII-era burlesque show in the main area. Max could only imagine what lay beyond the veiled doorways.

Eighth floor, sun and sand."

Max couldn't believe his eyes. *A beach? He has his own fucking beach with sand, a wave pool and a cabana?* Just outside the door, a beautiful Hawaiian girl sipped something from a long bamboo glass and turned a suckling pig over an open fire. There was even a convincing sun in the fake sky.

Goddamn fucking rich people.

"How does this building not collapse under all this weight?"

"The foundation is made up of columns of synthetic diamond coated with three inches of titanium. If Earth ever collides with another planet, this building will stick into it like a nail. When they separate, not only will it be unharmed, it will remain stuck in whichever planet takes less damage."

Cat kept going. "Ninth floor, aliens and antigravity."

"That's the sort of planning that put Mr. Heller where he is today."

On and on they rolled, each floor more decadent than the last. Sometimes, even with Cat's summary, he wasn't sure what he was looking at.

The glass went dark again as they reached the penthouse. The doors slid open, revealing a scene that would make Caligula blush. The room had the same churchlike effect as the hall downstairs, so the nude frolicking and drunken revelry seemed sacrilegious.

They stepped into a throng of leather-clad body-builders, flame dancers, celebrities and posh aristocratic folk. Some were in conversation, some in flagrante. The servants were beautiful, nude and extremely accommodating. Every taste was accounted for.

The architecture was as frilly and over-the-top as rococo, but updated and more tasteful. The walls were a mosaic of thousands of darkly-colored stones arranged in complex patterns and held in place by molded silver. The paintings were from different eras and different styles, but all featured bold colors and contrast that made the images three dimensional. They stood in, like windows to other worlds.

The string quartet at the top of the massive double staircase was playing fast but sad, something to dance to while your wrists bleed out. It sounded like the sort of thing Adhra would have liked.

The Count gestured with his cane. "Welcome to the happiest place on earth."

To his right, the Han was clinging to the rail at the bottom of the stairs. A bald Iiite woman appeared to have her leg buried mid-shin in his ass until she removed it and began smooshing on his dangling sack with her tapered leg-stump.

Why is that guy everywhere I go?

Cat snatched the poi chains from one of the dancers, then climbed onto his shoulders, screamed "Giddy-up!" and swung them around like a lasso while she rode him into the room to the right.

Greystoke smiled sadly. "You must excuse her. These parties have been the highlight of her year since she was eight."

"That explains a lot." Max had always advocated sexual freedom and hated age discrimination, but imagining a prepubescent Cat anywhere at this party filled him with three Baptastic cavalcades worth of animosity.

"Max couldn't see Emma's face clearly through the veil, but he could tell she was barely restraining herself. Hedorah looked offended as well. Max wanted to grab one of the silver candelabras and beat the Count into dumpling guts, but knew Heller's security would stop him before he could do any real damage.

"What are you looking at me like that for?"

Max forced a smile. "Like what?"

"Oh, never mind. I should have known you would find some way to be unhappy. Do try to have a good time. No one likes a party pooper." He knelt and allowed the Champagne girl to pour a bit of Cristal down her breast and into his mouth. When he had his fill, he stood and gestured to the doorway to the left. "Max, come with me. I will introduce you to our host."

"Nifty."

He pointed to Hedorah and Emma with his cane. "I will return for you in a moment. I'm sure you two can find something to amuse yourselves."

Hedorah tore off his shirt and disappeared into the crowd, leaving Emma to hug her briefcase like it was a teddy bear. Her hand slowly moved to her neck and Max's eyed darted to the band.

He leaned in and whispered to the Count. "This isn't really the best place for a rape victim to amuse herself."

The Count looked shocked, then apologetic. "I'm afraid he insisted on meeting you alone."

Max groped the air behind him until he found her, then closed his eyes and pulled her in for a hug. "It's going to be okay. You don't have to do anything you don't want to. Just grab a drink, and I'll call you as soon as we're done."

Her moist veil tickled his cheek as she nodded. He patted her on the back then followed the Count.

The next room had an island theme and was mostly taken up by a waterfall. The lagoon was full of the naked and notorious. Chaz Lightbeard and Dick Chompsky were splashing around with the McDougle's bikini team while Pope Jim II received a blowjob from the leader of the Baptastics.

Max stopped the Count and nodded at the pool. "What's up with that? Didn't Santorum just declare a jihad on the Catholistics?"

The Count smiled condescendingly. "Why would two men with so much in common hate each other? They are the world's foremost power-couple." He continued on.

Max followed, but didn't get three steps before someone grabbed his arm. He turned to find a shiny-eyed April Meadows spilling red liquid from a martini glass as big around as a basketball hoop.

"Max!" she hugged him, spilling red stuff down his back. "Isn't this party awesome? I should have known you would be here."

Max glanced back. Greystoke had disappeared. "Yeah, I didn't have much choice. Interesting place. You come here often?"

Her head bounced around like her neck was made of rubber. "No, first time. You?"

"Me too."

"Just after you left I got this E-vite. I figured it was spam, but then I Googled it and all this stuff came up. It's supposed to be a big deal."

Max nodded and jerked his thumb at the pool. "I can see why. There are probably a million great stories here, but I wouldn't recommend covering them."

Someone tapped on his shoulder. He turned to find a pissed-off looking Count. "You really must learn to follow direction."

"You're the one who ran off. April, have you had a chance to meet your overlord yet?"

She looked confused.

"April, Vlad. Vlad, April."

Vlad arched his eyebrow and presented her with a card from his breast pocket. "Count Vladimir Greystoke, actor extraordinaire, master magician, Order of the Owl twenty-seventh degree, at your service. You must be Ms. Meadows. I'm so glad you were able to attend."

April burped loudly, then turned red and stared at the floor.

"Yes, well, allow me to borrow Max for a moment. I was just on the way to introduce him to our host."

Her eyes slowly rolled towards Max. She hiccupped, slapped him on the ass and slurred. "You go get 'em."

Max nodded and allowed the Count to lead him away. As they approached the door, she screamed, "Hey, don't forget you owe me an interview!"

The party fell silent. All eyes were on her.

Greystoke grabbed Max's arm and dragged him into the next room.

"What the fuck, man? Did she have a bomb on her I didn't notice?"

"More or less."

There was a large, posh bar on his right, offering all sorts of mind-altering substances. Max wanted a drink, but now he thought it might be a bad idea.

Greystoke led him to the center of the room where antique drink dispensers huddled together like terrified children at a vampire's banquet. He grabbed a large, silver ball, pumped out two fingers of light brown liquid for each of them and handed one to Max. "Your friend has broken one of the cardinal rules."

Max accepted the glass, but didn't drink. "What's that?"

"Don't make an ass of yourself."

"What's going to happen to her?"

The Count downed his in one gulp and pumped another. "I really don't know. It is early in her career and the competition in her field is very lax, so she may be able to hold her current position. I doubt she will ever rise above it."

"Why is it such a big deal, though? I mean, the Media© expects celebrities to get drunk and act out."

"Celebrities must pander to the idiot masses, but we also have a responsibility to be better than them." He took another sip and pointed with his drink. "Everyone here is an artist in some way. Some use their skills to create laughter while others mold the world. Lack of control can lead to all sorts of problems.

"If the wrong picture from this party were to find its way onto Blurbface it could fracture the infrastructure of collective reality. You have already taken a big chunk out of it. Another might well cause the whole thing to come crashing down, and then where would we be?"

"Free?"

The Count laughed heartily. "There is no freedom in anarchy. In reality, there is no freedom at all. Mr. Heller may have infinite resources, but even he is still bound by the expectations of others. All he has is dependent upon his network, hundreds of thousands of subordinates, each one searching for a mistake they can capitalize on to take his place. In many ways, he is the least free of all."

"I can sort of see your point, but I don't get why you think it's necessary to fabricate reality. If you'd just let people do their own thing, reality would happen on its own."

The Count put on his lecture face.

Max started to say never mind, but he was too late.

"I will illustrate it for you then." He dragged Max into a corner by the veranda and waved his cane at the crowd. "Look at them: self-indulgent apes full of insecurity and cognitive dissonance, each with their own god complex and a taste for violence. Our nature is destructive to ourselves and everything around us. Can we at least agree on that point?"

Max glanced at the drunk guy taking a selfie as he tiptoed along the veranda railing. "Can't disagree there."

"A long time ago, a few wise men came up with a game that gave us something to do other than rape and bash each other's heads in. Imagine the time before that, a truly free society where our nature went unchecked. Read the ancient texts, if you lack imagination. The Bible, for instance, is a compendium of rape, incest, murder, thievery, revenge, betrayal and torture, but at least there were fewer instances of necrophilia and cannibalism than previous times. Can we agree that, today, it would be unusual to respond to a rape by convincing everyone in a city to self-mutilate, then slaughtering them all before they could recover?"

"How would you even do that?"

Greystoke shook his head. "It doesn't matter. Do you feel that that sort of thing would be reviled by people today?"

"Yeah."

"That is because the game has led mankind to progress, to evolve self-control. The rules have been refined over the years. Each tweak makes the game more effective, but also more complex and fragile. Each rule is so intricately balanced with the others that the removal of one could collapse the rest of the game. For instance, if people stopped pretending little green pieces of paper were worth having, the economy would collapse. People would no longer be able to get the things they need to survive. If they stop believing they are safe, they will become paranoid and violent."

*Why can't I ever just keep my mouth shut?* Max noticed the spokesman for the Super Car sitting on the head of a marble statue, masturbating with a look of great concentration. *How is that okay?*

Greystoke continued. "When people find out their religious leaders are atheists, they question the validity of their moral system. When one questions morality, one finds there is no concrete evidence of good or evil. It's all relative to the individual. Knowing this, they begin to indulge themselves at the expense of others. When others see them raping and pillaging—well, monkey-see monkey-do. Civilization either becomes an anarchistic mess or a police-state. The illusions we create are for the common good. They keep the game going and society civil.

"Imagine a clerk at a hardware store. She isn't likely to go abroad on minimum wage, but she knows going to work on a regular basis will provide her with enough money that, if properly managed, will cover all of life's necessities and the occasional treat. Destabilize any part of that, and there's nothing to stop her from stealing a chainsaw and running amok."

He put his hand on Max's shoulder. "You are a game master, now. You are responsible for crafting and maintaining those illusions. You can play the game however you like, as long as you don't let on it's a game."

Max's butthole clenched at the realization that the Count had a point. All things considered, it was amazing humans had progressed at all. "Why didn't you just say that to begin with?"

"I did. Do you finally understand?"

"I'm not sure I entirely agree, but I see your point."

"I cannot tell you how happy that makes me. Now, let's go and meet our host. I believe he is in the dressage arena." He led Max to the door on the far wall.

Max noticed a change in the air the moment his foot touched the long Persian rug. The doors were ornately carved from dark, heavy wood, and the huge mirrors hanging between them gave the impression of standing among an infinite number of magic portals. There was something deeply sinister beneath all that beauty, a tone, a vibration that grew exponentially more potent with each step. By the time Greystoke opened the door at the end, Max felt his heart beating irregularly, flopping in his chest like a horse with a broken leg.

Max was ushered into a small stadium where a jockey clung to a large black horse as it stood on its hind legs, dancing an awkward soft shoe. The recessed arena was surrounded by padded bleachers upholstered in crimson leather. The upper area was empty save for one mustached individual on the opposite side of the room. Even at a distance, Max could feel waves of power coming off him.

I could swear I've seen that guy before.

As they made their way around the arena, the horse went down on all fours and trotted out the door to their left. Heller had big, laughing eyes—predatory, imposing orbs that drew Max in while filling him with dread. His face was pear-shaped with a tiny mouth and a little pencil mustache that curled with his thin bluish lips like worms baking on the pavement of his face.

Max offered his hand. "Have we met before?

Heller looked at his hand like it was made of anchovies. "I can say with some degree of certainty that we have not." His voice had a quality like insect wings brushing against a screen door.

"Well, thanks for seeing us. I know you're a busy man."

Heller frowned and looked at the door they had come through.

Greystoke stepped forward. "Maxwell has performed splendidly today, even in the face of violent adversity. His altruistic action-hero persona is testing better than our four best-loved characters combined. I dare say he's a natural."

Heller pressure washed Max with his eyes.

Fuck, this guy is creepy. Does he want me to say something? Should I compliment his house? That would probably bore him. Goddammit brain, spit out something useful!

The silence became a vacuum. Those eyes seemed to pulse and grow.

This must be what it's like to be a feeder mouse.

Heller's gaze relaxed. "Enjoy the party."

Greystoke took his arm and led him back the way they had come. When they were out of the room Max jerked away. "What was that all about? He barely even spoke to me."

"You really shouldn't question these things. All that matters is that it went well."

"How can you tell?"

Greystoke put his hands on Max's shoulders. "Relax. The hard part is over. All that is left is for you to enjoy yourself, but not too much."

"Yeah, but..."

"Shhh. Enjoy the party."

Greystoke spun him around and shoved him towards the bar. When Max turned around he was gone.

Fuck it, I need a drink.

Max walked up to the bartender and said, "Surprise me."

Something thick and pink was drawn from a tap. It had a head like beer, and smelled like a woman smeared with whipped cream. He held it up to the light. It was completely opaque, but glowed like a good weizen. Strawberry and spice soaked into his tongue like lotion, then sprouted wings and fluttered to his belly where they melted into a fuzzy warmth and radiated outwards, saturating him in coziness. By the time the warmth hit his head, he was already buzzed.

"What is this? It's like drinking the smiles of children."

The bartender smiled knowingly and helped another partygoer. Max wondered if he had made a terrible mistake. Bliss had taught him that not all alcohols are created equal. This would be a bad time for a repeat of the shopping-cart, sex-clown incident. He scanned the room. Nobody else was drinking it. He dialed the Count, but it went straight to voicemail.

He decided to walk around holding it and see if he got any looks that told him it was a test. He took a tiny sip and shivered as it made its way through him.

Maybe Cat can tell me what it is.

He left the lounge, made his way around the lagoon and past the elevator into the room Cat had run off to. The walls were lined with recognizable paintings, some of which he thought were in the Louvre. Beautiful, famous people mingled among the sculptures, drinking wine and making pretentious hand gestures.

This isn't really Cat's scene.

There were three other doors, all closed. The first led to a hermetically sealed wine room that required a pass code to get in. The second was a small parking garage with a huge elevator and fifteen top-tier gas guzzlers.

Fucking rich people.

He closed the door and scanned the room again. Still no Cat.

I guess she's behind door number three.

The last one opened into a long, empty hall identical to the one on the other side of the building. He stepped in and closed the door, sealing himself off from the cacophony of rich people trying to talk over one another. Tinnitus rushed in to fill the vacuum, making him feel lightheaded.

He massaged his ears until the buzz grew fainter.

Damn, I hadn't noticed how loud it was in there.

He felt like he was trespassing, like if he opened the wrong door he might see something that would get him killed.

I hope it's okay for me to be back here. He probably would have locked the door if it was off limits.

He took another sip and tried to look nonchalant as he walked to the farthest door and opened it. A soft floral breeze drifted past him as he stepped outside.

Wow, the guy has his own indoor enchanted forest.

Blossoming tree fingers sifted moonlight onto a grassy, orchid-lined path that ended at a crossroad about thirty feet ahead. Firelight was faintly visible through the trees to his right, which echoed with laughter and splashing water.

He walked to the crossroad and saw that it went on a good distance in both directions before curving out of sight. Straight ahead he could make out figures running in the woods. A woman screamed happily as she darted through the bushes to dodge her playful pursuer. There was something serene and innocent about this place, which clashed horribly with all the rest of the house.

He ignored the fire and walked around the path to the left. Once the door was out of sight it was impossible to tell he was in the city. The farther he walked, the more he wondered if he really was. Heller's house was huge, but he'd walked farther down this path than he had to get to this side of the house.

After a few minutes, the path opened onto a pond with large round rocks around the far end. Soft wind tickled the water just enough to jiggle the stars.

Weird, I usually notice when the moon is full.

He hadn't seen this many stars since his grandmother had died. Her house had once been a farm, but when Grandpa died, her kids all moved to the city, leaving her to sit on her porch watching nature reclaim all they had taken from it. He'd felt sorry for her, but not so sorry as he would have been if his parents had stayed.

The rare pang of sentimentality was carried away on a lavender-scented breeze. He felt so relaxed and safe there that he took another sip. The warmth pulled him forward, urging him to sit on the embankment and soak his toes. He kicked off his shoes, sank his feet, and laid back on the soft grass, pleasantly befuddled.

This was totally unlike him. He hated nature, and was never able to relax. His whole life he'd felt pursued, like something terrible would happen if he let his guard down. His childhood was driven by curiosity, then after his disillusionment it had been the need to know and understand. Once he understood, it had been the need to purge what he had learned, to cleanse the shore of his mind with wave after wave of alcohol. He wondered if he had ever felt peace before that moment.

There was movement in the rocks. He lifted his head and saw a nude woman lying propped on her elbows at the highest point. He could have sworn she wasn't there before.

She was beautiful and long, like she had an extra segment in her torso that most women lack. Still, he didn't have the urge to go fuck her, nor did he feel he should avert his gaze.

She smiled and let her head fall back, arraying her Neapolitan dreadlocks like a hippy peacock. She had the sort of hair that said, *Yeah, my parents are rich, but I'm cool anyway.* She rolled her head and said, "You should sit up here. This is the best view in the whole garden."

"All right." Max brought his drink, but left his shoes and socks where they were. He climbed onto one of the smaller rocks then hopped from one to the other until he was adjacent to hers.

He lay beside her, taking it all in. The rock, being the highest point on a large hill, provided an excellent vantage point to keep an eye on Cheeky and Puff as they chased each other around the trees. The slope was gentle and covered in enough trees and bushes for one to pass through or hide in with equal ease.

Max smiled at the beautiful woman next to him. "It's all downhill from here."

The wind shifted like a giant liquid tongue tasting the earth. The trees swelled like nipples, and the Earth let out a tender sigh. He didn't know or care what this place was, but he planned to hide there until the party was over.

Moonlight washed down the woman's throat like cappuccino. "Hm?"

He smiled and took another sip of his drink. "Nothing. Nice place you have here."

The woman lay back down and closed her eyes.

"Do you know a girl named Cat, Greystoke's daughter?"

She smiled and tilted her head as if remembering something nice. "Everybody knows Cat."

"Have you seen her? As soon as we got to the party she jumped on some cowboy and rode him in this direction. There are a lot of weird people here. I'd hate for her to get hurt." His words sounded silly. This place made all the shittiness of the world seem like make believe.

"What party?"

"The same one you're at. Heller's big to-do."

The woman bolted up and looked at him, really looked at him for the first time with those big dark eyes. Her eyes darted to his glass. "Oh, I forgot what day it was. I should probably be going."

She jumped into the water and swam to the embankment where her clothes lay neatly folded under a bush. He stared at the yakuza style tattoo covering her back.

Is that a canary?

He stood. "Is something wrong?"

"No, it's just getting late." She pulled her dress on and struggled with the zipper. She was frantic, but trying not to alarm him.

"What's your name?"

"Why do you want to know?"

"I don't know. Is it a secret?"

"Lucille."

"Nice to meet you Lucille. Is there something about this party I should know?" She had run off before he could finish the sentence.

"Weird." He lifted his glass and found it empty. "What the fuck happened to my drink?"

Something wasn't right. A lot wasn't right. Going back to the party was the last thing he wanted to do, but he had to make sure Cat and the others were okay. He felt they were fine, but the feeling felt fake, like somebody or something else was feeling it for him. In either case, he wanted more pink drink.

He hopped back down to the embankment and retrieved his shoes.

"If that pink stuff was some kind of crazy drug or supercharged alcohol that wouldn't have been so easy. I'd know by now if that stuff was bad."

He hurried down the path and found the door. As soon as he stepped into the hallway the sense of calm began to fade. His head felt different, like he'd inhaled a lot of dust and his sinuses were swelling up. The vertebrae of his mind were slipping out of place, pinching all the usual nerves.

Now he really wanted that drink.

*No, I need to find Cat first. She's like a kitten in a dryer here.* He pictured her tumbling around, going 'Wheeee' until her spine snapped.

He opened the door to his right. It was another hallway that went on for a good distance with doors every fifteen feet or so, and other halls branching off.

Great.

He closed that door and opened the next one down, filling the hall with light and sound. The walls pulsed with patterns and colors.

The air vibrated with binaural beats. There were people in the room, but it was hard to make out how many because their white leotards were pulsing along with everything else. They were doing a slow, interpretive dance that didn't seem entirely voluntary.

If Cat was in there she would have dragged him in, so he shut the door and moved on. The next four doors were locked. He knocked on a couple, but nobody answered.

The last door opened into a hunting lodge with dead animals all over the place, leather furniture and a gaggle of sluts servicing five douchey guys between the ages of thirty and sixty. They all shared a handful of chiseled features, but some of the permutations were better than others. In order of ascending age Max named them Sporty, Scary, Cocky, Fatty and Posh.

"Adam! I told you to lock the door." The one with the dead eyes and the big creepy mouth threw his tumbler at the one who looked like a football player. It glanced off the red leather couch and shattered below the moose head.

Sporty ignored him and stuffed his mouth with tit. Creepy shook his head and resumed fucking the mouth of the girl he was sharing with Fatty. Fatty was beet red and pouring sweat. Behind him the tall woman with walnut-colored skin and a massive purple strap-on that matched her eyes and hair moved her hips back and forth looking bored. She cocked her head at Max and smiled like a demented pixie.

The stench of sweat and santorum was unbearable. Max didn't see Cat, so he was about to shut the door when the oldest addressed him.

"Aren't you Maxwell Quick?"

"Yeah."

Posh waved the twins away, stood and zipped his pants. "Savior of the world! Come in. I've been dying to meet you."

Max didn't want to be rude so he stepped inside and closed the door. Posh approached him and offered a perfectly manicured hand. It felt like he was shaking a very firm satin pillow.

"My name is Alec Rothafella, and as you have probably guessed these are my brothers Danny, William and Stephen. That's Adam Rothafella on the couch. No relation.

"Come. Have a seat. Can I offer you a drink, a blowjob?"

Two of the girls led Max to a leather armchair, pushed him into it and turned into a gropey octopus. Max stated in a polite but firm voice that he was fine, and the girls went back to Adam.

"I've heard of you guys. You're the oldest old-money family. You own IMD and Glob-Oil. They say you secretly rule the world, or something like that."

Alec laughed. "Don't tell me you believe that sensationalist claptrap."

"I know how things really work, and I know you have the money and power to do whatever you like. Comic book characterization aside, you sort of do, don't you?"

"Not really. We protect our interests. I'll be damned if I'm going to be the one to destroy a fortune that has been with my family for over two thousand years, but aside from that I could care less what happens out there."

He leaned back and crossed his legs. "Now, our father was known to pull a string now and then, and his father was a professional busybody. They did all sorts of things that had major cultural ramifications. They weren't saints by any means, but as far as I know they never ate the hearts of virgins or turned into lizards." He made a poor excuse for a dragon face and flicked his tongue around.

Cocky came, making a noise like a horse.

"But enough about us. Tell me about yourself. What are your hopes, your dreams?"

The Count had made it very clear never to let on that he believed in change. Lizards or not, these guys could drown him in cognac and suck the flesh from his bones before he knew his clothes were off. "I spent most of the last fifteen years in a grimy stupor, then I accidentally rid the world of our mutant overlords. I'm not sure what you're supposed to dream about after that, but I hope my life doesn't turn back to shit."

"I wouldn't worry too much about that. Tell me, what was it like, this grimy haze?"

"What's the worst thing that's ever happened to you?"

"I once lost ninety-eight million dollars in the course of three hours. Terrible day. Every investment I had took a nosedive at the same time."

Ninety-eight million's pocket change to these guys. "That is pretty sucky."

"Yeah, but I made it all back the next day."

*Of course you did.* "Anything more personal?"

"Personal?"

"You know, not so much money oriented."

He looked thoughtful for a moment. "When I was five my nanny had me help her hang herself from a chandelier in our home in Aspen. She was a wonderful woman. Erica was her name. It wasn't until years later I learned the story. My grandfather had fallen in love with her, but she was already happily married. He wasn't used to not getting his way, so he made her husband disappear then tried again. The second time she rejected him he flew into a rage and assaulted her.

There were rumors she was pregnant." He whispered "pregnant" as if it was a big secret.

"She did it to teach us all that our actions had consequences. It said so in the note."

"That's pretty bad."

"She was like my own private mom."

Max stared at his hands.

"I suppose you're going to say your haze was like that but worse, or all the time."

"No, not really anything like that. It was a totally different kind of shitty. It hurt to think. I hated everything. Nothing was fun. It was like dying and going to hell, but hell is a waiting room filled with fat, stupid assholes. The assholes get everything you want and spit on you every chance they get, plus there's no hope, because you can't die. I felt like that was all I'd ever have."

Alec smiled like he was on a billboard. "You're a sufferer. I like that. I've always envied sufferers—the connection they have to the misery of existence. My world is made of shiny plastic. It looks good, never rots, but it doesn't have any real value either."

"If money keeps you from enjoying life, why not get rid of it?"

"Poor people are unhappy, too, but they can't drown their sorrows in Coteaux Champenois La Côte aux Enfants." He held up his champagne flute, took a sip and smiled. "Are you sure you wouldn't like a drink? The wine cellar here is phenomenal."

"No thanks. By the way, what is that pink stuff they have on tap?"

"Nectar?"

"I guess. What is it?"

"Liquid extravagance. It heightens the senses, opens you up to things you ordinarily wouldn't experience. Heller brews one batch a year and only serves it at this function. I plan to have a couple before I go upstairs."

"What's upstairs?"

"The orgy room."

"Orgy room? This whole place is an orgy room."

"No, people are free to do whatever they like wherever they like for the most part, and they do, but the orgy room is something else entirely. Have you ever attended an orgy?"

Max shook his head.

"Oh, it's wonderful. You've never really experienced the human body's potential for pleasure until you've lost yourself in a sea of strangers. You dissolve into sweaty flesh, all that friction, all those pheromones soaking in. You don't know whose foot is in your mouth, whose tongue is in your ass, and it doesn't matter. You're a germ in a Petri dish, a biological imperative made flesh. You really must take advantage while you're here. It's hard to get a good orgy together these days."

Max smiled. "Maybe I'll take a dip after I find my girlfriend."

"You brought your girlfriend?"

"More like she brought me. Cat's apparently been coming to these since she was a little girl."

"You don't mean Cat Greystoke?"

"Yeah, that's her."

Alec made an O face. "Oh my God, did you guys hear that? He's *dating* Cat!"

The brothers registered shock and confusion. Fatty asked, "Why?"

"Why's that weird? She's a lot of fun."

Fatty answered. "Fuck yeah, she's fun. Every guy at this party knows how fun she is."

Posh added, "The orgy room is frequently referred to as Felicity's Pleasure Palace."

Fatty and Creepy high-fived over the woman's back and made a foghorn noise.

Max put on his douchiest face. "I didn't say we were high school sweethearts. Her dad hooked us up so we could be famous together. She's a sweet girl, but I don't really see white picket fences in our future."

Alec's smile was patronizing. "All right, well, to each their own. She's probably in the orgy room now, but good luck finding her in there. She tends to swim near the bottom. She thinks all the juices are good for the skin."

Max couldn't help picturing her naked and dripping with the fluids of hundreds of old rich people. She looked so—happy.

"She is very soft."

"She is."

Max was jealous and creeped-out, but mostly sad that Cat had such low standards. Things were only going to get less comfortable the longer he stayed, so he forced a smile and stood. "Well, it was nice meeting you guys, but I should probably get back out there."

"It's been an honor, Mr. Savior Sir."

Max shook his hand and made polite gestures to everyone else as he left. Outside he took a deep breath and leaned against the wall.

Will today ever fucking end!

He gathered what little nerve he had left and fast-walked to the bar, ignoring everyone who tried to stop him. There were too many shitty people, too many vapid conversations, and way too much mindless self-indulgence. His self-control was waning. There was no telling what he might say or do if he got cornered again.

The bartender had stepped away, so Max served himself. He downed half the glass in one gulp then gave himself a refill. A few seconds later he felt like his molecules were being massaged.

That is some good shit. Maybe one of the guys can synthesize it if I bring back a sample.

He doubted they had go-cups, so he locked himself in the bathroom and let a little soak into his hanky. The Nectar was filling his head with lights, like a cartoon hammer. It no longer bothered him that somewhere in this fortress of depravity his girlfriend was probably drinking sperm out of a bucket, or fellating some old guy with her mouth full of live worms. That was who she was. Why should it bother him? He thought of the sea of flesh upstairs waiting to envelop him in sticky bliss.

Why the hell not?

He left the bathroom and jogged up the stairs. Halfway up, the smell hit him. It was like the garbage can he'd had as a kid, times a billion.

Heller's maids must make a fortune.

There was something else in the air, possibly incense, that balanced the slimy musk and kept him from gagging. It was sugary with hints of crème brûlée, piña colada, and cookies.

Max passed the band and followed the balcony to the open double doors. The moans of pleasure blended into a disarming drone that beckoned like sexual slot machines. He stood at the steps to the recessed flesh pit.

Fuck me! There must be three hundred people in there.

The room was huge. Red and black sashes hung from four massive marble pillars. A few people were hanging in fishnets from the mirrored ceiling. Others were tied up and dangling Japanese-style. There were chairs, couches, sex-swings, fuck-benches, even a rack, all draped with glistening flesh. Some were mostly buried; others bobbed along the surface. The tangle of limbs was difficult to make out at first, but there were more women than men and a lot more young attractive people than there were oldies.

Max was drunk enough to want to do a cannonball, but sober enough to know it was a bad idea. He stripped off his clothes and allowed a valet to take them into the adjacent room to keep them clean.

A baby oil shower? Hm, might as well.

He stepped under the showerhead and pulled the cord. Warm oil drizzled out, anointed him, turned him to water. Every nerve hummed a pleasant tune. Every hair danced along in slow, supple rhythm.

All right, time to get me some VD.

He stepped into the mass feeling sillier and more free than ever before. The flesh opened up to him, drew him in. For a second he felt like he was being sucked into the mouth of a giant stink-monster. Then came the tongues. A slavering rip-tide pulled him deeper. The undulation of so many oiled bodies made it hard to stay in one place for very long. He could be sucking on a breast and suddenly have a hairy butt in his face, but before he could say 'yuck' it would be replaced by a vagina. It took him a minute to get used to, but the Nectar was helping him go with the flow.

Once he settled in it was all quite lovely. He was a worm floating at the bottom of a bottle of sex. His whole body was super-sensitive, on the verge of discovering a new kind of orgasm, when he heard a muffled voice say his name.

"Huh."

Something shifted beneath him and he was pushed up to the surface. When he didn't hear it again he assumed it was nothing. April popped up next to him, her head rolling in ecstasy.

"April?"

She saw him and flopped towards his cock. "Mammmm."

Her tits were as fake as the Count's accent, but her tongue was the real deal. He was being sucked back down, and April was following when he heard his voice again, clearer this time and with an edge of anger. He looked towards the sound and saw Cat, dripping just as he had pictured, but considerably less happy.

"Asshole!" she pulled him up and slapped him so hard he spun around.

"Oww! What the fuck?"

April was sucking on some other cock now, probably too drunk to know the difference.

Cat tried to twist his nipple, but it was too lubricated, so she slapped him again then ran out of the room like a Jesus Lizard.

Max had no idea what he had done wrong, but he went after her, half-swimming, half-rolling across the surface. It took him a couple of minutes, but he made it. His erect cock twitching like a divining rod, he ran down the stairs, slipped, and slid all the way to the elevator on his stomach. A few people paused their conversations to giggle in his direction, but most everyone seemed unimpressed.

He stood and addressed the Champagne girl. "Hey, did you see a naked girl run through here?"

She looked at him like that was the dumbest question she'd ever heard. Three naked girls ran by as if to illustrate her point.

"Cat Greystoke, specifically."

The girl cracked a little smile and nodded towards the lagoon.

"Thanks." He ran into the next room, slipped and slid into the pool. A few people clapped. "Goddamn stupid oil."

He splashed around a little, hoping to get the oil off, then climbed out and ran to the bar. After a quick scan, he saw Cat speaking vehemently to her father in the back-left corner. Her hair was so full of goo it stood out from her neck like a rubber wig. Max jogged over to them in time to hear Cat say she wanted to go home. The Count glowered at him.

"What did I do? I don't understand."

Cat slapped him again, then stalked towards the elevator. The Count stared him down from head to toe. "What did I say about behaving yourself?"

"I did. I think I did. I mean, she was in the orgy room first."

"You thought it would be a good idea to join her?

"I was just trying to fit in. Anyway, she has no right to be mad. From what I hear everybody in the city has had a go with her."

Greystoke looked as though he might hit Max with his walking stick, but he took a breath and calmed himself. "I am aware my daughter's spirit is somewhat more liberated than most, but I would appreciate it if you would show her a modicum of respect."

"Sorry."

"In your experience, have you found Felicity to be a great fan of logic?"

"No."

"Reason?"

"No."

"Fairness?"

"Only when it benefits her."

"So, once again, you thought it would be a good idea to wade into a pile of naked strangers, why?"

Max knew anything he said would only get him into more trouble, so he silently watched his erection deflate.

✳✳✳✳✳

When Max and the others got back to the limo they found Cat curled on the floor naked and sobbing. It was the same horrendous howl from the pizza place, but louder, more annoying. It invoked the same piercing discomfort as a fire alarm.

Hedorah covered his ears and turned away. "No way I'm getting in there with that."

Emma used Cat's discarded dress to muffle the noise.

Everybody was staring at Max like he'd microwaved a kitten.

"Make it stop." The Count shoved Max inside and slammed the door.

The stench of drying semen made his sinuses feel pregnant. Cat's face looked like a busted pen. She wailed louder and rolled over so she wouldn't have to look at him. The Rorschach her makeup left on the carpet looked like a gingerbread man with broken wings.

Max plugged his ears and climbed onto the seat. Part of him wanted to apologize and cry along with her. The other part wanted to slam her head in the door over and over until she was quiet.

He knew he would have to figure out what he'd done before he'd know how to apologize, and that meant thinking like her.

Okay, I'm a socialite from a quirky, erotic graphic novel. I've been going to orgies since I was eight. I think like a kid. Gee, I wonder if there's a connection there. Anyway, a mysophiliac, sociopath with dissociative disorder walks into an orgy. What's the punch-line?

The volume kept going up. Her throat was choked with ugly little veins that looked about to burst.

Damn it, I can't think with all this fucking noise. How can I make her happy? Maybe if I pee on her. Wait, she has no attention span. That might actually work.

He crab-walked over to her, unzipped and peed on her cheek. She looked at him with big soggy eyes as rivulets ran over her lips and up her nose. She seemed to ask, 'You really mean it?'

Max smiled, amazed he'd done the right thing. She lurched forward and gave him a hug with her mouth. He was hard on his back before he knew what was happening. She smiled and worked her tongue. She grabbed his ass and pushed her face so close her lower lip hurt his balls. It was like she was trying to give him lung. He came, twitching like her mouth was a light socket, but she kept going.

He grabbed her under her arms and dragged her up onto his chest. "I came. You can stop now."

She looked disappointed for a second then hopeful. "Better?"

Max let out a little laugh. "Yeah." She would often ask him that after sex. She was convinced that men existed in a perpetual state of sexual frustration and sperm was just pee you had to work to get out. Her weird innocence made him think of the old shake and bake commercials: 'It's an orgasm and I helped.'

"Really?" Her level of excitement let him know she had meant something different.

"Uh, yeah. A lot better."

She squealed, wrapped her arms around him and squeezed so hard he couldn't breathe. He didn't mind, though. It kept him from choking on her stench. He was dying to know what she'd meant, but knew better than to let on.

"Good. I was worried."

"Why?"

"She's a pro. She blows people to get her job. She blows people for information. I was afraid she'd have a better technique."

Oh!

He laughed and hugged her head. "You never have to worry about that. Nobody is better at any kind of sex than you."

"You really think so?"

"Oh, hell yeah." He almost added a comment about how she should be a porn star to show the world how good she was, but he remembered she had already given every guy in town their own private and/or public show. It was gross, but turning gross into sexy was one of her super powers.

They cuddled until Hedorah opened the door and stuck his head in. He gagged. "Oh God."

"Just a sec." Max waved him away.

While he pulled on his pants, Hedorah complained. "Can we get another limo? This one smells like a porn theater, shame, and popcorn.

The Count shook his head. I have been made a mockery of enough for one night. I will not have it known that my daughter is such..." he took a deep calming breath, "such an aberration she ruined a limousine. It will be tolerable once we roll down the windows."

He jerked the wadded dress out of Emma's hands and threw it at Cat. "It would be most helpful if you would put this on."

She complied, and everyone climbed in. Hedorah started to roll down the windows, but Greystoke stopped him. "We are not leaving prom. Hold your breath until we are out of the gate."

Max would have thought seeing Greystoke this upset would be funny. It wasn't.

Should I say something? If so, what? Sorry your daughter's a psychotic cum dumpster? I think I'll keep my mouth shut.

Hedorah, Emma and the Count glared at them from the opposite end. Once they passed the gate and the windows were rolled down, everyone looked slightly less annoyed. Emma moved to the center seat to Max's right and motioned for him to join her.

She whispered something, but it was impossible to hear over the wind. He made the universal sign for 'I can't hear you,' and she repeated it in a normal voice. "Did you recognize Heller?"

Max shrugged. "He looked kind of familiar."

She pulled out her phone and flipped through the pictures. She showed him a picture of Heller sitting at a big conference table with Jacob and a bunch of high-ranking M.I.L.F.s. It finally clicked. Heller was the mystery man.

"Oh, well that makes sense."

"Is that all? I sort of expected more, I don't know, horror?"

"Why? We already knew Heller had ties to the M.I.L.F."

"This is more than ties. Even the M.I.L.F. thought this guy was scary. He hardly ever spoke. When he did, nobody spoke back. They just did whatever he said. I think he was the Mittons' proxy."

"That's not good." Max handed the phone back and stared at the stain on the carpet.

He'd learned from "Yes, Mister President" reruns that elections didn't cause change because it was the advisors and administrators who really ran everything. What hope did he have of changing the world while working under the same assholes who quietly manipulated the last guys? If a puppet is self-aware, can it influence its master?

Emma slipped her phone back into her handbag. "So what's the plan?

"Same show, bigger arena."

# THE SPIRITUAL LIVES OF POTATO MEN

Max was lost in the planes, but that was okay. It was the good sort of lost. Someone was looking for him. He wanted to run, to be crushed to that buxom bosom by the manly arms of gravity, but the battery was dead on his internal GPS.

The hot mozzarella burned his feet as he plodded nakedly toward the enormous potatoes that sat in silhouette before straining clouds, which glowed in the light of a waning eclipse. The clouds spread their legs to every horizon, raining purple freezer bags like Mardi Gras beads as he plodded toward the field. The lighter ones fluttered beautifully as their meatier counterparts sped past to explode, splashing slick, salty liquid, like bloody baby oil in his face and mouth.

Every drip sang a challenge to Max's aridity.

The cheese was thinning around the spuds. With every step the earth sank deeper, splashing his feet with puddles of hot grease, as the ground bore teeth to chew his heels and toes. If only he'd thought to wear shoes, or clothes. A nice thick soul would have made it harder for the wisdoms to take root.

He was standing on the hymen of reality. Safe for now, but if he stopped moving or stomped hard enough, he might tumble into God, or out of a womb, possibly both.

A million bulging chatoyant eyes ogled his nakedness.

The potatoes bulged with wisdom, so he asked, "Where have all the cowboys gone?"

Max's right nipple responded. "Ask not what your cowboys can do for you, but how much pink paste is in the burger."

"Why speaketh so unnaturally, nipple man?"

His left nipple spoke with a forked tongue. "Nor that, but rather how many beans a burrito might hold when wrapped in the hand of the Buddha."

"Have you always been this emblematic?"

"Yes," they responded. His nipples' tongues coiled together like copulating snakes.

Max, excluded, brought pastry cakes, which tilled the earth and turned the tubers turning. Cleft-palate, vag-faced monsters blossomed with scaly purple leaves as the passage shivered. Max had their full attention.

The eyes puffed up with observations and exploded, showering him with glittery black dust.

He didn't so much hear as feel their message as he pulled a lip aside and entered the closest one.

"Sorry I'm late. You wouldn't believe the sort of day I've had."

✳✳✳✳✳

Max jolted awake. His mouth was full of hair and the bed was growling at him. There was a small wet spot where he had chewed a hole in its fur. Cat was curled at the bottom of the pouch. She'd fallen asleep sucking his toes again. He was surprised he hadn't kicked her in the head.

He spat the fur over the edge and climbed down, careful not to wake her. Despite his enthusiastic erection, sex was the last thing he wanted. The image of his nipples making out flashed in his mind. It was much more disturbing than it had been in the dream. He was afraid to look down, but he did. His nipples were hard and silent.

Thank god.

The bed continued to growl. Cheeky was lying between the feline's ears in a Baileys coma, but the vibration was making him twitch. If it didn't stop growling Cheeky might roll off and kill Cat in a drunken rage.

"Shhh!"

He mouthed that he was sorry and stroked its ear.

Hopefully the hair would grow back. It had to suck to be genetically engineered into furniture. Bio-Corp said they were designed to be happy this way, but he knew better than most how little they cared about an animal's happiness. He told himself they were better off than veal and tried to make his Bio-Bed as comfortable as it made him, but every so often his disbelief would come crashing down, reminding him he was doing something terrible.

You poor, comfortable bastard, I wish I could quit you. Then again, if people stopped sleeping on you, you would all die.

It was five fifty-six a.m. He had only been asleep for three hours, but there was no chance he was getting back to sleep without a hard reset. Even if he could, he didn't want to risk slipping back into the dream still lingering in the habitrails of his consciousness. He pushed the squishy tragedy out of his mind and pulled on his pants.

I think I'll go for a walk. That's supposed to clear your head, right?

He headed for the door and noticed a pair of tiny glowing eyes staring around the corner. Puff's contempt for her morbidly obese cousin was as cute as it was morally reprehensible. She was kneading the floor about to pounce like a fuzzy-wuzzy little bully.

Max moved between her and her target, but she pounced anyway. Max caught her by the tail and dragged her flapping into the hall. He wrestled her onto his shoulder and held her there until she calmed down.

"That's a good Puff. Let's go kill something somewhere else." He shut the door quietly and headed towards the garden.

Cheeky had picked the perfect name for her. Her feathers were as soft as her fur, and despite her lean appearance she was covered in a thick layer of squishy fat. Her skeleton must have been more bird than cat. "You're so weird—and awesome. Don't tell Cheeky I said that. He might eat you." He scratched around her tiny horn.

She nuzzled his cheek. Her horn caught his earlobe and went straight through.

"Ahh, pointy." He kept his cries to a whisper and tried to pull her away. She dug in with her claws. "Fuck! Stop being so goddamn pointy."

He wrapped his fingers around the back of her neck and rubbed her gently to calm her and eventually managed to get all her barbs out of his flesh. He held her head so her horn was pointed away and ambled toward the garden.

This time of night the majority of the castle was dark, but every twenty feet or so the motion sensors would kick on another section of lights. Max knew he was the cause and the lights were the effect, but he felt like something was leading him. The Boccaccio's stared with pitying eyes, like they knew something he didn't.

Another segment flickered on, and Max's stomach jumped into his throat. Where this hall T-boned the next, Ernie sat on a low display case full of malformed fetuses.

Puff dug her claws into his shoulder and hissed.

"What the fuck, man?"

Ernie hopped down and walked out of sight.

Max had the creeping suspicion he wouldn't be getting back to bed any time soon. He sighed and told Puff. "I wouldn't know what to do with more than three hours of sleep, anyway." He quickened his pace and followed Ernie towards the main entrance.

Max called to him and redoubled his pace, but Ernie was walking with a slasher's gait. The motion lights didn't come on for Ernie, so every twenty feet he would fade into darkness then reappear when Max came into range.

The next light came on in time for Max to see Ernie's cape flutter around a corner. Max let Puff fly away and chased after him, but when he rounded the corner there was no one there. The light from the

Count's study reflected off the mirrors in the hall, providing a clear view of Ernie's absence.

Max was sure Ernie had gone this way, but he checked the other halls to be sure.

"Ernie? Where the fuck did you go?"

No one answered, so he continued to walk toward the light. It's got to be him in there. Greystoke wouldn't get out of bed before noon if his bedroom was on fire.

Max entered the study and found the Count passed out on his desk. He had a third of a bottle of Oban open by his right hand and he was drooling into a large book with yellowed pages. Max walked around behind him, careful not to make a sound.

The book was written in a language he didn't recognize, a cross between Cyrillic and Futhark. The left page was a picture, but the Count's head was over most of it. Max pulled out his phone and took a picture of his bombed benefactor.

You never know when you might need to blackmail someone.

His phone buzzed letting him know the battery was low. The Count jerked his head up and looked around in a panic. Max considered ducking behind something, but decided that would be silly.

"Boo!"

The Count spun around, knocking his bottle into the waste basket beside the desk. "Max? What are you doing here?"

"Watching you drool."

He angrily wiped the spittle from his cheek. "Might I ask why?!"

"It's a long story."

"Indulge me." He took three tissues from the box to his left and blotted the pages dry.

"I had a creepy dream about giant harelipped potatoes. I didn't think I could get back to sleep, so I took a walk, saw Ernie, followed him. He disappeared. I saw the light was on. I came in. You woke up. Here we are. Riveting, isn't it?"

"Who is this Ernie, and why is he in my home at this ungodly hour?"

Max wasn't sure how to answer that. "Uh, he's this magic guy who's helped me out a few times?"

"A magician?"

"No, more like, I don't know, an alien, a god. Something like that. I'm fairly sure he's not human."

"Explain."

"He's the one who zapped us back to this dimension when we were stuck in Witches 'R' Us. He knows the future, flies, you know, stuff people generally can't do. Oh, and his head's sort of a TV, the old, fat kind you see in museums."

"And why are you just now telling me about him?"

Max shrugged. "Didn't seem important."

"How could that possibly not seem important?"

"Well, let's see, I met him just after fighting my way through an evil enchanted forest, and just before being labeled the messiah. At the time, I was sort of in shock from seeing my girlfriend turned into a giant chicken with chainsaw-arms. She was ordered to kill me, but instead she killed the magic meat machine the super-mutant overlord was trying to take over the world with, and got sucked into some kind of vortex. On my scale of weird, Ernie's like a three."

"Only you could make divine intervention seem mundane. Very well, this Ernie seems to have led you here for a reason." He took a deep breath and exhaled slowly. "Tell me about your dream."

"I was naked and it was raining freezer bags of bloody lube. My nipples were talking. I don't remember about what. All around me there were these giant potatoes with lots of eyes on them, which exploded. The potatoes sprouted purple leaves and turned around, and they had these big doorway-mouth things. I knew they had brought me there to tell me something, so I stepped inside. After that I woke up."

"Well, that is different." He thought for a moment then flipped a few pages back in his book. "These potatoes of yours remind me of a conduit order I was just reading about. They call themselves simply, The Holy. Upon acceptance to the order, they have their arms, legs and sex removed. They are blinded and deafened, then set on a purple pillow where they spend the rest of their life spouting prophecies."

"Freaky. How do they survive?"

"Acolytes feed them, bathe them, empty their colostomy bags, take notation, etcetera. When one of The Holy dies, the most faithful acolyte is chosen to replace him."

"Who wouldn't want that?"

The Count cocked his head. "It isn't as insane as it sounds. They don't need eyes because they are masters of remote viewing. They don't need ears because they can read your mind. Whereas most conduits serve as a link between two specific things, one plane and another, or nature and man, The Holy are able to tune in to any frequency like psychic walkie-talkies. It's a highly venerated position. If they are looking for you, it must be something big. I imagine Ernie knew you wouldn't find them on your own, so he brought you to me."

"What would they want from me?"

"I honestly have no idea, but it is a stroke of luck. I have been looking into the, shall we say, outbursts, which had become so fashionable of late and came to the conclusion your pigeonmaster theory may have some weight to it, after all. I need a conduit to find out more. I *had* hoped to find someone less unpleasant to deal with."

Max laughed. "I'd be unpleasant too if somebody whittled me into a potato."

The Count nodded. "Indeed."

"I'm guessing we have to leave right now, or something terrible will happen?"

The Count pushed his chair back and stood. "I certainly hope not. I'm going to bed."

"So, I can get some sleep?"

"Of course. The Holy aren't going anywhere."

"In my experience, when a higher power wants your attention, they tend to want it right then."

"If it's so urgent, why didn't Ernie simply appear to you in your dream and tell you where to go?"

"I guess you have a point."

The Count sat in his chair by the fireplace and pushed the button that raised him out of the room.

"Whatever." Max shrugged off the foreboding hollowness in the pit of his stomach and toddled back to bed.

# CREPES AND CIRCUS

At one o'clock the next day, a breakfast of fresh fruit and Nutella crepes was served in the main dining hall. The coffee was strong and thick with sweetened condensed milk. Cat had her usual: bacon-wrapped bacon muffins drizzled with a sauce of brown sugar and caramelized bacon.

Cheeky sat on the table between her and Max, trying to lick out his crepe, but getting more on his face than in his mouth. The chef had rolled his crepe into a little chocolate burrito to make it easier to eat, but Cheeky had immediately unrolled it and smashed his face into the center like a drunken thirty-year-old at his second birthday party of the night.

Max stared at his crepe. Sitting there, eating, taking his situation for granted felt wrong. Outside, reality was going bad. It had only been a day since his run-in with the rabid zombies, but every hour had brought with it a new lever of horror. Max swallowed a wad of sweet brown goo more out of politeness than hunger.

He'd dreamt of those giant needy potatoes all night long. How was he supposed to have an appetite, knowing somewhere out there a group of masochistic religious zealots was counting the colostomy bags until he arrived?

He burped up a little splash of chocolaty stomach acid, then washed it back down with orange juice. "I really don't see what good a press conference is going to do."

The Count dabbed his mouth with a napkin. "In times such as these, what people need most is reassurance."

Max traced the purple paisley on the silk table cloth with the tip of his finger. "But what am I supposed to say? I don't know what's going on. It could be anything from a boatload of PCP sinking into the water supply, to solar flares, to aliens."

"The masses abhor specifics. They only want to know that someone is handling it."

"But nobody is handling it."

"An insignificant detail, which you would do well not to mention. Show no weakness or doubt. Simply ride the crest of your heroism, and the people will love you."

"Who cares if they love me? Last night someone glued fifty-something people together in a giant clump and then used a chainsaw to carve them into a squirrel. Then, the squirrel came to life and took over the park. We've got to fucking prioritize..."

The Count cut him off. "Calming the masses will make this situation easier to deal with. Do you *want* to wade through rioters on your way to The Holy?" The Count took a hasty sip of coffee. "No? Then give the people what they need, the feeling that someone is taking care of them, surrogate parents with enough money and power to protect them from the big scary world."

"Cynical much?"

Greystoke furrowed his brow. "If the masses were up to the task of knowing things and taking responsibility for their lives we would all be living in a democratic utopia." He set his fork on his plate and dabbed his lips with a napkin. "Responsibility is terrifying to most people. History teaches us that regardless of what is going on, all the masses really want is a flag to wave. Speaking of which, I have a little surprise for you."

He produced a little black box and slid it across the table to Max.

"Is this a proposal?"

Greystoke's leer was reptilian. "Of sorts, open it."

Inside the fuzzy little box was a pin with two right arms, one Iiite one human, interlocking at the elbow on a dull black disc.

"What's this?"

Cheeky slid over for a peek then went back to his plate.

"This is your flag: a bold, yet simple symbol of your intent the masses can rally behind. Iiites and humans lock arms in shiny solidarity against the scary Darkness surrounding them. You will implore your viewers to wear them to show their support. You will say that the ten-dollar donation will be used to safeguard the world and bring about a new era of peace and understanding. Your cut is thirty percent."

"Why only thirty percent?"

The Count had never looked more delighted. "You are making progress. As a reward, I'll give you forty."

Max's cheeks burned. Was he already that jaded? Still, he knew he didn't have a choice. If he was going to be hocking pot-metal, he might as well get his extra ten percent. Money equals power, and he had a long way to go before he would be as powerful as his enemies.

Cat snatched the box and scrutinized its contents. "It's not cute."

Greystoke rolled his eyes. "Not everything can be cute."

"Why not?"

"Sometimes we have to take things seriously."

"Why?"

Greystoke shook his head. "Please stop asking stupid questions."

Max smiled and scratched her behind the ear. "She has a point. How much better would the world be if nobody ever took anything seriously? There'd be no stress, no war, no hate, no poor self-esteem..."

Greystoke added, "No food, order, safety, human life."

"I'm pretty sure food existed before the concept of seriousness."

"Food existed before conception in general; however, were it not for the concept of necessity, man would not have lived long enough to invent humor."

"Also a good point."

Cat slammed the box on the table, knocking her fork onto the floor. "Cuteness should have a flag, too. Make me one."

"And what would you like it to be? A happy strip of bacon, perhaps? Should it have googly eyes? Perhaps we should make it smell of cupcakes?"

"Yes, yes and no. It should taste like cupcakes and smell like cinnamon rolls. And they should play mp4s. And the face should look like a cat. No, a kitten! Why aren't you taking notes?"

"I believe I can remember that."

"You better." Cat nibbled the bottom corner of her muffin.

At the far end of the room, the door opened, and the butler announced, "The mongrel is here to see you, sir."

Max shook his head and whispered, "Why do you keep fucking with him? You're just making things worse."

Hawk walked in and punched the butler in the gut. "That'll be all, Bigby."

Bigby backed out of the room clutching his stomach.

Hawk strode towards them, his face aglow with smoldering hatred.

"General Hawk, so good of you to join us. Would you care for a crepe?"

Hawk nodded hello to Max then slammed his hands on the table in front of Greystoke.

Cheeky jumped and landed in a battle stance.

"Cut the shtick, Swami. Why'd your goons drag me all the way over here when I should be lockin' down security?"

"Calm down, man. There's something we need to talk about."

Greystoke smiled and gestured toward the chair opposite Max.

Hawk begrudgingly took his seat.

Cheeky relaxed and crawled into Max's lap.

"So, why am I here?"

"Muffins!" Cat tossed four muffins in the air.

The Count leered sadistically at Hawk. "As you are aware, you no longer have enough men to walk Max down the red carpet, let alone provide security for the largest Media© Circus in history."

"Oh, fuck you. I can keep an area that size secure with six cats and a bullwhip."

"Really? Would you bet Max's life on it?"

Hawk's teeth crunched.

Greystoke looked like he was going to say something mean, but held himself back. "Max is an official A-lister now. He may well be the most famous person in the world. Unfortunately, there are a great many drawbacks to being so successful. For instance, were he to go into a crowd, his fans would likely tear him limb from limb and sell his scraps on the internet. He must avoid all contact with mundies. You never know who might be a crazy stalker that wants to hollow him out and sleep in his rib cage."

Cat smiled and picked up her knife. "Mmm, inside hugs."

Cheeky hissed.

Max set his fork down. "Wait, are you saying I can't watch the opening bands?"

"Yes, I am, but if you like I can have them put on a private show for you some time. You no longer have to view concerts while gasping for air, trying not to be crushed between a sweaty hippy and an irritable meathead, constantly keeping an eye out for crowd surfers and flying shoes."

"But that's what makes it fun."

The Count raised an eyebrow and turned back to Hawk. "In any case, Hawk, Max will need more security than ever before. To that end and at great expense, I have hired I-Force to provide security tonight."

"Great. Why didn't you just say that? Their training and equipment'll make tonight a fuckin' cakewalk."

"Indeed, they have everything well in hand, meaning your talents may be more useful elsewhere."

"What the fuck do you mean by that?"

"Don't be thick. I am saying they don't need you."

"You're tryin' ta fire me? Max, this dumbfuck's tryin' ta fire me." Hawk stood, picked up his chair and walked toward the Count.

Cat took off her shirt.

"Dude, chill. Nobody's firing you. Put the fucking chair down."

Hawk hurled the chair against the wall, smashing it to bits and deeply gouging a section of wood paneling.

Greystoke snarled. "That chair was a valuable antique even before it belonged to Vincent Price."

"I told you to stop rattling his cage."

Greystoke was too angry to respond.

"All he's trying to say is that we think it would be a good idea if you stayed close to me. I don't have the Nrrds to watch my back anymore. They've all beaten their swords into circuit-boards and forgotten I exist. I-Force's good, but they're just hired guns. You're my friend, and you've worked just as hard as I have, but got none of the credit. I think it's time we changed that. Let's be famous together. What do you think?"

"I think this idea's up past its bedtime. I'll stick to what I know."

The Count chimed in. "That is not an option. I-Force does not work with outsiders."

"I did a stint in I-Force. I know their procedures."

"All the same, they will not work with you."

Cat threw her knife on her plate and stood. "I'm bored." When her outburst garnered nothing more than a fleeting glance, she stormed out of the room.

Hawk came in close and whispered to Max. "This smells fishier than his mother's twat."

"This was my idea."

Hawk whispered, "You know I'm a better strategist than I am a soldier."

"Every press conference I've had has ended in some kind of crazy massacre. I'm hoping the fourth time's a charm, but if it's not and I-Force drops the ball, I want you by my side instead of in some control room somewhere."

"But—," Hawk cleared his throat. "Cameras make me nervous."

"Dude, after all the shit we've been through, are you really trying to tell me you're afraid of having your photo taken?"

"I ain't the best at making impressions."

"Don't be nervous. Everybody's there to see me. Tell you what, I'll introduce Cheeky first."

Cheeky perked up and cooed.

"K Corp bought exclusive rights to Cheekworms, but they aren't selling well, so they're paying us a bundle to do something I was going to do anyway. Plus, they're providing the venue for free. Did you know they actually demolished a Super K to make room for this? Apparently, they considered a store a small price to pay for the massive publicity, or as they said, the honor of helping the messiah."

Hawk rolled his eyes. "Did you know I helped pick the location? Of course not. We never talk anymore. You know how hard it was to find a location that big with all the quarantined areas?"

"I saw the map. It's bad out there, which is why I keep telling him," he jerked his thumb towards the Count, "we need to forget about the pageantry and focus on fixing the problem."

Hawk sneered. "Well, it's good to know you haven't *completely* forgotten about the end of the world. You sure about this, though? The Cunt's not gonna dump a bucket of pig blood on me or anything?"

Greystoke smiled.

"You two have got to work your shit out."

"Fat chance of that."

"So you're okay with this?"

"Hell no, I'm not okay with this. But I'll do it if it's what you want."

Greystoke clapped twice. "Excellent. Bigby, mimosas all around!"

✳✳✳✳✳

At six-thirty, Max and Hawk peered through a gap in the big, red stage curtains. It was already dark, so giant floodlights had been set up to illuminate the three Ferris wheels, two dunking booths, two roller coasters, a free-fall, teacups, bumper cars, and an army of food trucks. That was only what was visible through the gap. It was an impressive display, but he could have done without all the ads.

No wonder Hawk thinks I've sold out. I can't scratch my ass without knocking over three K co. flags.

The opening bands had been a huge success. He'd worried that the Iiite band Constant Condescension's flamenco-surf-black metal opera might have been too much too soon, but normals were taking to non-commercial music like dieting fatties to S-mart low-calorie desserts. Greasy Little Fingers was one of the first and best non-com surface bands to gain mainstream recognition, and not just because the singer was Greystoke's nephew. They showed real talent, playing raw, balls-out rock and roll with enough speed and swagger that Max could forgive their vapid lyrics. At least they weren't about toothpaste. The shows would have been much more enjoyable if he hadn't had to watch them on the TV in his trailer while professionals accentuated his features in ways that made him seem strong yet approachable.

The only hiccup was that Hawk would rather be shot with a gun than a camera.

Hawk used the curtain to dab the sweat from his face then let it go and stared at the peach smear he'd left behind. He turned to Max with an embarrassed smile. "Hot as a bitch's titties out there."

"Yeah." Max glanced down at the jersey and shorts they'd been told to wear. He hated having to dress like a politician, but at least it breathed well.

Hawk looked slightly less ridiculous, but more uncomfortable despite his vastly more positive view of sports.

"Can you believe that crowd? There must be thousands of them."

Hawk frowned. "If I didn't know you so well, I'd swear you were looking forward to this."

"I wouldn't go that far, but it is kind of gratifying."

"Is that why we're here? We're in show-business now? We get all gussied up in idiot drag and dance around like retards so we can sell pins to morons?"

Max nodded sadly. "Pretty much."

Hawk looked like he was about to slap him.

"I'm kidding. Don't worry. I'm not losing my edge. It's just, you know, revolution is the easy part. Killing the enemy can only take you so far. At some point you have to rebuild, and that takes money and support. Unfortunately, *this* is how you get those things."

"Sounds like Greystoke crawled up in your skull and took a big ol' shit." Hawk pointed at the crowd. "There's your support. They got money too. You don't have to lick Greystoke's ass anymore."

"I'm still not to a point that I can afford pissing him off."

"Fuck that wand-jocky. You're already famous. You can't just un-famous somebody. That's a load of codswallop."

"I don't know, man. Greystoke's a douche, but he's good at what he does, and I definitely see how he could un-famous me if he wanted to, or worse."

"You act like you know a bunch of shit I don't."

"I do."

"And why is that? You used to tell me everything." He ran his palm over his fresh crew cut. "See, this is what really gets me. I could put up with the Count if he was just a douche bag we had to deal with to get our plans done, but he's turnin' ya into him."

"No. I just…"

"Do you not see this?" He pointed at Max's outfit. "You're wearin' a goddamn softball jersey, and you're doin' it to manipulate the folks. You think you're in cahoots, but you're just a prized pet. You think you're gonna sell your gilded cage one day and buy freedom with proceeds. That ain't how it fuckin' works."

"Dude, keep it down. People are staring."

"Fuck that shit. You're in his house. Cut his throat while he sleeps, and be done with it!"

Now everyone was staring at them.

"Shh." He smiled for the gawkers and slapped Hawk on the shoulder. "Yeah, I should totally do that for making me wear this." When the crowd lost interest, he came in close and whispered angrily, "Look, Greystoke is a fucking lackey. Killing him won't do shit, but playing along gets us access to the boss monster. Not to mention, the world's going platypus shit, and Greystoke's the only one who knows how to deal with it."

"Well, pardon me. I forgot you were the president of his fan club."

Max gritted his teeth. "I know what all this looks like. It sucks plenty without your bitching about every little thing. You were less of an annoying little piss-pants back when people were shooting at us. Not too long ago we were literally swimming in shit. I know this isn't your wheelhouse, but fucking cowboy-up and deal with it."

Hawk blinked back tears.

Oh, for fuck sake. Here he goes again.

Max knew his words were harsh. Part of him felt bad, but the other part, the part that was about to go out there and wow the masses, was sick of his constant belly-aching. Hawk hadn't done anything useful since they'd taken down the Fist. Max was beginning to wonder if Hawk could ever be happy in a peaceful world. Maybe he didn't have the capacity to evolve.

He let his words resonate.

Hawk's lips quivered as black tears streamed down his cheeks.

"You should see yourself. You look like Rusty after the first time he saw A.I."

The more weakness Hawk displayed the more cruelty well up inside Max. He felt terrible, but he couldn't stop himself from saying, "You know, when Cat stayed home to pout, I assumed I could go five minutes without a bitch making everything about her."

Hawk narrowed his eyes. "You haven't lost your edge, just your soul." He turned and stalked off toward his trailer.

Max smiled. He was making progress. At some point, Hawk had thought he had a soul.

An intern with black-rimmed glasses and a matching ponytail sped by. "Five minutes to curtain." She never looked up from her ePad.

She has the best of both worlds. Work with the stars, but live with the masses. I wonder if she'd switch with me?

✶✶✶✶✶

Max found Cheeky in his trailer. "Really? Cheeky needs makeup too?"

The stylist looked at Max like he'd just vomited on his shoes, but went on blushing the last of the cheeks. Max put his hand on the arm of Cheeky's chair and let him climb onto his shoulders.

"Hawk needs a touch up."

The stylist let out a little growl and rushed out, grumbling about amateurs.

Max stroked Cheeky's nose with his fingertip. "Aren't you a little soldier. I'd have never thought you'd put up with all that tickling. Are you excited to be on TV?"

Cheeky grinned. He had that look he got sometimes when he got so excited he peed, so Max pulled him off his shoulders and set him back in his chair. "We only have three minutes. You should probably have a tinkle."

Cheeky shot off to the bathroom, but came back so fast Max wasn't sure he'd actually peed. "Did you go?"

Cheeky nodded.

"Are you sure?"

His little friend narrowed his eyes and pursed his lips.

"Okay, no need to be sarcastic." He let Cheeky climb back onto his shoulders and rushed out the door. His intro music was pumping away. Marco from Greasy Little Fingers gave him a high five.

Being famous is pretty fucking cool.

The ePad girl grabbed his arm and dragged him the rest of the way. "Where the fuck have you been? Five minutes to curtain does not mean wander off." Ignoring Cheeky's hiss, she shoved him onto his cue and ran to the wings.

The curtain came up. The crowd was screaming. He was whooping and running around like an idiot. He felt like a kid again, a big rock 'n' roll kid getting flashed by groupies in the front row. He'd spent most of his life trying to be the opposite of this. He'd perfected stoicism to the point he didn't remember what it was like to feel excited. Now he wondered if he'd made a mistake.

"Hello, hello, hello. What is be happen, yo?!"

The crowd screamed even louder.

God, I hope they know I meant that ironically.

"Everybody feelin' good?"

The crowd went, "Woooo," and three more girls flashed him.

"All righty then, let me give a quick shout out to my boys Constant Condescension," he paused to let them cheer, then added, "and Greasy Little Fingers." He paused again. "And let us all give thanks to the K for throwing this shindig."

Judging by their response, the crowd liked the K best of all.

He reached back and scratched Cheeky behind the ears. "I'd like to introduce you all to my little friend here. His name is Cheeky. Say hi to Cheeky, everybody!"

The crowd said, "Hi, Cheeky."

Cheeky went up on the Jumbotron waving with all his nubs.

"He's my best buddy, and I never could have saved the world without him. He's been fighting by my side since the start, and it's high time he got some recognition."

He let the crowd roar for nearly a minute then waved for them to stop. "Okay, everybody shut up. Sorry, Cheeky. It's time to get morose up in this bitch. Just kiddin'. We all know shit's got weird lately. There's violence, monsters, hungry-ass zombies and this heat. Goddamn, don't get me started on the heat. Luckily though, violence and monsters are my specialty. I came here today to let you know this shit's bein' handled."

He paused to let the crowd scream some more.

"I'm gonna get it all straightened out, but I can't do it alone. I need your help. I need each and every one of you to work with me on this." As he spoke, the telescopic poles began to sprout all around the stage and in strategic points around the crowd. "Pledge to me that you will not go crazy and/or kill anybody, but rather join arms with your fellow man and march towards a brighter future, a future of love, peace, and partyin'."

Marco ran out on stage with his guitar, shredding on Vivaldi, while the flags bearing his symbol unfurled. The girls came out in their sparkly black bikinis, and Max danced his few choreographed steps as banners dropped on either side of the stage. Fireworks shot out above the crowd in a magnificent display, which ended with his symbol emblazoned on the sky in fire.

Max stopped dancing. "This is the flag we rally behind. This is the symbol of our future. Iiites and normals united against all odds, against all threats, working together to make a better future for us all!"

He put one of the pins on his shirt then pulled wads of them out of his pockets and hurled them into the crowd. People dropped to their knees, fighting over the free swag. Competition was fevered. Punches were thrown. It looked as though a riot might break out.

"I think some of you have missed the point. We have tons of those at the merch table for just $9.99, and proceeds go to saving the world. Buy as many as you want. Give them to your friends, your family, your pets, whatever, but don't forget what they stand for."

The crowd calmed.

"That's better."

Someone screamed. A hole opened up around a woman who was straddling a guy and stabbing him in the face with a broken cotton candy dowel. Several pins lay around her knees, but nobody wanted to get close. She pulled the back off one of the pins and slammed it into his forehead. It stuck there like a wet beer cap.

She stabbed him in the face a few more times before an I-Force officer could get to her. She stabbed him in the eye, then went berserk running back and forth stabbing random people with her eye-on-a-stick. Panic broke out. Touchy-feely became grabby-stabby. Max's fans were trampling one another trying to escape the carnage.

Dammit, why does this always happen?

Marco's guitar playing grew faster and darker. He appeared to be in a trance. His eyes were locked on one spot on the floor. He was drooling the same white goo as the construction guys.

"Fuck." Max's skin prickled. He felt nauseous.

Security came from behind the curtain and stood between him and the crowd.

"Hey, everybody, calm the fuck down! They're just pins. They're a symbol of good intentions. You're supposed to wait for somebody else to twist it into a reason to kill. Stop skipping steps!"

Hawk ran out on stage. Bessy was shinier than ever. Max could see his face reflected in her barrel as she was leveled at the crowd.

Surely he's not...

Hawk opened fire. Plasma cut the rioters into melty strips that collapsed together like shuffled cards.

"No! Bad Hawk!"

Cheeky yowled like a stomped bunny.

I-Force flooded the stage, keeping Hawk in their sights as they formed a protective ring around Max. There was a clicking noise at his feet as the soldiers' boots shot out metal plates, which locked together to form a circular platform about a foot wide.

They said, "Step on." in creepy synchronicity.

He did.

Hawk turned towards him with big drippy eyes and a white gloppy mouth. The security guys grabbed each other's belts with their left hand, forming a protective knot around him, then shot grappling hooks into the sky with their right. A passing chopper jerked them off the ground and away from the scene.

Max lost sight of Hawk. Even when they set him down safely on Greystoke's roof, he was afraid to ask what happened to him. Hawk was a good dog, loyal and sweet, but Max knew what happened to pets that foam at the mouth.

✶✶✶✶✶

Greystoke sat on the couch in his underground study watching footage of the massacre and drinking bourbon out of a tall glass. Max stood behind him drinking out of the bottle. He couldn't get over how intentional it all looked.

Max watched himself spewing propaganda, throwing something into the crowd, the people reacting like it had been a fistful of PCP while Marco jammed on his guitar. Then the military came out and shot everybody. The video ended with a giant plasma ball flying towards the camera. It might as well have been anarchist performance art.

Max plopped down next to him and rested his bottle on the soft, black leather. "What the fuck was that?"

Greystoke shushed him. His eyes were locked on the screen like it was made of boobs.

Cheeky hopped up and nuzzled Max's ear, silently telling him everything was going to be okay. Cheeky was a bad liar.

The video started over from the beginning, on auto-loop.

"I should have known this would be like porn to you."

Greystoke cut his eyes at Max. "Oh yes, nothing sexier than utter failure. What you have done here is the equivalent of trying to make a sandwich and accidentally inventing airborne cancer!"

"You can't blame me for this. This was your plan. I did exactly what you said. I even fuckin' danced. I don't dance!"

"Yes, well I don't foresee any arguments on that subject. It was like watching a chimpanzee suffer a heart attack."

"Fuck you!" It took every bit of Max's willpower not to hit him.

"Who do you think is to blame for this debacle? Is that me up there with the giant plasma rifle killing your fans on live TV while the guitarist from Greasy Little Fingers reinterprets Vivaldi into black metal?"

Max took a healthy glug from the bottle. "That wasn't Hawk. Something took him over. It was like Dadance all over again. As I recall, that was also your plan."

"There you go again, blaming everyone but yourself." Greystoke rushed forward and grabbed Max's throat like it was a microphone stand. "I warned you not to involve the ape!"

Cheeky hissed and head-butted the Count.

"Bloody hell." He let Max go, looking confused and offended. He turned and walked around his desk. "No. Apes are far more intelligent. His greatest aspiration is to someday evolve into the thing that will eventually evolve into an ape. You not only demanded he participate, but also allowed him to bring his shiny bitch girlfriend along. I shall henceforth refer to her as Yoko after her less destructive namesake whose presence also entailed shrieking and disaster."

Max grabbed a huge yellowed tome from the side table and hurled it at the Count. "You need to chill the fuck out. We're wasting time. What happened, happened, and it fucking sucks, but the sooner we start our recovery the better off we'll be. I'm sure a lot of people saw that—."

Greystoke interrupted. "Sixty-seven million."

Max coughed. "Yeah, well some people didn't see it. And every second we aren't on the news letting them know what really happened, they're out there thinking about what they saw, telling their friends, discussing their take—."

"Yes, free thought. Your favorite thing and the biggest pain in the ass I know, present company excluded." Greystoke walked over to his minibar and poured another six fingers.

Max silenced him with a look. "Free thought is a good thing. What happened makes a lot more sense than anything the conspiracy theorists can come up with."

Greystoke chuckled. "You think they will believe you because it makes sense?" He had to pause, he was laughing so hard. "That is precisely why they won't believe you. The masses love a good story, especially ones that play on their fears. They would rather be right than safe. They all want to be the one who finally predicts the end of the world accurately. Can you imagine that idiot's smile as the comet comes towards him? 'I did it. I was right. I'm not crazy.' Happiest man on Earth."

"We don't have time for this. We need to get Hawk, see to the survivors, spin this thing in our favor and most importantly figure out how to stop this from happening again."

Greystoke sighed and fell heavily into his desk chair. "You're right. We are completely, irrevocably fucked, but it will only get worse if we don't act."

"What happened to Hawk after I flew away?"

Greystoke frowned. "Unfortunately, he is still alive. He murdered my staff and escaped into the sewer. As much as I hate to say anything in his favor, Hawk is quite good at making people die. Tomorrow's headline will likely be, "High Ranking Riot Nrrd and Friend of the Messiah Rampages Through Iiite Marketplace Killing Indiscriminately." I literally cannot think of anything worse."

"Well, at least we agree on something. Look, we tried it your way, now it's my turn. Where can I find The Holy?"

The Count pursed his lips. "Their order resides inside Mount Robson in the Canadian Rockies."

"Why?"

"Cheap rent. In any case, the entrance is at the top, only accessible to the best mountain climbers and those with helicopters. We can be there in a couple of hours."

"And they'll be able to help us, right?"

"They don't help anyone. They will be able to tell us more than we know, but I wouldn't get your hopes up. Whatever is happening is very big. I don't know if I will be able to stop it."

"Good thing nobody expects you to. Saving the world's my job—dammit." He stared at the floor and sucked a strand of crab meat from between his back teeth.

Mmm, V.I.P. food.

Max drained the last of the bourbon, then pointed at the door. "Let's finish this conversation on the chopper."

# MAXWELL QUICK AND THE HOLY PAIL

Greystoke's helicopter was a vast improvement over droid travel. It had leather recliners, TV and enclosed space. Plus, minibar! He'd asked Pope to install one in his droid a million times, but all he ever got was lectures on physics, biology, and poor decision making.

The Rocky Mountains jutted up below him like great accusatory nipples, grey pointy mysteries, demanding tribute. "Shouldn't there be snow up here?"

Greystoke studied the passing mountains like he expected to find Waldo. "There was last week."

Max grimaced. "Global warming?"

Every day it got hotter and purpler outside. He knew what was happening. In a way, he'd always known. The idea was too terrible for him to consider, but he'd come too far to ignore the truth. This was happening, and it was up to him to do something about it.

We're all going to die.

Greystoke offered a reassuring smile. "Are you prepared to see what lies beyond the veil?"

"What the fuck is that supposed to mean?"

"There are things that lie beyond this world, yet in it at the same time. All worlds permeate all others to a degree, like culture, like weather, but there are places and things most men would rather stay hidden. Some truths that, once known, can never be forgotten."

"Drop the melodrama, already. I dipped my fingers into a vortex inside a kid's head. My girlfriend turned into a giant chicken with chainsaw wings. I was beaten into this mumbo-jumbo by a little old lady who eats souls, after a bunch of rapey squiggles sent me to a tainted fairyland Sid and Marty Kroft designed on bath salts. And that was all before shit got weird, so please stop acting like I'm some kid you're taking to the fair."

Greystoke smirked. "I apologize. This must all be very dull for you. Gum?" He pulled a little silver case out of his coat and opened it, revealing three thin stacks of orange strips.

"Sure, grandpa, I'd love some." Max stuffed a piece in his mouth and chewed it sarcastically.

The Count put a piece in his mouth and continued to smirk. Are you familiar with ley lines?"

"Yeah."

"Do you know much about the Earth Mysteries?"

Max shrugged and shook his head. He could feel a lecture coming on.

Greystoke saw his reaction for what it was. "One of these days you are going to realize that knowledge is not a nuisance. It is a rare blessing; one you should appreciate. You act like a high school student who thinks knowing too much is going to make him a Nrrd. A bit late for that."

The chopper descended sharply and flew through a hole running through the center of two conjoined peaks. The sky on the other side was different, brighter, bluer. Max felt an immediate release of tension. His jaw unclenched as the snow-topped peaks dropped away. The chopper slowly turned, offering a panoramic view like a thousand inspirational posters taped together. The clouds shimmered like coming dreams. They were everything, protoplasmic spunk shot into his vitreous humor. He could swear, somewhere someone was laughing at him the way a child does when an adult falls down.

He and Greystoke spoke in unison. "What was that you were saying?"

They leaned in and kissed. Greystoke's tongue tasted like mulberry and juniper. Maybe it was the gum. Light welled up inside him so fast he felt it might spew out his mouth. Greystoke's eyes retreated into his skull and switched places. Max nodded in agreement.

The chopper landed near the edge of a veiny blue plateau. The pilot turned off the engines, opened the door, and helped them down the steps grinning all the while as though he had just said something everyone thought was very clever.

Max followed the Count to the center and down an ancient spiral of stairs that sagged like cheap couch cushions under the weight of dead seekers' boots. Fifteen feet below was a disc scarred by symbols seeping red beneath their feet. The Count cut his hand and scrawled a swooshing salutation in blood.

The scars shone brighter. The earth broke apart into stones that fell mechanically away, folding in acceptance, gaping in welcome. The mountain turned beneath their feet and the hole sucked them in like a hungry fish.

The lights flickered on. They were in a waiting room done in red and gold like an old theater. The walls were covered in soft crimson paper, the floor in matching shag. Magazines were spread over a long table, its dark oak dulled but not entirely obscured by dust. The selection was outdated and disappointing. Max wondered if there was a periodical package everyone with a waiting room was legally obligated to subscribe to.

Greystoke approached the dark window and read the post-it note with great dissatisfaction. "Come visit us in our new location in Heller House. Egad. This will be awkward."

"The ancient order moved?"

"It would appear so. It seems they have allowed themselves to be collected. Whosoever selleth themselves to him shall have everlasting prosperity. Heller is today, the boot and the lathe. No way asunder, but by him." Greystoke's eyes were wide and drifting with metallic flakes of understanding.

Max was as confused as ever. "We came all this way for nothing?"

"Not nothing. This is quite significant."

"But now we have to fly all the way back to Heller House?"

"No, they were kind enough to cast a temporary door spell."

He opened the door beside the reception window. On the other side was another, much newer waiting room. The seats looked cushier and the lighting was better, but it had none of the warmth or charm of the one they were standing in.

Greystoke sneered. "Progress." He pulled out his walkie-talkie and told the pilot to go back without them, then ushered Max into the new office.

"Why the fuck are people still using planes and cars? I mean, how much could we reduce our carbon footprint if we—"

"Magic comes at a price. Some can pay, others can't. The wise choose not to."

"What's the price?"

"Suffice it to say, it is very high."

Greystoke shut the door. It shimmered and turned into an elevator. The tightness came back to Max's jaw. He wanted a cigarette, except he hated cigarettes. It's how he stayed quit.

"Everybody's happy to drone on about shit that doesn't interest me, but every time I ask a question they go all cryptic. As king of the Nrrds I demand a sensible answer."

Greystoke laughed. "I share your frustration. I would like nothing more than to illuminate you my boy, but your questions are always vague and poorly timed, the equivalent of what is the *best movie*, or how does *stuff* work. You are an intellectual toddler, and I don't mean that as an insult. You simply must study basic math before having a run at calculus."

Max wanted to punch the shine off Greystoke's teeth, but he knew he was right. He'd have to learn a lot just to figure out whether he had a chance to figure out how to save the world. Greystoke was the one who understood this stuff. All Max brought to the table was a sense of obligation. So, instead of punching him, he pulled a tab out of the queue machine and plopped down in one of the grey, chrome and foam chairs.

Good lumbar support.

A second later, a young man in a black, hooded robe came through the door and called his name. Max looked at the tab and saw his name. He didn't know why he was surprised. He and the Count were the only ones there.

They followed him down a long white hallway lined with dark ironwood doors. Muffled curses seeped through the cracks as they followed their guide to the big black door at the end. The adept stopped and turned. His freshly sewn eyes were crusted over. Max cringed vocally.

The adept raised a brow. Thick green fluid squirted out the corner of his eye and rolled down his cheek.

Max stepped back and looked away. This time it wasn't light splashing in the back of his throat. *Wait, did the Count and I really kiss? No, that—uh.*

"Are you unprepared?" The adept turned his head as if shifting his gaze between Max and the Count.

Max overcompensated. "I'm all kinds of prepared. There's a badge Scouts earn by stalking me to learn the true meaning of prepared. I'm good."

"The Altuber does not see strangers easily, and his mood is particularly dark today. I recommend you take a moment to stay yourself before you enter. The sight of the Altuber is overwhelming."

Was that a string of puns? Should I laugh? Do monks joke? He's not laughing. Too late. The laugh window has closed. "I've heard that."

Greystoke gave him a, "behave" look. "Shall we proceed?"

The stifled laugh slipped around his diaphragm and escaped like a loud sneeze. "Ha! I mean, Hell yeah. Let's do this."

Yep. Awkward.

The adept opened the door slowly, gravely, like he was using a French press to make coffee for the devil himself and every ground in the cup would earn him a million years in the pit of hungry maggots.

Max stepped into an oval room decorated in a 16th century dungeon motif. Walls of stacked stone curved to form a high dome. The floor was packed earth. Everything stank like a port-o-dump smeared with aloe. He wanted to make a joke about how it needed a woman's touch, someone to put flags around, brighten the place up a bit. Instead, he cleared his throat and walked toward the crapulous lump gurgling atop a large purple cushion.

Two acolytes were spooning opaque glop over his pale blubber, which hung like a pile of raw baguettes. He looked like a melted toy, all white and runny, his head all but swallowed by the biggest stack of chins since the Sonians declared eminent domain on China. The only feature it had left was a mouth too wide and teeth too sharp ever to have been human.

Holy was not a word that came to mind.

*Where is his robe? You'd think he'd at least cover up that colostomy tube. Why's it so big? It's like a fucking garden hose. And why the fuck does it empty into a bucket? I don't want to have to smell that.*

"Well, look who it is." The blob's voice was as bloated and sticky as the rest of him. "Maxwell Quick, the messiah." He laughed. "I wasn't sure you were coming."

"I dreamt about you *last night*. I think I did pretty well considering I'd never heard of you."

"Yes, well, time passes differently for us. It's monotonous sitting up here all day, every day, nothing to keep me occupied but the stings and tingles of vindictive flesh."

Max nearly had a sarcastagasm, but maintained control. "Right, so I got your message, kind of. What can I do for you?"

"How refreshing. My guests usually want to know what I can do for them." He chortled like he'd just invented the one-liner. "This plane has a problem. Normally I wouldn't care, but our order just relocated here, and it would be quite unfortunate if he had to move again so soon."

An adept lifted the bottom fat roll while another applied ointment to his undercarriage.

"Yeah, I've had to move around a lot lately myself. No fun. So, do you know what's happening?"

"Of course I do. I know everything. I've seen everything, been host to gods. There *is* a reason I look like this, you know." The gorbellied goof quivered at the sound of his witty repartee.

"Well, enlighten me."

"You are already familiar with The Darkness. You encountered it before at Witches 'R' Us, but what you have seen is only the tip of an iceberg that is ripping through the hull of your reality."

"I was afraid of that. This Darkness have a name?"

"He has many names, but none define him so well as The Darkness."

"Okay, whatever. How do I kill it, blow it up, whatever?"

"Kill it?" The lump laughed so hard his adepts had to hold him on his perch. "He wants to kill it!"

It looked as though the blob may never stop laughing, so Greystoke butted in. "Please excuse Max, your Holiness. He is new to all of this."

The laughing gradually petered out. "Oh, I didn't know it was state the obvious day. Let me play. You are both idiots, the world is doomed and I'm wasting my time. Bring forth the pizza pillow!"

One of the acolytes ran out of the room. The other stayed to scrub between the folds with a gloppy white towel.

Max cleared his throat. "You called me here for a reason. Tell me what I need to know."

"Fine. You cannot kill The Darkness. Even if you could, I can't imagine the damage it would do to all of existence. It would be like killing carbon.

"Imagine a fractalized double helix running across every frequency, through every dimension. Each spiral has two poles connected by another series of poles. Each pole is an aspect that translates into something observable in every reality. Now imagine the biggest double helix of them all. All the other helixes are tangled around it, sliding up and down, always wiggling, shifting forms. The Darkness is one end of that center pole. The other end, obviously, being light."

"Nifty."

"Do I detect sarcasm?"

"No."

"Good. Now, to the point. The IS—this world will henceforth be referred to as the IS—is drifting ever closer to the Dark side of the pole. The closer it gets, the stronger The Darkness's gravity becomes and the faster the IS is sucked in. Normally the IS hangs in the center, the realm of chaos with roughly the same amount of positive and negative ripples.

"Many attempts have been made to explain The Darkness. Every religion has some maligning entity who feeds on suffering, but I believe it was H.P. Lovecraft who personified it best in his parables of the elder gods. They came in many forms, but really only a few variations, usually some combination of sea monster and insect with an overabundance of mouths, tentacles, and eyes. Much like the Tarot, Lovecraft used the juxtaposition of symbols to explain concepts far too vast to put into words. Too bad he was such an awful writer."

"So, you're saying our world is being sucked into Cthululand?"

"More or less. The laws of physics will continue to bend. Delirium will envelop the minds of men and the earth will become a breeding ground for pain."

"So, no major changes?"

"Very funny. Unfortunately, sardonic humor is inherently negative and therefore feeds The Darkness. To win, you must think of everything in terms of positive and negative and in broader terms than yourself. Does it empower the light elements or the dark? Does it create more pleasure or pain in the world?

"Back to my previous metaphor, the best way to think of this is that The Darkness is Shub-Niggurath, the Goat with a Thousand Young. Every negative influence is one of her young, who go out and reproduce, populating the world with more and more little black goats. The more there are, the more there shall be."

"So I have to slaughter millions of proverbial goats. How does that work, exactly?"

"An act of kindness in hell."

The Acolyte returned with a pizza in the shape of a toilet seat and draped it around the blob's chin collection. The Holy issued guttural cries of ecstasy as it gnawed at the drippy, meaty wreath.

Max stared silently, expecting an explanation. None came. "So, I should die and then help a little old lady cross the street of a million nipples?"

The blob started to laugh, but choked on a mouthful of cheese. One Acolyte braced him from behind while the other kicked him hard in the stomach, propelling the food back into his mouth. He chewed it a few more times, then swallowed. "That won't be necessary. Hell is coming to you."

Max shook his head. "I don't understand. I mean, I think you're saying I can't attack the evil directly, that I have to balance out the evil with good deeds. But how the fuck am I supposed to do that? I mean I can be the nicest guy in the world, but that won't make me any less dead if I'm eaten by a flying octopus."

The blob giggled grotesquely and let out a burp that would impress Godzilla. "People who have caused great lasting change have almost always been martyrs. Gandhi was able to defeat the British by starving himself. By dying, Jesus showed the power of selfless love."

"Yeah, I'm not letting anybody nail me to a tree."

"It won't be that easy. Grand gestures go a long way, but no one act will convince humanity to give up their favorite toys. Fairness, success, revenge—The Darkness feeds on everything that makes one person feel good at the expense of another. The most powerful acts of kindness are the ones you do to those who have hurt you. You must convince people to let go of their egos and embrace their true selves, but you must first do it yourself. Ego will never win against ego."

The Count let out a belly laugh. "Good luck with that. Maxwell makes metaphysical solipsists look like altruistic hippies."

Max glared at him for a moment then took a step towards to the blob. "How does that work, exactly?"

"There are many paths leading to the destination. You must simply find the one that is right for you, and do it fast. I recommend finding a guru, possibly your spirit animal."

"I don't think Marvin's going to be much help."

"Go about it however you like, but be quick. The Darkness has taken a human form. At this moment, it walks the Earth in the body of your friend, sowing seeds of doubt against your cause."

"Nothing new there."

The Count asked, "Are you referring to Hawk?"

Max sighed. "Of course he is."

The blob chewed off another wad of pizza. The remainder tumbled down his back and into his colostomy bucket. He swallowed and licked the sauce from his lips.

Max felt like a penguin at a gift-wrapping station. "You know I'm a sociopath, right?"

"Sociopath is a made-up word, like all the others. Everything is in a constant state of change, so people use words to nail those things down, to stagnate them into submission. You are not the man you were a year ago. You are not even the man you were a week ago. Evolve freely and in whatever way you choose. That is the gift of self-awareness."

"But self-awareness is the ego studying and defining itself."

"You must understand yourself to know you are a lie. Every morning you are a new lie, similar to the previous lie, but not the same. It is within your power to be an entirely new lie, a lie of your own design. That is the gift of free will."

"But will is based in ego, right? You can't will what you don't want, and we only want things because they gratify the ego or help maintain the ego's ride."

"Freedom means liberation from the constraining forces of the false will. That is the gift of submission."

"Wait, what?"

"Your mind is divided. You are half robotic, a meat computer programmed from birth, and half divine. Each has a will of its own. You must shun the false will of the flesh to know the true will of the spirit."

"I'm getting a headache." Max turned to the Count. "Can we go?"

The Count looked like he was thinking. "What would happen if you channeled The Darkness and we exposed it to some powerful symbol of good?"

Max cocked an eyebrow. "It's an elemental force, not a fucking vampire."

"It is just a thought. There might be a way to weaken it by poisoning its core."

"Well, it's settled then. All we need's an army of Furry Pals."

Greystoke smiled. "That may work!"

"It frightens me that you didn't sound sarcastic just now."

"If there is a hell dimension where vile crawling things feed on suffering, there must also be a dimension inhabited by creatures of pure love. If we could infest the negative planes with creatures of light, The Darkness might weaken its hold on our world."

"Or get desperate and dig in harder."

"Stop playing devil's advocate. You are supposed to be learning to be positive and hopeful."

"Yeah, well neither of those things are in my wheelhouse. I think we should pawn this off on somebody better suited, like anybody."

The blob turned as if to take another bite then snorted at his shit-bucket. "Your imperfection is the reason you were chosen. If you can save yourself, you can save the world."

"I'm no cheerleader, and this is no comic book. If our only hope is for me to transform into a big purple dinosaur and give the world a hug, we're all gonna fuckin' die. I've been the poster boy for misanthropy since I was, like, eight. I wanted to be a serial killer when I grew up. If there was a button I could push to kill every human on the planet without hurting any animals, I'd punch it. What moron decided I was the guy to buy the world a cola? Point me at 'em, so I can rip out his lung and fuck it like a dead dog!"

Greystoke strode toward him. "Calm down. We can do this." His voice was an archer with a quiver full of doubt.

"No, we can't. This is crazy. We're better off moving to a dimension The Darkness hasn't gotten to yet. See, that's how I think. I tried to be a good guy. I wanted to make some kind of difference, and look where it got me, pulling my hair out in a stanky dungeon with Pizza the Hut and a senile magician who thinks he can save the world by opening a portal to Disneyland. Fuck this! I'm going home to have weird demeaning sex with the fucked-up piss-mop you call a daughter."

Max turned to leave, but Greystoke grabbed his elbow. "That will be quite enough!"

Max whirled around and nearly broke his fist on Greystoke's temple. Rather than go down like a good little bitch, the Count judo-flipped Max face first into the dirt.

Max tasted soil seasoned with a thousand years of feet, then blood. He was unconscious before his legs hit the ground.

*****

Max came to on a cot in a sterile, white cell, not unlike the ones in Greystoke's basement. Greystoke and Pope stood just outside the door, talking quietly.

Max tested his front teeth. They gave a little and clicked, but nothing was out of place. He groaned, shooting lightning bolts from the tip of his nose to the back of his brain. *I guess the piss-mop comment was a bit much.*

Max forced himself to sit up and propped against the wall. "Sorry about that. I guess I kind of freaked out." Max squinted at Pope. "Why are you wearing a security uniform?"

His friends seemed annoyed their conversation had been interrupted.

Pope looked him over as if taking inventory. "I've been working for Heller ever since you abandoned me here."

"We didn't abandon you."

Pope's face showed no trace of emotion. "Did you retrieve me from the holding cell before you left?"

"I didn't know they had a holding cell. I figured they kicked you out and you went home."

"I wasn't given that option. It's all for the best, though. Mr. Heller offered me a job. They have an excellent training program here. They stripped away all my weaknesses overnight, even my asthma."

"That sounds—creepy."

Pope punched in a code and the door hissed open. "It does. I must say, though, being a Stepford husband isn't all that bad. There are a lot of benefits to being fearless and self-assured. I doubt I would have any luck attracting a female now, if I was interested in sex. That was another weakness they removed."

Max leaned forward sharply and smelled blood. "They made you a eunuch?"

"No. They just took away the need for physical gratification."

"I think that might be worse."

Greystoke interrupted. "We have more important things to discuss."

"I think it's pretty important to find out how and why my friend's brain has been tinkered with. Did they explain this training to you beforehand? Was it consensual? Are you on drugs, or did they just pop an ice pick in your head?"

Pope stared blankly. "I appreciate your concern, but it was my decision. If anything is to blame for my decision it would be the weaknesses that led to my abandonment and the emotional state it created. I am better now. There is no need to waste further time on this subject."

Greystoke tapped on the glass with his cane. "If you are finished, we rather need to be going."

He was still mad.

"Sorry I called Cat a piss-mop."

"Your reaction was natural, according to the Holy. Your ego was trying to defend itself. I'm sure The Darkness had a hand in it as well."

"Yeah, maybe. I'm still sorry."

Greystoke averted his gaze. "I am less bothered by what you said than the fact that it is true and it is my fault. Her mother and I wanted to raise her to be free and powerful, the sort of person incapable of obscurity. We succeeded."

Father of the fucking year. Good thing he didn't want to raise her to have a strict moral code. We'd be living in a fascist theocracy with her as the pope. I guess I should say something reassuring.

"Don't be so hard on yourself. Cat might be a bit extreme, but she doesn't hurt anybody. In fact, she's all about making people happy. According to the Holy, she's a positive influence on the world, whereas I'm negative."

Greystoke blinked twice and cracked a little smile.

Holy fuck, I did it! I said the right thing! I don't think that's ever happened before. Woo hoo! Maybe he won't kill me now.

"Come on, then." Greystoke waved him out of the cell with his cane.

They followed Pope through a series of hidden doors to the main entrance. Outside, the limo driver opened the door for them. Greystoke and Max climbed in, but Pope remained on the steps.

Max waved him in. "Come on, we need to move."

Pope tilted his head. "I work and live here now. There is no reason to leave."

"There are several reasons. One, you are a member of my entourage. Two, you're a scientist, not a flying monkey. Three, Hawk's gone all Linda Blair, and I need your help getting him back. Oh yeah, and the world's ending."

"I would love to help you, but I'm afraid I am under contract."

"So you can't leave? You're a prisoner?"

"Not a prisoner, I choose to keep the contract. I have weekends off. Perhaps I could help you then."

"Fine, keep in touch." Max slammed the door and waited in awkward silence for the driver to walk around the car. As they pulled away, Pope turned and walked back up the steps in that same stiff robotic manner he'd always had. If it was anybody else, Max would feel obligated to rescue him, but Pope was probably better off this way. He hadn't really been human to begin with.

"Stepford Pope is a pain in the ass too."

Greystoke laughed.

Greystoke's in a suspiciously good mood. I am down two of my closest friends and assets. I can't keep losing leverage like this. At least he seems to want to help. I guess he can't dominate the world if it ends.

Then again, he is sitting on the largest Aklo library unknown to man. Maybe he thinks he can turn this to his advantage. He has to know better than to bargain with unfathomable evil. Right?

"Max." Greystoke was staring at him.

"What?"

"As unlikely as it seems, you are the man for this job."

Max looked out the window.

"If you were not capable of this task, you would not have been singled out."

Max grunted.

"Can you think of any chosen one who has failed at their task?"

"Jonah comes to mind."

# MAX TAKES MANHATTAN

Max sipped his scotch and watched the patchwork of modern life crawl by from 15,000 feet. The stench of Cat's nail-polish made it taste like a moist towelette. He glanced at her, wanting to tell her to put that shit away, but it was the only thing distracting her from him.

There was purple polish everywhere, now. She had started out painting her toenails, then got bored and moved on to her legs. The designs weren't bad, but she kept moving, smearing them into glittery bruises.

Cat noticed him looking and put down the polish. "I'm bored." She banged her head against the helicopter's window it time with the song on the radio. "This is boring. Why couldn't we take the droids?"

Max fingered the bottle of ether Greystoke had loaned him. They had spent the first two hours of the flight having sex and another talking, but they still had one to go, and her attitude was degrading fast.

"I told you before, it's a four-hour flight."

"So?" She hugged her knees, smearing purple nail-polish all over her Han-Man V-Neck.

"So I don't want to dangle from a rope for four hours."

"But we'd get to fly over the whole country."

"Yes, and we are, but instead of clinging to a rope for dear life we have reclining seats and booze. And we got to fuck. We couldn't have done that on the droids."

"Yes, we could."

Max had a Dr. Strangelove flashback.

That's how I'm going to die, with Cat riding me like Slim Pickens all the way to hell. I have to remember to keep her away from cowboy hats.

Max downed the rest of his scotch and poured another. "As exhilarating as that sounds, I don't want to meet God with four hours of smog in my clothes. This isn't a pleasure trip, you know."

Cat sneered. For the first time, Max could see a family resemblance.

"I hate New York*."

Max took another sip. "You didn't have to come."

"Everybody's weird there."

"Since when do you think weird's a bad thing? A society based on 1980's hair metal *horrifies* me, but it should be right up your alley."

Cat got that lucid look he'd come to fear.

Max quickly added, "We won't be there long. I just need to ask for his help."

"He won't."

"He might."

"If you had servants fulfilling your every need and a giant cocaine bucket that was always full, would you leave to fight bad guys?"

He hated it when she was lucid. "Valid point. Still, I have to try. His followers could make a big difference.

"His followers are going to love The Darkness. Haven't you ever seen a heavy metal album cover? There was even a band called The Darkness."

"I wonder how that works. If The Darkness makes them happy, and happiness is a positive thing, would that hurt it?

"The Discordians are the ones you should be asking. This is Eris's world."

"I somehow don't see chaos worshippers being much help against an entity that creates chaos."

"Chaos is a balance of order and disorder. If you get too much disorder it's not chaos, it's just disorder. Eris likes to keep things fun and interesting, and too much disorder is no fun."

Oh, that's why she hates New York. If everybody else is weird, she's normal, and normal is boring. She'll probably be lucid for the rest of the trip.

"Tell you what: when we get back I'll help you organize the Discordians." He said it snarkily, then realized it wasn't much crazier than his current plan.

"Not with that attitude."

"Seriously though, you summoned a holy cockroach that time. Think you could do it again?"

Cat pulled a bunch of napkins out of the dispenser and began wadding them up.

"Not right now. We're in the air. There's no ventilation. Plus, last time everybody got knocked out before he came. I don't know if that's a part of it, but we need the pilot awake."

She continued wadding napkins. "He'll be fine, probably. What else are we going to do for six hours?"

"Anything else. I'm serious. If we try that up here I'm ninety-nine percent sure we'll die."

She tossed wadded napkins all over the place, then pulled two mini-bottles of clear booze out of the fridge and removed the caps. He thought she was conceding, but then she put her thumbs over the holes and slung it like holy water while chanting what sounded like backwards Latin.

"What the fuck are you doing? Stop that. Don't waste good booze."

She dug in her purse and pulled out a pink disposable lighter. "Not wasting."

"You do know liquor isn't flammable, right?" He looked down and his heart jumped into his chest. "Fuck! Who put Everclear in the minibar? Who's gonna drink that?"

She flicked the lighter and lit a wilted napkin ball. He wrestled the lighter away from her before she could light another, but their shifting weight rocked the chopper, rolling one ball into another with a speed and efficiency that implied the ritual had already worked. He tried to stomp them out, but Cat tackled him.

"Stop it!" She stuck her hand down the back of his pants and prodded his rectum.

He tried to squirm away, but her fingers were like hentai demons.

Little fireballs bounced all around them, filling the cabin with smoke. The pilot was screaming and flying like the cockpit was full of bees. All this was accompanied by a very scary beeping.

Something tickled his inner ear. He stuck his pinkie in and wiggled it around. A weird pressure grew in his head, seeping toward his fingertip.

Something bit him.

"Oww!" He withdrew his finger. A little cockroach flew out of his ear and perched atop the fridge. Cat let him go and sat up, clapping excitedly.

"Ready for a second date already?" Gulik morphed into the naked Mexican lady. This time she had a penis.

Cat's face fell into confusion.

Max climbed back onto his seat and grabbed his drink, which had miraculously survived the turbulence. "Don't start that again." He finished his drink and held the glass in his palm in case he needed a weapon.

"No, usted es divertida." He shifted back into a roach. "What do you want?"

Cat tried to catch him with a tumbler, but he was too fast. She chased him all over the cabin, screaming, "I want wishes."

Gulik made a 'hyo yugen' noise. A blue light appeared in front of him, and a cow the size of a hedgehog shot out, hitting her in the face. She fell to the floor, unconscious. The cow screamed and exploded into hundreds of tiny hamburgers.

Gulik landed on her forehead. "Fucking groupies. You were saying?"

"I assume you know The Darkness is seeping into this world, taking it over?"

"I might have heard something about it."

"Cat was saying Eris might not like that, since Earth—or the IS—or whatever is usually in her realm. She thought Eris might want to help."

"Wow, you still haven't figured it out?"

"Figured what out?"

Gulik sighed and shook his tiny head. "Nothing. She knows. She's already got something in the works."

"So it's all going to be okay? I don't need to worry about it."

"No you need to be very worried about it."

"Why? You don't think her plan will work?"

Gulik sighed. "Anybody ever told you you're slower than a dead slug in a jar of molasses?"

"I doubt anyone has ever told anyone that before."

"Well you are. Look, what do you think she should do to fix this?"

"I don't know. She's the goddess."

"You think she should do something to counteract The Darkness."

"Yeah."

"Gods usually choose a champion to carry out their plans. Maybe she should pick somebody who's really negative and teach them how to change. Then, maybe that guy can teach the world how to change itself."

"…"

Gulik pursed his mandibles. "I'll get right on that."

Max shook his head. "You're saying it's me? I'm the plan? All this shit about being the chosen one is true, literally?"

"I thought you knew that."

"I never really believed it. Not, chosen as in by a God. Fuck!"

"Why not? People have been saying it this whole time. Hell, she told you herself."

"No, I think I'd remember meeting a goddess?"

He crossed his top two sets of arms. "Yeah. Whatever, my mistake."

"Well, can you help me then? The Holy said I need a guru, or a spirit animal to guide me, and we are working for the same boss."

"I'm no guru, and you already have two spirit animals. Where is Cheeky, anyway? You never bring him anywhere, anymore. How do you think that makes him feel?"

Max poised his eyebrow. "Said the rapey cockroach."

"You want a clue, here it is. You are one of the few people ever to have two spirit animals. Three if you count the one you killed. And you never use them. You met Marvin one time and all you did was hurt his feelings. You killed off most of your friends in the war. You let one get brainwashed. Another one, you hurt his feelings so bad he got possessed by The Darkness and became the AntiQuick. If you want to be a positive influence on the world you're going to have to stop being such a dick."

"It's not my fault Hawk's so sensitive."

"I don't have time for the whole 'you defend yourself and I rebut' thing. I'm right. If you think about it, you've been told a bunch of stuff by a bunch of people that should make sense now. You won't get everything yet, but you should have a good idea of what to do. If you promise not to bother me again, I'll try not to tell anyone I had to spell it all out for you."

"Fine, can you tell me anything else? Can God help me?"

"I thought we went over that."

"No, I mean the big shiny guy in New York."

"Do I look like a gypsy?" He shifted into the form of an old gypsy. "Do you see Tarot cards anywhere on my person?" His hand filled with Tarot cards. He dropped them. "Didn't think so. You want me to help? I'll help. I'll shave some time off your trip."

The chopper fell still and silent. Max's heart jumped into his throat, then he realized there was no sense of falling. Gulik opened the door, said, "Later, tater," and flew away.

The air was uncomfortably hot, definitely over one hundred degrees. Max poked his head out and saw he was on the roof of a short skyscraper. The knee-high wall running around the edge was covered with leather and silver spikes and the pea gravel was colored to look like jellybeans.

"Yup, that's definitely New York."

The doorframe felt sweaty and soft. He pulled his hand back and saw it had left a dent. "What the fuck?" He pressed a little harder and made an imprint of his hand in the metal.

"That's weird."

He turned to find Cat sinking into the floor. "Shit!" His feet were sinking in as well. The cabin was warping as the ceiling buckled under its own weight.

He grabbed Cat's hands and tried to drag her to the door, but the added pressure pushed his feet through the floorboard. The roof buckled, pulling the walls closer and sealing them in the front half of the cabin.

Max clawed at the wax until he had a hole big enough to stick his head through, and screamed, "You've made your point. You can stop now."

There was no reply. Gulik had disappeared into thick, brown air.

Max ripped a larger hole and strained every muscle in his body stuffing Cat through it. He tried to crawl out, but his left leg was tangled in a thick rope of wax. When his foot finally came free, it was missing his shoe. "Goddammit."

He punched the blob a few times to make it ooze the other direction then stuck his hand in and retrieved his footwear. It looked like a cold anchovy.

"Stupid supernatural beings think the world's their sitcom." He beat the shoe on the edge of the roof a few times to get the muck out, then put it on. Greasy residue had soaked into his clothes. He noticed a pungent floral smell.

"Oh, fuck no. You cannot make me go to meet God stinking of scented candle." The smell stayed the same. "Great, he's gone. Now I have to buy new clothes."

He walked over to Cat and tried to wake her. She mumbled something about pudding pops.

"Wake up. Your asshole God melted our whirlybird." He looked up and realized the pilot wasn't with them.

"Shit!" He ran and poked around in the rapidly flattening cockpit goo. He could see the blue and gold of a uniform through what used to be the glass, but no movement. He dug into the top layer with his fingers, but stopped when they came out dripping with red and tan.

"Eh." He looked at the sky and asked, "What did he do? You know you're hurting your cause with this kind of shit."

Cat laughed. She was swimming in the stones like she was trying to sit up.

Max ran over and checked her for concussion. Her pupils were different sizes.

"Where'd the pretty bad thing go?"

"I don't know. Look at my hand. How many fingers am I holding up?" He held up three fingers.

She cocked her head. "Again?"

"No, for the first time, how many fingers?"

"Why was I asleep?"

"He hit you in the face with tiny cow."

"Aww, I wanna hug a tiny cow. Where is it?" She seemed to be coming out of it.

"It blew up. Now how many fingers?"

She furrowed her brow. "Aww."

"Fingers."

She sat up and noticed the oozing black puddle. "What happened there?"

"Gulik was making a point about how I shouldn't ask him for help. He zapped us here, but turned the chopper to wax, which melted in this heat. What is up with that, anyway? It's, like, a hundred and five degrees up here."

She scratched a little dried blood off her lip. "Where's Serj?"

"Who's Serj?"

"The pilot."

"Oh, he melted too."

"Serj melted? He just adopted a kitten. I'm sad. Hold me."

She hugged him awkwardly, him squatting, her leaning on him, almost knocking him over. He didn't want to be rude, but knowing her, she'd stay there until she fell asleep.

"Hey, you think they have ice cream in New York?"

"Mmm, ice cream."

"You want some?"

She let him go and climbed to her feet. "Ice cream, ho."

It was the first time he'd heard her utter a sad, 'ho'.

As his adrenaline faded, Max realized the thumping in his ears was the sound of distant bass guitar. He walked to the edge of the roof. Bryant Park was only three blocks away. He could see the top of the giant dragon-throne and a big cloud of hair fluttering beyond the buildings like a street anemone.

Max consulted his phone and found that Dr. Sass's Dream Cream was one and a half blocks in the wrong direction. He set his GPS and led Cat through the door and down the stairs to the elevator on the top floor.

He pressed the down button and looked through one of the office windows. The desk was made of chrome molded to look like pygmy bones. The office chairs were bio-mechanoid with buzz-saw blade head rests. It had the same black shag and cherries-on-black-glitter wallpaper as the hallway. He'd heard the whole city was like this, but never quite believed, until now. The fact that Gods were real and this place hadn't been destroyed by divine wrath worried and comforted him at the same time.

A little guitar solo played as the doors slid open. Inside was an inspirational poster. A man with a huge black perm smiled and pointed at him. The caption read, "Cool doesn't drool."

"What the fuck does that mean?"

Cat scoffed. "I don't speak metal."

They rode down listening to a song with the refrain, "I wanna be somebody cool."

"This song is the antithesis of cool. Saying that, even just singing along to that makes you lame. How do these people not see that?"

"It's their religion." Cat did a line off the complimentary coke table.

Max cocked an eyebrow at her.

"What?" She smiled. "When in New York..."

"You know that's about ninety percent baby powder. I heard the city supplies decent stuff, but every person it goes through cuts it a little more. Apparently they are too coked out to understand it's free to everybody including them."

She rubbed some on her gums and smiled. "My gums smell like diapers."

The doors opened, and they exited into the lobby. It was mostly black marble with big pillars crawling with dragons of varying sizes and shapes. The windows were framed with chain.

A fat guy in a gimp suit was asleep behind the front desk. He must have been that way for a while because his drool had run down a groove and was dripping off the goatee of the big shades-wearing Baphomet mounted on the front. As they walked towards the door, Max jumped as little blasts of fire shot out of the floor on either side of them. It happened every few seconds.

Max had heard the conspiracy theory that the overuse of pyrotechnics was God trying to make Earth more hospitable to his true form. Another speculated that it was all a plan to make New York a tropical environment so they could grow their own Coca plants without greenhouses. Max figured it was idiots.

Cat ran in circles, delighting in the little puffs of flame. Her giggles woke the guard, who threw up the devil horns and screamed, "Hail God. Hey, who are you!"

"Nobody. We're just checking out your building. It's totally...rockin'."

He muttered something about tourists and sat back down.

Max reciprocated devil horns and walked towards the door. "Stay cool."

They stepped outside and soaked in the Heavy Metal atmosphere. All the buildings had been made over, some covered in leather, others chain-link. The streets were lined with barrels of fire and littered with beer cans and broken liquor bottles. Nobody drove in New York. Nobody was ever sober enough.

They followed the GPS to the left.

Small groups of people staggered this way and that, usually singing, or rather screeching like the devil had their genitals in a vice. The air was oily with evaporated sweat. The holy land smelled like a hobo's thong.

"Why would anybody choose to live here?"

Cat's voice was sarcastic. "I don't know. Why *would* somebody want to live in a city that runs on sex, drugs, and rock 'n' roll, where God lives right down the street providing a free soundtrack for the coke-fueled orgy that stretches across five city blocks?"

"Careful, you're starting to sound like you like it here."

Cat stuck out her tongue.

They navigated around the broken glass, needles, and other hazards that lay in drifts along the sidewalk. "I guess it would be more tolerable if I was drunk, but I don't think I could deal with all the terrible music or the clothes I'd have to wear. Speaking of which, let me know if you notice a clothing store. I feel like I've been Jell-O wrestling."

The voice of his GPS came over his implant. "Arriving at destination."

"Ice cream!" Cat ran across the street, jumped over an unconscious hobo, and burst through the door.

Max hurried to join her.

The inside was done in an evil clown motif with checkered floors and funhouse mirrors covering the walls. Leering clowns were carved into everything else. The spinning tunnel he would have to walk through to get to the bathroom seemed like an especially bad idea.

The clown behind the counter gave him the devil horns as he walked in. Max assumed he was the owner. Anybody else would have been fired for looking so shitty at work. His greasepaint was cracked, scabby, and covered in scratch marks. Either the makeup was old, or he was wearing it to cover a horrible rash.

There's enough under his fingernails to do it over from scratch. Max imagined a rim shot. He was tired.

Cat squinted at the flavor selection. "I don't know these flavors. What does Valnilla taste like? And what kind of blue candy is that?"

The clown smiled like a porn producer and shouted, "It's Vanilla with gummi Valiyums in it. What can I get ya, sir?" White flecks fell from his moustache as he spoke in a loud drawl.

"I'm just with her."

"Come now, you're in an ice cream shop. Eat some fucking ice cream. It ain't gon' kill ya. Not one scoop, anyway."

"Fine, just stop screaming at me."

The clown popped his eyes and laughed a disconcerting gape-mouthed ha-ha-ha. "First time in New York, huh?"

"How can you tell?"

"Newbies always comment on the way we talk. Think we're being rude, but the fact is we can't help it. Everbody in this city's got a near-terminal case of tinnitus. You folks tourists?"

"Not exactly. I came to seek an audience with God."

"God's audience is hard to miss. They're a couple streets that-a-way." He pointed at the spinning tunnel.

"No, I mean I need to talk to him."

"I know what you meant. I'm funny, not stupid. Now what kinda ice cream?"

"Do you have anything without pills?"

"There's the Nutter Butter."

God, I hope that doesn't mean what I think. "Anything else?"

"Picky one, ain't ya? We got Chocolatini, Kahlua Surprise, Clowntastic…"

"What's the surprise in Kahlua Surprise?"

"Instead of Kahlua there's espresso and meth."

"I could use a pick-me-up. Can I get a sample?"

"No."

"Fine. Give me the smallest one you have. What do you want, Cat?"

"I want the same, but the biggest." She stuck out her hand and made the gimme gesture.

Max grabbed her wrist and lowered it. "Oh, hell no. You're hyper enough. How about a Clowntastic? What's in that, by the way?"

"LSD."

Cat smiled and nodded.

"Is this a specialty shop, or are there drugs in everything in this city?"

"Bit o' both." He put a big scoop of psychedelic swirl into a chocolate-dipped waffle cone shaped like John Wayne Gacy's head. Then he pulled out a tiny novelty scooper and put about a teaspoon into a little plastic skull ring.

"Is this another joke?"

"That'll be twenty bucks."

Max waited for the clown to laugh and pull a cone out of somewhere inappropriate.

"Licking it off my fingers is extra."

Cat snatched her ice cream, stuck her tongue in the center and waggled it around until she made a volcano. "Sprinkles?"

The clown stuck his hand into the bucket of sprinkles and screamed, "Yah!" as he tossed them over the counter like confetti.

Max threw a twenty on the counter, accepted the ring and sucked the ice cream into his mouth. "Wow, you can really taste the meth."

"You like it?"

"No."

"Well fuck you too. I recommended the Nutter Butter."

"And what's in that?"

"Peanut butter. It's for kids."

Max squeezed his eyes shut and inhaled slowly. *At least it'll wake me up.*

He devil-horned goodbye and led Cat back to the street. "I think you were right about this place."

She stuck her mouth in the bowl and came in to kiss him, saying, "Trippy drippy turtle lippy."

Max backed away, but she kept coming until he held her back by the hair. "Any other time, but right now I need to focus. I can't fuck this up."

She stuck out her rainbow-swirled bottom lip. A few drips of tainted cream dripped into her cleavage. It was very tempting, but he couldn't let evil swallow the world just because he had a hot girlfriend.

"Maybe after we get done we can come back and get a gallon to take home. How *are* we going to get home anyway? I'm not sure New York still has an airport."

She shrugged and took another lick.

"We should figure that out." He dialed Greystoke and waited while the phone rang eight times.

Voicemail picked up. "You have reached the home of Count Vladimir Greystoke, actor extraordinaire twenty-seventh degree. Please state your business after the tone."

Beep.

"Hey, it's me. Call me back. The chopper melted. Don't ask. I'm on the way to meet God now. He's about a block away. Have you ever been to New York? Place is fucking weird. Half the buildings have spikes sticking out of them. Sorry for talking so much. I think my ice cream's kicking in. It had meth in it. I figured I could use something to help me focus. Anyway, I'll hang up. Sorry again. About the jabbering, not the chopper. I assume it's insured, and it wasn't my fault. Cat set it on fire, but that's not why it melted. A magic cocksucker did that." He laughed and hung up, knowing Greystoke wouldn't get the pun.

Cockroach, cocksucker. That ice cream's fucking strong.

They rounded the corner and saw the outskirts of what used to be Bryant Park, now New Heaven. In the outer ring, those recovering from time in the center mingled with those who had just arrived. The Metists were carrying on conversations, though he didn't see how. Even this far away, the music was deafening.

I should have brought earplugs.

Pressing through the crowd and into New Heaven proper was harder than getting Cat out of the chopper. Every couple of seconds one of the devout would try to have sex with one of them. New York had always been a Mecca for sex offenders, but now they had God's endorsement.

Twenty feet in, the waves of groping hands wove an impenetrable net of prospective penetration. Cat didn't seem to mind. Her pupils were the size of goldfish bowls and she was chanting, "I'm down with the clown. Down with the clown. I'm down with the clown."

God stood a block-and-a-half away with one leg on his massive dragon-throne, posing with his triple-necked guitar, screeching, "I gave rock and roll to you, gave rock and roll to you."

Max was transfixed.

God was as impressive as he was hokey. His skin glowed bright orange against the black mist of his perm, which was held back by the ram horns growing out of his temples. His pupils were black skulls roasting in the center of fireballs. Smoke poured from his nostrils, possibly from the cigarette dangling from his lower lip, possibly from the demons he presumably bit the heads off of earlier in the show speckling his goatee with blood.

Great spiky shoulder pads connected the red, dragon-skin cape to the chain bandolier, which crossed his chest and met in the center at a pentagram the size of a car. Over his bellybutton was a cocoa leaf tattoo with "Metal" written above it in fancy gothic letters. The T in Metal was an inverted cross complete with a nude, crucified female. Her hair was tangled in the horns of the demon-head buckle on the spiked leather belt hanging sideways across his emaciated stomach. His pants were black spandex with actual lightning striking down his legs at regular intervals and most frequently around his bulge, which writhed like an anaconda all the way down to the vampire-skull kneepads. If not for them, it might have stretched all the way to the spiky bands at the top of his platform boots.

The pièce de résistance was a pair of leather-studded gauntlets with buzz-saw blades coming out of the wrists. Max turned to see Cat's reaction and found her fellating a pimply teenager through his lime green leotard. Max wrapped his arm around her stomach and tried to power through the crowd, but even with the meth pumping his heart like a stress ball, the crowd was too dense.

He let her go and wiped some drool off his chin.

He hoped it was drool.

Max spoke in a normal voice. "God, if you really are a God you should be able to hear me. I need to talk to you about a matter that greatly concerns us both."

The music stopped.

The crowd rumbled its disapproval.

God dipped a handful of coke out of his tribute bucket and sucked it down in one breath. In a piercing falsetto, he asked. "Who dares interrupt God's concert?"

Sing-talking while referring to himself in the third person, that's a good sign. "That would be me. We need to talk."

He continued to sing-talk. "God does not need anything. He is God. God's servants have God's wants well in hand, and what they do not provide, God takes. But it takes balls to interrupt God's concert. Speak, ballsy human."

"I was hoping we could speak in private."

"Very well, God would like a drink." God reached out and plucked him up like a cigarette he'd dropped. His cape blew out behind him, turning into massive leathery wings that bore them into the sky. They flew over the melted chopper and landed on a nearby rooftop.

God shrunk down to human size and flopped into a leather hammock while a teenage girl with the biggest hair and the smallest bikini Max had ever seen rushed him a chilled bottle of Bookers. The little knife sticking out of her G-string covered more skin than the rest of her outfit combined.

God pressed the bottle to his lips and turned it up, taking a third of the bottle in one gulp.

Max cleared his throat. "Do you know what's going on?"

"The break before the encore. Do not waste my time, human."

"You know how things are heating up, getting dark, crime is spiking, all that shit."

"God knows all."

*Why did I think this was a good idea?* "Well, then you know an evil force is slowly devouring the universe. I was hoping you could help me fight it, you being, you know, God."

"What now?" God sat up and spoke normally, really looking at him for the first time.

"It's The Darkness, this elemental—no, more than an elemental force, more like a building block of metaphysics. It's the source of all negativity. Pain, hate and everything else bad is its influence on the world. I'm trying to stop it, but I need all the help I can get. You up for it?"

"Dude, are you serious?" His forked tongue gave him a slight lisp when he wasn't singing.

"Yes."

"That explains a lot." God ran his tongue back and forth between his fangs. "And you're trying to stop it?"

"Yeah." Max tried to do the metal screech, but his voice box nearly imploded.

God laughed at him. "Good luck with that. This world is fucked. I'm gettin' while the gettin's good." He downed his drink and puffed back up.

"Seriously? What kind of shit god just runs out on his followers?"

"Hey man, they started it. I just went along with it. Truth is, everybody from Sirius is like me. We're not gods. We just evolved better." The artist formerly known as God gave him a pitying look then flew toward the stage, trailing a guitar solo behind him. "Attention, everyone! Your world is fucked. Enjoy your unending cornucopia of misery, suckers." A massive swirl of blue appeared behind him and sucked him in.

"Really, that's your reaction? Not even a, so long and thanks for all the coke? Dickhead."

"You made God go away!" The bimbo grunted and hurled her tray like a professional disc golfer. Luckily she was tiny and weak, so it missed him by three feet and twirled to the street below. She drew her knife, accidentally cutting her panty-string. The tiny band of zebra-striped material fluttered down her thigh as she ran.

Max grabbed her wrist and wrestled her to the ground.

Hmm, I thought speed made boners impossible.

He tossed her knife out of reach and tried to soothe her. "Calm down. I didn't make him go. He's just a dick. I came to him for help. You heard me."

"You made God go away!"

"Look, I'm bigger than you. You're not going to hurt me, and I'd rather not hurt you."

"I just made concubine! I was going to receive the sacrament tonight." She struggled with a tenacity only a pissed off teenager can muster.

"I don't have time for this." He looked around for something to tie her up with. There were chains all over the place, but nothing to fasten them with. The only other thing was the hammock.

He dragged her over to it, dumped her inside and tried to yank the support strap loose with his left hand while fending her off with his right. He almost had it when she poked him in the eye with her fingernail. He saw stars and nearly lost his grip on her.

"Okay, fuck this." He grabbed her by the hair and dragged her to the edge of the roof. "Calm down, or fall down." She continued to flail and stomp his toes. With an exasperated gasp, he grabbed her by the ass and flipped her over. He immediately felt bad.

Maybe she'll land head first and her hair will cushion her...

Nope.

Well, that's a fucking waste.

Max rubbed his eye and looked at his hand. "Great. I'm bleeding."

He pulled out his phone and dialed Greystoke. It went straight to voicemail.

"Dammit man, where are you? We have a problem. God flew off like a dick, and the Metists blame me. I'm on a roof about two blocks from an entire city of coked-out cultists whose God has just abandoned them. Oh, and Cat's in there somewhere, tripping her ovaries off. Not my fault. Anyway, if they don't know she's with me she might be safe, but I have no idea how to find her, or get out of the city. One of your magic doors would be really handy right about now. Call me back."

He looked over the edge. The Metists were rioting, running through the streets setting everything on fire with torches and liquor, probably trying to flush him out. The black leather coating on the buildings wasn't enough to mute their screams.

Those fuckers can really project.

A mob was forming around the girl's body. It wasn't long before they looked up.

"Shit."

Max ran to the elevator and found it was already on the way up. He took the door to the stairs and read the sign.

Floor 69.

"I should have had more ice cream."

He ran down the stairs three at a time. Ten floors down, a guy in a spray-painted jean jacket burst through a door and swung a bat at him. Max grabbed the bat and busted him in the sunglasses so hard he landed on his head eight steps down. At the next landing, Max jumped over his body and doubled his speed.

"Come on, gravity." He jumped an entire flight, tripped and hit his head against the wall.

"Oww, fuck you, gravity.

He grabbed the rail to steady himself and continued on. Fifteen floors later he had to take a break. Drugs or no, his legs had had enough.

He slumped in a corner, hugged his bat and listened.

Silence.

Weird. Maybe the building isn't overrun. It'd be funny if that was just some random guy who stayed at work doing angel dust and happened to hear me while in a psychotic rage. Or maybe he's security. Probably security, heard me running, assumed I wasn't supposed to be here. Maybe I'd do better going down slow and quiet.

His breath had mostly returned, so he stood and ambled down another flight.

The sign said, "Floor 43."

Maybe I should try the elevator again. At least I have a bat now. Maybe I could pass myself off as one of them. I doubt anybody got a good look at me. Shit, I should have traded clothes with that guy. I can't really hide, smelling like this.

He glanced up the stairs and shook his head. The only way he was going back up was if a flood of cultists carried him.

 Stupid panic.

He listened at the door for a long time before getting the nerve to open it. When he did, he found an empty lobby. According to the sign above the front desk, this floor was occupied by Aspen, a division of Hellcorps.

"Maybe Heller could get me out of this."

He dialed and Pope answered. "Hello."

"Pope, hey. You at work?"

"Yes."

"I'm in a bit of a pickle, and Greystoke's not picking up."

"That does not make me any less at work."

"No, it's good you're at work. I think Heller might be the only person who can help me. I need a magic door that goes from his Aspen office, that's the company in New York, not the place, to—just about anywhere else. I have a few thousand enraged cultists after me. If I can't get out of here soon, they're going to make me an album cover."

"Holy gherkin, brash man. Let me put you in contact with the house magician. I'm sure he won't mind being dragged out of bed." After a moment of silence, Pope made a thoughtful noise. "He is out of town until Monday. There is a company chopper, though. The keys should be in the top drawer of the receptionist's desk, tag number 23."

Max opened the drawer and grabbed the keys. "I found 'em."

"Do you think you can get to the airport?"

"I don't know. The streets are filled with bloodthirsty headbangers. Any chance there's a droid handy?"

Pope clucked. "Why would there be a droid in an office building?"

"I don't know. I'm used to them being everywhere. Any other mode of transport, a jetpack, hoverboard, web gauntlets, magic fairy wings...?"

"There are Segways in the parking deck."

"Not funny."

"Is too. Look, I don't know what to tell you. New York is on the other side of the country. I sent an email to security asking them to guard you on the way to the airport. That's the best I can do from here."

"You sure Heller can't make me a magic door himself?"

"Heller doesn't do, he orchestrates."

"I have to wade through hundreds of thousands of rioters whose national anthem mentions both demon rape and mummification in razor wire, and the best you can do is get a couple of mall cops to go with me?"

"Yes."

Max growled, hung up and plopped into the receptionist's chair. "What was I thinking, coming here? I've done a lot of stupid, desperate shit, but this time it might actually kill me."

He opened the other drawers and searched for anything that might prove useful. Pencils and shit. A staple puller. Maybe if I was attacked by mice. Eightball of coke, that's worth about as much as a pack of cigarettes here. This bourbon's only eighty proof. He took a couple of quick chugs to calm his nerves and put it back. Ooh, pepper spray. Maybe I'll be attacked by the one fucker who's not too high to feel pain.

He stuck it in his pocket and was about to go digging in one of the offices when he heard a guitar solo. He turned toward the elevator in time to see two guys dressed like the one he'd killed rushing out with baseball bats full of nails.

"You're gonna fuckin' die."

Shit, their bats are scarier than mine.

He barely had time to ask, "You security?" before the big one swung at his head. Max grabbed his arm and used his inertia to flip him into the swing of the other. The nails stuck in the big one's lower back, and Max let him fall, disarming them both.

The little one let out a squeak of surprise and took a step back as Max stomped on the big one's neck. Fear partially dissipated the drug cloud from the little one's eyes. Max pointed his bat at him and asked again, "You security?"

"Y-y-yeah."

Max stepped towards him, and he fell on his ass. "You're supposed to be helping me get out of here."

"You made God abandon us. I'd rather die."

Max took another step and he scuttled backwards into the corner behind reception.

"I didn't make him do shit. He's not God. He's not even a god. He's a stupid dick who ran off because I asked him to help defend the world against the evil that's coming to destroy it. After all you've done for him, he abandoned you without a second thought. It's him you should be mad at. Not me."

Max put his foot on the big one's back, and twisted the bat free. It reminded him of a wet hairbrush. He shook off the blood and slung a crimson rainbow onto the wall. The security guy whimpered, but he didn't move.

Max grabbed the other spiky bat and returned. "You going to help me or not?"

"Fuck you. I'd rather die."

Max raised the bat and stepped forward, sending the security guard into a convulsive fit. He stopped and shook his head. "I'd be doing you a favor. Just stay out of my way."

He pushed the down button on the elevator, and the doors opened. Inside, he pressed L, not breaking eye contact with the security guy until the doors closed.

He pressed his forehead against the doors. *I cannot believe I pulled that off.*

The bats felt good in his hands, like a part of him that he'd been missing all his life. His arms and chest were tight with manliness. He stepped back and flexed a little, posing with his weapons like a little kid.

I might make it home after all. Thanks, meth.

He was still tweaking his battle stance as the doors opened, and another security guard rushed in. Max reflexively brought the bat down on his forehead and kicked the corpse into the five guys behind him. This batch was far less suggestible than the last. They tossed their buddy aside and came at him.

There wasn't much room to swing, or hope of getting past them, so he punched the basement button and beat them back until the doors closed. A few seconds later they opened again. The lights flickered on, revealing a large storage area with fences separating the junk of various companies. Max stepped out cautiously then put a chair in the door to keep the doors from closing.

Now what?

There were no windows or doors. The only way out was a manhole.

"Better than nothing."

He pried it up and gagged.

"Oh God, it smells like diaper bisque."

He pulled his shirt over his nose and used the flashlight on his phone to check the tunnel. The sewage level was low enough that, if he was careful, he could use the grated walkway without permanently damaging his shoes. Still, a Segway would have been nice. He momentarily considered going back up to the parking deck, but decided not to risk it.

Why does it stink so much more than the poop back home?

He set his GPS to guide him to the airport and climbed down. The light on his phone lit the tunnel for about thirty feet ahead of him, but his battery was half gone. He told his GPS to find the airport, synced his retinal implants so the little arrow would appear, then stuck it back in his pocket and let his implants adjust to the dark.

"This was a lot more fun when I had a team of tech-laden soldiers with me."

He followed the prompts south while keeping an eye out for doors that might lead to Iiiteville. He knew there had to be some Iiites around somewhere, but he wasn't sure what to expect from them. Would they be all Metaled out like the normals, or did Iiite culture trump everything else? He spotted a door, but hesitated to open it.

Shit, what about Cat? I can't leave her here, and I can't find her on my own. This is not optional. Just don't think about all the reasons they might want to kill you, or their physical superiority, how you don't have a gun, or—I shouldn't give pep talks.

He took a deep breath, choked and stepped through the door into a long empty hallway. It looked the same as the buffer zones back home, but green, sparser, and with more graffiti. There were lights and plug-in air fresheners every few feet, but not much else. The carpet was the long-term kind that looked shitty, but didn't mildew as fast.

He continued south until he came to another door and found a hall identical to the one he was in, except it smelled better.

They probably layered the buffer zones to combat the extra stink.

He followed his nose through several similar doors and down several similar halls and eventually came to the suburbs, or rather what used to be suburbs. It was his first time seeing an Iiite shithole. He didn't even know there was such a thing. Aside from being a shithole, everything looked normal.

At least they aren't metal themed.

Max stepped over a slumped hobo as cautiously as he might a zombie. He could hear noises of delinquency echoing from the direction he was heading, so he took a right into a more populated area.

Pawn shop, massage parlor, planned parenthood, employment agency. Wow, I really hit the jackpot.

He quickened his pace, hoping he would make it to a nicer area before he was spotted, but the ghetto rolled on forever. Music clattered from a dingy little bar, fast and angry, with a good beat. It was probably the meth, but Max couldn't resist going in.

Inside was dark, and the acoustics were terrible. The band sounded better outside. Three bare light bulbs dangled from holes in the ceiling above the bar in a fifty-foot room with walls so full of staples you couldn't read the tags anymore. Here and there he saw black and white posters advertising shows for bands like Pickled

Sputum or Coat Hanger and the Necktie Suicides. Against the left wall, a band was playing on a six-inch high stage for eight kids who were all jerking around like they thought dancing hard enough might turn the world beautiful. The smells of piss and cheap beer intermingled to the extent it was impossible to tell them apart.

Max smiled.

This is my kind of place.

The good life was nice, but he always felt out of place. He liked the gutter. He always knew where he was in the gutter.

Something familiar caught his eye over by the bathroom. It was a poster for a show the following night with a logo of two arms fist bumping.

"Chemical Compound? I didn't think they were big enough to tour this far."

He pulled out his phone and looked for the number Charlie had given him. Unfortunately, he had completely forgotten the guy's name. Even if he had remembered to program the number into his phone, the chances of him finding it was next to none.

Stupid auto-import technology. I added like five of these people.

He approached the bartender, who was sitting on the well with his back to the room, playing a game on his own. He didn't notice Max until his mission failed. He turned around and they shared a look of astonishment.

"Max?"

It's the guy!

"Hey."

"Dude, it's Charlie. You remember me?"

"Of course. You saved my life. When was that, a week ago, a month? So much has been happening lately I can't keep track."

Charlie smiled nervously, like he could recite the number of seconds that had passed, but knew better.

Max smiled back. "I saw your flier over there. I was going to call you, but I seem to have lost your number."

"You want a nudge?"

"Sure."

They pressed the proper buttons and touched their phones together linking, friending, following, and otherwise consummating their friendship for all the interwebs to see.

Charlie was so happy his voice shook as he asked, "What are you doing here?"

"Trying to avoid death. You know, the usual. How about you? Could I..." He made the universal sign for "give me a beer."

Charlie snatched a beer out of the icy water, popped the top and handed it to him. "On the house."

"Your boss doesn't mind?"

"This is my cousin's place. I'm covering for him while he's on vacation. My band's playing here tomorrow. You should check us out."

"I'd love to, but I really need to get back home. Thing is, I'm kind of trapped here. It's a long story, but my transportation's gone, my girlfriend is lost on the surface, and all the Metists want me dead. I kind of made their God forsake them."

Charlie laughed. "You what?"

"Like I said, long story. I'd fill you in, but my stopping in here is a short break in the latest of a long procession of huge life-or-death crises. Sometimes I wonder if I was a terrible person in a previous life and my punishment was to be reincarnated in some stupid sadist's art project. If I wasn't a sociopath, the last few months would have driven me bat-shit crazy."

Charlie's eyes registered disappointment and a little disgust. "Buck up, dude. Your life is interesting."

Max took a big sip of his beer. "Maybe I pissed off a Chinese gypsy."

Charlie leaned over the bar. "How can I help?"

"Thanks, but you don't want to get involved. I have to find one person in a city-wide riot of bloodthirsty drug-fiends. Then I have to get home and stop the world from being swallowed by evil."

Charlie chuckled. "Relax, man. The underground is a strong, tightly knit community. We got ya covered."

"Would you believe me if I told you I was hand-picked by an obscure goddess to fight a badness so huge and old it eats entire realities?"

"Haven't we all?"

Wait, what the fuck am I doing turning down help? I know I'm going to regret this, but at least I'll have a chance to live that long. "Where is the rest of your band?"

"I don't know. Doin' the tourist thing, I guess. But screw them. Those guys are lucky if they can make a frozen pizza without losing a thumb. I'm talkin' bout the Niites. My cousin's the head of the New York Chapter. I got all his contacts. If you'll watch the bar for a minute, I'll go to make some calls."

Max nodded gratefully.

"Enjoy the show. These guys are local, but I'd put 'em up against anybody."

Max nodded. He walked behind the bar while Charlie went up the stairs by the bathrooms. The bottom shelf held a bat full of nails. *Maybe that's a New York thing?* There was a little metal plate on the base that said, "The Manager." The rest of the wall was four shelves of bottom-shelf booze. He'd bet money they were watered down, but then this wasn't the type of place you drank liquor.

The band was great. They had the rawness and conviction of Minor Threat, the intelligent snarkiness of Dead Kennedys, and the technical ability of a good metal band. He didn't see a merch table, but made a mental note to get their name.

The show ended with the lead singer locking arms with one of his fans and spinning so fast that, when he let go, he ran head first into the stack of amps. Max wasn't sure if he had done it on purpose, but it the most authentic artistic display he'd seen in years, possibly ever, and definitely in person. He liked it here. If it wouldn't mean the end of the universe, he'd probably stay a while.

The dancers laughed, hooted, and high fived each other while the drummer, a skeletal teenager with a spider tattoo peeking out from his grimy wifebeater, nudged the singer with his shoe. The singer rolled over and sat up. Blood poured from his hairline, trickling down his bare chest to soak into the band of his underwear. He smiled like a man who'd put in a good day's work, sprang to his feet and made for the bar.

The drummer sneered. "Russ! The fuck are you goin'?"

"Where's it look like I'm goin'?"

"It looks like you're going away from the shit we gotta break down."

The singer screamed, "I'll help you in a fuckin' minute! I got fluids to replenish."

The rest of the band shared looks of annoyance with the dancers. The girl whose head was shaved except for blue pigtails looked the maddest. Max judged her to be about fifteen, but everything about her radiated ferocity. Her black T-Shirt was cut off just below her jail bait and said, "What I don't fuck, I eat" in drippy red letters. Her silence made her crush on the singer as obvious as the one the drummer had on her.

Ahh, youth.

Russ cocked his head and looked Max over. "The fuck are you?"

Max cocked an eyebrow and handed him a beer.

The singer poured it down his throat and motioned for another. "Let me get some for those assholes too."

Max put four beers on the bar and popped the tops, but Blue Hair darted over and snatched them before he could pick them up. "Thanks."

Russ pursed his lips and gestured for another round.

Max wasn't sure how alcohol laws worked in the sewer, but he didn't want to get Charlie's bar shut down. "I should probably see some I.D."

Blue Hair dropped two of the beers and threw one of the others at his head. He ducked and the beer exploded behind him, taking a bottle of cheap bourbon with it. "There's your fucking I.D."

Max's back was soaked, and his hair was dripping with foam, but he couldn't help being turned on.

Russ waved his finger disapprovingly. "He's right. You're obviously too young to be trusted with alcohol."

She snatched one of the half-empty bottles at her feet and hurled it at Russ. It flew past his head and skittered to the far wall. "Shut up, and get your fucking band out of my way."

"Or what?"

"Or I'll shove that mic stand up your ass and make picks out of your nipples."

Russ strode slowly toward her. "I like your spunk. Let me know when you hit puberty, and I'll give you some of mine."

She kicked him in the balls, then kneed him in the teeth as he fell forward. His scrawny chest splatted in the puddle a millisecond before the backlash slammed his face into the concrete floor. Blood was pouring out so fast it pushed the beer away rather than mixing with it.

It was an impressive display, but Max didn't want to lose street cred by acknowledging it, so he leaned against the wall and said. "Get a room, you two, geez." Beer squished out of his shirt and ran down his crack. He stepped away and scrutinized his soppy silhouette.

I don't think this is what Charlie meant when he said watch the bar.

Before Russ could get up, the drummer grabbed him by the neck and dragged him to the stage. "Quit fucking around and help us pack up."

When he was let go, he pushed himself up, slurred, "Fuck you, Grant." and then passed out, smacking his face yet again.

Two other girls, a little older and a lot less cute than Blue Hair, ran over and high-fived her. The short one, who looked like a cross between Patti Smith and Lou Reed, slapped her on the ass. "Woo! Thora for the win."

The taller one looked like a pissed-off American Indian version of Helen Hunt. She punched the short one in the nose. "What did I tell you about being handsy?"

Drops of blood fell from shorty's right nostril and soaked into her Crass shirt. She laughed and wrapped her arms around the tall one's waist. "Come on, baby, you know you're my girl."

Baby grabbed her wrists and peeled her off. "No, you're *my* girl, and if you don't stop groping every chick who gets closer than five feet, you're gonna be a *dead* girl. Get me a beer."

Shorty pinched her girlfriend's nipple the way an old person steals a nose. "Sure thing, darlin'." She scampered over to Max and raised two fingers.

He popped two more beers and handed them over.

"Where do I know you from?"

"The news, probably."

Recognition struck her face like a flying gerbil. "Wait, you're that guy, the one that blowed up the M.I.L.F." She waved to her friends. "Hey, get over here. This guy's famous."

Sweat prickled Max's back as they approached.

"This here's Thora and Sinnah. They call me Shorty."

Sinnah furrowed her brow. "You really famous?"

Shorty elbowed her in the stomach. "Look at 'im. That's Max—something. I forgot his name, but he's, you know, that revolutionary guy."

Thora nodded. "Oh, yeah. I think you're right. What the fuck are you doing here?"

"I'm just watching the bar for Charlie. He's making some calls for me."

Sinnah looked suspicious. "You sure that's really him?"

Max pointed at their beers. "That round's on the house if you promise not to make a big deal about it."

Thora set her beer on the bar. "What kind of calls? Is something going down?"

"You could say that."

"Cool! Are you gonna blow stuff up? Can I watch? Can I help?"

"No, I mean, I don't know. Maybe. Probably not. I need to find my girlfriend and get out of the city."

The girls looked disappointed.

Sinnah put her arms around the other two's shoulders. "Sounds boring. You wanna start setting up?"

Max smirked. "You should probably do that. God just abandoned his followers, so they're all rioty. If she's still alive, finding her's going to be next to impossible."

The mention of violence gave them all girl-boners.

"Fuck the gig." Thora jerked away from her friend and pressed herself against the bar. "I've dreamed of being in a riot since I was like, six."

"Shit yeah. What's your girl look like? Is she cute?"

Sinnah stomped on Shorty's toe. "You just want to be able to say you have a famous person's crotch rot. Does sound like fun, though."

Max cocked an eyebrow. "Why is everybody down here so fucking helpful—and bloodthirsty?"

The office door popped open and Charlie jogged down the steps waving a tablet. "Dude, I found her!"

"What? How? You don't even know what she looks like."

"It was easy. I just found a pic of you two online then uploaded her face to the biometric scanners. This is NYC, dude, cameras everywhere. There is this, though." He held up the tablet and pointed to Cat. She was naked and lapping at a puddle around a fire hydrant, seemingly oblivious to the chaos around her.

"She's on a lot of acid. Not that she needs an excuse for that sort of thing. Cat is, shall we say, orally adventurous."

Charlie chuckled and scratched his upper lip. "Takes all kinds, man." He pulled up a map of the city and pointed to West 34th Street near Tenth Avenue. "She's right here, and we are," he slid the map with his finger and pointed to the intersection of Fifth Avenue and 42nd Street, "here. It's a straighter shot traveling underground, but the nearest surface exit is three blocks up, and three blocks is a long way to go in a riot. I have some friends on the way to pick her up. They're big dudes, so they shouldn't have any problems. We can meet up at this manhole and get you both out of the city using the Underground Railroad. It's not the most comfortable, but it's cheap and close. Sound good?"

Max didn't know what to say. It had been ages since he'd been able to relax and let somebody else come up with a plan. "Why are you a bartender?"

Charlie's eyes glazed, but he tried to play it cool. "I'm an artist, and art pays squat."

"Yeah, but when this is over we should talk, assuming we're not dead. I'm sure I can find you a part time gig that pays better than selling malts to miscreants."

Grant came over. "Hey, what's goin on?"

Sinnah grinned. "Show's cancelled on a count'a riot."

Grant looked understandably confused, so Thora added, "We're gonna help this famous guy rescue his trippin' girlfriend."

He ran his palm over his clean-shaven scalp, squeegeeing away a healthy quantity of sweat. "Why?"

Shorty chimed in, "Because it's adventure time, bitch. You wanna come?"

He shot Max a look of incredulous disgust. "You know Thora's fifteen, right?"

I guess bringing a fifteen-year-old to a riot is a tad on the irresponsible side.

Before he could respond, Thora had pushed Grant down. "Age is just a number, asshole." She kicked him in the leg. "You're not my fucking dad."

Sinnah kicked him too, but playfully. "Yeah, what kind of punk are you? Ageism isn't cool."

Grant punched at her shin, but missed. "Fine, whatever, but I'm coming too."

Aww, he wants to protect her even though she's obviously not interested.

He wasn't in a position to turn down help, but Iiites or no, he knew it was pretty messed up to put a bunch of kids in harm's way. On the other hand, these kids were no younger than the ones he'd mass-murdered on his first raid. They were obviously not opposed to violence, and who was he to impose his concept of age-appropriate activity on a group of strangers?

Charlie helped him to his feet. "Don't worry, man. Some friends are bringing the girl to us. We're just going to escort Max to the pickup and then to the Underground Railroad."

Thora kicked him in the knee. "Speak for yourself. I'm gonna riot."

Grant shot Max another hateful look.

"Hey, it's Charlie's plan. I appreciate all the help I can get, but I'm not making anybody do anything. That said," Max raised his voice so the whole bar could hear him, "anybody else want to help rescue my girlfriend? Any takers? There's threat of bodily harm."

A little over half the bar flipped him off. The rest ignored him.

Max snatched the bat off its pedestal. "All right, then, let's go not get killed."

Charlie and the girls ran for the door like excited children, but Grant walked more slowly, pacing Max. "If she gets hurt, I'm going to kill you. You know that, right?"

✳✳✳✳✳

Twenty minutes later, Max and the miscreants were at the manhole, but Cat was not.

"Where the fuck are your friends?"

"I don't know, man. Nobody's picking up." Charlie connected to the Biometric Surveillance System and scanned for Cat again. "Oh, what the fuck?"

Max snatched the tablet away from him. "Ah, shit. Not this again."

Droolers ran in and out of frame in a crazed frolic as they chased down and mutilated anything that moved. It was way worse than the last time. In one frame, he saw two guys with spiky bats taking turns hitting each other in the crotch, a group of children tearing a dog apart, two different rapes, and one guy doing a header on himself.

The buildings and cars were on fire. In the midst of all that carnage, Cat was dancing and singing, wearing a large intestine like a boa. It circled her throat and her left breast, but the other end was raised and striking at anyone who came too close.

"Dude, what do you mean, this again? You've seen this before? It looks like a Clive Barker zombie porno up there."

A Mohawked Iiite ran across the screen dragging a woman by her foot. When he was almost out of the shot, he hurled her through the window of a burning codpiece shop then ran back the other direction.

"Yeah, see, I wasn't joking about the soul-eating monster thing. The Darkness invades reality turning everything it comes across into its most negative, murdery form."

Sinnah smirked. "You're tellin' us New York City* is overrun with deadites?"

"Pretty much."

"And you're serious."

"Yep."

"Awesome!"

Charlie stared at her in disbelief. "Are we looking at the same image?"

Thora explained. "This is better than a riot. The possessed don't narc."

Grant pointed at the manhole cover. "That's blood dripping through those holes. No way in hell are we going up there."

Charlie shook his head. "How do you fight it?"

"I'm still trying to figure that out. I came here to ask God for help, but when he heard what was going on, he said he wasn't really a God and then ran like a bitch."

"Can those people be saved, like if they get out of range, or something?"

"I don't know. Never thought about it. I hope so, for Cat's sake."

Grant furrowed his brow. "You aren't seriously considering going up there? Your chick's one of them now."

"I don't think so. She's not attacking anybody or drooling. The infected usually drool a lot."

"Yeah, but..." Charlie pointed at the intestines around her neck."

"I know how it looks. If it was anybody else I'd agree, but that's just how she is."

Sinnah smiled. "She's my kind'a chick. Let's go get her."

Grant roared. "What the fuck is wrong with you people? Wouldn't going up there mean getting infected like everybody else?"

"You guys probably would, but not me. The Darkness is sort of saving me for dessert. It likes to fuck with me. I'm pretty sure that's why Cat isn't infected. She's bait."

Grant deflated a little bit. "So you're going to handle this yourself, right?"

"I don't know what good any of you could do."

Thora scrunched up her face. "Fuck that. I'm going up."

Before anyone knew what was happening she had scampered up the ladder and punched the manhole cover out of place.

"Let's rage!" She thrust herself through the hole.

Grant ran after her.

Max snatched the tablet away from Charlie. "This is not good. You should run now."

On the screen, Thora pulled the intestines off Cat and dragged her toward the manhole. She didn't seem infected, but Max wasn't getting his hopes up.

"Nah, man, I came to help."

"Seriously, you should get somewhere safe. I'm nowhere near lucky enough for this to work, and you don't even have a weapon."

"She's almost back, anyway."

Everyone crowded around the screen watching Thora drag Cat toward the manhole. Grant was still on the ladder screaming and gesturing furiously for her to hurry. They were about five feet away when one of the bodies grabbed Thora's ankle. She was running so fast the body came with her, but she lost her balance and skidded to the manhole.

"Fuck!" Grant lifted her face. "Are you okay?"

Cat went back to dancing.

Max shifted his eyes to the ladder. "Check her once she's down here. And grab Cat. What the fuck are you waiting for?"

There was a growl, a short scream and a gurgle, then Grant fell, splashing Sinnah with his neck-geyser.

Sinnah shrieked and jumped back. "Not fucking cool!"

His head landed a few seconds later.

"I fucking told you."

Charlie froze, except for his trembling beard.

Something else hit the ground near the ladder. Max looked over in time to see another smaller glob splat near the drummer's feet.

"Shit."

Thora tore down the ladder face-first like a giant, rabid squirrel. The Iiites screamed as the lights flickered and dimmed. The Darkness was coming with her.

"Run!" Max grabbed Charlie and propelled him down the hall away from the trio of slobbering teens.

Max swung "the Manager" and Thora's cranium splashed like a water balloon. The other two ran toward him, gurgling yogurt and screaming with untempered rage. He kicked Shorty in the stomach and took a swing at Sinnah. One of the nails caught her cheek and ripped the right side of her jaw free from her skull. She wasn't fazed.

Max pulled back, but they kept coming, scrambling towards him like animals. He kicked Shorty in the head and heard a crack. Her head drooped awkwardly. She fell, but continued to crawl toward him.

Sinnah tackled him and tried to stick her fingers in his eyes. He grabbed her hands, but he couldn't get her off him. She was screaming white stuff onto his face. It tasted like the inside of a snack cake that been stored in a box of Laundry detergent. Shorty was trying to bite him, but her neck was broken. All she could do was drag her head across, snapping hopefully and smearing him with more white glop.

He heard footsteps running up behind him. Sinnah's head exploded, and she flopped over to his left. Charlie brought a lamp down on Shorty's head, which bounced and jiggled like a tetherball.

Max twisted to his feet and swung a homerun. Bits of Shorty's skull ricocheted down the adjacent hall. Panting, he turned to his friend. "You don't listen too good."

"You're welcome."

"Thanks, but I don't know how much longer you can be here without turning evil."

"I feel fine. You know, aside from having just killed a few of my friends. Shit. We killed the Menstruals."

"Get out of here, man. The more you think about what just happened, the more likely it is to happen to you." Max checked the screen and saw Cat was still pretty close to the manhole. He ran to the ladder and climbed high enough to call to Cat without being seen.

"Cat! Cat, get over here." He watched her spin around on the little screen. "Cat, it's me. I'm right below you in the sewers, come down here."

She walked over to the hole and waved at him. "Where ya been?"

"Looking for you. Now, come on. It's not safe up there."

She looked around like she didn't know what he was talking about.

"Trust me."

She shrugged and hopped into the hole, breaking his nose with her crotch. He lost his grip and landed on his back.

"Oww, my knees." She rubbed them with her palms, grinding her pelvis into his smooshed smeller. "Kiss 'em, make em better."

Max twisted free and sneezed until he was lightheaded from blood loss. He pinched his nose and asked, "Can we please leave this anal wart of a city now?"

Charlie nodded to the left. "The Underground Railroad is a few blocks that way. We should hurry."

"Yeah, I'd rather not be stuck on a train with a bunch of them." He grabbed Cat and examined her while she tried to unzip his pants.

"Don't forget to pick up the ice cream."

Charlie grabbed the ladder and began to climb.

Max grabbed the seat of his pants. "What the fuck are you doin?"

"Making sure they don't come after us."

"You're exposing yourself to the badness and drawing attention. Fuck that." Max picked Cat up and slung her over his shoulders. "Lead the way."

Charlie gave a sideways nod and took off down the passage. He led them through several corridors and down some stairs to a rail station where they used his pass card to board the nearest car heading East. It was late enough the only people riding were drunks, hobos, and thugs, none of whom were up to messing with a guy ballsy enough to use public transport while dripping with gore and carrying a naked chick.

Max gave the gawkers his best creepy smile and plopped down onto the blue plastic bench. His clothes made the sound of a wet sponge dropped into a sink. He pulled Cat down beside him and patted her thigh. "How are you doing?"

"Best date ever!"

Charlie got a strange look on his face and turned white. He wrapped both hands around the support pole, hung his head and vomited a handful of gritty beer onto his shoes.

The train lurched forward.

Charlie breathed a sigh of relief and wiped his lips with his blood-streaked palm. "I think we made it."

Max forced a smile and averted his eyes.

"We did make it, right?"

"I wish it was that simple. This is happening all over the place. For all we know, the next platform's already been infected. Even if we make it back to Castle Greystoke, it's only a matter of time before the infection spreads there too. This trip was a disastrous waste of time."

"Don't be so down on yourself, man. You saved your girlfriend, and I'd have probably died back there, too, if it wasn't for you."

"If it wasn't for me, the city might not have been infected in the first place. I'm the reason their God left, and the riot I caused was the door The Darkness came in through." He paused to grind his teeth. "Every single time I try to do something good, The Darkness shows up and turns it into an Andreas Schnass film. Maybe it's me. Maybe I'm like Edgar Allan Poe, but epic. The best thing I could do to help the world is die."

"Nah, man…"

"Shut up, Charlie."

"Dude."

"I appreciate all your help, but please shut the fuck up."

# TO CAST A DEADLY FAIL

After the initial nightmare of figuring out where they were and what trains would take them home, the trip had been refreshingly boring. Over the eighteen-hour trip, Max managed around five hours of tortured broken sleep. Charlie said he'd never sleep again, so he took guard duty. For a man in shock, he did a pretty solid job. Max was only peed on twice, and one of those was Cat.

Max was close to falling asleep for the sixty-seventh time when the train squealed into the K-234 station.

Charlie grabbed Max's shoulder and shook him gently. "Dude, we're here."

"Let the octopus answer itself." Max tried to roll over and snuggle deeper into the hard plastic bench.

"Come on, Max. You have to get up."

"Hamburgers!"

The doors slid open and Cat wandered onto the platform. "Dude, your girlfriend is naked and all alone out there."

Max refused to acknowledge him.

"If you stay on this train, you'll end up in Mexico. Get up!" He grabbed Max's foot and dragged him onto the floor.

"Ouch, fuck! What the hell?"

"We're here. Come on."

Max pushed himself to his feet, shook off as much of the hobo fluid as he could, then stepped out the door. Cat was arguing with one of the five I-Force guys about whether or not she had to put on the clothes they'd brought.

*Why did I have to quit smoking?* Max swished some spit around his mouth and swallowed as much morning breath as possible. "Put it on."

"I don't like this jumpsuit. It gives me mom-ass." She let out a twenty-second fart, stood with arms akimbo and popped her lower back, unleashing several smaller gusts.

Two of the I-Force guys laughed, two looked disgusted, and one cracked a pervy smile. Max put his hand on the small of her back and made threatening eye contact with each of them. "Pregnancy couldn't give you mom-ass. Just put it on so we can go get some coffee."

Cat pouted and snatched the jumpsuit out of the agent's hand.

Charlie laughed.

"What's funny?"

"You know, you wanting coffee."

"How so?"

"You're crashing off a meth high. You can't seriously want coffee."

"There is nothing more serious than my need for coffee."

Two of the agents helped Cat into her clothes, both "accidentally" touching her as often as possible.

"Screw coffee. You need some rest, dude. We all do."

"Sleep is a lie my enemies made up to torture me with false hope."

"You look like an owl pellet that got run over by a car."

"Well, I feel worse, so huzzah for facades. Give me a shower and some caffeine, and I'll be back to looking like an undisturbed pile of cat shit." He swooned, but regained his composure before he fell down. "If I don't have a gallon of sweet life-giving fluid swirling through my guts in the next ten minutes, I'm going feral!"

The pervy one said. "There's an espresso machine in the limo, sir."

"That'll do until we get home. You're on caffeination duty. Run ahead and get it started. Keep them coming all the way home, and call ahead so there will be coffee when we get back. I want at least enough to swim in."

Agent Perv saluted, then jogged up the steps to the surface.

Charlie looked concerned. "That's not good for your heart, man."

"If my ticker goes boom, I'll buy another. I'm rich now." Max ambled toward the steps, and everyone else followed.

The surface stank of festering meat and car exhaust. Filmy air broke through his defensive line of blood, piss and vomit like a ghostly quarterback, piling sweet tones of curling putrefaction onto the devil's orgy in his sinuses.

It was 12:10 in the afternoon, but looked like eight o'clock at night. Pedestrians all seemed to be rushing away rather than toward anything.

The city's on the verge. All it'll take is one server getting an order wrong, and it'll be New York all over again.

"Fuck."

He ducked into the limo.

Happy thoughts Happy thoughts. Happy thoughts.

Charlie put his hand on the top of the limo and stuck his head in. "I need to check on some friends. I'll catch up with you later."

"What the hell, man? I need you, and it's not safe out there."

"I'll be fine. The Darkness didn't take me before."

Agent Perv handed Max a coffee cup half-full of espresso. "Whatever, I'm too tired to argue. Good luck." Max downed it in one gulp and shut the door. "Anybody have any anti-depressants?"

They responded with an array of quizzical looks.

"I'm serious."

Everyone shook their head or shrugged.

Max accepted another cup of espresso and poured it down his throat. "Why aren't we moving?"

Perv spoke into his wrist, and the limo pulled into traffic.

Max dialed Emma. Hedorah picked up on the third ring. "Hey, I thought you'd forgotten about us."

"Yeah, sorry I haven't been in touch. You wouldn't believe the shit I've had to deal with lately."

"You might be surprised. A bunch of Jengists near my grandmother's house ran low on materials, so they started using people. They were wrapping them in plastic sheeting to keep them straight, then stacking them along with everything else. They claimed the whole neighborhood, got Emma and her grandmother. I had to pull them out with a droid."

"Damn. That's—I don't know what that is."

"I'm just glad they were near the top."

"Yeah, me too." The image of a giant tower of stacked humans collapsing reminded him of the day they took down the Fist. All those faces screaming. "What's up with the Nrrd herd?"

"Magog went crazy a couple of days ago. He's sedated for the most part, but we wake him up every few hours to do tests. Higher brain function has been shut down completely, his R-complex is on fire and his peptides are all out of whack. We're trying to filter out some of the Vasopressin, but it's not working. His basal ganglia are growing, applying extra pressure to—"

"That's all very interesting, but there's something else I need to talk to you about."

"What?" He sounded irritated.

"The thing causing all this is the same as what took over Witches 'R' Us."

"Are you just now figuring that out?"

"No. Look, it's getting stronger. If we let it get as bad here as it was there, we're fucked."

Something red and head-sized splatted against his window.

"What do you want me to do?"

"This thing feeds on negativity. We have to calm people down by any means necessary. Do you have any kind of super anti-depressant, something that could chill out the whole city?"

"Hmm, maybe. Feelgood has been studying the theory that the 528Hz frequency promotes healing and feelings of love. I could have him hack into the national broadcasting system and add a buzz."

Max took another gulp of espresso. "Will it work?"

"I doubt it. Frequencies can affect the brain, but this thing, whatever it is, is changing the vibrations of the earth. It'll be like trying to listen to smooth jazz on your phone at a Slayers of Babies concert."

"Try it anyway. Anything you can think of that could distract people from the craziness, make them happy, peaceful, whatever—do it. Take to the streets handing out ecstasy. Talk beautiful people into walking around naked. Give sexual favors to strangers. Buy the world a waffle. I don't know."

Cat raised her hand, but didn't wait to be called. "Make the whole city smell like fresh-baked cinnamon rolls."

"Pump comforting smells into the air."

Hedorah laughed. "If we're all going to die, we might as well go out with our lungs full of cookies. I'll dig around and see what I can do." Max heard the scratching of facial hair on the receiver and the flick of a lighter. "You ever feel like we were better off when all they had to worry about was a vindictive shadow government?"

The limo jerked. Max felt something meaty crunch beneath the wheel.

"Hey, I just wanted to watch TV, drink craft beer and eat tacos, but you guys were all like, 'Hey, come save the world from the big scary monsters. It's your destiny. You don't have a choice.' Bunch a bullshit."

"Maybe you should let us nail you to something. It's worked before."

"At least I'd know what was going on."

Hedorah snorted. "Nice hearing from you, Max." He hung up.

"Dick."

Max put his phone away and peered around the flaking blood on the window. They were in I-district. Everything looked green and peaceful as they approached Castle Greystoke, but the number of police had doubled.

The limo passed the main entrance, went up the hill and around to the secret cave entrance. Max cast his eyes to the floor. He wasn't willing to bet his life that Ernie was sitting on his shoulder again.

Where's that fat bastard been lately? He could have magicked me back home and let me get some sleep.

Max could feel the symbols nagging him, each letter a loose tooth begging to be wiggled. He squeezed his eyes shut and buried his face in his hands, but the deeper they went, the stronger the impulse grew. He focused on the pain in his stomach. He'd developed a weird, constant pressure in the lower left side of his abdomen days ago, but hadn't had time to think about until now.

I can't remember the last time I pooped. It's probably a stupid stress reaction—or bowel cancer.

Cat passed him another cup of espresso, which he gulped down gratefully. His stomach gurgled, shooting acid up the back of his throat. Things were in motion, now. That lump would be gone soon, but hopefully not before he made it to the bathroom.

When the limo pulled up to the secret door, Max was the first one out. He waddled over, punched the hidden panel, then ran for the bathroom. His feet left the ground as he was sucked in by a strong wind, which swirled furiously around Greystoke, who was chanting in the center of a large pentagram. Inside the circle, the floor was littered with various inanimate and post-animate objects. Outside was a tornado of first editions and priceless artifacts.

Greystoke stopped his chanting and screamed, "Get inside the circle."

"In a minute." Max snatched at the door knob every time he flew by. On his fourth attempt, his fingers caught in the ornate brass handle. He grabbed the lion's face carved into the door and hoisted himself halfway inside. He grabbed the toilet paper dispenser, kicked off his shoes and pulled the door closed with his toes. He was on the toilet with his pants around his ankles before all the muscles he'd pulled had a chance to complain.

The toilet's monitor lit up and smiled at him. "Greetings, Master Quick, what do you have for me today?"

Stravinsky's Firebird pranced awkwardly out of the speakers like a drunken goblin in a tuxedo. Seconds later he felt so light he could float. Greystoke was still screaming, so Max turned up the volume, leaned back, closed his eyes and listened to the music.

Mmm, I wonder if I could take a little nap while I finished up.

His bowels answered with a series of quotes from Krumpps movies. Max hated those movies almost as much as he did their fans. He flushed the toilet to cut down on the smell.

The caffeine had his muscles humming, but his head was miles away, brimming with jagged, nondescript thoughts that jostled for room like amoebas in a Petri dish.

Greystoke stopped screaming. A moment later there was a knock at the door.

Max lifted his head and groaned. "I'm busy."

The Count shouted through the door. "Do you know how far you've set me back?"

"I didn't do anything."

"Twenty hours. I have literally spent every moment since you left preparing for this ritual and you burst in seconds after it began to work."

"Can we talk about this later?"

"No, we bloody well cannot."

"All I did was walk through the room. If you wanted privacy, why didn't you rout the limo to the front door?"

Greystoke stomped away and slammed open the door to the parking deck. Max couldn't make out what was being screamed, but it sounded like the Count's rage had been redirected to one of the security guys.

Cat scratched at the door. "Maaax. Let me in."

No way in hell I'm making that mistake again.

"Be a good Cat and go check on my coffee for me?"

"Let me in!"

"No. I need this."

The door handle rattled like she was doing something to it.

"What are you doing?"

The door popped open, Cat pulled down her pants and straddled him. "I need this too."

He rested his head on her chest while she peed through his legs. The warm sprinkle trickled down his scrotum soothing his cold contracted flesh. He was too tired to care about anything anymore.

The caffeine had turned to energy, but rather than fueling him, it had broken free to ravage his nervous system like chain lightning in a house of mirrors. His chest was shivering, his arms twitching, and his teeth were rattling despite his jaws being clenched. His mortality had never been more apparent, but swaddled in Cat's flesh wasn't a bad way to go. She was soft and warm. He felt loved. He could feel himself slipping away, into what form of oblivion he didn't know or care.

"Ye Gods!" Greystoke's white lambskin gloves slapped against the marble floor. "The world is about to end and you two are—I don't even want to know what you're doing. Put your bloody clothes on and get out here this instant. He slammed the door.

So much for that.

He pulled his head out of her cleavage. Her eyes were soft and moist. She looked embarrassed.

He wanted to say something sweet to comfort her, but he could never think of those kinds of words. He craned his neck to kiss her, but got a nostril full of tongue instead.

There's the Cat I know.

He tangled his fingers in her hair and pulled her away. She smiled like they'd just hidden the body of her abusive uncle, slapped him in the face, and scampered out of the room.

She's so fucking cute.

He rinsed his crotch with the retractable sprayer then flushed and rinsed.

"Max!" Greystoke's mood was not improving.

Max responded in a cool, even tone. "Your attitude is only making your enemy stronger. I don't know if it's The Darkness or the sleep deprivation, but I'm pretty sure if you scream at me one more time I'm going to pull out your eyes and stuff the sockets with used condoms full of broken glass."

...

That's what I thought.

Max wiped, pulled up his pants and joined them in the study. "What the hell was that, anyway?"

Greystoke tossed back two fingers of a Scotch he had once screamed at Max for sipping too fast. "I was creating a doorway to a plane that I hope will cancel some of The Darkness's energy."

"You tried to summon Furry Pals, didn't you?"

Greystoke frowned. "A flashlight will cut a hole in the dark. I believe that the same principle could apply to intelligent energy. The sudden change created an energy storm. I was protected by a magic circle, but you two just came very close to being disintegrated."

"So why are you doing this inside your house?"

Greystoke paused to stare at a drift of magic thingamajigs. "I need to rest. As do we all."

"That would be awesome, but I'm afraid I might wake up on a Bio-Shoggoth, next to a cenobite." Max rubbed his face and realized he'd grown a short beard. He hadn't had a chance to shave since before he met the Holy.

Max shook his head violently, trying to focus. His sinuses tingled like he'd done a line of pepper, but he couldn't quite sneeze. "I have to call Al and see what the Iiites can do to chill the people out. You need to open that doorway, outside this time. Gulik said I need to talk to my spirit llama. We need to find Hawk and perform an exorcism. Plus, I need to placate Cheeky and apologize for not getting him a souvenir."

Greystoke shook his head. "One cannot bring order to chaos while in a state of delirium."

"Were you not listening just now?"

Greystoke turned to the head of security. "Help my friend to his bedroom."

The guard nodded to one of his subordinates, who pulled out his weapon and shot a dart into Max's thigh.

"Hey, what the fuck, man?!"

Cat popped her thigh with two fingers the way junkies do on TV. Greystoke nodded and the guard complied.

Max felt seasick. The caffeine and the sedative were playing tug of war with his mind. "You've just killed us all."

The caffeine slipped, and Max plunged face first into a muddy puddle of unconsciousness.

# LONG NIGHT OF FLUFFY DOLLS

There it was, The Darkness, personified in drippy tentacled wrath. Its black, veiny wings blotted out the sun as skyscrapers crumbled like teeth in its wake. Its shape was vaguely human, with a massive torso and spindly limbs that made it also vaguely spider-shaped. Countless eyes bobbed in its black oleaginous flesh to fix Max in its jaundiced stare, then pop out and be sucked back like a piece of spaghetti in an endless cycle of swallowing and regurgitation.

It stomped a bookstore. Dull white teeth pushed through the blackness, grinning.

Max, inside his giant snugglebear, gnashed its felty palate and let rip a tremendous happy noise, shattering windows for miles around. Finally able to breathe freely, the building's bricks softened into gingerbread with buttercream grout and gumdrop gargoyles.

Max spoke the sacred words. "All the leaves are off the oak, and all the sheep have followed the spoken word. I'm coming, Constantinople. Here I come."

He charged, stomping prisons into parks, each footfall springing with life, the beasts of Eden howling at his heels. Max howled along and closed the gap, hooting through the rose-tinted eyes of his intentions. The beast gaped; shrill tendrils of compressed darkness spread like a catcher's mitt to receive him.

It was too big to hug, too sharp to snuggle. The wings crashed against him in wave after wave, his tender plushy flesh absorbing, dissolving like a cheese puff.

As Max drowned in his own flesh, he heard a voice like a child with cancer-choked lungs. "Hugs are the vice of the weak."

✶✶✶✶✶

Max jerked awake and found himself as stifled as before. He tried to rip off the covers, but his hand hit something warm and furry. The thing squeaked and tumbled off the bed.

"Puff?"

He used both hands and tried again. He heard two more thunks and noticed a faint rainbow glow spreading across his wall.

Whatever they were, a heap of them were holding him down. It took all his strength to force himself into a sitting position. More

235

things rolled off and hit the floor with little gasps and squeaks of dismay.

The lights were getting brighter. He could see them, now: teddy bears—living, glowing teddy bears.

The last to fall was a pastel blue. As it stood, Max noticed a cupcake-shaped patch on its belly. It asked, "What'd you do that for, mister?"

Max screamed and struggled to free himself, but there were so many bears on either side of him all he freed was a hiss from his Bio-Bed. The bears were crawling back on top of him.

"Get off me! What the fuck are you?"

The blue one smiled. "I'm Marty Bear!"

"Right."

A candy apple red one said, "I'm Billy Bear!"

The rest lit up and said their names all at once. They were all about the same size, but each was a different color and had a different symbol on its belly. Some of the symbols were from nature, like trees or stars. Others had manufactured goods like a wrapped gift or picnic basket. They were all so cute, so horrifically cute.

Max held his covers up like a shield. "What do you want?"

One of the yellow ones spread its arms. "We want to be your friends!"

This has to be another nightmare. Why am I not waking up?

Marty added. "We saw that you were having a bad dream so we came to help you feel better!"

"It's not working. You can leave now."

A green one crawled toward him. "We have not yet begun to nurture!" It yanked the sheet out of Max's hands and glowed brighter.

They all got brighter. There was a humming in Max's head, a white noise that slowly drowned his fears. He felt better, much better. After a few seconds, he was downright blissful.

He wrapped his arms around the green one and pulled him into a snuggling position. He'd never felt anything so soft. The way it pressed itself against him, the way it filled him with light, it was better than ecstasy sex. The light spread like shea butter on his dried-out soul.

The others piled on top of him, each individual light distinct, but melding into an overwhelming wholeness that reminded him all he had to do was relax and feel good. All of reality was soft, vibrating fur and he was a welcomed flea.

He was drifting off again, but that was fine. When he woke, they would still be there. They would always be there.

✳✳✳✳✳

A loud smack was followed by a faint buzz. Max's cheek stung, and his inner light was drifting to the bottom of a septic tank. Max squinted at the Greystoke-shaped silhouette and grunted his displeasure.

Greystoke slapped his face again. "Wake up and help me!"

"Oww, stop that. I'm up. I was having a nice dream. Why do I smell blood?" He touched his nose and found blood. "You broke my face."

The Count whacked him in the shin with his cane. When Max grabbed his leg, he noticed it was bloody too. Not just him, the whole room was littered with chunks of multicolored bear meat. The two Iiite butlers in the doorway fired several short bursts into the hall with assault rifles.

"Okay, somebody needs to tell me what the hell is going on."

Greystoke's airs had drifted away momentarily, revealing an old, frightened man. "My plan backfired. I found what I was looking for, but when the gate opened it was more than positive energy that came through. It's a full-on invasion."

"Oh." Max wiped some of the blood off his face with the dry side of his pillow. "Yeah, I figured that was a bad idea."

Greystoke slapped him again. "Now is not the time!"

"Oww, calm down. Those things are weird, but they're not that bad. They're kind of cute."

"*Those things* are still coming through. I can't close the portal."

"Is freaking out a component of the banishing spell?"

"If I knew the banishment spell I wouldn't be freaking out."

"Just—" Max rubbed his whiskers. "Just shut up. Is there any coffee nearby?"

Either the butlers were becoming better shots or the bears were thinning out.

"There is no time for coffee, you idiot."

"Shh, those bears might be exactly what we need. The Darkness makes people afraid and uncomfortable then feeds on the negative energy. I think these bears do the opposite."

"That may be, but they never stop feeding. Soon everyone in the world will be trapped in an endless snuggle. We will starve in our beds without noticing our hunger."

Max cocked an eyebrow. "I don't feel like we have enough information to jump to that conclusion. If it makes you feel any better, we were doomed before you fucked up. At least death by snuggles is more pleasant. How long ago did this start?"

Greystoke glanced at the wall clock. "I opened the gate forty minutes ago. It feels like a lot longer."

The butlers let loose another volley of gunfire.

"So you saw the bears coming through and, what, immediately started shooting them?"

"They had put half my staff to sleep before I noticed they were here. I was defending myself, as I am now. May I remind you we are being invaded by an alien life form we know nothing about? If moral distinctions must be made, I believe it would be prudent to make them after the invasion is dealt with."

"If you stop talking like an aristocratic buff-puff, we'll be done in half the time.

"I merely observed the facts and carried them to their natural conclusion."

"Great, so calm yourself with the knowledge that you're immortal, since, you know, you've been alive your whole life." He slapped Greystoke preemptively.

Greystoke was too stunned to respond, so Max continued. "Considering the alternative, I think I'm going to have to side with the shiny bears. Let's just seal off the castle and see what happens."

"You're willing to risk destruction of life as we know it simply because it comes in a cute package?"

"No, if you're right and these things want to suck us all dry forever, we'll have to try to stop them. I just think we should let them do their thing for a minute and see if it repels The Darkness."

Greystoke was beginning to look himself. "They truly are repellant."

"That's the spirit. The first thing we have to figure out is whether or not these things are in the service of some sort of conscious higher being. The bears could be to the light what he feisty zombies are to The Darkness, and I'd rather not find out how the Light reacts when it gets pissed off."

The shooting escalated.

Greystoke grimaced and screamed over the noise. "Stop shooting the bears. Keep them away from us, but don't kill them."

The younger butler turned. "How are we supposed to do that?"

"I don't know. Gently nudge them away with your rifle."

The butlers looked at each other for a second then shut the door.

"Don't do that! They could amass outside and trap us."

Max shook his head. "I don't think they want to trap us. I'm pretty sure they just want to make us feel better. They seem to be attracted to negative energy. The more upset you get the more the butlers shoot.

Greystoke straightened his back and cleared his throat.

"Let's make sure no more of them get into the castle. Then we can focus on figuring out what they are and how this is going to work."

Greystoke pointed with his cane. "We can lock the whole castle down from the control room."

"Then we'll do that."

"If I had known disaster would imbue you with so much prudence I would have induced the apocalypse months ago."

"I hope you're joking, but I have a feeling you're not."

Greystoke flashed his best mysterious smile.

"Come on." Max got up and opened the door. The hall was littered with tiny mutilated bodies, but otherwise clear. He motioned for the others to follow.

One of the butlers asked, "Would you like us to rescue Felicity, sir?"

"Do you want the world to end because the time we had to save it was spent explaining to my daughter why she can't keep an entire race of living teddy bears as pets?"

Max laughed. "Yeah, she's fine where she is. So where did the witches go when Witches 'R' Us got too creepy for them?"

"Any number of places. Like any other business, Witches 'R' Us had its competitors."

Max smirked. "How does *that* work? I mean, do magic corporate conquistadors open portals and take over whatever is on the other side?"

"No. They isolate a small point in reality and pump raw power into it until it inflates, creating a tesseract, which exists inside but underneath the skin of another reality like a cyst. The frequency of the new world is some percent of an octave closer to another preexisting frequency. We exist in the 49th octave. The closer a world gets to the 48th, the more conducive it is to black magic, while the ones nearer the 50th are better for white magic. The cost and exclusivity of use is directly proportional to the frequency."

Max sighed. "I'm not sure if I should be more worried that people can do that or that your explanations are starting to make sense."

They turned a corner and saw a pile of bears so big they couldn't tell who was under there. The Butlers raised their weapons, but the Count waved for them to stand down. They watched the pile carefully and crept past.

They were almost in the clear when the one on the top of the pile raised its head. "Hi, my name's—"

Greystoke pulled a small pistol with a silencer out of his jacket and put a bullet in each of its eyes. His head flopped down, pouring blood over his friends. The others didn't notice, so they continued down the hall.

When they rounded the corner, Max punched Greystoke in the arm. "I thought we weren't doing that anymore."

"I apologize. It was reflexive." He tucked the pistol back into its shoulder holster. "Why did you want to know where the witches went?"

"They might be able to tell us what these bears are, maybe even help us."

"Not likely. The bears come from an *extremely* obscure realm. It took every bit of my power to make the connection."

"Sorry, I didn't mean to challenge your hipster magic. You got any better ideas?"

Greystoke shifted his eyes away. "Our best and closest option is at Heller House."

"Oh yeah, I went in there. Nice place."

They arrived at the control room. Greystoke stood in front of the terminal and made a sign in the air with his hands.

"Access granted." The door slid open, and they went inside. The door closed automatically.

The room was a little larger than a walk-in closet. A small rack of assault rifles was mounted on the left wall. The right was covered in monitors that displayed various areas inside and outside the castle. The back wall was empty except for a refrigerator and an unshielded toilet.

"Shouldn't there be a guy in here?"

Greystoke flipped a switch on the desk, and a red "Lockdown" lit up above it. "One would think. Though, I believe I remember something in the information packet about I-Force officers joining their agents in the field when under attack."

Medieval-style grates lowered to cover the windows and doors to the outside.

"That will keep the new arrivals out, but what do about the ones that are already in?"

Max ran his tongue over his upper teeth and inspected the screens. Most of the bears were crowded around a door Max had never been through.

"What's in there?"

"China, mostly. It's a storage room. One of my staff must be hiding in there."

Max compared the horde at the door to the other groups and raised an eyebrow. "Your lawyer, maybe."

There were fourteen bear-piles in all. The smallest of which was the three bears that had snuggled up in Cat's bed. Max pointed. "Maybe we *should* wake her up."

"I thought we were in agreement."

"Yeah, she'll freak out when she sees the bears, but—" Max noticed several other types of creatures roaming the halls. A large purple thing with a huge mouth and tiny eyes was walking into the study. Several childlike creatures with huge eyes and rainbow jumpsuits, each accompanied by a gaggle of little walking puffballs, were exploring various bedrooms. Looking closer, he saw littler blue things the size of mice wearing little white pants and hats marching single file through the dining room.

"—But this seems like her kind of craziness. If anybody can talk their language, it's her. Can't you see her, like, uniting them in our cause and leading them into battle against The Darkness?"

"Under no circumstances is my daughter going into battle. That is what you are for."

"The fuck I am. That's what we pay I-Force for. Anyway, you know what I mean. Those things are creepy as hell to us. If they pick up on that, we're probably going to end up like them." He pointed at a pile. "Cat would think they were cool, so she'd probably be safe."

"If your theory is correct, she would be ideal, but I am not willing to bet her life."

"If I'm wrong, we're all fucked, anyway. She's already got three of them on her. What's the harm in trying?"

The thing in the study put its paw on the glass of one of the displays. The taxidermy griffin woke up, smashed through the glass, and commenced rubbing itself on the purple thing's shins.

"These things have a lot of juju."

Greystoke stared, speechless.

"So—are you going to let me wake her up or not?"

The Count took a deep breath. "I suppose it is selfish of me to leave her at the mercy of those things. I will consent to your retrieving her, but nothing more until we understand their agenda."

"Okay. Any chance there's a way to send the feed of nearby cameras to my phone?"

"I wouldn't know."

"Figures. We'll do this the old-fashioned way. Watch the monitors and let me know what's coming."

"I'm afraid that won't be possible."

"Why not?"

"A radio jammer blocks all wireless frequencies while in lockdown. I could use the landline to call out, but you wouldn't get the signal."

"And you can't turn it off?"

"Not without opening us up to further invasion."

"What about your guys? How would they communicate?"

"I don't know. Their procedures never interested me."

"So I'm on my own?"

"You can take one of the butlers."

The butlers looked away, each hoping Max would pick the other.

"I'm probably better off on my own." Max used the monitors to plot a course then walked to the door. It didn't open. "How do I get out of here?"

Greystoke gestured to the left of the door. "Press the big white button."

Max pressed the button and stepped into the hall. He jogged right and ducked into the secret passage behind the tapestry. There were no cameras in the passage, but he doubted the creatures had time to find the entrances.

He reached the burnt-up bedroom and listened through the bookshelf.

Sounds clear.

Max pushed the bookshelf in and peeked. No critters. He squeezed around, sprinted to the door and listened. It was silent at first, but just before he stepped out there came a pitter patter of lots of tiny shoes on marble. It sounded like it was moving away from him, but in the direction he needed to go.

Shit. It's probably one of those creepy kid things.

He didn't know another way to get to Cat's room without passing several of the bear-piles. One way or another he was probably going to run into something before he got to her.

Don't freak out. That's the key. They just want to be friends. I want to be their friend, sort of. So it's all good.

Fuck, I hope I'm right.

He took off his shoes and stuck one under each armpit. He didn't hear anything else coming, so, as quietly as possible, he sneaked in her direction. At the next hallway, he peered around the corner. Cat's door was only about twenty feet away. Tiny voices echoed down the hall, but he couldn't tell where they originated.

Where the hell did they go?

He crept around the corner and made for the door, but when he was halfway there, the kid stepped into the hall. She was three feet tall with pink glittery skin and hair like yarn. Her huge eyes widened with surprise and she stumbled backward and fell into her puffball entourage.

Terror blanked Max's mind. Before she could recover, he bolted the opposite direction. It didn't matter where he was going as long as it was away from that thing. He tried to turn down the right hall, but, unable to overcome his momentum in socks, he skidded past, rolled off the wall and continued straight.

He focused on the last door before the next hallway. Start sliding early. Maybe grab the table. I can do this.

A purple wall appeared in front of him. Next thing he knew he was on the floor staring up at one of the big ones.

"Hello friend!" It had the dumbest voice he'd ever heard, low and exaggerated like a retarded Muppet.

Holy fuck! Goddamn that's big. Smile!

Max was laughing, and he couldn't stop. Tears streamed down his cheeks as he rolled onto his side. The thing laughed with him and danced around joyfully.

When his bout of insanity was over Max said, "You got me, buddy. Good one. I guess that makes it your turn."

"Yay, my turn." The thing jumped for joy. "My turn for what?"

"You found me, now it's your turn to hide and I'll find you!"

"Oh, that sounds like fun." It cocked its head to the side. "But I'm confused. You weren't hiding. You were running."

I guess it's not as stupid as it looks.

"I was trying to hide again before the girl that saw me could touch me out."

"Oh, okay." It turned to go hide.

Wait, maybe it would be safer to bring it with me. It could establish me as a friend.

"Hey, hold on a second. I just remembered something."

"What's that?"

"It's time for my friend to get up from her nap. Why don't we go get her and she can play, too?"

"Oh, yeah! The more the merrier."

Max led it back to Cat's room. The kid was nowhere to be found.

I guess I really did scare her. All these creatures are plushy, furry, colorful or otherwise super cutesy. To her I must look like a hard giant with beady little eyes. She's probably seen one of the massacre sites and thinks I'm responsible.

He opened Cat's door and found her snuggled with her three new friends.

If these guys turn out to be harmless, I bet we could market them as stress reducers and sleep aids.

He reached over and gently roused the blue one. It slowly raised its head and rubbed its eye with its paw. When it saw him, it snapped awake and smiled. "Hi, my name's Bobby Bear. You want to be my friend?"

"Nice to meet you, Bobby. Of course I would. My name's Max."

The big purple guy chimed in. "My name's Burney. Want to be my good friend, too?"

Bobby crossed his arms. "Nope. I don't think so."

Burney raised his hands to his face in horror. "Oh, no. Why not?"

"I don't want to be good friends. I want to be best friends!" The bear ran and jumped into Burney's arms.

"Oh, Bobby, you're so silly." Burney hugged him tight and rocked from side to side.

The other bears were waking up. The purple one sat up first. It yawned and stretched. "Hey there, my name's Baka Bear. Want to be my friend?"

Their introduction ritual was grating on Max's nerves. He wanted to snatch the little fucker up and spike him like a football.

These things would probably be okay with that as long as I said it was a game.

"Of course I would. I'd like to be buddies with the little yellow guy too."

The yellow one narrowed its eyes at him. "I'm not a guy. I'm Babette Bear. Babette as in *girl*."

"Of course you are. Anybody could see how pretty you are. In this world, guy isn't exclusive to males. It's a general term."

"Oh, that's weird. Words are more literal where we come from."

Max forced a smile. "Friends?"

Everyone replied in unison. "Friends!"

Cat groaned and sat up. "What's all the hubbub—oh, Marty, mother of Goddess." She snatched Baka and Babette and hunched over to cuddle them with her whole body. "I love you sooo much!" She wiggled her butt and squished them harder.

It looked really uncomfortable, but the bears were giggling.

Burney and Bobby said, "We love you, too," and jumped on top of her.

Running into Burney had been like running into a big squishy wall. He didn't budge, just made a little "oof" that was likely more from the surprise than the impact. Something that stout should weigh more than enough to flatten a girl Cat's size, but she was giggling along with them.

Let's not over think this.

Max jumped on top of Burney and hugged him from behind.

Eventually Cat's curiosity outweighed the novelty and she shifted, dumping Max and Burney onto the floor. She sat up with Baka and Babette in a chokehold. "Really though, am I dead?"

Max stood up and popped his lower back.

The bears didn't seem to understand the question. "What is dead?"

Max crawled into bed beside her. "Your father managed to open a gateway to their dimension and new friends have been flooding in ever since."

"Ah, that makes sense."

"Really?" Max caught himself before he said anything negative. "That's awesome. Hey, just for fun let's tell each other about our days. You first, Babette."

She put her paws together and fluttered her lashes. "You're such a gentleman. Okay, well, I woke up and ate a big bowl of sunshine. Then I brushed my fur and went out to meet Baka and Bobby at the marshmallow fields so we could practice our ball dancing. There's a big competition coming up, and I just know we'll get first place, 'cause we've been practicing all week.

"We were almost done for the day when the portal opened up. We could feel so much sadness on the other side, we knew we had to come and help."

"So, all you guys came to be our friends and make us feel better?"

"That's what good friends do."

And our reaction was to gun them down. God, we suck.

Cat squeezed them tighter. "That's so sweet. I could just eat you up."

The bear's eyes widened. "Please don't eat us!"

Max patted them on their heads. "Don't worry; it's just a figure of speech."

Burney wiped imaginary sweat from his brow. "That's a relief."

"There is something you should know about this world, though. And I gotta warn you, it's pretty scary."

Bobby dove under the covers and the other two cowered into Cat and squeezer their eyes shut.

Burney hugged his knees to his chest. "We don't like being scared. Good friends don't scare each other."

"True, but best friends stick together when things get scary. Best friends know they have nothing to fear as long as their friends are by their side."

Burney giggled. "Oh, yeah."

"Well, the thing you felt that drew you here, it's worse than people being sad because they don't have enough friends."

"But friends can get through anything together. You just said so."

"That's true, we can get through this together, but you should know what's going on. Cat, you want to try to explain this?"

Cat looked like a cartoon bird that had just flown into a window. "No."

The critters were beginning to tremble.

"I think you can do it better. Please?"

Cat scrunched up her face. She looked Babette in the eyes then smiled and scratched the top of her head. "Okay. Have you guys ever met somebody who wasn't a friend and didn't want to be? Somebody who was a big meany no matter how nice you were to them?"

"Why would somebody not want friends?"

"Well, that's just it. He likes to make people sad."

Max added, "You know how you can glow and put people at ease? It's like that, but the opposite. It makes people mean, afraid, violent."

"Why?"

Max shook his head. "I don't know. It's just his thing. He's called The Darkness and he feeds on misery."

"Darkness is scary. Why don't we call it TD?"

Cat cocked her head. "Why didn't I think of that?"

Max's eyebrow jumped. "That's actually a great idea. I'm sick of saying The Darkness all the time."

"And I don't know what misery is, but maybe if we feed him lots and lots, he'll have a happy tummy and start being nice to everybody. Then he'll make lots of friends and we can play together."

"Misery means bad feelings, and TD can never get full. The more he eats the more he grows, and the bigger he gets, the hungrier he is. The worst part is he's not so much a person as an intelligent form of energy seeping into this world, turning everybody into him."

"That's terrible."

Cat nodded. "You bet it is, but we can stop it together. Will you help us?"

Bobby crawled out from under the covers and stood akimbo. "Of course we'll help. We're friends, aren't we?"

"Awesome."

"What should we do?"

"Cat, why don't you show them the districts that needs friends the most?"

"Why don't you do it?"

"I have to go to Heller's and handle something real quick."

"Are you putting me in charge?"

"Yeah, do you mind?"

Cat grinned. "Mind? I have a cute, plushy army. I dreamt of this in my mother's womb!"

Max laughed and patted Bobby on the back. "Thanks for helping, guys—and girls." He turned to Burney. "By the way, what's your superpower?"

"What do you mean?"

"Do you have any unique abilities? Like, they can glow and affect people's moods. What can you do?"

"I give the best hugs of anybody. Ask around, I'm famous for it. I have a real big imagination too."

Max remembered the sculpture coming to life. *Probably best not to ask for a demonstration.* "That's a great superpower."

Baka Bear added, "We give great hugs too."

"Anybody who needs a hug is in good company."

I don't think I can handle much more of this.

"I'd love to stay and play with you guys, but I've got to go meet another friend now."

"Can we come too?"

"This isn't going to be much fun. Besides, Cat needs your help organizing all our new friends. You can make a game of it. The first to get a hundred friends together wins an extra scoop of ice cream at the victory party."

"We love ice cream!"

Bobby declared, "I love ice cream the most! I'm going to win!"

Babette shook her head. "You can try, but I think I'm going to win."

"The sooner you get started, the sooner there'll be a winner."

Cat and the critters ran out the door chanting, "Ice cream. Ice cream. Ice cream."

Max gave the camera a thumb up and gestured to disengage lockdown. The grates creaked to life and his phone rang. He peeked out the door to make sure nothing was listening in, then answered.

"Hey, we're good. They want to help."

"Are you absolutely sure?"

"They're like furry little kids with magic powers. They don't even know what death means."

"They do now. Cat seems to be explaining one of the larger piles of corpses."

"That can't be good."

"Whatever she's saying, they seem to be taking it well."

"Good. I told them the first one to recruit a hundred friends to help us would get an extra scoop of ice cream, so you might want to make some calls, get as much ice cream as you can."

Greystoke sniffed. "It's bound to be cheaper than I-Force."

"Yeah, we should probably wake everybody up and tell them not to kill anything else." Max entered the hall and made his way toward the door with all the bears in front of it." I'm going to rescue whoever's in the china closet now. You think the butlers can do the rest?"

"I'm sure they can manage."

"Just tell them to pretend they're in a kids' TV show. They'll be fine as long as they act friendly."

Greystoke grunted.

"This was your idea."

"I am painfully aware of that. Meet me on the roof. The streets are clogged by those things, so we will have to take the spare helicopter."

The china room came into view. The number of bears outside hadn't changed.

"If Heller's so powerful, why doesn't *he* do something about this?"

"No good can come from questioning Heller. Keep that in mind when you see him. The answer to your question is that he doesn't do things, he pays others to do things. That is how it works."

"So why isn't he paying anybody to fix this?"

"He is—you. And if I were you, I would have a damned good excuse ready to explain why you've made such a mess of things."

Max hung up and approached the bears, who were trying to jimmy the lock with a folded-up receipt. "Hey guys, what's up?"

A little pink bear explained. "Somebody's trapped in there and they're really unhappy. We're trying to get them out."

"That's terrible. If they don't come out, they'll miss the ice cream party."

"Ice cream party?" They all turned. He had their full attention.

"You haven't heard about the ice cream party?"

"No."

"What about the important mission?"

"What mission?"

"You have to go on the mission if you want to go to the victory party, silly. Everybody's in the garden is talking about it."

"Oh no."

"Tell you what, I'll help whoever's back there and you can all go get caught up."

"You'd do that for us?"

"Of course I would. That's what friends are for."

"Thanks, mister, you're my bestest friend."

"Mine too!"

All the bears agreed Max was their bestest friend, then scampered off towards the garden.

I'm going to hell.

Max knocked on the door. "Hey, who's in there? You can come out now."

No response.

"It's okay. They're gone."

He pressed his ear against the door. Silence.

"Anybody in there?"

Fuck it.

He pulled out his license and slid it around the door to pop the lock. The door swung into a dark room. He flipped on the light, but all he saw was a series of antique china cabinets and a Victorian era table set.

"What the hell?"

He was about to leave when he heard a rustling noise above one of the cabinets. He pulled out his knife, dragged a chair over, and climbed on top to find Cheeky curled up asleep and Puff lounging on him like a couch. Puff yawned and stretched out her paws.

Max scratched the top of Puff's head. "Don't worry, you're not being replaced."

Cheeky woke up and looked around as if he didn't know how he got there. "Hey, buddy. It's nice to see you." He rubbed his fingers over Cheeky's face, squishing on it in the way that made him complain, but put him in a good mood.

"You want to come on a mission with me?"

Cheeky rolled into a standing position. Puff flew to Max's shoulder and nuzzled the side of his head. "All right, you can come too."

Max scooped Cheeky up and headed to the elevators.

"How'd you get locked in there? Neither of you have hands."

# A LONELY CABBAGE WEEPS
# AT DAWN

Castle Greystoke perched like a lone gargoyle atop a small mountain by the coast. Max stood at the edge of the helipad staring over the grounds, past the suburbs to the city, which sprawled calmly in direct defiance of the blight smeared across its breast like so much rancid semen.

Greystoke tapped him on the shoulder and motioned that the chopper was ready to go. Max, Puff and Cheeky climbed aboard and settled into one of the two plush, red recliners. They were worn, but cozy. The cabin had the feeling of an old jacket. It wasn't as nice as the other one, but he could tell it had soaked up a lot of good times. His only complaint was it had also soaked up twenty years' worth of cigar stank.

Greystoke climbed in and took the seat across from him.

Instead of a minibar, there was a single handmade fountain. As soon as they were in the air, Max placed a tumbler under the nozzle and turned the knob, filling the glass halfway with a thick amber liquid. Its smooth, rich vapors were reminiscent of Cognac, and it caressed his palate like a first kiss.

"I can see why you like to travel so much."

Greystoke half smiled, and stared out the window. Puff climbed his leg and flopped onto her back using the valley created by his crossed legs as a papasan chair. Greystoke put his hand on her side and absentmindedly twiddled her ear.

Max reclined the seat halfway and let Cheeky wedge himself between his left side and the arm of the chair. He was almost happy until he looked out the window and saw the rainbow of strange plushy creatures marching toward the city.

Max sat up for a better look. His retinal implants provided a detailed view of the unimaginable horrors unfolding up ahead.

Ignoring the drifts of multicolored flesh lining the McRoad, the bears ran, glowing with arms outstretched toward the bloody functionaries of Hell. Together their light was so bright Max felt a contact high from two thousand feet. The majority of zombies and raged-out living were easily calmed, but the bigger things were less cooperative.

One such creature, with a man's torso and incredibly long arms and legs, swung his rake-like hands, tearing the bears open and flinging them deeper into the city. The purple dinosaurs gathered around its legs and picked him up. They stumbled as a group, trying to keep their balance as the monstrosity burrowed through the backs of one after the other, flooding the street with little white clouds of dino-innards.

The monster reared back and decapitated one of the last two left on his right leg. The sudden shift in balance toppled them all, dropping him into a decorative fountain, which snapped off his arms and legs as he landed. The creatures seemed to be apologizing as they rushed to smother it with hugs.

Max scratched Cheeky's chin to keep him from looking out the window. "Your plan seems to be working. Not so great for our new friends, but as fuck-ups go, it could be a lot worse."

Greystoke snorted. "Could it? Say we win. The Darkness is vanquished. Then what?"

"We're calling him TD now."

Greystoke scowled. "We either live out the rest of eternity in a children's show, trick or force them back through the portal, or kill them all in cold blood. The first option is unbearable, the second impossible, and though my scruples may not be Whovian, killing innocents en masse is something I would rather not have on my conscience."

Greystoke continued to gaze out the window in awe. "Look at them go. Not a speck of fear. No thought for themselves. They're running toward certain death to save a race of rapists, conmen, thieves, and murderers. I suppose they don't know any better."

Max smiled sadly. "I don't think it would matter to them if they did. Makes you feel like shit, don't it?"

Greystoke nodded.

They were flying out of range of the battle to where the streets were deserted ruins of a once bustling commerce center.

Max pointed out the window. "See how empty the streets are? I bet TD is as attracted to the bears as the bears are to it."

"Mm."

As the chopper passed over the park, Max noticed the body of a woman lying by the monkey bars. She'd been pulled apart. Her guts decorated the ground around her like an exploded portrait of Venus. A second later he noticed the baseball diamond. The dirt around first base was darker, redder than the rest. Red skid marks slashed the ground around the pitcher's mound.

Greystoke tapped the com button with his cane. "You can go higher now. I've seen enough."

The engines whined and pitched them upward and away from the carnage.

Max turned to the Count. "If it's that bad, why haven't we been affected?"

Greystoke reached into his jacket and pulled out a shiny, silver disc the size of a hockey puck. He'd seen it before on the Count's desk.

"Your paperweight protects you from evil?"

"Isn't it lovely? Not too heavy, not too light, austere enough that it is barely noticeable, but it complements everything around it. Cat went through a phase when she would take it down to the road and roll it into traffic. It caused quite a few accidents, but never got a scratch."

"Well, that's nice for you. You got an extra one?"

"No, this was a gift from an old friend, a scientist, if you can believe it. It's an extremely powerful magnet made from an alloy he developed to shield astronauts from radiation. The electromagnetic field creates a near impenetrable barrier against all forms of energy."

"It protects you from sunburn and magic-missiles. Nice."

"It has proven useful more than once."

"But won't that mess with the magical tesseract thingy?"

Greystoke cocked an eyebrow. "The thingy will be fine." He opened his coat and pointed to the right inside pocket. "This pocket is normal. However," he pointed to his left inside pocket, "this one has undergone a long and complex series of scientific and magical treatments. With the disc inside and the pocket zipped, the effects cancel each other out."

The com button lit up, and Greystoke pushed it. The pilot said, "We're here, sir. Prepare for landing."

Max stared out the window at the Hellerpad. Instead of the normal H, the pad bore Heller's stylized logo, two pillars with a long snake curled around them in a figure eight.

The chopper landed smoothly. Max went for the door, but Greystoke blocked the way with his cane. There was a loud click and the platform sunk into the roof.

"Heller thinks he's Batman, doesn't he?"

Greystoke's eyes bugged and he popped Max on the head with his cane.

"Ow, what the fuck?"

Greystoke mouthed, "Show respect."

Max glared and rubbed the side of his head.

The platform slid into place with another loud metallic clank, and a man in a tux opened the door. "Good evening, gentlemen. Mister Heller will receive you in the lodge."

He led them to the room where Max had met the Rothafellas. It still stank of sweat and santorum. Mr. Heller sat by the fireplace with a large ornate pipe in one hand and a small leather-bound book in the other. He looked up as they entered and waved with his pipe for them to have a seat on the red leather couch.

Max and Greystoke stepped inside, but the servant put out his foot to block Cheeky and Puff. "I'm afraid the animals will have to wait in the hall."

Before Max could object, Greystoke put his arm over his shoulder and hurried him to the couch. The servant shut the door.

Heller stared like a bug, each eye looking at them from hundreds of different angles. Max held eye contact as long as possible, then turned to the Count. They appeared to be making eye contact, but when he looked back at Heller those cold compound eyes were still upon him.

Heller closed his book and set it aside. "Gentlemen, I'm glad to see you are doing well."

Max nodded. That wasp-like voice buzzed in his ears for several seconds after he finished speaking.

Greystoke bowed in his seat. "And you as well, sir."

Heller puffed his pipe several times then sat back and crossed his legs. "Things have gotten out of hand, haven't they?"

Greystoke frowned. "That remains to be seen. I am formulating a plan, but I need more information."

"You call those *things* a plan?"

"I assure you the creatures are only a small part of my grand design. They will weaken The Darkness and afford us time to set the greater scheme in motion."

Max cocked an eyebrow at the Count. *What the fuck is he talking about?* He was about to ask about the nature of the creatures when Heller stood and shook Greystoke's hand.

"I'll be happy to give you the resources you need."

Greystoke shook Heller's hand and all but dragged Max out the door. Cheeky was giving the servant's right leg a nuclear Indian sunburn while Puff fluttered around the man's head, scratching a solo game of tic tac toe on his face. The servant silently stood his ground, shielding his face with one arm and trying to slap them away with the other. The dignity with which he fought was simultaneously inspiring and tragic.

Max snatched Puff out of the air. "That's enough, you two."

Cheeky stopped playing and followed them down the hall and through the door to inside-out world. Max could feel the magical buzz in the air smoothing his wrinkled mind. His muscles relaxed, adding a slight curl to the corners of his mouth as Puff and Cheeky chased each other through the trees.

"Hey, don't go too far." Max stopped and shut the door. "So what was that all about?"

Greystoke smiled. "I assume your pets resented their detainment."

"No, that." Max pointed at the door, which felt worlds removed from the hallway that contained the room he was referring to. "Shouldn't we see if he knows anything? And why did he offer you resources without asking about your plan? And what is your plan? I didn't even know you had one."

"Heller has already supplied me with a good deal of information. The meeting was a mere formality."

The Count was hiding something. The missing thing swirled around the edges of Max's brain like smoke. "Any chance you'll let me in on that?"

"That is all magical nuts and bolts. The information you need is here."

"Where is here, exactly?"

"This is Venustas, a sort of man-made magical time share for practitioners of the occult."

"If Heller's so rich and powerful, why doesn't he have his own?"

Greystoke smirked. "There are a multitude of reasons why the magical elite cooperate with each other, but to put it simply, the creation of a world such as this requires a magical force equivalent to one hundred thousand neutron bombs focused on an area the size of a doorway. This is not something one does for the luxury."

"Okay, so how many wizards does it take to screw in this sort of light bulb?"

"What does it matter?"

"Just trying to understand."

"Honestly," Greystoke shifted his eyes to the trees, "I don't know."

"How do you not know? Magic's all, like, your thing."

"There are powers beyond even my experience."

"If magic were a conglomerate, you'd be a store manager, maybe a district supervisor?"

Greystoke scowled.

"So why aren't the CEOs handling this?"

"They are, but your role is the nail on which the plan is hung. Being the one who started all this, you are the only one capable of putting an end to it."

"Why?"

"A proper explanation would take hours, which we do not have. You need to speak to a woman named Lucille. She frequents a lake just down that path." Greystoke nodded to their left.

"I think I met her last time I was here."

Greystoke's smirk returned. "Of course you did."

"What's that supposed to mean?"

"Simply that your knack for blundering in the right direction is uncanny."

"Whatever. I've got blundering to do. I'll catch up with you later." Max called to Cheeky and patted his leg. Cheeky came running with Puff flying behind, and together they strolled down the path.

The sweet-smelling sprinkle of flowers and the soft moss beneath his feet put Max in a halcyon humor.

If people can make this, why bother with the rest?

Déjà vu poked him in the forehead as he rounded the corner. Lucille was sunbathing in the same spot as before, so he removed his clothes and walked towards her. She followed him with her eyes, but otherwise ignored him.

Cheeky made a grumbly noise and darted into the woods.

Max spread his flesh within an inch of hers, crossed his arms behind his head, and smiled at the sky.

After a few minutes of pleasant silence, Max convinced himself to get on with it. "Your name is Lucille, right?"

She rolled onto her stomach and turned to peer coyly through hair like wind chimes of maple syrup. "You're really hung up on names, aren't you?"

Max laughed. "No, I'm actually shit with names."

"Well, in that case, I'm flattered."

"You're not an easy person to forget."

She smiled but closed her eyes and laid her face on the rock as though she was going to sleep.

"Rumor has it you're the person to talk to about extra-dimensional weirdness."

Her smile faded, and she turned away.

"The Darkness has turned my world into a heavy metal video. I'm still not sure how, but everybody says it's my fault, and I'm the only one who can stop it."

She giggled and turned to look at him. "That's what this is about?"

"*Yeah.* I mean, flirting with you is a hell of a lot more pleasant than fending off the source of all evil, but people are dying, and it's my fault."

Her eyes misted, but she was smiling like she remembered something. "No, it isn't."

"Well, you're the only one who doesn't think so, and that's probably because you don't know the story. Do you know the story?"

"I know more than enough to tell you you're wasting your time."

"How's that?"

"You can't kill The Darkness. Best case scenario, you force it out of your world, but it's not likely to go back where it came from, so you would probably just be screwing some other world. Its migration is a part of nature, so blaming it on a mortal is ridiculous, even if they did open the door to get a sweet but unnecessary power boost."

"Huh?"

"This didn't start with you. It's been going on forever, like global warming. This part of it started when a bunch of dumb kids tried to summon the devil at Witches 'R' Us. The Darkness came, but it was too subtle to notice at first. They left thinking the guy who had sold them the summoning spell ripped them off. Over the course of years Darkness crept in and took everything over. Xav thought he could trap The Darkness and harness its power."

"You mean Xavier Mitton? You knew him?"

"Mm hmm. The machine was my design."

Max popped up and spun around to stare at her. "You—why the fuck would you do that?"

She crinkled her forehead. "It's kind of a long story, but I'll give you the Cliff's Notes if you calm down."

Max cocked his head and forced himself to speak softly. "Sorry, I hardly know anything about you, but that, you know…" He put his fingers at his temples and mimed his head exploding.

"I've known him since we were kids. We dated for a week in high school, but he got clingy, so I broke it off while we could still go back to being friends."

"Hold on, I have so many questions, but—ah—so many questions."

"One, I don't have all night."

"Sorry, uh, how did you know him?"

"That's your question?"

"Too many to process. I picked the first one that wasn't sexual."

Lucille laughed and pinched his nipple.

Max crossed his legs, suddenly regretting his decision to join her in the buff.

"We met at school. Daddy likes to throw his money around. *Nothing but the best*, you know? Iiites had the best school so he sent me there."

"Who are your parents?"

"I said one question."

"Sorry, continue."

"Xav had a fucked-up life. As soon as he could understand words, the leadership told him he was the savior of his people and everything was riding on him. That was on top of all the normal growing-up stuff. Kids picked on him for being a freak. But they hated him because everybody said he was superior. If he did well, they hated him out of jealousy. If he screwed up they hated him for being a fake that was going to mishandle their future.

Sadness waxed her eyes. "Inside he was just this normal kid.

"One day, a bunch of kids grabbed him and tossed him in the main flow reservoir. It's a huge lake of all things flushed. I heard him crying on my way home. He was so pitiful. I felt sorry for him. I took him home and we bonded over cinnamon oatmeal cookies and Penultimate Fantasy 7."

"So you thought you'd help him get his revenge by harnessing the infinite power of evil?"

Lucille cast her eyes to the water. "No, my point is that he wasn't just a monster. He was a person—flawed, yes, but under the circumstances he could have been a whole lot worse."

"Yeah, I get that. I just don't care. He was a fucking war criminal."

"He didn't have a choice, though. Heller wanted somebody to fill that role, so he made one. What do you think would have happened if he said no?"

"Wait, *Heller* made the Mittons?"

"Who else?

"I don't know, an Iiite, I guess."

"You thought the Iiites were so afraid of freedom they genetically engineered hideously deformed monsters to rule over them?"

"Does it make more sense for Heller to do it?"

"I feel like we're getting off topic."

"We are. I don't care."

"Fine. Heller is the ultimate control freak. He knew he'd never fully control the Iiites through normal means because they would always see him as an outsider. Iiite leaders didn't need his money, and their public image couldn't have gotten any worse, so no blackmail. He could have arranged a collapse like he did with the government then finagled in his own guy, but it was easier to convince them he could grow them a super genius. He left out the bit about the bomb being attached to their hearts before they were born."

"Wait, did you just say Heller was behind the government collapse too?"

"Heller's behind everything."

"That sounds a little—impossible. How the fuck do you know all this?"

"You ask a lot of dumb questions."

"Xavier told you?"

"Duh."

"He not only knew he was a puppet, he shared that information with you?"

"Everybody has somebody they tell their secrets to. For him that was me. I think he was in love with me." Lucille smiled like she was bragging.

"Right. Xavier was a big cuddly bunny, and Heller, the man I basically work for and the reason I'm here, is the ultimate baddy."

She grew anxious. "Did you come in through Heller's house?"

"Yeah."

Lucille raised her right hand and said some gibberish. Max felt millions of tiny electrical shocks like static electricity discharging all over his body. He crawled back from her. "Hey, stop it. I'm not a bad guy. I started working with the Count so I could take people like Heller out."

"Why didn't you say you came in that way?"

"Why does it matter?"

"Shh, you can't possibly be that clueless."

"Yes I can. Nobody ever tells me anything useful."

"You were covered in Heller's cooties."

"You mean the little robots? I didn't think they would work out here. And who cares if he knows my heart rate."

"You don't think he has a receiver out here? This place connects to his house. He just recorded everything we said."

"They can do that?"

"That's their main purpose. He doesn't advertise it, but everybody knows."

*Dammit Greystoke.*

"When you tazed me just now, that disabled them?"

Lucille whispered. "Yeah, but there could still be bugs out here. I hadn't thought about it 'til just now."

Max whispered back. "If he heard all that, nothing else we say is going to matter much."

She started to shrug, but noticed a little black mole scurrying across the rock. "I guess not." She pinched its back and scrutinized it intently for a few seconds before letting it go.

"Thanks, by the way. I should have known better than to trust Greystoke. Not that I trusted him, but I thought I could at least trust his motives.

"What do you think his motives are?"

Max counted them on his fingers. "Money, power and fame."

"That's what everybody is after. If you want to know his motives, you have to know why he wants that stuff."

Max thought for a moment. "Well, he's always talking about how he started out 'a poor' and got where he is through hard work and brilliance. Heller made him who he is, and he could take it all away. I guess pleasing Heller is what keeps the Count from rejoining the poor, so it wouldn't make sense for him to tell me what Heller wouldn't want me to know."

"Ding, ding."

"He would rather let the universe be destroyed than go back to being nobody. That's fucking tragic."

"If you opened the Count's chest, you'd find a craven little henchman inside, pulling levers and speaking into a microphone.

"What's next? You gonna tell me TD is my mother and you eat kittens?"

"TD?"

"I get tired of saying The Darkness all the time, so I call him TD. Plus, since he runs on fear, it can't be good to constantly refer to him using the most ominous name imaginable."

"That's cute, and kind of brilliant."

Max blushed. "So—Heller's like fifty. Even if he fell out of the womb reading global domination for dummies, some of this stuff was before his time."

"He's not fifty. There's no way to tell how old he really is because he doesn't age. I'm not completely convinced he's human."

"Of course not. He can't just be a supremely powerful puppeteer; he has to be a space alien as well." Max scooted over and sat facing her Indian style. "Get to the part where it makes sense to help Xavier slap a leash on primordial evil."

The middle of her forehead bunched up. "You can be nice, or we can stop talking."

"Sorry, you're right. I appreciate the ever-loving fuck out of all this information. You have no idea the cryptic bullshit I usually have to deal with. If I ask Greystoke what he had for lunch he responds with three riddles and a goddamn side quest. So thank you. Please tell your story."

"So—the machine. Xav and I were really into theoretical magic. Like magic is unexplainable science, right? Theoretical magic is where you take sciencey facts and magical facts and perform experiments. It was one of those experiments that brought The Darkness, sorry TD, to Witches 'R' Us in the first place."

"Why does it not surprise me Xavier started all this?"

"Not Xavier."

"What, you did this?"

"Guilty."

"You don't strike me as the sort to bring about the apocalypse."

"You don't come off all Commando McSpy, either."

"Fair enough. So, wait, you tried to summon the devil? Why would anyone want to summon the devil?"

She frowned and rolled onto her back. "We were stupid teenagers with access to too much money and no accountability. We just wanted to see if it would work."

"And you're okay with the outcome?"

"I'm at peace with it. I mean, I can't regret it because it made me who I am. It woke me up, made me a real person. Anyway, it doesn't matter. The IS is just a tiny insignificant speck of the ALL."

"How many hippies shat in your head this morning?"

She rumpled her forehead at him. "This interview is over." She rocked forward and dove into the lake.

"Hey, don't go. Look, I'm sorry. It was a joke. A friend of mine used to ask me that all the time. He was a military guy, long story. Come on, please!"

She emerged on the far side of the lake, pulled her yellow sundress over her head and walked toward the path. Max ran down the rocks to head her off, but slipped and fell into the water. The water was shallow, so he was up and running in seconds. His feet found every jagged rock and thistle that lay between them.

"Please, I'm sorry. Obviously you care. That was a horrible, insensitive thing I said." Though it was a reasonable response considering you said it didn't matter that you destroyed the universe.

She slowed but didn't turn.

"I've had a really fucked up day. I didn't mean to take it out on you."

She stopped. When he caught up to her, he saw she was crying. He wrapped his arms around her, and she cowered into him, trembling. He held her until she stopped and pushed him away.

"That's what the machine was for."

Afraid he would say something stupid, he waited silently for her to explain.

"It was supposed to fix it."

"You built it to stop The Darkness?"

"Yeah, but Xavier fucked it up. I tried to talk him out of it, but he was losing the war. He was desperate. He thought he could use it as a weapon, and he could, sort of, but the more he did, the weirder he got. At first I thought it was the pressure, but then he got obsessed and started saying all this crazy stuff about becoming a god."

"And then I blundered along and broke the machine that was keeping it in check."

She bobbled her head.

"And then Ernie zapped me back home, but TD had my scent and followed me, but why? I freed it. Shouldn't it be grateful?"

She smirked. "You expect pure negativity to be grateful?"

"I see your point, but what an asshole."

"That's evil for ya."

"What do I have to do to make it go away? This isn't one of those cheesy, I-have-to-sacrifice-myself-to-save-the-world-because-nothing-is-more-powerful-than-selfless-love scenarios, is it?"

"I'm pretty sure that would just make you dead."

"Can we make another machine?"

She shook her head. "TD's moving too fast."

"So, what then?"

Lucille shrugged.

"I was told you'd have some sort of insight."

"If I knew how to fix this, you think I'd be spending all my time staring at a lake?"

"How would I know? We just met."

She thumped his right testicle.

"Oww, fuck!" His knees buckled. He fell, crushing a pointy stick with his ribs.

She grimaced. "Sorry, I didn't expect to connect so perfectly."

When the pain faded enough to speak, he asked, "Are you a paper football champion or something?"

"I play a lot of Catacombs."

"What the fuck is Catacombs?"

"It's a board game. You thump heroes into monsters. It doesn't matter. Let me help you up."

He took her hand, but instead of standing he pulled her into his lap. "Kiss it, make it better?"

She pursed her lips and thumped his nipple.

He smiled. "That I don't mind so much."

"I thought you had a girlfriend."

"I'm pretty sure she's fucked every humanoid she's ever met."

"What about saving the world?"

"You were my last hope. I'm out of ideas." He ran his hand down her back. "If there's nothing I can do to prevent my horrible death; I might as well pass the time enjoyably."

Lucille jerked loose and stood. "Not every girl is a raging slut waiting to ride your trouser train."

Not every girl spends all her time naked in the woods having long, deeply personal conversations with strangers.

"Sorry, I didn't mean to imply anything. You're gorgeous and I'm a human male who's just spent the last I don't know how long sitting naked with you in a romantic setting without trying anything."

"You just did try something."

"Only after you touched my balls and told me there's no hope for mankind. Give me some credit."

"I did, you lost it."

"Why are you making such a big deal out of this?"

"Sex is a big deal. It's the most magical act a human can do."

"It is pretty awesome. That's why I wanted to do it."

"No, dumbass, I mean magical literally. In terms of energy, everything in existence pours into our head and down through the body to our root chakra." She grabbed her twat like a construction worker. "When you have sex you're not just sticking a blood-gorged tube into a slippery hole. You're creating a circuit between two bodies of psychic energy. Your minds, souls, egos, wills, everything syncs and becomes a conduit, one big nerve the ALL uses to experience itself in a magical way.

"Meaningless sex and bad sex are spiritually degrading. You don't make that connection. You just do what makes your body feel good. When the body and mind are out of balance in the body's favor, it fucks everything up and pushes the ALL out, or more like constricts the hole the ALL can come in through, and feeds the ego, which is the root of all human suffering."

"I get it. You don't want to have sex."

"No, you don't get it. Nobody gets it. There's nothing wrong with having lots of sex with lots of people. What's wrong is when it's treated like a bodily function. I don't have sex or fuck, but I make love as often as I can with as many people as I can. You're cute, but you just spent the last hour badgering me for information, and then your big move was asking me to kiss your balls. You're not somebody I want to have that kind of connection with."

Max stood and brushed the dirt from his ass cheeks. "You're right. I'm sorry. My last couple of girlfriends were pretty over the top sexually. I'm used to Cat wanting sex all day every day. I guess it's made me presumptuous. I promise, despite all evidence to the contrary, I'm really not a douchebag."

She smiled. "That's just what a douchebag would say."

"Can we go back to the lake? I want my clothes. Maybe if we talk some more we can come up with a solution."

She shrugged. "I've got nothing better to do."

Max followed her back toward the lake. "The thing I don't get is, if there's no way to beat this thing, why do supernatural beings keep telling me I'm the chosen one?"

"The chosen one?"

"Yeah, those words keep popping up, the chosen one. Technically, I guess I've been chosen a bunch of times. TD chose to make my life a living hell. Eris chose me to make TD's life a living hell.

The Nrrds chose me to lead them to their deaths. Greystoke chose me to be the next cash cow for the fuckers I supposedly overthrew. Just once it would be nice if *I* got to choose what happens to me."

Max cried out as he stepped on another pointy rock.

"Why don't you?"

"Well, it's not like I don't try. Destiny sounds like a load of camel pucky, but apparently it's a thing."

"There are higher beings, lots of different kinds, and some of them like to toy with mortals. They can pull strings, mess with your head and make stuff happen to you, but that doesn't mean you don't have free will."

Max found his clothes, stepped into his pants and pulled them up. "I used to think that too."

"Well, you were right."

"When I was being substantiated, the house told me my destiny was so set in stone, so fucking special its rules didn't apply to me."

"You were substantiated?"

"Yeah, a bit." Max pulled on his shirt and pointed to the big rock. "You want to sit down?"

She arched her eyebrows. "You don't get substantiated a bit. You either pass or fail."

"It passed me like a kidney stone."

"What did it tell you, *exactly*?"

"The little old lady said my third nostril was clogged and I was destined for enlightenment. Then she turned into a big scary monster and started gibbering at me in a way that made my insides rattle. After that, I jumped out the bathroom window into nothing, which turned into a volcano where a couple of rednecks made sport of me."

She laughed and walked toward the rock. "We might be able to fix this after all."

He stepped into his shoes and let his feet settle in as he followed. "Hm?"

"Gods are one thing, but the process of substantiation is totally unbiased. It's a construct of your true self communicating directly with your subconscious while your conscious watches. If it said you'd be enlightened, it'll happen, and if the world ends and we all die, there's not much chance of you reaching enlightenment. What else did it say?"

"I don't know. It was a while ago."

"Think. It's important."

Max settled next to her on the rock and tried to remember something useful. "I was tired and didn't really know what was going on. I passed the door riddle and met the old lady. I told her to make it fast, so she took me up to the shower and tossed some cats in with me. After the cats turned me into coleslaw, she dragged me into another room where she beat the fuck out of me. That was all before she knew anything. Then she said there was a ritual to substantiate me, but it wasn't possible, whatever that means." He sighed.

"I asked her how to get rid of the Night Noodles, which was why I went there, and she said they were my benefactors and they served Eris and I shouldn't piss her off."

Lucille's eyes twinkled like pools of broken glass. "Maybe that's the key. Do you see the Night Noodles much?"

"Not really, but Cat's a Discordian. She summoned Gulik twice, and let me tell you that guy's a smug, rapey dick. He melted my helicopter."

"And what did he tell you?"

"Apparently, I'm Eris's champion. He said it's all up to me, and I should use my spirit animals more." He gestured to where Puff and Cheeky were chasing each other through the trees.

"A saint told you that you were chosen by a goddess?"

"Yeah."

"Why didn't you lead with that?"

"I did."

"I guess so, but the way you said it—look never mind. This is great news. Gods don't give tasks to people who can't carry them out."

"She's the goddess of chaos. She probably picked me because of how ill-suited I am."

"Maybe, but she's still a god. Gods are predictable. The more followers and real estate they have, the stronger they are, and they all want to be stronger. I don't care how entertaining you make it; she's not going to let him steal her IS. If Gulik said to let your spirit animals guide you, you should do it." She turned to where they had just been. "Where did they go?"

"I don't know. They were right there a second ago. Cheeky! Puff!" He waited and listened, but didn't hear anything. "Cheeky, get your lumpy ass back here!"

He listened. Still nothing. "How can a forest be this quiet?"

"Should we look for them?"

"Is there anything out there that might hurt them?"

"Shouldn't be."

Max screamed, "Cheeky!"

Lucille made a generic animal summoning noise with her tongue.

"It's not like him to ignore me, and he couldn't have gotten out of hearing range that fast." He climbed down and walked over to the last place he'd seen them. "Cheeky! Puff! Get the fuck back here!"

The trees rustled as the things in their branches flew, jumped, and skittered away.

Max rumpled his forehead. "Well, that's not good."

"Don't worry." She closed her eyes and babbled something. When she opened them, they glowed as if a blue nightlight had been plugged into her sinuses. "Follow me."

She led him straight into the brush, ducking and brushing flora aside as necessary. Greenery of every shape and hue crunched under Max's handmade footwear. He felt like a kid again—an awkward kid who was more than usually concerned about bugs. "Are there ticks here?"

"No. There's a general ward against insects."

"Smart."

Every time Lucille bent to pass under a branch her little yellow dress would rise, taunting him. The thicker the brush, the more he found himself staring directly into her holeyest of holies. His mind zipped back and forth between concern for his pets and the musky muliebrous mounds, which he was probably following too closely. The deeper they went into the woods the closer he followed. It was like a gravity well of pheromonal bubblegum. He could barely keep his tongue in his mouth. He wanted to compliment her sphincteral geometry, but thought better of it.

"Are you sure you know where we're going?"

"Mm hmm, we're almost there."

"How do you know?"

"I can see them glowing."

"They shouldn't be glowing."

"Because of the spell, dumbass."

"Oh, right."

Maybe if I pretended to trip, I could smoosh my face in there for a second. No, she's too smart for that. Maybe she'll stop suddenly and I can walk into it.

The foliage thinned, and the ground sloped at a twenty-degree angle. She was moving faster with less bending over. He sped up, drawn forward by a need more pressing than self-respect. The next time she started to bend he lunged, but her bend was shallow and his lunge wonky with desperation. He tripped, and instead of the silken pillows of animal magnetism he got a faceful of tree bark.

She glanced at him, her eyes loaded with curiosity.

He brushed the splinters from his face and kicked at the woody protrusion. "Stupid root!"

She smirked and kept moving.

The best thing men have going for them is that women can't bring themselves to register how utterly pathetic we are.

He followed, grumbling and pressing on his nose. He decided it wasn't broken.

She stopped abruptly. "Uh oh."

Figures.

"What do you mean, uh oh?"

She pointed to a spot about twenty feet away where the forest floor ended in a large ravine, then lowered her hand, pointing to a spot about halfway there. "They're down there."

Max threw his arms in front of his face and ran forward. He skidded to the edge and watched a clump of dry leaves dissipate as they fell to the riverbed forty feet below. Cheeky was still. His body twisted over a large rock seeping glop into a trickling stream. Puff was perched on a smaller rock stretching to sniff the yellowing water.

"Cheeky!"

Puff looked up, but more at the cloud of leaves than Max.

Lucille joined him. "Crap, that doesn't look good."

Max frantically searched for a way down, but the sides were smooth and sheer, as if the ravine had been made by a giant ice cream scoop.

"Fuck!"

"Don't freak out. I got this." She touched his arm and babbled more magic-speak. "Do you trust me?"

"Not really."

She narrowed her eyes and shoved him over the edge.

"What the fuck!" His mind was spinning like a slot machine, but about halfway down he realized he was falling slower than the leaves. He craned his neck and saw Lucille jump. "This is freaky!"

He shifted his weight just in time to land on his feet. The water was only about six inches deep, so he stomped over to Cheeky and scooped him up. The little body twisted in his arms, wheezing like an empty bottle of dish soap.

"It's okay, buddy. I'm here."

The suckers latched onto his arm and he felt the all too familiar sensation of his life force rushing out of him.

Cheeky's wounds were closing.

Max kissed him on the head. "You take whatever you need, little guy."

Unlike the previous times, he felt invigorated instead of drained, like the supply was endless. He was reminded of Lucille's lecture about magic sex.

Why is it different this time?

Within seconds Cheeky was fully healed and nuzzling him gratefully. Max gave him a big hug. "Don't you ever do that to me again." He pulled him away and looked him in the eyes. "What happened?"

Cheeky shot an accusatory glance at Puff, who cocked her head and blinked innocently.

"You've got to be more careful when you play. And don't go so far away when we're in a strange place."

Cheeky glared at Puff, snarfed then rolled his eyes to Max. He looked more embarrassed than anything.

"Is he okay?" Lucille approached them slowly.

"Yeah, he's fine. Cheekworms have a weird regenerative ability. Shit, do I look older?" He touched his face. It felt normal, so he stuck his hand down the back of his shirt.

Thank god, no back hair.

She shook her head slowly. "Why would you look older?"

"No reason." He shifted his attention to Cheeky. "So, it's been brought to my attention you might know more than you're letting on. You'd tell me if there was something I needed to know, right?"

Cheeky's expression hardened. He looked Max over doubtfully.

"What? *Is* there something you want to tell me?"

Cheeky smacked his lips three times then opened his mouth and rolled out his tongue. Instead of licking him, the tongue split down the middle then shot up Max's nostrils—way up.

"Is Max ready to move on now?" He could tell it was Cheeky talking. The voice was too cute to belong to anybody else, but why was it coming from inside his head?

"What the fuck, man? Get your tongue out of my nose." His words sounded more cartoonish than Cheeky's.

Lucille looked like she might try to intervene, but Max waved her away.

"Does he do that a lot?"

"First time for everything."

"What is he doing?"

"He's talking to me. He asked me a question."

Cheeky asked, "So?"

"Please tell me you aren't nasally violating me to tell me you are ready to go."

Cheeky snorted. "Cheeky love Max, but Max primitive, stupid monkey. Max can be more, is more, but only if he knows."

"Fuck you, man, at least I have decent grammar skills. What do you mean knows?"

"Monkey-speak is inefficient, but if you would prefer I speak with unnecessary verbiage, I will indulge you."

"Cheeky, please, this is uncomfortable."

"Says the man with his tongue in his mouth."

"I assume you're nostril raping me for a reason. What am I supposed to know?"

There was a swoosh and they were suddenly disconnected. Cheeky fell backwards, yowling in pain. Three inches of tongue dangled out of each of Max's nostrils.

"Cheeky?!"

Max jerked his head around looking for what had attacked them.

Lucille pointed down the river to their right. "The cat did it. It went that way."

"Puff?"

"Yeah. She started looking antsy when Cheeky's tongue split. She got worse while you were talking, then shot over there and cut his tongue off."

Cheeky latched one sucker onto Max's hand and re-grew his tongue. It barely took anything. Max realized he was starting to like it when Cheeky fed on him.

Max yanked the severed tongue out of his nose and massaged his nostrils. "Why would she do that?"

"Maybe she thought she was protecting you?"

"Yeah, because cats do that."

"Maybe she thought it was string?"

She is supposed to be my spirit animal. Maybe Cheeky was hurting me and I couldn't tell. What the fuck am I thinking? Cheeky wouldn't hurt me. Maybe she got jealous. Maybe TD got into her.

Max checked for signs of The Darkness. The air was almost cool with a slight breeze. The moon was bright as a dentist's kid's smile. He felt only as on-edge as he would expect after one of his pets attacked the other.

Lucille stared downstream. "Should we go after her?"

"I guess." Max looked at Cheeky. "All this time you've never said a word, why now?"

Cheeky frowned and his eyebrows jutted forward.

"Yeah, stupid monkey, I get it. I'm not sure I want to talk to you. Let's go find your cat."

They walked around the bend, but all they found was another fifty-foot straightway that bent to the left. Max called out, "Puff! Here kitty. Nobody's mad at you. It's okay."

Cheeky's expression said, "Speak for yourself."

They came to a drainage basin where the path dwindled and there were no stepping stones. Max looked down at his already ruined shoes and stepped in. The water came up just below his knees, but it was slowly creeping up his legs to menace his phone. He pulled it out and slogged around the corner with Cheeky and Lucille following close behind.

Ready for this adventure to be over, he activated his retinal implants and scanned for heat signatures. Memories of the operation flooded back, making him nauseous: that scalpel coming closer, cutting into his eye. He hated those implants, but they had saved his bacon several times during the war. There were critters all over the place, but nothing quite Puff-shaped.

They kept walking. Puff obviously didn't want to be found, so they stayed close to the rocky walls and stole peeks around the corner with his camera.

There was something off about this whole thing. He was about to ask Lucille what purpose the ravine served when a small, oddly shaped heat signature faded in on the other side of the stone wall. Puff was around the next bend cleaning her face with her paw. Max put his finger to his lips and motioned for the others to stay put, then crept around the corner as quietly as possible. He turned off his implants and saw Puff looking at him, still cleaning herself, but more cautiously.

Max spoke in soft, soothing tones. "Hey. Stay cool. We're not mad at you." He walked over and crouched beside her.

"So why'd ya do that?"

Puff looked up with wide innocent eyes then blinked one long "I love you" and went back to licking her shoulder.

"What's your deal, Cat? You're not a normal cat, obviously. Gulik said you're one of my spirit animals. Are you like Cheeky? Is there a pompous dick behind that fuzzy little face?"

Max's words slid off Puff like piss on a duck.

"I guess not. Come on, let's find a way out of here. He moved to pick Puff up, but she darted between his hands and flew farther downstream. She landed near the base of a huge, writhing tree that shimmered slightly in the mist of breaking water. It looked like a willow, but its branches were full of shiny blue fruit. There was a large cleft at its base where the stream narrowed and emptied as if the entire river were there just to feed it.

Puff dove inside.

"Oh, what the fuck? Cats are supposed to hate water." Max stomped toward the tree. The river deepened and the water rushed faster. "You guys can come out. The little fucker moved downstream again."

The closer he got, the more alive the tree bark seemed. It was moving the way everything moved on good acid. There were flowy patterns in the bark that felt like messages.

What is this thing?

His foot slipped, and the river carried him splashing toward the tree. He slammed against one of the large rocks around the base. It was smooth and slippery with algae, but he had enough inertia to propel himself onto it. He carefully pulled his legs underneath him and crouched on all fours.

Lucille screamed something, but her voice echoed strangely and was lost in the roar of the water.

Max called back, "I can't hear you."

She repeated herself, but he still couldn't tell what she was saying.

"I still can't hear you! Puff went in there!"

Cheeky was swimming towards him fast.

"Cheeky, no! Stay!" He turned back to the tree and screamed. "Puff! Come out of there now!" As he tried to stand, his weight shifted, and his legs slipped down the sides of the rock. His scrotum broke his fall, but didn't stop him sliding into the water and down the hole.

✱✱✱✱✱

Max woke up. He hadn't been so parched since the Iiites' interrogation chair. A slight wind blew across the dusty moonlit plane filling his face with grit.

Where the hell am I, and why can't I move?

He struggled, his conscious mind as yet unwilling to process what his eyes reported; that he was buried up to his neck in dense black dirt.

"I am not a fucking cabbage!"

Not far behind him, shoes lazily scraped the ground. Someone was doing something, but he couldn't turn to look. For all he could tell they were dancing.

"What the fuck is this about?" Max's chin beat against earth so dry that clouds rose up to motorboat his tongue. He spat, and rather than soaking into the ground, his spit sucked up more dust creating several small balls of mud on top of the dirt.

"Answer me, asshole!" He raged against the quagmire, but all he managed to release was sweat. "Show yourself, you sick fuck!"

Max could tell the boots were getting closer because the dust clouds drifting past were getting bigger. Every so often Max heard a pattern in the scrapings, thump, thump, scrape thump swish.

Whoever he is, he's definitely enjoying himself.

Max dug his chin into the dirt and scraped away what he could, but he was no Chaz Lightbeard. A familiar chuckle came from above. He leaned his head as far back as he could, but his captor stood just out of range.

"If your goal is to bore me to death, you're off to a great start."

The figure leaned over, dropping his face within inches of Max's. "Wee howdy."

"Hawk! Where the fuck have you been?"

"Oh, I been all over, busier'n an eight-armed slut on orgy night."

"Right. Well, I'm glad to see you're okay, but I can't help wondering why you're not digging me up."

"Typical Max, can't help thinking about yourself." He reached down and pushed his fingernails through the skin at Max's hairline. Blood trickled down Max's cheeks as the flesh was slowly pulled away. The act was delicate, almost loving, but that did nothing to ease the pain of having his face peeled like an orange.

Max's screams were muffled by his own flopping skin.

The wind picked up, coating Max's eyes and face-meat with a thin skin of mud. He felt drier with each passing moment. The desert was sucking him like a lozenge.

"Why?" Max asked as his lips were pulled away and ripped from his jaw.

Hawk grinned and stretched Max's face over his own. "Oww, stop hurting me. My Name's Max. Everybody has to do what I say because I saved the world all by myself. I get all the pussy and fame that the others can't have because I led them to their deaths. People are just tools for me. I feel no connection to my fellow man because people are stupid and primitive and any association with them could only serve to remind me what a useless waste of skin I am. I opened a gateway to let pure evil into my world because I have no concept of right or wrong. I have no soul, and I know it. Maybe that's why I smell like cat pee when I sweat."

Hawk did a little three step tap dance with jazz hands then smiled down at Max with his own wonky lips.

Max had neither the words or lips to argue, nor lids to shield him from the grim tableau. He hoped the brown grit caking his eyes would grow thick enough to block it all out so he could seep in peace. He was so dry, so cold. He yearned for the relatively balmy fingers of death, but despite massive blood loss, he was more conscious than ever.

This is what it all boils down to.

Figures.

Not exactly as I imagined it, but close enough.

He thought back to his early monologues; I won't do this, I can't do this, oh fuck it, I'll make it work. At some point, he started thinking he could change things, save the world for real.

Once it began, this could not have ended otherwise. But an end is always the beginning of something else. Right?

The sheet of dirt in Max's right eye became so thick it buckled and tumbled down his cheek like a slinky. Hawk was still wiggling his fingers as if waiting for applause.

This is a perfect representation of our relationship.

The Darkness was holding up a mirror, rubbing his face in his inner shit. Max felt guilty for the way he'd treated him, but it had always been a necessary evil. Right?

The guilt that had been growing inside him popped like a boil, spattering his brain with millions of instances of pointless cruelty. The air was going out of his logical inner tube. New thoughts were bubbling in, memories, a thousand crumpled brows, slick lashes, kicked puppy-dog eyes. What purpose did they serve?

He tried to speak and found he was able to make clear statements despite the lack of lips. "You're right. I'm really sorry. I've been a massive cunt."

Hawk jumped like an explosion had gone off near his head.

"This is all my fault. If I hadn't been such a dick, The Darkness wouldn't have taken you over.

"I'm fucked up. I don't mean that as an excuse. Just, I never meant to be an asshole. I can't help the way my brain works, but if you're still in there somewhere I want you to know I'm sorry. You're my best friend."

Max began to sob. Without eyelids to direct them, his tears squirted from his skull like windshield wiper fluid. "Whatever happens here, I don't want you to feel bad about it. I forgive you. I hope you can do the same for me."

Hawk laughed like he was coughing. "You think this is a movie? You think you can fuck me up with some deathbed confession bullshit? The damned is damned, boy, and you're a damned fool. Apologies are meaningless. Every mournful, yowling moment of your life has been a prayer to feed me!"

Something clicked, and a pressure began to grow in Max's esophagus. He smiled. "I see your point. I've always focused on what's wrong. I guess I thought I could identify and remove all the imperfections from my life. I was fixated on the negative, on you, I guess, and I never appreciated what I had. I wasn't dumb, or poor, or unhealthy. Hell, I'm quasi-fucking-immortal. I mean, not so good in this situation, but still." He jerked his thoughts back on course.

"I had Cheeky, Puff, Hawk, Cat and maybe this new chick, lots of others along the way, lots of others I let down by being a selfish asshole. But that's your fault. Isn't it? You were in my head before I was born. You were there while my mind was maturing, whispering in my subconscious, twisting basic instincts to rationalize processes that made you stronger. I meant well, but you fucked my head up.

Sure, I made choices, but human brains are only processors. Nobody can really be at fault, can they? At some point, some people become self-aware. With some effort, they can change the way their mind works. I've read about it. Metaprogramming. I used to think noticing dickish behavior in others and not doing those things made me self-aware, but that was just my program defending itself."

Max cocked his head thoughtfully. "Shit pops into your head at the weirdest times."

Hawk grabbed him by the hair, pulled him out of the ground and turned. Behind him was a full-length mirror. Max looked himself up and down. Below his neck swayed a soppy cardiovascular system. His heart looked like a dried plum and moved like it had a mouse inside.

"Your psychobabble cannot be used as a floatation device."

Maybe I'm a cabbage, after all.

Max grinned and laughed so hard he squirted tears. Where they fell, the dusty earth sprouted with new green life. All around him flowers bloomed as he spoke. "You know what? I've led an interesting life. So if you're going to kill me, fine. I still win because I managed to get the shit out of my head before it happened. But you're not going to kill me, are you? You can't because none of this is happening to my physical body. I slipped into another magic psychotherapy session, and whether you're the substantiator or a real manifestation of The Darkness, you can't hurt me. Even in the real world you can't hurt me. You can kill my body, but I've seen more than enough to know death is just a transition to the next part of life. I am a pupa. I like that word. Pupa."

His scalp slowly expanded, covering his muscles with pink, healthy flesh. A spine dropped out of his neck hole. Branching bones bloomed with muscle and sinew. He was knitting himself a new birthday suit. Within seconds he was standing on his own new feet.

Hawk let go, consternation peeling back his eyes. "You're not playing fair."

Max laughed, enjoying his new lungs. Laughing had felt weird without them. "Really? That's how you lose?"

Hawk grunted and threw a punch, but Max easily stepped aside. His adversary landed in the dirt.

"Don't be sore, man. It's all just nature taking its course. I know you can't help being what you are, but you have to let the pendulum swing back. My world doesn't belong to you." Max offered him a hand. "No hard feelings?"

Hawk yowled in pain. His body curled and became small and white. His adversary stared through slitted pupils and stumbled, flapping its ruffled wings like a discombobulated pigeon.

"Puff? What the fuck?"

The kitten steadied itself, smiled, and puffed up. Its fur fell out, revealing black reptilian skin that sprouted spines and talons. Its tail split into seven long necks each with a different abomination at its end. The abominations snapped their teeth and jabbed the sky with their horns, and the sky was torn asunder and blood rained down upon him. Black fire spewed from its many mouths as it roared.

"Big and scary, I get it. So you were Puff all along?"

The beast stopped its posturing. "No."

"You little stinker, you were spying on me."

"No I wasn't."

"Come on, you got weak and accidentally showed me your true form. Admit it."

"Fine, there is no Puff!"

"No, Puff was real. She might have been a part of you, or rather you might be a part of TD, but that just proves that she can be nice, even adorable, and if TD can be Puff, even for the purposes of deception, it's capable of something other than its own nature. I propose that any conscious mind has the potential to change itself. You could go back to being Puff, if you wanted. Even TD as a whole could change its nature."

"Stop calling me TD!" It stomped its clawed feet. "Your arrogance knows no bounds."

"For once, it's not arrogance."

"I am a fundamental part of all that is. I give the gift of suffering to all who need it, and you think I should abandon my nature to be a cuddly plaything for your amusement?"

"You can't be happy being what you are. You sort of are unhappiness. I watched you playing with Cheeky. You liked it. You liked having your head scratched. Don't lie to yourself. There would still be suffering without you, but there'd be a lot less. And don't bother making the argument suffering builds character or makes people feel validated."

The beast snorted. "Those are valid arguments."

"No, that kind of emotional validation only creates shame spirals and misery."

"Suffering does build character. Without trial by fire, the human soul is a squalid bezoar, which is hacked up in death and immediately relegated to the trash."

"I'm not going to debate this with you."

"Because you know I'm right."

"No, because I know we wouldn't be able to change each other's mind. All I'm saying is you could be happy if you chose to be, just like I could have, but didn't for most of my life."

The beast grew giant wings and spread them. "I am The Darkness! I am misery! I'm the bungee cords that hold the tarp on reality. No, I am reality! All that is good in the world is just a tarp held onto a rusty old wreck by bloody hooks and dry rot."

"Maybe so, but you're also my little Puff." Max reached out and ran his hand down its chest.

The monster shrieked, collapsing back into Max's fuzzy little pet. It twitched, blinked once and shot through the mirror as if it were an open window.

The lump in Max's esophagus twisted and grew. He hunched forward and wharfed Cheeky into a slimy puddle of his drippings. It was oddly pleasant, like puking on ecstasy.

"Dude! Why were you inside me?"

Cheeky responded wirelessly. "I came to help."

"Thanks, but why were you in me? And how? There wasn't much me there at one point."

"I was in your heart. That's why I was able to help."

Max laughed. "Let's not make this cheesier than it already is." He scooped Cheeky up and hugged him tight. "Thanks, man. Sorry I've been stupid."

"It's okay. You can't help it."

"Where are we, anyway?"

"Some cultures call this the tree of life."

"Ah, and that mirror is the way out?"

Cheeky nodded. Max picked him up and stepped through. There was a momentary feeling of falling, then he woke up on his back at the base of a waterfall with Cheeky on his chest.

"All right! I'm starting to get the hang of this.

Cheeky shot him a look to let him know he was more pleased with himself than he should be.

There was a rusting in the brush and Lucille appeared. Her dress was dirty and her hair full of twigs. "You don't listen for shit."

"Hey, awesome! I wasn't sure I'd be able to find you."

She was taken aback. "You're awful chipper. Did you bump your head?"

"Probably, but it doesn't matter. I know what to do now."

It took her a second to register what he was saying. "You do?"

"Yeah, it's all going to work out!" He took her hands and grinned.

She grinned back but her eyes betrayed her doubt.

"No really. It's all going to be okay!"

On their way to the exit, Max heard a familiar cough. About twenty feet into the woods, in a small clearing, he saw a teepee with a wacky, armless, inflatable tube man of smoke wiggling out the top. The flap opened and burped out the Count, who slapped at a patch of ash on his shoulder then did a double take as he saw them walking down the path.

Greystoke and Lucille eyed each other strangely, as if each thought the other might throw up in their pocket, given the opportunity. Max smirked. "Wow, I could cut the history with a knife. I want details, but it'll have to wait. We have a God to kill." He pointed at Greystoke. "You'll be happy to hear I've got this sewn up tighter than a Baptastic's asshole."

Greystoke tilted his head slightly and forced a smile. "But of course you do." He turned to Lucille, "Still in good health, I see."

"And look at you, totally recovered from your bout with femininity. What's it been, three years?"

"Five."

Max waved his hand between them. "*Hellooo*, Max here. Leave the ice storm for later. Time is money, or rather lives."

Greystoke snorted. "Well then, by all means. Lead the way, Messiah."

Max headed straight through the woods toward the exit.

Greystoke's smug expression fell from his face like a roofer in dress shoes. "That is not a path!"

Lucille and Cheeky followed Max. Greystoke hesitated for a moment, then growled nasally and ducked into the woods.

"The path of least resistance never gets you anywhere." Lucille let a tree branch snap Greystoke in the face.

Greystoke made a noise like a choking turtle. "Do be careful. That hurt."

As soon as the Count emerged onto the path, Max said, "I need a press conference ASAP, big as you can make it, at least one reporter from every news agency, blog site, and water cooler this side of Sirius. Do whatever you have to do to draw them in, just get them here."

"So you can tell them…"

"The solution."

"Which is what?"

"You'll find out along with everybody else."

Greystoke's eyes sliced at Lucille like katanas. "Would it not be better to share this information with as many people along the way as possible? What if something happened to you before the conference? I'd hate for the whole world to perish because you wanted a dramatic reveal."

"There isn't time to explain it twice."

"There will be a ride there."

"You need to be working on setting it all up on the way there."

Greystoke lowered his gaze, ground his teeth, and nodded his consent.

Max stuck his hand inside Greystoke's jacket and pulled out his phone. He grabbed Greystoke's hand and pressed the phone into his palm. "We might only have one shot at this. Get it right."

The Count hooded his eyes.

"Relax, man, I got this."

# CIRCUS OF THE DUMB

The Count stood three idiots from the stage, rubbing the satin in his coat pocket for comfort and occasionally bopping a miscreant in the head with his walking stick to bid them keep their distance. He in no way appreciated this new, more self-assured form of belligerence Lucille had inspired in his charge. In only a few hours she had utterly destroyed every scrap of amicability he had worked so hard to cultivate with that cretin.

He looked around at the feat he had accomplished: a full-scale Media© event in a time of crisis, produced safely, with representatives from every purveyor of Media© and a full audience in attendance, all in less than four hours. As requested, the sky was blue with yellow squiggles.

All this for a man unwilling to share his plan. And then to be banished into the audience like some intern whose usefulness has expired!

This impudent malfeasance would be addressed in due time. For now, all he could do was chew his tongue and hope the foundation for Max's audacity was based in something substantial, rather than, as he suspected, the desire to impress the dispassionate gorgon who had turned his own heart to stone.

Max's presentation, whatever it was, would begin shortly. The cameramen were pressing in, trying to squeeze in front of him. One stepped on his toes, scuffing his shoe just below the spat. The Count quietly placed the tip of his walking stick in the center of the man's foot and unleashed his spring-loaded stiletto. The man looked at him, then down at his foot as the blade was slowly removed. Blood bubbled up like lava and trickled little streams down the ridges on his white trainers. He opened his mouth to scream.

The Count silenced him with a look. "Now, now, let's not make a fuss. You have an important job to do." He gestured to the stage with his cane.

The music started, some sappy antique from the dark days of music. "All you need is love. All you need is love."

The man forced a smile and turned his camera toward the stage.

The Count smiled. Despite Max's initial bungling, he was sure this would be a success. *How can it not be after all I've done?*

Max walked slowly onto the stage wearing peasant clothes. The Count felt like a little man had pushed a fistful of fish hooks up his rectum then tied the line to the bumper of a little car, got in and drove away leaving him empty.

"Oh no."

Where fanfare should have been there was instead a vast sea of dull eyes, cocked heads and smacking gum.

The music ended as Max took the microphone from its stand. He waved curtly. "Hey, everybody. I thought I'd leave out the bullshit for once and get straight to the point. I have defeated The Darkness."

After several seconds of silence someone threw their fist in the air and screamed, "Fuck yeah!"

Others joined him, and soon everyone was screaming jubilantly and dancing to the music of freedom.

When did this happen?

The music commenced its blaring, and the curtain behind the stage dropped. Behind it, a choir of white-robed hippies joined in with a sickeningly joyous chorus. Felicity came onto the stage wearing a plush bacon costume. Two plushy felines appeared on either side of the stage dragging small cannons, which they lit and fired over the audience. Multicolored envelopes fluttered into the crowd.

Greystoke caught one, opened it and poured the googley-eyed, cat-bacon monstrosity into his palm. *I had wondered what she would do with these.*

Cinnamon wafted through the crowd.

The felines reloaded the cannons and fired again. More explosions erupted in the back. The Count turned to see the issue of a further four cannons fluttering merrily into the waiting hands of the public.

There goes 1.5 million.

Max screamed over the music. "These pins commemorate our victory today, but a month from now when everything's back to normal, I hope you'll keep on wearing them as a symbol of all the things that make you happy. Every time you see one of these pins it should serve as a reminder that life doesn't suck. There are cats and bacon and cinnamon rolls and music. They play music, by the way. What was it, five hundred gigs of storage?"

One of the felines nodded.

"Yeah, five hundred gigs of storage with Blacktooth and Wi-Fi, so you can put anything on there and play it through your phone, or whatever."

Despite being only marginally better than a prize one might find buried in cereal, the pins garnered quite an impressive reaction from the crowd. Felicity had stolen his idea and successfully adapted it to further her agenda. The Count had never been so proud. It almost made up for the proper mess Max had made of his part.

Something changed in the air, like a sudden drop in barometric pressure. The cheering was choked out by gasps of shock and confusion. The music became jumbled and disintegrated.

The Count scanned for breaches, signs of violence, but there were none. He turned his attention to the stage and saw Hawk yanking the microphone out of Max's hand while the latter stood transfixed like a stoned pastry chef in a sweet shop.

Many in the crowd recognized Hawk from the last time Max was on TV, but he put out his hand to calm them. "Hiya, folks. No need to be alarmed, not by me, anyway. I mean, everything he just said is a fuckin' lie, but I doubt any of ya was dumb enough to buy into it."

The crowd was growing more restless by the second, so the Count slipped around the side of the stage and nestled himself in a cove of I-Force guards.

"I used to believe everything he said, but that was before the powers that be got their hooks in him. I don't know what he's tryin' ta sell ya, but folks are still getting ripped apart out there. He says he's handled it, but all I see he's done is conjure up a bunch a fuzzy little monsters to put everybody to sleep. Is that your plan? Knock us all out so we can't hurt each other?"

Max snapped out of his shock and snatched the microphone back. "Wow. This is bold, even for you." He addressed the crowd, "Everyone, I'd like to introduce you to The Darkness." He air quoted The Darkness. "He possessed my friend, but I beat him anyway, and now he's here as a last-ditch effort to trick you all into being afraid of him again." He turned to Hawk. "Look at you. You're so weak you can't even infect anybody anymore. Just fuck off back to hell or wherever and leave us alone."

The crowd screamed and applauded.

"Nice try, but I think it's pretty obvious I'm not infected anymore. No thanks to you. You all saw me get knocked up with evil. After that, the Iiites nabbed me. Bunch'a kids did all kinds of tests and they come up with an antidote. That's how we handle our problems in the real world, not a bunch of hippie claptrap about love conquers all. If Max had spent any time trying to find a real solution instead of jettin' around the globe to meet with mystics and stuff his ass fulla crystals, he'd probably have nipped this in the bud a long time ago. Whatcha got to say for yourself mister messiah?" Hawk held the microphone out for Max to respond.

The crowd booed, but it was hard to tell who it was intended for.

Max kept smiling and motioned off-stage for someone to bring a second microphone. Someone ran one out. He thanked them and turned back to Hawk.

"I don't know if this antidote thing is true. I hope it's true, because that means you're okay, but I doubt it. Either way it doesn't matter. TD is still defeated. He feeds on fear and hate. All we have to do to starve him out is focus on stuff that makes us happy and he's like a declawed cat. He can glare and hiss and swipe at you all he wants, but since he can't hurt you, it's kind of cute."

Hawk shifted his eyes to the ground looking sullen. "I don't know if you snapped under the pressure or Greystoke's finally managed to bring you over to the dark side. What I do know is you're up here fillin' people's heads with pretty lies instead of doin' anything to help 'em."

Hawk addressed the crowd. "Now, unlike Max, I brought proof." He waved stage left and four Iiites wheeled out a large cage containing a frothing male in a shredded business suit. The crowd gasped as the man growled and beat himself against the bars.

"As you can see, this fella's got himself one heavy dose o' darkness, but observe as he is immediately restored to humanity."

"Now I know you're not Hawk," Max said. "Hawk never had this much showmanship."

One of the Iiites had a long stick with a syringe on the end. He walked around the back of the cage and jabbed it into the man's ass. Within seconds he stopped screaming, smiled, and sat on the floor of his cage.

Hawk squatted to address him. "Excuse me, sir?"

The man looked up in a daze, seemed to notice the cage and responded. "Yes?"

"What is your name, sir?"

"Phil Mahoney. Where am I?"

"It's all right, sir. You're safe. You got infected, but you're better now."

Max squatted too. "How do you feel?"

The man giggled and rolled his head. "I feel wonderful."

"Do you love me?"

"Of course I do. I love everybody!"

Max nodded and stood. "All they did was get this guy high, which was my idea, anyway. I'm glad to see it worked, but you can't keep everybody high forever. This might be a great short term solution, but it only proves what I was saying. His love is artificial, but TD still can't affect—"

Hawk butted in. "Your plan was to dump drugs in the water supply to save your own ass. This here's not just ecstasy, it blocks The Darkness for a long time after the person comes down. The only problem is we're still working on producing the stuff in the quantities we need to help everybody. We're going as fast as we can, but we're gonna have to start off using half the supply to inoculate the unaffected in at-risk areas while the other half is used to treat the infected as they try to press in. This way we can stop the spread of infected areas. Once we've got a few more plants making the stuff, we can make a push to take back the compromised districts."

"You're going to inoculate a bunch of Sonians rather than treat infected Savanians? And he says I'm a shill."

"You had your way you'd give it all to your Klipsch buddies."

"No, I wouldn't."

The corners of Hawk's mouth jutted irregularly. "You really think these people are that stupid?"

The crowd booed. This time it was obvious for whom.

"No, but you obviously do. I came here with a message of victory. We already won. Right now, not in a few months after somebody's made a fortune and thousands more people have died. You say you're not infected anymore, but this is the best, no the only thing TD could do to save itself." A pin bounced off the side of his head.

Someone in the crowd screamed. "Get off the stage, asshole."

Others piped in. "Liar!"

"False messiah!"

"Hippie bourgeois cunt."

Now everyone was throwing their pins at him. "Hey, chill out everybody. I'm here to help."

"Why don't you go help yourself to another bottle of Champagne!"

People started removing the backs before hurling them.

"Ouch, guys come on." He turned his back to the crowd, shielded his face and looked The Darkness in the eyes. "Bravo, but I maintain that you are capable of reason, so I know you'll come around eventually."

The Count ground his teeth so hard he felt a tooth crack. "Enough of this! Get us out of here before it can get any worse."

His guards locked boots and flew him to safety while several others rushed the stage and did the same for Max.

This is the last time that imbecile has any say about anything.

# 100 TEARS

Greystoke cursed in six different languages, while Max stared silently at the mahogany floor of the study. The Count called Max everything from "an unaccountable dribble in the ballet of chestnuts," to "Mighty Shiva, destroyer of all things." When it was obvious Max wasn't going to respond, and his voice began to break, he slapped Max in the side of his head and stormed out, slamming the door so hard the Camilla Rose Garcia painting hopped off the wall and shattered its frame.

Greystoke's words rattled around his skull like small caliber bullets.

What was there to say?

Greystoke was right.

He had failed.

# REALITY BLEED THROUGH

The next day, Max slept in, but he'd have enjoyed it a lot more if his dreams weren't all about his pores being full of worms and his teeth falling out.

"Fuck me."

He rolled onto his back and stared at the ornately carved ceiling while memories of his failure pounded his soul like a retarded gorilla with a squeak toy. If that wasn't bad enough, his optic nerve had come to life and was fighting a turf war with his brain. He massaged his eyes, and the pain subsided, so he opened them and realized nothing in his surroundings looked familiar.

"Where the hell am I?"

Wanting to be alone and drunk, he'd taken a decanter from Greystoke's study and wandered into the unused wing. The rest of the night was missing.

"At least I'm not a complete failure."

He sat up and rolled his shoulders to work his nerves back into place, then climbed into the chair by the antique roll-top desk and rested his face in his hands.

His head felt hollow, like everything useful had been removed with an ice cream scoop; no ideas, no hope, just the crushing weight of failure. He had the answer. He'd won. All he had to do was let them know, but he'd been so excited he forgot how fucking stupid they were, how addicted to fear.

Max could feel The Darkness squirming within him. It could have him if it wanted, but it was taking its time, making a point. The Darkness knew him well. It knew his brain was trained to give up easily. Hate returned like a horny ex-girlfriend. His psyche wanted to reset to its default settings. Part of him wanted that validation, but something held him back. He was too self-aware to let it happen.

"Sorry, TD. You might have won the world, but you can't have me. I still know what I know." He thought of running his lips over the fatty lumps on Cheeky's head. Deep within him, The Darkness danced like a salted slug. His head cleared a bit, and the knot in the back of his neck slackened.

"That's what I thought."

Max sucked in a heaping helping of musty air and exhaled slowly, imagining all the bad stuff pouring out his mouth like smoke. After a few more times, he felt almost good. He didn't know what to expect when he left the room, but he made up his mind to be as happy as possible for as long as possible, which, to his thinking, was the best anyone could do.

✶✶✶✶✶

Max found Cat watching muted news in the Bonsai Banana room. He had no idea why Bonsai was so special to her. He was one of hundreds of color-coded cartoon characters that existed solely to push the boundaries of merchandising. This room was a shrine to their success. Everywhere he looked, thousands of little green bananas tangled and heaped, each one squinting like it was about to shit pure joy. All that green made him feel a little high.

Cat swiveled her big banana-chair and stuck out her bottom lip. "They're killin' all my friends."

Max sat in the other banana chair and swiveled to the banana-rimmed TV. A little purple bear ran in slow motion toward the camera. When it was about five feet away its face imploded and shot out the back of its head. Its feet left the ground as it flipped twice through a cloud of its blood and landed on its back.

"What the hell?"

Max watched scene after scene of brightly colored creatures rushing to hug merciless death squads. Cat unmuted the TV. "...taking back the streets. These brave men and women are doing what the police could not, and many are beginning to question what it is we're paying for."

"They're makin' squish videos with the little blue ones."

"Wow."

They played the slow-motion bear murder again.

"Leading sources predict that, with the new vaccine, the alien invasion could be over as soon as mid-July."

"But getting people high isn't going to affect *them* at all." Max turned off the TV. "It's too early for this shit."

Cat smirked and picked up a little Bonsai clock. It said 6:30 p.m.

He glanced at her oversized Bonsai sleep shirt.

"Where ya been all day?"

"I passed out in some storage room. It's how I process."

"I'm sorry your day sucked."

Max laughed and smooched her on the forehead. "You're so fuckin' cute."

"You're cuter."

Max shook his head. "No, I'm fuckeder. Your dad made it clear I've lost all rights and privileges. I'm his bitch forevermore."

She opened the minifridge and handed Max a kiwi-banana smoothie pouch. "Daddy's attention span is worse than mine. He'll get over it."

"I appreciate you trying to make me feel better, but I don't think it'll be that easy." He stabbed the straw through the foil and sucked its thick, chemically contents. "Of course he gets over being mad at *you*. You're his daughter. I'm a commodity he's trying to cash in on, and my stock just went through the floor."

She patted his knee. "Don't worry. I'll make him be nice."

Max wondered how he could have a girl like Cat, and still be so infatuated with Lucille. Cat was sweet and gorgeous. She would do anything for him, including buffer her father's rage. The sex was beyond description. She was weird and fun, but he didn't love her.

What is wrong with me?

"In the meantime," Cat pulled off her oversized sleep shirt and squeezed the rest of her smoothie over her chest, "you still look thirsty." She leaned back. The gloppy green stuff goose pimpled her flesh and hardened her nipples as it slid down her breasts and into the smooth inward curve of her stomach.

I suck so bad.

"I think you might be right." He tore off his shirt and lunged.

Everything tastes better with a hint of unwashed girl flesh.

He pictured a little vial of Savory Savanian with a picture of Scarlet on the label. They probably had something like that in one of the specialty shops. He imagined Greystoke spritzing a little on his rack of lamb.

Eww.

He forced those thoughts out of his head and focused on quenching his thirst.

Cat produced another bag, put it against his face, and punched it open. He should have been upset, but the burst of pain and fruit turned his headache into a kinky accessory. He stabbed his tongue into her bellybutton and fumbled with his belt.

He looked up and saw she had draped a bag over her left cheek.

He was so hard it hurt.

Any other time he wouldn't have been up for it, but in the moment, he decided to give the lady what she wanted. He reared back and brought his palm down hard, but instead of popping, the little green bag flew across the room and hit the wall.

"Aww, fail." She placed another bag. "Do it right, fucker."

He cocked an eyebrow, gritted his teeth and tried again, close fisted. Green stuff went everywhere. He blinked it out of his eyes, grabbed her legs, and twisted her into the jackhammer position. He'd just hit cervix when he heard a gasp and turned to find Lucille pinned against the doorframe by shock and revulsion.

"Fuck! Hi."

She dropped her doughnuts and backed into the hallway.

"Where ya going? Hey! Goddammit." He looked down at his dazed girlfriend.

And here's where it all goes to hell. He let go of her legs.

She fell hard on her back. "Ow, why'd you stop?"

"Can we finish this later? I think a work thing just came up." Max jumped into his pants.

"What? No. You don't have work things anymore. Get ta fuckin' me."

"Sorry. I'll make it up to you." He dashed out the door.

Cat's voice grew louder and angrier the farther away he got.

When he jerked open the front door the intercom screamed, "Fuck me, you stupid asshole!"

Lucille was unlocking her car.

"Hey, hold up!"

"This is obviously a bad time." She got in and shut the door.

She totally likes me.

"No, it's not ideal, but, come on. You're here. I'm happy to see you."

"I'm sure." She started her engine.

Max hugged the front of her car. "You're not going anywhere until you tell me why you came."

She took her foot off the brake and he was sucked under the car, bumping his head and badly bruising his wrists.

"Oww, what the fuck are you so mad about?"

The car stopped. For a moment he thought she might back over him, but the engine cut out and the door popped open.

"You're right. I'm sorry. I don't know why I did that." She got out and walked over to him. "You okay?"

Max rubbed his wrists. "Yeah, I've had worse."

"Sorry."

"No biggie. It was worth it."

"How so?"

"Now I know you feel the same way."

She furrowed her brow. "What's that supposed to mean?"

"We have a connection that Cat and I will never have. She's great, but it's not going to be a permanent thing. I've been extremely attracted to you since the day we met, and I don't just mean sexually. I'd like us to be more than business associates, and it's pretty obvious you would too."

She scrunched up her mouth and glared at his nose for ten seconds before responding. "Get in the car."

Max grinned.

"Now, before you make it worse."

"Make what worse?" he asked, as he complied.

She got in and turned the key. "She had to be watching us. The last thing you need right now is a vindictive ex."

"Yeah, I'd like to think she won't mind, but I suppose that was pretty terrible of me."

"Ya think?" She drove slowly towards the gate.

"Go faster. We need her to believe this is an emergency."

"Oh, right." She sped up. "I was trying to act casual."

Max laughed a little too hard, earning himself a high-browed stare. The rubber band snapping his mind from extreme depression to joyful exuberance was stretched to its limit. He had to pick one emotion and stick with it before something snapped.

"So—you like me then?"

Lucille sighed. "What are you, twelve?"

"Yes. You like me. Admit it."

"I'm liking you less every time you say stuff."

"Sorry, I'm not usually like this. It's just, usually the girls I'm with—they're great, and I feel like I should love them, but I don't. With you, it's different. It always felt like I was pretending, before. In the back of my head there was always a little voice calling bullshit. Is this what bewitching means? Did you hoodoo my hoo-hoo, or something?"

She smirked, but kept her eyes on the road.

"It's okay if you did. I wouldn't mind."

She cocked an eyebrow at him, but remained silent.

"Even that's different. One of my exes used mind control drugs on me. They were a lot of fun, but I resented it. I never did figure out what was up with her."

Lucille was looking less and less amused.

"So why did you come?"

Her shoulders slumped a little. "How could I not? Between that monumental craptastrophy yesterday and the news today, I thought you could use some cheering up."

"Oh, yeah. You know, I'm weirdly at peace with it. I can honestly say I did my best. I never wanted to be a savior, and I never had a chance. Things happened the only way they could have."

"You can't be serious."

"What? My psyche is very efficient."

Lucille laughed. "A little too efficient. It's not over yet."

"The fuck it's not. I've lost all the support from my backers. Everybody hates me. Shit, the last person who could have helped me, I just walked out on in the middle of sex, which, in retrospect, was most likely her attempt at helping me get over my massive failure. God, I'm a dick."

"Yeah, fair warning, you ever do anything like that to me and I'll take your penis."

Max laughed.

She stared straight ahead. The slight tweak in her lips was not facetious. "Greystoke knows."

"What does Greystoke know?"

"I guess you'll hear about it eventually. Greystoke tutored me for a while. I was young and impressionable. He was larger than life, sort of a walking amalgam of everything that melts the panties off adolescent girls. We became involved. After a while, he got bored with me. He got infatuated with another of his students and flaunted their relationship to torture me. So, I turned him into a girl."

"You cut off his dick?"

"No, I literally turned him into a girl. His body hair fell out, he grew breasts, and his penis withered into a vagina. I was reading a lot of feminist literature at the time."

Max laughed uncomfortably. "He is one ugly girl."

"After two years, I matured enough to strike a deal with him."

"Are you serious? I mean, can you actually do that?" Max couldn't help but picture himself as a girl having a ménage a trois with Cat and Lucille. Lesbian sex always looked like so much more fun.

"Be a good boy and you'll never find out."

✳✳✳✳✳

It took Max three tries to get Tantric sex right, but when he did, he felt ready to give up regular fucking for good. In truth, he'd still jump at the chance of a sad hand job in a port-o-dump, but he *felt* like he was ready.

Lucille taught him to come with his brain, to feel with his eyes, to slow down. She took the bodily function out of the equation, explaining, "The orgasm takes place in your mind and in your soul. The ejaculate is only a punctuation, a sacrament of the flesh to make new flesh. Sex for pleasure has no need for sperm, so hold onto it.

"By keeping your body in check you strengthen your soul, which is a little piece of God. Instead of dissipating, the energy that funnels into you during sex stays inside you, strengthening your inner God. Now, look past my flesh to the goddess inside me. Marvel at her

292

beauty as she radiates out through my skin. Recognize me as your Goddess as I recognize you as my God. See yourself in my face as I see mine in yours."

It had been very difficult to concentrate on her words, as his lingam was in the balmy embrace of her yoni. The difficulty was further compounded by the uncomfortable pretzel she had tied his legs into. Her heels dug into his kidneys while they did weird, sexual sit-ups. He tried to chant her mantra, but found it very difficult to replace the one he already had.

I'm gonna come. I'm gonna come. Please, no. No. Fuck, I'm gonna come.

Before long, his fears manifested as reality, earning him another lecture on the necessity of a pure mind free of anxiety.

She explained that sex is a sort of trance and whatever thoughts you enter into it with will be magnified to form a self-feeding loop. As the energy fills you, it pumps up that loop. The loop envelops you. At some point, the loop bursts as orgasm. But the purer the loop, the more it can hold. The object is to make the loop loving acceptance. Slowly inflate it as big as you can without it bursting, then stop and keep all that positive energy within you.

Max thought it sounded kookier than a truckload of cuckoo clocks falling down a ravine and landing on a cartoon platypus, but nodded as though they were in complete agreement. His policy was to never look a gift yoni in the mouth.

She immediately launched into round two, which was much different. The position was still awkward yoga bullshit, but there were no sit-ups. Now that the pressure was off, he was able to relax into it. At first it was nice, but sort of boring. No, boring was the wrong word. He could never be bored with boobies in his face. Peaceful?

He liked being able to take his time to study her body. Usually if a guy asked a girl to sit still and let him stare at her breasts, she would kick him in the balls and walk off.

Tantra must have been contrived by guys who wanted to trick women into having hours of sex on the reg, while also validating the pathetic, immature impulses we don't want to admit we have.

He stared so long that the hypnotic lock faded. He began to admire other things, like the gentle swooping ribs sliding like ripples in steamy white coffee.

Her skin was pure and fresh like frozen yogurt.

He'd always wanted to lick her.

She tasted light and sweet like flowers somebody fucked on.

She was a slow-motion jellyfish swimming in waves of energy.

Her face. The contours of her chin.

Light clung to her like sweat. Her body was an exotic altar burning sweat like sacred oils, which penetrated all three nostrils, changing everything it touched, thrumming, spreading without moving.

Her eyes transcended physicality, linking their minds, creating a circuit. Every breath engulfed them in fire. The spiraling vortex of meat between their legs was slowly gobbling them up, grinding them, turning them into a psycho-sexual sausage. Just as some of the things she had explained were beginning to make sense, his bulbospongiosus muscle went off like anti-aircraft cannon. His teeth gritted so hard he heard a crack. He jerked away feeling like he'd stuck his dick in a light socket.

"Holy mother of fuck!"

"Don't worry. You're getting there, but you're still fucking me with your body. You're supposed to be making love to me with your mind. We'll try again."

"Really? Not that I'm complaining, but we've been at this for hours."

She pulled him to his feet and smiled. "All the more reason to do it right this time." She gently took hold of his nipples. "Do what I do."

He gently pinched her nipples and waited.

"Think of them like positive and negative terminals on a battery. Your arms are power cables. Your fingers are the connectors, made of the same stuff as the terminal. Put them together, and two things become one. Energy flows from one to the other then back to the first. The energy belongs to both, as both are one."

She gently pulled his right nipple while pushing his left. He did the same to her and was back in the spirit in under a minute. It felt like energy was flowing through his nipples. He was taking and giving. Was it possible to come without his penis touching anything?

On the up side, if he did come, all he'd expel would be a puff of smoke. Maybe he could play it off.

He relaxed into the timeless sensation. He looked through her eyes and saw she *was* a Goddess, not a cheesy supernatural entity, but an actual manifestation of the divine. There were galaxies birthing in her eyes.

"Now, we connect the other terminals. Be careful. There is a lot of juice down there, but there's plenty of time to let it flow. Feel the energy transfer as we slowly recline into a sitting position. Don't lose the connection with the other terminals. Just buckle your knees and fall back slowly."

He did as he was told, and they smoothly transitioned into an easy lotus. Their mouths and crotches locked like magnets, sparks and fire, bursting, swirling through the circuit like electrons. They were the building blocks and the builder, a fusion of every opposite, pure energy, making its own open system, feeding themselves, growing exponentially. They weren't burning, they were fire, electricity, plasma. They got so hot that heat lost meaning. Physics fell away, and they became the void. Together they looked down into reality with one omniscient eye seeing all the beauty that ever was.

From the outside, it looked like a star.

Eons passed.

They forgot what it was like to be down there. They wanted to touch things, to have separate perspectives, so they became a sun, to burn away their power.

They woke panting, nerves fizzling like live wires in a puddle of sports drink. Max fell back and Lucille came with him.

Everything sparkled like the nachos fluttering around their heads. Max tried to remember what he was on, but didn't remember taking anything. "My goddamn teeth are buzzing."

"Mine too."

She smiled and they kissed, slowly sucking each other's lips.

Max felt like a flower and a bee. Tears welled in his eyes. He laughed. "Cat would fucking love this. But you'd never get her to sit still long enough."

That was the wrong thing to say.

He expected her to slap him, but she laughed too. "Oh man, you should have seen us back in the day. Single most frustrating thing I've ever tried."

Max was stunned, "You fucked Cat *and* Greystoke?"

"Don't look at me like that. Her pussy's more omnipresent than McDougle's. Sooner or later everybody ends up in there."

"I got that impression. Say, you think you might like to have a three way sometime?"

She rolled off him and sat up. "You're seriously asking me that on our first date."

"Only because it would solve so many of my problems. I mean, if you two could share me and get along, I wouldn't have to hurt her feelings. If it wasn't for Cat, Greystoke would have probably walled me up in his basement last night. I don't want to think what might happen if they *both* want me dead."

Lucille nodded. "True. I don't believe in monogamy, and Cat can't even say it without bursting into flames, so you're probably good. We need to come up with a good excuse for running out on her like that. Whatever it is, you're going to have a lot of apologizing to do."

"Yeah, I know." He sat up and scooched over to lean against the wall.

Lucille hoisted herself into a swiveling office chair. "If you can survive until she forgives you, she'll probably try to instigate a three way the first time we're alone together."

"Probably."

"Still, we should pretend this never happened. She can be sort of possessive."

Max remembered Heller's party. "I know what you mean. I've been trying to figure out the rules to her crazy, but the only one I've managed is that anything is cool as long as it's her idea. I suppose that's the one way she's normal. Granted, most people wouldn't get the idea to entertain a group of children by ripping open a live chicken and wearing it like a hat while doing the chicken dance and crowing any-cock'll-do."

Lucille grinned. "She is proud of that story."

"What was it, her eleventh birthday?"

She laughed and swiveled with just enough force to make her breasts sway. "Something like that."

"Why'd you guys split up?"

She responded with a you-can't-possibly-be-that-stupid look.

"Aside from the obvious reasons. Seems like there was more to your relationship than weird sex and pissing daddy off."

She shrugged. "We didn't really break up, just went in different directions. Cat got religious, I got serious about magic, and we stopped calling each other."

"You miss her?"

"No, I mean, sometimes. She has a way of making you feel alive. It's not like we were in love. Like you said, that sort of thing's impossible with her."

"Mmm hmm." There was obviously more emotion there than she was willing to admit, but Max knew better than to press. "What are we going to tell her we've been doing all this time?"

"I don't know if telling her is going to be enough. She's a bit paranoid, if you haven't noticed."

"I did."

"We need to go be seen doing something important."

"We could go kick some militia ass."

"The militias are too popular right now. The public would hate you."

"Fuck those idiots. They already hate me."

"What do you think the Count would do?"

Max thought for a moment. "He'd probably sign the head of a militia and have him execute me on live TV."

Lucille nodded.

"We could kill somebody the public hates, the Cult of Abel*?"

"That might improve your image, but they're hardly worth running out on sex for."

"Yeah."

"What about that Hawk guy? He's the one who destroyed your plans. We could say he was planning some big nasty thing we had to stop."

"How would we even find him?"

She swiveled to her computer and tapped a few keys. "That won't be a problem."

Max stood and came close enough to read the screen. "He has a fucking website?"

"Plus Twaddle, Roller, Tumbly, Booker, you name it. His feed is more active than a teenage drag queen on Ecstasy."

"One thing you can say for evil, it's not lazy." Anxiety trickled through his guts like scalding cocoa. "But I don't know if I should try to cast out the demon or put a bullet in his face."

"Decide fast. He's got a Media© appearance at eight-thirty. If you could out him, somehow prove he's lying, that could get you back in with Cat and the idiot masses."

"How?"

"What if you fight lies with lies. Act crazy, attack him during one of his Media© events and he'll have to give you the antidote. You keep acting crazy while I stand in the crowd screaming the cure is a hoax. The Media© would report people tearing him limb from limb no matter how many serum darts they were shot with."

"That's a great plan except for the part where we're both killed by rampaging idiots. I think somebody would notice if I suddenly stopped being crazy and jet-packed out of there."

"Good point. I'm not in a martyr-y mood." She leaned back, put her feet on her desk and swiveled back and forth.

"There's always the obvious."

"What's that?"

"Giving him a dose of his own medicine."

"I thought we agreed the serum was a hoax."

"I doubt the serum does more than get people high, but if I could get the old Hawk to surface on live TV, even for a few seconds, he *would* tell people the truth. I asked the Nrrds to start experimenting with drugs a while ago. They probably have a prototype by now."

"Why haven't you called them yet?"

"I don't know. I stay pretty busy."

She tossed him a phone. "Call them."

Max dialed and Hedorah answered. "What?"

"Hey, it's Max."

"Oh shit." Max heard him switch to speaker phone. "Hey, Max remembered we exist. He must need something."

"Don't be a dick."

Emma's voice replied, "You *don't* need something?"

"Of course I fucking need something. Have you been watching the news?"

Emma giggled and whispered, "Stop that."

Hedorah giggled.

A horrible thought crossed his mind. "You guys aren't, like, fucking, are you?"

A lighter was flicked. Hedorah exhaled and said, "Not anymore."

"Eww, what the fuck?"

They made their excuses in unison. His that she wasn't so bad once all the inhibitors were taken away and hers that she didn't have time to find a stranger to satisfy her womanly needs.

"I honestly don't give a fuck. I just need to know if you found a cure."

He heard the wheeze of a Bio-Bed as Hedorah replied. "Not really. The best we can do with the hard cases, the ones that changed physically, is put them to sleep. We've got something that can bring the newly infected back to their senses for about forty-five minutes, but after that they tend to come down and get all pissed about being used as guinea pigs. Then they re-infect."

Emma added. "Fun fact, the stuff that comes out their mouths is frothed bodily fluids. The infection makes their guts convulse. I'm surprised it doesn't kill them. We have done some experiments with high-frequency resonators, but nothing has come from it yet."

"Forty-five minutes is better than nothing. Can you whip up a long-range delivery system for me?"

"How long you need?"

"A mile would be good."

"That shouldn't be a problem."

"When'll it be ready?"

"We have darts. We have a high-powered air-rifle with an assortment of barrel sizes that will shoot just about anything. I don't know, ten minutes."

"Cool, I'll be there in about twenty."

"Can you make it thirty? We were in the middle of something."

"Just hurry the fuck up." Max hung up and looked over at Lucille. "Some people have absolutely no concept of priority.

# CUDDLY HOLOCAUST

The road connecting Lucille's part of town to Emma's ran through a McDougle's drive thru*. There were other ways to get there, but the detour would have taken them just as long, but without the reward of a 32-oz. iced coffee.

As Lucille's engine struggled and sputtered, Max became aware of a group of noticeably under-evolved homo sapiens crowding around a familiar yellow truck in the parking lot.

Lucille followed his gaze. "What do you want to bet that's one of those militia groups?"

"I hope not. I think I know that truck."

"How?"

"This guy, Guido, gave me a ride to Witches 'R' Us one time."

"Is he with those guys?"

"I don't see him, but it's got to be the same truck."

"You want to say hello?"

"No."

"But what if they're out hunting bears?"

Max sighed. "I don't know. What would we do if they were? I barely know the guy. They'll probably shoot us if we try to stop them."

Lucille pulled up to the window, swiped her debit card, and took the coffees from the cashier. She put one in the cup holder and handed the other to Max. "You want to go see if your friends are done screwing?"

The image of those two naked thumped a nerve in his back. "Let's park over there and see what these guys are up to."

They watched the rednecks chatter and gesture for about fifteen minutes. There were seven of them ranging in age from forty to seventy. Most of them looked like fat sitcom-husbands: clean-shaven and dim-eyed, clad entirely in plaid and camouflage. They wore softball caps and long sleeves despite the heat. The old man in the driver's seat was different. His jacket was vintage, military issue. He had a white ponytail sticking out the back of his floppy camo-hat and more vigor in his eyes than the rest combined. Max couldn't make out most of what they were talking about, but his best guess was softball.

"This is dull." Max tossed his cup into the garbage can just outside his window.

"You want to go?"

"Might as w—ait, something's happening?"

The old man pounded on the side of the truck with his fist. The others hooted and piled in. One guy was nearly run over, but two others grabbed his arms and dragged him into the bed just in time.

Lucille smirked. Her eyes said you-know-you-want-to.

"Fuck it. Follow 'em."

She bit her lower lip and smiled. Moments later they were speeding after the truck at a distance the rednecks would have noticed if they weren't all loading guns and high-fiving each other. They were heading through K-222 toward S-184.

Lucille looked worried. "It's obvious what *their* plan is. What's ours?"

"I don't know. Talk them down, I guess. I'll try to show them there's nothing to be afraid of."

The truck screeched into a wide alley between two abandoned churches. Six armed rednecks crouched behind a barricade that had been augmented with garbage to provide better cover. Sounds of scraping and smashing came from the other side. The men piled out of the truck and joined their flannel-clad comrades.

Lucille parked and craned her neck trying to see around the barricade. "Can you tell what's going on?"

"Not yet. We need to get on the roof of one of those buildings." He pulled out his phone and accessed the transporter app. "I can have a droid here in a couple of minutes. Hopefully they won't do anything stupid in the meantime."

"I could put them to sleep."

"No, save the magic for when you need it. Unless, do you have a way to get us to the roof?"

"Of course. Come on." She got out of the car and walked around to his side mumbling something in magic-speak. She took his hand. "Okay, on three we jump together."

Max counted five stories. "Really?"

"Yeah, I made us light. We're just a teensy bit heavier than air."

On three, they jumped. Some logical limiter in Max's head made him jump straight up instead of up and forward like his partner, so instead of landing safely on the roof, Max dangled from her hand as they arced towards the wall. He screamed, imagining himself a live-action Wylie Coyote about to be taught a harsh lesson about breaking the laws of physics, but Lucille's foot came down on a windowsill and gracefully propelled them both onto the rooftop of the building opposite.

Max grabbed his wrist, which he was pretty sure was strained. "Shit, next time we should use the fire escape."

"Why'd you jump stupid?"

"I've never done this before. You could have explained how it works."

"I didn't think I needed to tell you to aim for where you wanted to land. Sheesh. You're welcome, by the way."

Max rubbed his eyes with his good hand. "Sorry, thanks." He crawled over to the edge and looked down.

Oozing out of the abandoned Sav-Mart across the street, a distorted mass of bloody jelly dominated the parking lot, squirming like piles of lampreys.

"See, this is what happens when you don't put refrigerated items back where they go in a store where the employees don't do it either. Mankind deserves this."

Lucille elbowed him. "Be serious."

"How? Look at that thing. Unless you can summon a storm of salt, all we can do is laugh. At least the rednecks were coming here to fight bad stuff."

Lucille backed away from the edge. "That's an abomination. TD is manifesting in his purest form." She plopped down on the roof and flopped backward. "It's over. The best thing we can do is atomize the planet to slow the spread to other worlds."

"Thank you. Melodrama was just what this situation was missing."

Max's droid approached her from behind. She squealed as it passed over.

"There you are." Max grabbed his plasma pistol from its holster and stuck it down the back of his pants, then pulled out his phone and searched the drop-down menu for functions that might be useful. None of its onboard weapons could tickle a creature that size. A distraction would be pointless. He could already see well. "This thing was not designed with giant hell-fish in mind."

He put the droid on standby and flipped through his other apps. "Well, I guess it couldn't hurt to let Greystoke know what's going on."

He took thirty seconds of video and attached it to a text that read, ":( ".

His phone rang before the video was finished uploading.

Max answered, but it was Cat on the other end. "Where the hell have you been?"

"Hi, sorry about that. Something urgent came up. Can you put your dad on?"

"No, not till I get an explanation. Do you like her better than me?"

"Just watch the video. You'll see why I had to run out like that."

After a few seconds of silence, he heard Greystoke cursing. "Here's daddy."

"What have you done now?"

"I've found concrete proof Hawk's lying."

Greystoke snorted. "Airing this video would only spread more panic. This is beyond my resources. Maybe Heller— "

"Hold on, something's happening."

Shouting echoed in the alley. Max ran to investigate, arriving in time to see the rednecks moving out. They were armed to the teeth and making a ridiculous amount of hand signals. He watched as they cautiously spread out around the creature and took aim with their rocket launchers.

Max knew this wasn't going to work, but he didn't see the point in trying to stop them.

The old guy appeared to be their leader. He hung back, oblivious to the fact that leafy green camouflage is useless in front of cream-colored stucco. His signal was not an order so much as a primal declaration of war, the abstract guttural scream leaders make when shit gets real and then hits the fan and the fan catches fire and the dirty flaming blades fly off and stick in the throats of all their friends like shurikens.

Missiles swam toward the creature like a cloud of enthusiastic sperm and did about as much damage. They might as well have hurled a fistful of snaps at it. If it wasn't for the noise the creature made Max wouldn't have thought it noticed.

The men fell back to regroup, arming themselves with machine guns as if those might somehow succeed where the antiaircraft missiles failed. These men had valor in spades, but only the lesser part.

Max noticed his phone was cursing at him and raised it to his ear. "Hey, sorry about that."

"What the hell was that?"

Max switched to video chat and turned the camera on the rednecks. "Some militia guys are attacking the monster. Their rockets didn't work, so I guess they're going to try lead poisoning." Max noticed movement in the far side of the lot. He laughed and shifted the camera. "Here comes the cavalry."

Colorful bears spewed from the alleys like rivers of candy, accompanied by stupid dinosaurs and the creepy things with antennas on their heads. Max was surprised at how organized their attack was. The bears surrounded the creature, linked arms and shot colored beams of light out of their stomachs, which came together to slowly form a rainbow dome around the abomination. It shrieked and shrank from the light.

The rednecks ran behind the barricade to cower.

The beast lashed out with its gooey tendrils, swallowing four and five bears with each swipe, but the bears were throwing down zombie-style. For every bear eaten, ten more rounded the corner to join the great circle work. In addition, the bears who were swallowed whole illuminated the creature from within, searing its throat like festive briquettes. After a few moments, the swallowed bears would tumble free, leaving the heads to swing and sizzle on gloopy strands. The monster flailed and wailed, its flesh peeling under the colored light like a slug boiled in salt water.

Greystoke cheered, "That's right, boys. Brown his sausage, but good."

Meanwhile, stupid dinosaurs sang and frolicked around the outside of the circle. At first, Max wondered if they were trying to annoy the creature to death; then he noticed that the more dinosaurs there were, the brighter the light became. There weren't very many of the creepy things, and the few in attendance didn't appear to be doing anything. Max couldn't tell if they were in charge or just there for the show.

The battle, with its splashy blood and splashier colors, was over before              you              could              say Pneumonoultramicroscopicsilicovolcanoconiosis.

"Okay, so maybe the portal wasn't such a bad idea." Max could hear the Count jumping around like a happy ten-year-old, but the other end of the video function hadn't been turned on. Max felt gypped.

The old man screamed again, and Max turned to see the rednecks rushing out in an attack formation. The first six hurled grenades while the second kneeled to prey upon their unsuspecting saviors with assault rifles.

"Hey! Stop that, you fucking assholes!" Lucille screamed and threw a half empty water bottle at the leader. It exploded beside him.

He wheeled around and pointed his weapon at her.

Max waved. "Hey, you wouldn't know a guy named Guido, by any chance?"

The gun barrel drooped and his head snapped to the side as if the last strand of reason snapped in his head.

"You're his dad, aren't you?"

The old man lowered his weapon and ran behind the barricade. "Do I know you?"

"Your son is a friend of mine."

"That's nice, and all, but I'm a little busy right now."

"That's what I wanted to talk to you about. Please stop killing the little bears. They're here to help us."

"Bullpucky. The enemy of my enemy is still a goddamn alien invader."

"They're not here to invade. We asked them to come because they're the natural enemies of the real alien invader. I don't know if you noticed, but you can't fight negativity with guns and bombs."

"I don't know if you noticed, but my son's friends are all idjits. Shut up, and let me save the world." He ran back toward the battle. One of the big creepy things stepped in front of him as he rounded the corner. He slammed into it and fell back, dropping his gun.

The creepy one smiled and stood akimbo. It said, "Binky dinky," and the shiny square on its stomach flickered on like a television.

The old man crossed his legs, rested his elbows on his knees and his chin on his fists. Max turned toward the battlefield and saw the other rednecks were sitting in similar positions around other creepy ones. The bears and dinosaurs were dancing and playing together as if the battle had been a fun game.

"What the fuck?"

Lucille shook her head and shrugged.

One of the creepy things turned off its bellyvision and frolicked away singing, "Do do. Do do. Do do."

Max lifted the phone to his ear. "You see that?"

Greystoke had already hung up.

The rednecks that had been gathered around it got up and ran towards the bears and dinosaurs, but instead of attacking they joined in.

"Mmm hmm."

Another bellyvision went off and more rednecks joined in.

Max groaned. "I'm going to have to go down there, aren't I?"

Lucille stared into the parking lot. "I'll come too, but let's wait another minute. Those TV creatures give me the creeps.

"Me too. What do you think they're doing to them?"

"Some kind of hypnosis, maybe?"

"Great, mankind's only hope is a bunch of squeaky voiced, brainwashing monsters? How am I supposed to sell that?" He switched to his carnie voice. "Step right up folks, get your brains cleaned here! Are you bothered by incessant negativity? Do your thoughts trend towards the problems and disappointments of your day? Is life confusing and hard? Do you wake up thinking things like, 'Oh, God, not again?' Are you now, or have you ever been suicidal, homicidal, tired, wired, or otherwise denied the happiness you desire? Well then, Doctor Dinky Dinky is just the thing you need. He calms, cools, cheers, consoles and cleans out your microwave. Doctor Dinky Dinky will collect your thoughts and organize them in a way even a child can understand. He's a hoppin', poppin' miracle on two purple legs, my friends. Come on in and see him today."

Lucille looked more worried than impressed.

Max's stomach turned inside out. Even if it was possible to send The Darkness back to where it came from, how were they going to get rid of all these other things? What would the world be like in a year if they couldn't find a way? His stomach sank even further when he considered what else might be frolicking beyond the gate. Each new creature was creepier and more powerful than the last. He still hadn't figured out what some of the things' powers were. The childrenoids worried him the most. He never saw them out fighting the good fight. Maybe they were management? Their little gaggle of puffballs could be spies or secretaries.

*I have to stop thinking about this before they sense me freaking out and climb the building.*

He walked to his droid and took a look at his chemical inventory. There was adrenalin, cocaine, PCP, Amblen, arsenic, Valiyum, Xan-tabs, and Dr. Feelgood's special cannabinoid cocktail.

Lucille furrowed her brow. "Well, hello, Mister Thompson."

"What? You never know when you might need to live better through chemistry. You want something?"

"This is a weird time for a rooftop party."

Max shook his head. "I can't go down there like this. They'll see I'm agitated and pile on to make me feel better. I want to know what they did to those rednecks, but not first hand."

He bit off half an Amblen and offered the rest to her.

"Isn't this a sleeping pill?"

"This is so much more than a sleeping pill. It's like a Quaalude with an opium center somebody dipped in acid and sprinkled with fairy dust. If you lie down, you'll be asleep in no time, but until you do, you'll feel like you've stepped into a kid's movie from the 1970's. I can't think of anything more appropriate."

They chewed their pills and washed them down with Feelgood's Tonic.

Lucille's history with drugs wasn't so much an open book as a page with her name at the top. He'd assumed, what with her involvement with Cat and her interests in the occult that she would be well versed in the art of reality modification, but her eyes were wide and vulnerable and her ick-face made it clear medicine was something she avoided whenever possible.

As the tonic swept across his brain like springtime, he realized the firelight playing across her face only existed to augment her beauty. Her lips were a cup brimming with love. He drank deeply, but slowly, savoring every drop, his hand on her neck, her hair tangling around his fingers like the inverse of a spider's web.

They stopped briefly to stare into each other's souls. Sly smiles grew to gaping grins and the process began anew. This continued for about fifteen minutes, and would have gone on if not for the fairies pressing themselves too closely around them. Nosy buggers, but they were the only entourage he had.

They scanned the parking lot to confirm the creepy things had left, then availed themselves of the droid's safety harnesses and told it to fly them to the street below.

As they landed, Max called out, "Heeeey buddies! Y'all wanna play?"

All the creatures, rednecks included, threw up their hands and said, "Yeah!"

"Awesome! Let's have fun!" He high-fived a dinosaur and joined the nearest circle.

They were doing some sort of freeform hopping where every third hop was punctuated by either a shaking of the tooshie and the chanting of "Bumf" or wild flailing of the arms and an exclamation of "Spartle."

Max was afraid speaking might be taboo in such a circumstance, but hoped his "friends" would forgive him if it was. He hopped close to a little green bear. "Hi, I'm Max. What's your name?"

"I'm Bailey Bear. Nice to meet you."

"Bailey, that's a great name. I bet you're a real good friend."

"You ain't whistlin' Dixie." The bear chuckled and swayed his arms a bit more as he hopped.

"I saw what you guys did to that big squirmy thing."

Bailey's bouncing halved in energy. "That was too bad. Sometimes you just can't be friends, no matter how hard you try."

Lucille hopped over and scratched the back of his head. "Don't be sad for the friends you don't have; be glad for the one's you do."

"But friends are the most important thing."

Max nodded. "They are. That's why we're trying to teach TD how to be a friend."

The little bear scoffed. "Good luck with that. Even the Teleluvvies can't help TD."

"What's a Teleluvvie?"

The bear glanced around. "I think they all left. They're good friends, but bad at playing."

"Why's that?"

"The only game they know is one where they stand around in groups and say their name over and over. They're a simple people, but they can make friends faster than anybody."

"Why's that?"

"They're empaths. Their tummies create a neural web of all the people that can see it, and they can enter that web and fix all the little problems making them unhappy."

"So, they sort of tidy up a person's mind? What do they do with all the rubbish?"

"That's the best part. Anything that makes their new friend unhappy just goes away, like magic!"

Holy fuck.

Max pointed to the old man who was teaching a nearby circle to do the hokey pokey. "So, he'll be a good friend from now on?"

"For ever and ever, no matter what!" The little bear smiled proudly and bounced along a little faster.

Max needed a second to process, so he lagged behind. When the little bear lapped him, Baily and a redneck were having an intense discussion about yummy treats that come out of cans.

Max bounced over to Lucille. "I think we should go."

She nodded. They hopped back to the car and headed toward the Nrrd Base.

Max buried his face in his hands. "You heard that, right?"

"The bit about erasing people's minds?"

"No, the bit about pudding."

"No."

Max snorted and flopped back against his seat. "This is all so fucking typical."

Lucille's eyebrows hovered near her hairline.

"The theme of my life. Everything always gets worse, crazier, less manageable. The second I think I have a plan, everything changes and I have to run after some other rabid goose that's hopped up on PCP and running for president. It's like there's a higher power watching my every move and shitting on me like a swarm of Tandoorian pigeons. Oh wait, there is! My only escape is death, and even that's a maybe."

Lucille turned her eyes to the road. "What do you think happens to a Discordian's soul when they die?"

"You are not setting me at ease."

"Sorry. It is an interesting question, though. A soul's trajectory is usually calculated by the average emotional state minus the state of mind in death, divided by religious belief times understanding. But the nature of chaos negates a simple mathematical correlation, and your closeness to the Goddess—let's face it you're pretty much her paladin—would make randomness the strongest influence. There's no heaven or hell associated with her, and she doesn't seem the type to reward her servants. So my prediction is that, when you die, your soul will be flung randomly into the ether.”

“Thanks, I feel much better now.”

“Just something to think about. I’d try not to die until this is all over.”

“Sage advice.”

# SUCCESSIVE SLIDINGS OF DISPLEASURE

Emma had bought a squat, yellow mansion on the outskirts of I-333. With its modest four stories, it looked like a dollhouse that had fallen off a truck on the way to the real houses down the street, but relativity lost all meaning where People were involved.

The valet took Lucille's keys and opened the door for them. They passed through a small vestibule and found a large room filled with 50's futurist furniture and collectible vinyl figures. She had hundreds of the damned things, as if her first purchase when she got rich was a lost Kidrobot warehouse. He'd expected something drab, like her, but this place looked more suited to the Buddy Bears.

Emma appeared in the kitchen doorway, wheeling a silver cart full of fancy coffee paraphernalia, and looking like a grey tie on a birthday clown.

I guess even she needs a place to exist.

She wheeled the cart over to a low couch and invited them to sit by the window.

Hedorah appeared in a doorway above them, trying to carry a rifle and two briefcases while lighting a cigarette. He got it lit, but dropped one of the briefcases on his toe. "Fuck! Goddammit. Hi, guys." He grabbed the other case, resituated everything, and hobbled down the stairs.

Emma poured coffee from a pot that looked like the Death Star into a crystalline mug that changed colors as it heated up. "We finished your gun, but I'd like to go on record saying this is a terrible plan."

Max took a small sip. "Mm, nice coffee." He took a bigger sip and set the cup on the coffee table. "The plan sucks, but we have to do something. Wait a second, when did I tell you the plan?"

Hedorah set his load on the table. "You're trying to temporarily disinfect one person from a distance. It's gotta be Hawk. What do you think he's going to do when he snaps out of it?"

"No idea, but it'll be televised."

Emma cocked her head. "See, that's not a plan. Why don't you let us help you make one?"

"Thanks for the offer, but plans haven't worked out for me lately."

Emma rolled her eyes.

"Really, we don't have time to plan. At the rate shit's going, we'll all be dead or drooling by tomorrow night."

"Are you sure you aren't just falling for the Media© hype?"

Max pulled out his phone and showed them the squiggly-thing video. "This is what's going on outside of your comfy little money-bubble.

"That's new. What happened after that?"

Hedorah listened to the rise and fall of the abomination with the curiosity and enthusiasm of a five-year-old, but didn't quite freak out until he heard about the Teleluvvies. "Oh my god, please tell me you bagged one of those."

"Of course not. I didn't want to go near those things."

Well, can you go back and get me one? Please?" Hedorah was so excited his eyes were shaking.

Max wanted to punch him for being so predictable. "Fuck no. Weren't you listening?"

"Dude, they're mind wipers. That means remote neural manipulation!"

Max glanced through the purple angora curtains to make sure there weren't any extra-dimensional creatures surrounding Emma's house. "From the looks of it, there wasn't much to manipulate, but yeah."

"That's not supposed to be possible. Especially not selectively. The implications, I mean, it's not blowing my mind, it's fucking carpet-bombing carpet-bomb factories in my head. If I could figure out how it works, I could do anything. Imagine learning every language in under a minute. Psychic meshing means shared experience. The sexual potential alone—you have to capture one."

"In the entirety of my life, I don't believe I've ever meant *no* more than I mean *no* at this very moment. No."

"Don't be a dick."

Max tried to crush Hedorah's head with sheer force of will. Hedorah looked to Emma for support, then to Lucille, incapable of comprehending why the others weren't as stoked as he was.

Max knew this would go on indefinitely if he didn't put it into terms even a Nrrd could understand. "Even if having my mind wiped wasn't the most pant-soilingly horrific thing I can imagine, even if it wasn't morally reprehensible in more ways than I can count, and they weren't the strongest weapon the world has against The Darkness, and it wasn't likely to cause an inter-dimensional incident with the potential to destroy the world, and even if I knew how, I would still be too fucking busy trying to keep everything in the known universe from being swallowed up by pure fucking evil."

"It'll only take a second. Just tranq one." He looked at Max like he was an idiot and pantomimed squeezing a trigger.

Hedorah wasn't getting it, so Max grabbed the gun and the case of darts off the table and nodded to the door. "We have to get going. Nice seeing you guys."

"Man, all the shit I've done for you and you're seriously telling me no?"

Max started toward the door. "Yup."

"You mean you'll do it?"

"No." He stopped and turned. "You're a fucking mathematician. Do you even know how to vivisect?"

"Every scientist knows how to vivisect."

"Well, every scientist is a morally repugnant waste of skin." Max followed Lucille out the door.

Hedorah was momentarily stunned. "Fuck you. I stopped fucking to invent you something."

Max kept walking.

"Enjoy your new toy. It's the last thing you'll ever get out of me, or any other Nrrd. You're a fucking sellout, which is impressive since you never gave a shit to begin with." He flicked his cigarette at Max and slammed the door.

Max had never liked Hedorah. He had a low tolerance for captious shits who hated themselves and dedicated their lives to alienating everyone because their mommies and daddies didn't hug them enough. Still, it would suck to lose his tech hook-up. Hedorah and Emma were the only Nrrds he still had any contact with.

I should probably apologize. No, if I go back I'll probably end up kicking his teeth in. I really want to kick his teeth in.

He joined Lucille in the car. They were halfway back to Castle Greystoke when Max broke the silence. "Sorry, that was a bit awkward."

"It's not your fault. That guy's a fucking monster."

"Nah, just a jackass. He'll get over it."

"So he's not going to turn the other Nrrds against you?"

"Who knows?" Max smirked. "He'll probably just get drunk and trash his room."

"What, is he twelve?"

Max laughed. "Emotionally, yeah."

"How did he get where he is?"

"He didn't die in the war. The world is a little light on geniuses now."

Lucille rumpled her forehead. "It's hard to imagine him in a war."

"Just picture him cowering."

"It's hard to imagine you in a war too."

Max laughed. "Just picture me cowering."

Lucille smiled.

They wound their way up the bosky drive toward Castle Greystoke's main entrance. As they approached, Max noticed several armored cars surrounding the fountain.

"That's odd."

She pulled up by the door, but no valet came to take her keys.

Max opened his door. "Something's definitely wrong. Stay in the car, but keep it running. I'll call you if everything's okay."

"Screw that. I'm coming with."

"I'd feel much better knowing there was a running car I could escape in."

"What if you need backup?"

"I'll be fine. Don't make me jinx myself any more than I already have." He searched the windows for signs they were being watched, then gave her a quick kiss on the temple. "Be right back."

Max climbed out and cautiously made his way up the steps. He looked through the window and listened, but there were no signs of life. The door was unlocked, so he stepped inside.

"Cat? Vlad? What's up with all the cars?"

Nobody answered.

Okay, I should probably come back later. Maybe he gave all the servants the night off. I can't see him doing that, but anything's possible, right?

He slowly crept down the hall toward Greystoke's study. He peeked into every room he passed. Everything seemed fine, but where the hell was everybody?

The light was on in the study. Max crept closer and called again. "Vlad? You here?"

He stuck his head inside and found Pope sitting behind Greystoke's desk. "Pope? What the hell are you doing here? Where is everybody?" He stopped just inside the door.

Pope straightened his uniform and greeted him with a smug smile. "Hello, Max. Long time, no see." He looked like he was auditioning for a role as "Gestapo Commander" in a comedy about Nazis.

Max cocked an eyebrow. Pope was acting weird, even for him. "Yeah, nice to see you. Did Hedorah call you?"

"No, I'm afraid my new position doesn't allow much time for socializing. I'm here on business. Mister Heller wants a chat."

"He has my number."

"Mister Heller doesn't call, he summons. I like that. Man knows what he wants and when he wants it."

"As nice as it is to see they're giving you all the Drink Aid you want; I should probably get going. I wanted to have a quick word with the Count, but, seeing as how you're in his chair and he's not bludgeoning you with his cane, I guess he's unavailable."

"On the contrary, he's very available. He and Mister Heller are expecting you at Heller House."

"All right, I'll stop by later."

"Is there somewhere else you are supposed to be?"

"I have to go shoot a friend."

"It can wait."

"Not really. The fate of the world kind-a-sort-a depends on me doing this."

"You're always so melodramatic."

"No, Hawk's become the false prophet, and he will bring about the end of days unless I shoot him with this special drug cocktail Hedorah cooked up. We hope it'll dislodge TD long enough for Hawk to admit to being possessed on live TV, thereby ending the disinformation campaign that's keeping people from doing what needs to be done. After that I'm hoping Greystoke can help me retool the corny, but true message everybody hated. Hippie shit's due for a comeback, anyway."

"All the same."

"Whatever, man. Bye." Max turned to leave, but his way was blocked by two of Heller's goons. "Dude, that's not necessary. I really will come by when I'm done."

"Heller doesn't wait. He sent for you hours ago."

"Then he does wait and one more hour isn't going to kill him."

"It's more likely to kill you."

"Man, we took down the Iiites together. We snuggled for warmth in an abandoned factory. Seems like we'd be beyond threatening each other's lives."

"I came here to ensure your safety. Look, we have our orders. Even if I let you go, there are thirty other men in and around this building that wouldn't. It would just get me in trouble. You don't want to get me in trouble, do you?"

Max took a deep breath. He could see at least two more guys in the hall. Given Pope's hard-on for accuracy, escape was probably out of the question.

"Fine, dammit. Maybe if we hurry we can finish in time for me to save the world."

Pope stood and followed him out of the room. There were six more men in the hall, three on either side of the door, and they all had automatic rifles. He considered dashing to and fro in the hope they would all kill each other.

That would be idiotic.

They led him to the front door where Lucille was standing, horrified.

"Max, what's happening?"

"Apparently, Heller is summoning me. Won't take no for an answer."

"But..."

"Go ahead with the plan. I'll join you as soon as I'm done."

"I've never shot a gun before."

"It's easy, point and click."

A Teleluvvie waddled around the corner of the mansion. It raised its arms and the square on its stomach flickered to life. For a second Max wondered if he might be able to talk his way out of being brainwashed, but nothing about its cold glassy eyes implied reasoning skills.

The goons followed his gaze and dropped the creature like a paper bag full of cancer.

"Like that, but with a cooler gun. The sights on that thing can read the genetic signature on a grain of rice from ten miles away. You'll do fine."

Her expression changed from fearful to determined. She stared at the goons and chanted some magic gibberish, but nothing happened.

Pope stepped up to her and put his hand on her arm. "Nice try, but we're all shielded from magic."

She kicked him in the balls. As he hunched over she kneed him in the face. "Not shielded from that, are ya, bitch?" She broke out in little red dots.

"Lucy." He tried to step between her and the majority of the guns, but she was surrounded. "We don't have time for this. Please, try. I'll probably be there, but if I'm not, you have to do this."

Fear returned to her eyes.

"It'll be fine."

She nodded, and the red dots went away.

Max grabbed Pope's shoulder and dragged him to his feet. "Come on, I haven't got all night."

✳✳✳✳✳

Max's motorcade pulled up in front of Heller House, but the goons wouldn't let him out until the other goons lined up on either side of the door to make a human hallway all the way to the front door. Pope opened the door, and Max stepped out.

"You really think that third layer of goons is necessary? You said to yourself, he might red rover through the human wall if it's only two lines of arm-locked bodybuilders. Better add a third just to be sure."

Pope pursed his lips and waved for Max to follow. As he did, the goons closed in behind him, forming an impassible scrotum to complement his shafting.

He entered the building with Pope and eight others who escorted him swiftly to the elevator. He knew it wasn't possible for him to feel the little robots infiltrating his body, but the knowledge they were there induced a psychosomatic reaction that felt like a bad flea infestation.

The outer ring of goons peeled away as they boarded the elevator, but four stayed with him. The parade of hedonism filing past the glass elevator doors was less enjoyable the second time around. Max realized this was more than the show and tell of a braggadocios old man. It was a threat, a show of power meant to remind every visitor of his superiority.

Most disturbing of all, the restaurant, the bordello, the indoor beach, every single floor was empty. If the situation was reversed, Max would have made sure Heller saw everything was business as usual. He'd have thought clearing out the building would imply weakness. He was wrong.

The only thing that conveys a feeling of doom better than an empty skyscraper is when the elevator reaches the top floor, stops, and begins its descent without the doors opening. Fear jabbed the soap bubble of his confidence like a sharp pin. He could almost hear it pop as he fell physically and mentally toward an abyss of absolute despair.

Max couldn't keep the panic from his voice. "Hey, it looks like he doesn't need to see me after all."

Pope smiled, but didn't respond.

Sweat prickled his flesh, drowning the little robots in neon fear.

Dammit! I cannot let him get to me. Focus! Maybe he'll see I'm shitting myself and get overconfident. Heller may have more money and resources and power and knowledge and—shut up brain! I can't forget the basic truth that Heller can't really hurt me. He can hurt my body. He can kill me, but death will only free me from this clusterfuck. But what if Lucille's right? What if I die and Eris punishes me for failing? If this is how she treats people she likes, what the fuck does she do to people who let her down?

Max watched the lobby slide past.

That can't be good.

The subterranean floors were obscured by large metal doors engraved with numbers, which didn't correspond to any numerical system he was familiar with. Rather than 1-2-3 the first few doors were marked with 23, 32, 1-75, 846.289.01.

Focus! Whatever is waiting for me down there, fear will only make it worse.

Max emptied his mind and forced his lungs to take in slow, deep breaths, but the cortisol was already in his system. Max's efforts had barely stopped his teeth chattering when the elevator stopped at the door marked with a seven-pointed star.

Oh, yay. Weird stars are always a good sign.

When the doors opened, the goons shoved him into a large room carved out of solid granite. Max stood at the edge of a large empty circle, on one point of the huge heptagram chiseled into the floor. On the opposite side of the room, thirteen steps led to a dais where twelve robed figures chanted around a pool. Above the pool was an unusual formation of luminescent red crystal, which looked like a woman's face and fed the pool with rosy water issuing from her mouth.

Max looked back at Pope. "Heller wants me to join his larping group?"

The doors closed and the goons went wherever goons go when their gooning is completed. The figures were busy praying to the water, so Max examined the room. The symbols on the walls reminded him a bit of the ones under Castle Greystoke, but he got the impression this was more a multilingual thesaurus than a grimoire. Whatever it was, his brain wasn't growing tentacles. So, that was something.

Max walked deeper into the room. He recognized the people on the dais. Some he'd met, like the brothers Rothafella and Greystoke. Others he knew from TV. There was Timothy V. Authority, the CEO of Universal Water and Power. The man on his left was John Santorum, then Pope Jim II, and Santo Montoya, who had recently replaced the disgraced Chaz Lightbeard as the CEO of Agrocorp. The faces of the two shorter figures were obscured by their hoods. Max walked to the other side of the room. As he suspected, Heller was in the center, but he was surprised to see Margaret Fitzer by his side. Her recent appointment to CEO of Universal Health certainly made her powerful enough, and Bio-Corp was certainly evil enough, but her sweet grandmotherly quality made her stand out like a Viking in a sewing circle. He'd never have guessed she would be mixed up in something as silly and nefarious as this.

They had to know he was there, but the water had their full attention. Max used the time to scan the room for trapdoors and suspended cages. None were apparent, but he waited on the third step just to be safe.

Why go to all that trouble to scare me, then ignore me when I get here?

Max checked the time on his phone. Hawk would be on TV in fifteen minutes. He had a text from Lucille asking what was going on.

He tapped out a quick response. "Not much, ATM. Waiting for a bunch of bigwigs to finish praying to water. Doubt I'll make it. Go on without me." He sent it, but got a connectivity error.

All his email had to offer was the usual trickle of spam, so he opened his new Clown Hunter game. He was still waiting for it to load when an unusual splashing drew his attention.

The waterfall spurted erratically around an invisible form that stood twenty feet tall and had a long flat mouth like a crocodile. The acolytes cried out and fell to their knees in worshipful terror.

Heller pulled an amulet out of his robe like he was flashing a badge. "Identify yourself, spirit."

The giant croc-man responded coolly. "I am Sobek-Ra. Do you not know me?"

Heller stood firm, but Max could tell he was afraid. "Of course we know you, master. We simply were not expecting an answer from someone so powerful. We meant to ask Eidothia what actions are required to free our world from The Darkness."

"Eidothia has fled this plane along with most of the others for fear of R'alek D'aathak. Only the creators remain."

"Then I pose my question to you."

"Do what thou wilt. This world is lost."

Veins bulged on Heller's head, but his tone remained deferential. "Surely not. We are gaining ground every day."

"The ground you gain is an illusion designed to keep you from fleeing. The creatures you summoned can slow R'alek's manifestation, but their effect on the human mind is making him more powerful. Humans are gunning down the embodiment of love. When no one is outraged by the death of the cute there is no more hope for the world."

Max stuck his phone in his pocket. "Sounds like something Cat would say."

Sobek-Ra looked at Max. "Do not feel bad, Maxwell Quick. This world was rotting before the breach. Even we who made this place have grown weary of it. Why do you think we have allowed the veil to slip so far?"

"Laziness?"

Sobek smiled. "Eris wanted a final epic tragicomedy. She chose you, not because of your aptitude as a savior, but because you, above all others, could make a good show of it."

Max wanted to respond so badly he smacked his lips, but the words bottlenecked in his esophagus.

Heller asked, "Is R'alek D'aathak the true name of The Darkness?"

"It is, but it would be foolish to attempt to use it against him."

"And you say there's nothing we can do? Can you not intervene on our behalf?"

Sobek crossed his arms. "Why would I want to do that?"

Timothy Authority raised his head. "This is your creation. It's your responsibility to help us."

The top half of Sobek disappeared, then Mr. Authority flew into the air and died like a jam-filled cookie on the lips of a child.

Heller bowed at the waist. "I apologize for his impudence, master. He was new."

Sobek resumed his regal stance beneath the fountain.

The knot in Max's tongue worked itself loose. "Fuck you!" He stomped up the steps. "Are you saying I did all this shit for nothing? That Eris just wanted the final season of "Humans" to go out with a bang? I'll give her a fucking bang! You tell her to get her fat, bitch ass down here right now, or I will hunt her through every world, dream, frequency and alternate reality there is, and when I find her I will fuck her in the eyes, and my sperm will devour her brain like hungry fuck-spiders!"

The acolytes ran down the stairs to cower at the far end of the room. Sobek laughed so hard he fell to his knees.

"What's funny, asshole?"

Sobek tried to speak, but he couldn't stop laughing.

"I brought *you* to your knees."

The laughing petered out, Sobek stood slowly. "Eris chose wisely, for once. If all humans were so amusing, we might be motivated to save this world."

"I'm calling bullshit. I'll be the first to admit humans are stupid, petty, violent, selfish, primitive, arrogant, wasteful parasites that have sucked all the resources out of your creation, consumed them and then shat them back out as poison, but we've always been this way. You made us this way, right *creator*? The only difference between now and whenever the fuck people knew your name, is that we stopped building you pyramids and kissing your ass. You want a pyramid?" He pointed to Heller.

"That fucker alone will build you twenty. The rest of them are probably good for five or six apiece. Call your buddies. We'll have a pyramid party. We'll get the Jengists in on it and make the whole east coast look like a punk fashion accessory. It'll be a good time. Whaddaya say?"

Sobek chuckled. "I like you. You are the epitome of all things human. Time will tell whether this creation was a waste of time, but I suspect it was not. Enjoy yourself in these final days."

The water around the figure all fell at once into the pool, splashing Max and soaking through his clothes. "Fucker!" He yanked his phone out of his pocket and did his best to dry it off.

Heller stalked toward him, screaming like a cloud of angry bees. "You recrudescent, rebarbative offspring of a bezoar and a teratoma! You have damned this entire cosmos to languish in agony for eons, if not eternity."

Max cocked an eyebrow. "Not according to him."

"If you had stayed your gormless little lips, I might have convinced him to help."

"Not according to him."

"Be quiet!"

Max wanted to respond, but found himself physically unable. He raised his fingers to his numb mouth flaps and smeared them around.

Heller took a cigarillo out of a slender silver case. "Come!"

Max walked forward against his will. The acolytes came as well, their expressions reflecting shock and fear. Heller stared intensely at Max, sucking desperately at the little cigar as if the answer to his predicament would spell itself in the ash. When the smoldering tip threatened to burn his knuckles, he dropped the butt and turned his attention to Greystoke.

"It is your indiscretion that has brought this upon us. Please, lift my spirits. Amuse me with your plan to set this right."

Greystoke trembled silently, his eyes searching the room for words that were not there. Heller smiled sadistically. He wouldn't speak until he had an answer.

As the minutes passed, the Count's fantods grew increasingly severe. Max was beginning to wonder if Heller had cast a head-explode-y spell on him.

A final jolt wracked his face, and he assumed the look of a man about to die. "I have considered every alternative and, as much as it pains me to say, I believe our best option is to migrate to a healthier dimension."

"Of course, why didn't that occur to me? Oh yes, it isn't possible."

"There is a way. I fully expected the creatures I summoned to fade away or die from exposure, but they have not. If they can survive here with no concept of science or magic, I am sure we will find a way. After all, you—."

Heller silenced him with a look. Then asked, "I what?"

"Nothing. Never mind."

Heller scowled. "Had you been paying attention these last few days; you would know the only dimensional doors that have not been bolted against us are the ones leading to worlds we created. Or are you suggesting we use Venustas as a panic room?"

"That could work as a last resort, but surely *some* natural plane will be willing to accept twelve refugees."

"We are more likely to find a realm willing to take twelve pregnant cockroaches."

"What about the door I opened?"

"You want to have your brain wiped and spend the rest of your life playing ring around the posy?"

"I suppose not."

Heller lit another cigar. "The only course left for us is to adapt. If you are going to live in hell, it's better to be a demon."

No matter how hard Max tried, his lips wouldn't budge.

Santorum spoke for him. "Are you suggesting we try to strike a bargain with evil?"

"Does anyone have a better plan?"

Santorum's nostrils flared proudly. "Anything is a better plan. You can't bargain with evil. Evil is never lawful. Evil won't like you or appreciate what you do for it. When evil is born, the first thing it does is kill its mother. Then it kills the doctor who delivered it, the father, the nurses—and it keeps on killing until somebody stops it."

Heller pursed his lips. "We are trapped in a room with a hungry bear. The bear is approaching rapidly, roaring with such ferocity it blows back our hair. Our chance of survival is negligible, but we have a choice. We can poke its eye out of sheer spite or we can try to pet it and hope for a miracle. Admittedly, both plans are terrible, but I would rather be mauled by a happy bear than an angry one."

Santorum scowled. "Screw this. I'm going to spend my last moments with my family." Santorum ripped off his robe, threw it at Heller's feet and walked toward the elevator.

The veins on Heller's forehead danced the worm. "Come!"

Santorum spun on his heels.

The buzzing in Heller's voice vibrated Max's teeth. "We do this together."

Max's lips were paralyzed, but his hands were free, so he retorted with his plasma pistol. Two shots whizzed by Heller's left shoulder and blew chunks out of the wall behind him. Heller was unaffected, but the heat from the blast burst Montoya's robe into flames.

What the fuck?

Max corrected his aim and fired again, this time passing over his right shoulder and melting a hole in the elevator door.

"Goddammit, what is wrong with you!" Montoya stripped down to his white tuxedo, and threw the quickly melting wad of material at Max's gun.

Alec slapped the flaming mass out of Max's hands and the gun came with it.

Heller looked more amused than anything. "Max still!"

Now, his entire body was paralyzed.

Heller glanced at the holes in his wall then back at Max. "Someone just lost their job because of that."

Greystoke looked furious, but slightly proud as he stepped forward, hand raised in the slapping position.

"Vladimir, still and quiet!"

Greystoke froze mid-stride.

The others backed away as Heller closed in on Max.

Well, that was obviously a mistake.

Heller walked up within two inches of Max and scrutinized his face the way one might look for flaws in a statue. His weird, bulging gaze grated against Max's skin like the unshaven mouth of a newly acquired uncle. His breath smelled like mundungus tobacco and expensive cheese. After a few moments, he stepped back and sighed. "I'm tired. Maxwell, strangle the Count and get off my property."

Max moved forward and crushed Greystoke's windpipe with his hands.

What the fuck am I doing? Stop that. Bad hands.

Fear and blood filled Greystoke's eyes, but he didn't so much as lower his leg.

Killing the Count felt a lot different than it had in his fantasies. He wanted to stop. Greystoke deserved to die for a lot of reasons, but at some point Max had come to think of him as a friend.

They had a short conversation with their eyes along the lines of. "I'm sorry. I can't stop."

"I would appreciate it very much if you would try harder."

"I'm trying as hard as I can."

"Stop killing me, you imbecile."

"Don't be a dick. This is your fault."

"Oh blast it, hurry up and get it over with."

"Fine, I will."

This was followed by an uncomfortable period of waiting that seemed to go on for hours, but was probably more like three minutes.

As a kid, Max had wanted to kill people in a million different ways, but never strangulation. He thought it would feel too personal. He was right, but it was also boring. There was no screaming or blood, just a constipated stare bordering on the comical.

Max was aware that the distance he felt was probably his mind protecting himself from the fact that he was strangling one of his few remaining friends on the eve of Armageddon, but he pushed that knowledge to the back of his mind and tried to think of something pleasant.

I'm getting hungry. What should I have for dinner? Tacos? Something healthier, maybe sushi? Does Lucille like sushi? I know, fish tacos with lightly blackened rare tuna and lots of cilantro. Yes. Definitely fish tacos.

When the light faded from Greystoke's eyes, Max let him fall and walked toward the elevator. Realizing his lips were still paralyzed, he waved his arms around to get Heller's attention. The doors opened, and he was almost inside when Heller said, "Maxwell, stop and speak."

Max turned and realized he had no idea what to say. He wanted to at least have a dramatic exit, maybe a quip or a declaration of vendetta. The best he could come up with on the fly was, "Thanks, I'll see myself out."

"Be seeing you."

Max told himself Heller's look of mild surprise was a victory. Stepping into the elevator under his own power was another victory. He was still alive. All things considered, that could have gone worse.

The doors closed and he felt a little pressure in his knees. He watched the mysterious doors slide downward one after another, half-wishing the elevator had buttons so he could check them out, but knowing he should beat it before Heller changed his mind.

Why did he let me go? I know his plans, and he has to know I'm going to try to stop him. I've come this far. Why let a little thing like utter futility stop me?

Maybe he figures as long as he's going full-on super villain, he might as well have a hero to keep it lively. Or, he might be hedging his bets, hoping I'll pull something out of my ass at the last minute. Then again, there was the whole fate worse than death thing. He could be operating under the assumption that if TD wanted me dead, I'd have died by now, in which case he's just letting TD play with me a little longer.

The doors opened onto the lobby, and Max walked out the front door checking the messages on his phone. It was after nine, but the last message from Lucille was from eight-ten.

"Fuck, can today get any longer?"

He tripped over something and almost tumbled down the steps. Pope had been shot in the head and left on Heller's doorstep like the trophy of a proud housecat.

Max snorted. "My bad. I guess your *new* boss is less tolerant of fuck-ups."

Max stepped over him and noticed there weren't any cars or guards to escort him off property. "Seriously? You're going to make me walk?" There was no response, so he summoned his droid and grumbled his way down the drive.

# THE RIGHT STUFF

Flying over all the wriggling evil made Max feel like a feeder mouse. The droid had definitely been the way to go. He hadn't seen a passable street since he left I-district. Everything was on fire and/or full of monsters. It was like H.P. Lovecraft's farm down there. Here a thing, there a thing, everywhere a thing thinged.

The city was a dog's breakfast. There was a sizzling sound like frying bacon as the acrid stench of hair, aluminum, and plastic wafted up like notes of spoiled wine. Whatever happened at that press conference had popped the demons' yokes and scrambled the masses like chopped meat. The Darkness was serving brinner.

He headed toward the area where Lucille was supposed to have shot Hawk, but he had no idea what to expect or what he was going to do when he got there. He couldn't even focus on forming a plan because his brain was stuck on the irony of him rushing into battle despite his finally being free to do otherwise.

The world doesn't want me anymore. The special interest groups are done with me. My girlfriends are all dead or missing. My best friend is possessed by absolute evil. The world is doomed, and all I have left is this droid and Cheeky—and Eris only knows what happened to him.

There's nothing to stop me going home. My DVR is definitely full by now, if it still works. It's probably in a dump somewhere. There's no telling. I haven't been back to my apartment since the Iiites trashed it and killed Spooky.

The funny thing is I don't care about that life anymore. I don't even mind all that shit I was forced to do. It was fun. I learned a lot, had a lot of experiences. Now, even though I know there's no hope, the gods are dicks and mankind doesn't want to be saved, I feel like I have a purpose. TD's ass is out there somewhere waiting to be kicked. Not that I know how to find it, let alone kick it. Even if I did, stupid assholes are going to kill us all sooner rather than later. If I was smart, I'd drink a glass of LSD and spend my last few hours at The Laugh Hotel fucking my way to Zen.

A gust of wind nearly blew him into a building. Then another left him spinning in place while the droid's adaptive sensor mechanism tried to cope with the sudden storm. The clouds to his right were growing tentacles. No, not tentacles—tornadoes. Lots of tornadoes.

"Fuck it, this looks like way more fun." Max had played enough video games to know a boss fight when he saw one, so he steered the droid into the storm.

Closing in on the heart of the storm, the tornadoes were all playing ring around the rosie on the dent he'd left when he toppled the Fist. That last building stood like a gravestone in the center of a huge circular park they'd made as a memorial to those who died in the Iiite war. Max smiled. He should have known this was where TD would be. What could possibly rub Max's nose in his own shit more than the site where his greatest achievement had been perverted into a tool to maximize the promotional value of destruction?

On the southern end of the park, Max could see droves of the infected flocking towards a fleshy mass the size of a large house. Max circled the creature, taking it all in.

Its blubbery flaps spread like layers of wings as the infected hurled themselves and each other into its assortment of mouths. Every time it grew a few feet of surface area, a new mouth would sprout so the creature could consume them faster.

*I wonder if Hawk is still in there somewhere.*

The various smaller creatures stopped jamming themselves down the big one's throat and greeted Max with a chorus of guttural rasps that vibrated his guts worse than the combination of pot, gas station burritos, and Japanese throat singing.

The manifold mouths smiled viciously and spoke in Hawk's voice. "Howdy there, partner. Come on down. I saved you a seat."

The infected backed away, forming a twenty-foot hole in front of TD, who was now the size of a small mansion.

Max set down in the center of the hole and sent his droid away, knowing this was a confrontation he would either walk away from, or not. Max grinned and walked toward it. "You got fat."

The creature laughed. "Don't be silly. This here's all muscle." The flesh moved inward, piling upward into a five-thousand percent scale replica of his old friend. Hawk towered, naked and glistening, his comically oversized god-wang swaying in the gale.

"You trying to impress me?" The wind was picking up. Chunks of skyscraper were coming loose and crashing into other buildings, but Max was unaffected. He was too heavy for the wind to carry, his flesh too solid for the rubble to scratch.

Hawk curled his arms into a double bicep pose. "What'cha say, darlin'? Wanna fuck?"

Max laughed. "Hawk *is* alive in there somewhere. Good to know."

The Darkness struck a side chest pose. "Hawk is sucking cocks in hell right now, but if you leave a message he'll still be damned for eternity 'cause of you."

"If you say so. Say, I'm looking for a chick named Lucille, little taller than me, hot. You seen her?"

"Does she have a bird on her ass and taste like magic?"

"That's the one."

"I imagine she's eatin' Hawk's asshole right about now."

"Might I inquire as to what happened?"

"Yes, you may. Silly bitch shot me up with drugs in the middle of my press conference. Caught me off guard. I lost control for a second, long enough for Hawk to come to the surface, tell all the good folks at home I'm full of horse shit. Thing is, killin' all that hope at once," he laughed, "well, it was like cramming a big juicy doughnut in my mouth, blowing PCP up my ass and making me come all at once. Mmm mmm good. I gave her the honor of being the inaugural snack."

Max nodded. "I suppose I should have expected that."

"I thought it was a wonderful plan."

"All right, I'm glad you had your fun, but I'm here to pick up my friends."

TD did a front lat spread and grinned.

Max smirked. "Cut the shit, man. You lost."

He stopped flexing. "Huh?" He swung his mighty finger around. "Either you're not payin' attention or you done lost your grip on reality. I hope that's not the case. I wanted to eat your soul *before* you snapped. I like to feel 'em wriggle on the way down."

"Nah, it's the opposite. I've gone sane. Are you going to send my friends out, or do I have to go in there and get them?"

"Come on in. The guts are warm." TD picked Max up, tossed him high and moved to catch him in his mouth.

"Wheeeee!" As Max fell, he noticed another, smaller hole in the crowd. Ernie was in the center grinning proudly while Cheeky ate popcorn out of his hand. Max waved, then did a cannon ball down TD's throat. It felt like jumping into a pool of Spagoooo's where the O's are alive. Thousands of little mouths gummed him hungrily, but all it did was tickle. He relaxed into it, opening himself up, giving freely the same as when he healed Cheeky.

The little mouths sucked as hard as they could. Max was pouring boatloads of himself down their tiny throats, filling their bellies, or whatever, with love. The goo around him quivered.

"Lucille? Hawk? You in here?"

Their voices were garbled, but clear enough to understand even through the wailing of countless others. "Calm down, everybody. I'm here to get you out. He can't digest happiness, so focus on me, think happy thoughts, and I'll have you out in a jiffy.

"By the way, Hawk, I'm sorry I was a dick. I didn't know what I was doing. I've been a shitty friend, but I'm going to try to make it up to you."

Hawk's voice was clearer and louder. "No need to go all emo on me. We're always good."

"Is Cat in here?"

Lucille responded, "I don't think so. Cat?"

"Cat?"

"Meow?"

"Cat, now's not the time to fuck around."

"Meow!"

"Cat!"

Hawk cleared his throat. "I think those are actual cats."

"Meow."

"I think you're right." Max reached into the goo and found a kitty. "Poor thing." He scratched it behind the ears and ran his hand down its back. "Puff?"

"Meow!" Puff rubbed herself against his hand.

"Hey, nice to see you too, buddy."

The quivering became violent shuddering. The goo thinned and the little mouths floated away like dead goldfish. Max fell in slow motion until his foot touched something steady, a butt cheek if he had to guess. He found another foothold in an elbow and raised his hands to help those falling around him.

After a few moments, his head poked through the top of the receding goo. After verifying that he wasn't being rushed by a horde of zombies, Max lifted Puff out and let her step onto the monster's skin. Puff shook off most of what clung to her, spraying him in the eyes and mouth.

"Dammit Puff!" He gave Puff a friendly but forceful slap on the ass, and she jumped to the ground.

When Max finished spitting and wiping goo out of his eyes, he searched the other heads as they poked through one by one. "Where are you guys?"

Someone tapped him on the shoulder. He turned and found Hawk standing right behind him.

"You always were an oblivious little cuss."

Max threw his arms around him and laughed. "General Hawk, now with a hundred percent less clothes. Why are you naked?" Max let him go and looked around and noticed everyone's clothes had been eaten away by the muck.

"Hell if I know. I'm just happy I ain't the Antiquick anymore."

Cheeky sat off to the side staring expectantly. Max waved and searched the crowd for Ernie, who'd apparently gotten bored and left.

"Where's Lucille?"

"Who the fuck's Lucille?"

About ten feet away, an oozing boil burst on the monster's side and something that looked like Cousin It dipped in tar splashed onto the grass.

Hawk cringed. "Eh, I think you missed a spot."

Max slapped him on the back. "I'm pretty sure that's her. I'll introduce you."

Hawk looked at him like he was crazy.

"Don't worry, she cleans up well."

"You fuckin' that?"

Lucille stood and wrung some goo out of her dreads. She ran her hands down her sides and slung the chunky black residue at her feet.

"Yup." Max smiled and nodded. "I certainly am."

The muck had receded to waist level, so Max and Hawk waded out. Cheeky tried to crawl up his leg, but the slime was too slippery. Max knelt and squished on his head lumps, then scooped him up and hugged him till he wheezed.

Lucille was eying Puff suspiciously and wringing her hair out one strip at a time. "Wasn't Puff a bad guy?"

"So was he." Max nodded at Hawk. "I reformed them."

"Pun intended?"

"Damn right." Max kissed her on the forehead. He spat out some goo. "Damn it, I almost had that taste out of my mouth." He turned his attention to Hawk. "So how's it going?"

"I am in desperate need of an alcoholic beverage."

Max was surprised to find he wasn't, but a tasty beer did sound refreshing. He pointed toward the Agrocorp building. "I think there's a bar in the food court."

Lucille shrugged. "I wouldn't mind something to get the taste of evil out of my mouth."

"Well then, whiskey it is."

# BEYOND LOVE AND EVIL

One month later, the world had found its equilibrium. Greystoke's death had closed the dimensional gate. The Paladins, as they had come to be called, forced The Darkness to recede to normal levels. The rednecks culled the Paladins to manageable levels, and the Teleluvvies turned most of the rednecks into harmless simpletons. The population was at a sustainable level for the first time since the Divine Disturbance*, and the survivors were coming together to reestablish the level of convenience they were accustomed to.

The Paladins were happiest when they were doing things to help their friends, and humans were more than happy to share the workload. Having no concept of money and an overabundance of goodwill, they inadvertently reintroduced slavery to popular culture. Some future generation might wise up, rise up and smite their oppressors, but for now, everyone was happy, and all was right with the world.

Cat, who had ridden the worst of the apocalypse out in a K-hole, insisted Lucille and Hawk move in to Castle Greystoke. Hawk was put in charge of security, but as there wasn't much to secure them from, the position was mostly honorary. Lucille spent the majority of her time studying Greystoke's books and teaching magic to the others. Cat and Hawk were poor students, but once they got past the initial awkwardness of group tantra 101, her classes became fun and interesting bonding experiences.

Life had become a warm cinnamon roll that swirled around them, filling their world with layers of sweet, moist delights. In short, Max was bored out of his fucking skull.

Hawk was the least contented of all. He loved hanging out with his friends, playing board games and perfecting the castle's defenses, but he was addicted to the thrill of hate. Having no enemies to slake his bloodlust took its toll on his psyche, and the meditation Lucille had taught him so contradicted his previous mental training that cognitive dissonance nullified the effect.

Max was alone in the study. He'd given up on the news boring him to sleep and was staring at his slippered feet, trying to decide what he wanted to do. These bouts of listlessness were getting longer every day. He rarely slept, and the extra time was threatening to drive him insane.

He was about to give up and try to go back to sleep when he heard Heller's name on the news. He turned up the volume just as it cut to

Heller standing behind a podium, surrounded by throng of A-list celebrities. The tiny man smiled like a guilty fox and waved his fedora at the cheering crowd. The pink shirt and zephyr peeking out from the pocket of his white suit made him look like an archetype of temptation as represented by a talking petit four in the nightmare of a gay teenager.

His voice was high and sweet, the buzz barely perceptible. "Thank you. And I hope to see you all there."

The bottom of the screen was captioned, "Festival of Lights to commemorate one-month anniversary of The Darkness's defeat."

It cut back to April Meadows. "Heller's first annual Festival of Light is not just the party of the year. This is the founding of a new holiday, and many say it's the only one that really means anything."

What's he up to, now?

"In other news, God has reappeared in Bryant Park."

Max turned off the TV and leaned against the desk. He'd been so relieved to be rid of TD that he'd forgotten to complete his primary goal.

Maybe that's why I've been so antsy. The whole point of all that shit was to make the world a better place, and it can't be better if the same fuckers are running it.

"Hey, Billy!"

The little red bear scampered into the room and straightened his bowtie. "Hiya, Max. What's up?"

"Would you mind getting Cat, Lucille and Hawk for me? I need to talk to them."

"Sure thing, pal-o-mine." He stopped in the doorway and turned. "And thanks again for these swanky new duds." He grabbed his lapels of his tuxedo jacket and pulled it tight on his back. "I feel like a real gentleman."

If I have to listen to another bear thank me for making him wear a uniform, I may well kill myself.

"I'm glad you like them. Hey would you ask Bobby to bring us some cocktails?"

"Righty-o." He scampered away.

Max lit the fireplace and poured himself a scotch to lubricate the grinding gears of his mind.

Hawk walked in ten minutes later. "Still can't sleep?"

Max squeezed his burning eyes, squishing cold tears into his eyelashes, then turned to smile at his blurry friend. "What's sleep?"

332

Bobby Bear came in with a tray of pink cocktails. Hawk accepted one and sat in one of the big leather chairs by the fire. "Some would say it's a might early to be drinking."

"Good thing we know better. And besides, you can't waste alcohol. It's disrespectful to the demons inside." He held out his tumbler and Hawk gave him clinkies.

Cat and Lucille stumbled in together. Cat's sleeping habits were feline, so she was just a bit groggy. Lucille, on the other hand, looked as though she might have just awoken from death. Her face was covered in red streaks and her eyelids were out of sync.

Max gestured to the chair beside him. "Hey, grab a seat."

Lucille groaned and rolled her head into glaring position. "What's so important you had to wake us up?"

He glanced at the grandfather clock. It was ten thirty in the morning.

"Sorry, I guess time's lost all meaning to me."

"Can we go back to bed?"

"In a minute. Since you're here why don't you have a drink?"

She scowled and snatched a drink off the tray, sloshing half of it onto the Persian rug.

Cat passed on the beverage and led her to the vacant chair. "Let's get this show on the road." Cat pulled down her skirt and flung her blouse into the fire.

"This isn't a sex meeting."

Cat removed her bra and, with one hand in the front and the other around the back, started masturbating.

Max knew nothing he could say would get her attention, so he continued. "This last month has been really nice."

Hawk scrunched up his face. "Are you dumping us?"

"No, of course not. Let me talk. The world is in better shape than I've ever seen it, you know, aside from all the rubble. But I have to wonder how long it'll be before Heller ruins it. He's still got all his connections and money. He's a terrible bastard and I think we should kill him at the party tomorrow."

Cat stopped masturbating. "Wait, what?"

"Heller's throwing a big shindig tomorrow night. I think we should sneak in and kill him and the rest of those evil shits before they find a way to fuck the world up again."

Hawk looked intrigued, but the girls were equally dumbfounded.

Lucille shifted into Indian style in her big leather chair. "I thought we decided that was behind us."

Max nodded. "Yeah, I changed my mind."

Cat narrowed her eyes. "That's stupid."

"He killed your father. You of all people—"

Lucille interrupted. "There are so many reasons not to do that." She counted them on her fingers. "Revenge is negative; it only perpetuates the cycle of violence. We could get killed or captured. Since He's a celebrated public figure now, killing him would make a lot of people hate us. I mean, I don't see any logical reason to risk our happiness to kill a guy who isn't currently a problem. He's already got all the money and power he can get. What do you think he's going to do?"

"It's the mindset that worries me. What good is all that money and power if you don't use it? And we're talking about a guy who brainwashes everybody he meets. He coats his houseguests with tiny robots that warn him when they have impure thoughts. Anybody that paranoid is going to do something stupid eventually."

Lucille rubbed some sleep out of her eye. "But evil is a hydra. A one-headed monster is a lot easier to deal with than a twelve-headed monster."

"That's why I want to kill the Council too."

"My point stands. Kill Heller and you have a twelve-headed monster; kill all of them and you have a free-for-all with every dick in the world."

"Maybe, but all those dicks are going to be eliminating each other."

"And taking a lot of innocents with them. World War I started because some rich fuckheads decided people were complacent and a nice war would remind them to stand up for their rights. You know how that worked out. Two wars, one depression, and about a hundred-million corpses later they had a culture where people didn't have the freedom to wear their hair the way they wanted. You know better than this."

Max stared at the goatskin rug at his feet. He hadn't expected this much pushback. "I don't know, maybe you're right. I mean, you're right. It's probably a stupid idea. Maybe Heller learned his lesson. Maybe he'll turn Heller House into a free theme park and spend his fortune providing ice cream and healthcare to the poor, but maybe he won't. If I'm right and we end up in another nightmare dystopia six months down the road, this is not an I-told-you-so I want to have to say. And really, I know it's stupid, but I miss questing. I need to kill something."

Lucille clenched her jaw.

Hawk's eyes gleamed in a way Max hadn't seen since before he was possessed. "You're both right. Heller's a threat, but killin' him ain't gonna do shit. Strategically, it's always better to neutralize a threat than kill an enemy, and I think I know a way we can do that."

He had everyone's attention.

"Hedorah just finished a prototype based on the Teleluvvie's ability to rewire brains."

Max shook his head and laughed sadly. "Just what the world needs, a handy-dandy tool to brainwash your friends."

Hawk smiled. "Oh, you'll love this. The invention is really just an app that uses the holographic screen on your phone."

"God, I hate science."

"Yeah, probably not something your average Joe should have on 'em all the time, but you gotta admit it's pretty neat. You just tell the app what sort of thing to get rid of and it does it. Quit smokin', quit cheatin', turn a jock into a nerd or an atheist into a true believer. So I'm pretty sure it can turn Heller into a good person."

"That's horrific." Lucille hunched forward and bit her pinky nail.

"How do you keep from brainwashing yourself?"

"Reading glasses. They warp the image just enough to make it harmless static."

"Can it make me think I'm a unicorn?"

Hawk grimaced and looked at Cat. "Not unless you want to be a dumb animal."

"Dumb animals seem happy."

Max asked, "You're not happy now?"

"Sure, I'm happy now, but I won't be when you get yourself killed. I'm planning for the future."

"I'm not going to get myself killed." He turned back to Hawk. "So you think we can sneak into the party, find Heller, wash all the evil selfish craziness from his brain, and get out without getting caught?"

"If we make him a good guy we won't have to worry about getting caught. If Hedorah says the thing works, it works. He's a lot of things, but foremost he's a scientist and scientists would rather eat their own kidneys than have their findings proved wrong. This party's all about PR, so Heller should be easy enough to find. That just leaves sneaking in undetected. There, I got nothin'. Your DNA's on file, so they'll know you're there before you get to the elevator."

"You can't neutralize the bugs?"

"Sure. I can knock out whatever electrical thingie-do you want, but they're gonna know something's up when their system goes dark."

"Good point." Max looked at Lucille.

"Why are you looking at me? I want nothing to do with this."

"Imagine this world the way it is right now, but with the richest, most powerful person being a benevolent benefactor instead of a malicious paranoiac. You told me Heller's probably not human and he doesn't age. Think about how long he could keep the world safe if he was a good guy."

Her expression softened and turned thoughtful.

Cat walked over to him and kicked his shin. "You said you wouldn't leave me again!"

"I'm not leaving. It's just a really important errand, and I want you to come too."

Cat smiled.

Lucille groaned. "I know I'm going to regret this, but I suppose I could change our sexes. That would be a reversible, but undetectable way to change our DNA. With the tricks I learned from Greystoke's books the change wouldn't take much time."

Cat's eyes bugged out. "Ooo, I wanna be a boy! You can call me Boomer, and I'm gonna ride a motorcycle and smoke tiny cigars out of long cigarette extenders so when I whip it out, people are gonna be all like, "Oh, that's what that means." And I want a face tattoo of a dragon." She pointed at Lucille. "I'm gonna call you Lucky and you're gonna be my scrappy Irish companion. You'll drink too much and cuss like a Frenchman, and you'll wear an old-timey detective hat so people know you have a dark past."

Max tuned her out and considered Lucille's proposal. It could work, and I have always been curious what it's like to be a girl.

He tried to think of a better option, but nothing came to mind. Cat was obviously on board, and Hawk looked over the moon.

"All right, fuck it. Sex changes all around. But no face tattoo."

Cat pointed at him, "Your name's Sparkletits, and you're gonna know your place, bitch."

# SPARKLETITS IN THE MANSION OF DOOM

Max had celebrated their plan with the weirdest sexual experience of his life. Now, they were in a rented limo on the way to infiltrate and brainwash the most powerful man in the world and all Max could think about was being double penetrated by her boyfriends while eating Hawk's pussy.

She tried to focus on programming the Tidier app, but the interface was designed for people who knew a lot about brain waves. It wouldn't have been an issue if Hawk hadn't let it slip that she was working with Max, stimulating Hedorah's vindictive twatiness and forcing them to hack his computer to get the program. There was no manual, so Max had to make do with the few scraps of memory she hadn't drunk away and a couple hours of internet research.

"I wonder if I could use this to make Hedorah likeable."

Hawk uncrossed her legs. "I sure as hell hope so. That's what we're supposed to be doing to Heller."

"We should swing by his place after we're done here."

Boomer whined, "You said we could have an ice cream party." He lowered his voice and got into character. "I mean, shut your dick trap Sparkletits. We're doin' my thing later."

"Fine, tomorrow then, but stop calling me Sparkletits. It makes me feel like a drag queen."

"I'll pass on the ice cream." Hawk ran her hands up the sides of her black silk gown and lifted her "bazooms" until they were bulging from the low-cut neck line. "I gotta watch my girlish figure."

Hawk looked better as a woman. A lot better.

Max's ghost boner made her feel queasy, but alive. "You going to switch back after this?"

"I don't know. I like it, but I won't know for sure 'til my first blood."

"I'm switching back before that becomes an issue, but if you want to stay a girl," Max smiled, "you won't hear any complaints from me."

The girls blushed and turned their heads. The boys had a peculiar knowing expression that rammed a jumbo fearcicle into her new lady parts. *What if they don't want to switch back, either? I'll be stepping in urine and picking ass hair out of my teeth for the rest of my life.*

Max frowned and looked out the window just as the Limo pulled onto Heller's street. It was weird seeing so many people in the park. They had a band playing in the Greek theater Heller had imported from the slopes of Mt. Parnassus. There were food tents and small rides set up wherever the trees permitted. If Max didn't know Heller, she might have bought into his propaganda about rebuilding the world.

Fucker's after pyramids.

She looked over the app once more and decided the commands were as good as they were going to get. It was supposed to remove bad memories and stimulate the mushy ones while attacking selfish and paranoid behavior patterns. She'd chosen to leave his IQ intact, thinking the world would be better off with a smart evil guy than a well-meaning idiot.

The limo stopped, and a black-suited thug opened the door. Max smiled and let him help her onto the red carpet. Boomer joined her and they strode arm in arm past the guards and paparazzi. Hawk and Lucky followed five steps behind them. They took the elevator to the penthouse and spread out in search of their target.

Boomer and Hawk went left to the lagoon, and Lucky went right to the statuary. Max was headed up the stairs to the orgy pit when he heard a familiar voice say, "Excuse me."

Max turned and saw Santo Montoya approaching her. He snatched two glasses of Champagne from a tray and offered one to her. Max smiled and accepted a glass.

"I am sorry to bother you." Santo gestured to the rose on his lapel. "I only wanted to show this flower how beautiful you are."

Max snickered. Bad jokes had always been a weakness, but this was the first time it had been a problem.

"Fuck me if I'm wrong, but isn't your name Bethany?"

Max shook his head, more at the line than the question.

"You are a model, aren't you? That's a very beautiful dress. It would look great on my floor."

Max was ready to stop being a woman. "Your face would look good in my toilet."

Santo leered. "Take me back to your place and we will see."

Max took a sip of Champagne then poured the rest over Santo's head.

"I see; you want to get me out of these wet clothes. You cannot wait for the sacrament of Santo Montoya."

"No. I am rejecting you. You are rejected. My grandmother could tell you're overcompensating. You make all men a little more pathetic simply by continuing to draw air. So fuck off, you tiny, desperate child." She turned and walked up the stairs.

"I have billions of dollars and a weak heart!"

Max looked straight ahead until she was on the second floor. The clothes check and orgy room doors were shut, but the goons in front of them implied they might open for the right people.

I guess Heller's being extra careful in case an average person gets in by mistake.

She kept walking, but felt conspicuous since there was hardly any traffic on the second floor. She noticed out the corner of her eye that Santo was still watching her.

Fuck! Why did I come up here? There's nothing but closed doors and an open view.

Thinking it was better to appear flustered than blow her cover, she quickly descended the stairs on the other side and ducked into the gallery. She grabbed another glass of Champagne and waited in the corner to see if Santo would pursue her.

A quick scan of the room revealed no familiar faces. When she was sure Santo wasn't coming, she opened the door and slipped into the hall.

Lucky jerked his face toward Max. He was on his knees using the sonic Lockpkr app on the first door to the left. "You scared the crap out of me."

"Sorry." She locked the door and joined him. "You know what's in there?"

"Something worth locking up."

"Or an occupied bathroom."

He smacked her in the shin with the back of his hand. "Shh, you're distracting me."

"Oww, fuck. No need to go all Ike Turner on me."

"Sorry, I'm not used to the muscles yet."

She nudged his butt with her foot. He turned angrily. "Why don't you try to open one of these others?"

"Not used to the testosterone, either." Max pulled out her phone and went to work on the next lock. She got hers open first, so Lucky joined her. They stepped into a storeroom full of kegs, cases of beer, and liquor. There was another door on the far side of the room, but nothing out of the ordinary.

They walked to the other door and listened. Hearing nothing, they opened it and saw a distillery. Twenty large metal vats lined the right wall. Hundreds of wooden barrels were stacked against the left and back walls.

Max raised her eyebrows. "Heller sure does like to party."

Lucky shook his head. "He only drinks to be seen drinking. All this is for his guests. If they're drunk, he has an added advantage when trying to manipulate them or gain information."

They noticed another door all but hidden behind a stack of barrels. Lucky grabbed the handle and smiled. "It's locked."

"It's probably where he keeps the good stuff. We're wasting our time here."

"There were five cases of Louis in that first room. I didn't think there was that much left." Lucky nodded at the locked door. "Whatever's in there is going to be interesting."

"All right. I thought we were here to find Heller, but if you want to do a dungeon crawl, I'm down." Max crouched and put her phone to work. What looked like a normal lock from the outside turned out to be a work of engineering genius. It used bits of every type of complex lock and more tiny moving pieces than his app could handle.

"I think you're right. He really doesn't want anybody getting in here."

Lucky pulled out his phone and concentrated on the top while Max worked on the bottom, but every time they had almost all the pins and discs in place, the first ones would snap back and they had to start over from scratch.

Max growled. "Goddammit! Should we kick it in?"

"No, that would be loud. Let me try something." He closed his eyes, rubbed his hands together and mumbled. When he opened them, his eyes had a faint blue glow. "There's a magic ward on this lock. Two, actually. One keeps it locked, and the other acts as an alarm system in case it is opened."

"Shit. Now I'm really curious."

Lucky pulled a straight razor out of his pocket and chanted in low froggish tones. He opened his shirt and sliced an x into his right breast in the spot he always wanted to be kissed. He pressed his palm to the wound then to the lock, leaving an x of blood. "That should do it. Let's try again."

It still took two phones to get it open, but this time the lock didn't fight them. They cracked the door, and the smell of chemicals wafted out. It was too dark to make out, but the lighted doorway reflected dimly in a series of large glass domes.

"Maybe this is where he grows his weed." Max switched to the flashlight app and shined it on the wall until he found the light switch. He flipped it on, turned around and saw three rows of large glass pods, each containing one naked child suspended upside down in pink liquid. Tubes ran from their heads and torsos into various collection devices.

"Well fuck me with a spoon."

Max walked up to the closest pod and stared into the grey sunken face of a little girl. Her eyelids fluttered, cracking just enough to convey that her childlike curiosity was still there.

"What the fuck is this?" Max turned to find Lucky pressed against the wall, tears streaming down his cheeks.

She rushed to him. "Hey, I know this is fucked, but I need you to stay focused."

Lucky blinked and looked at her like a dog who doesn't know how to convey what it needs. Max hugged him and let him cry a little more before pressing again. As each minute passed, the feeling they shouldn't be there grew stronger. Max was about to give up and drag him out when he finally spoke.

"Nectar." His voice came out sounding like the kids looked.

"Hm?"

"Nectar."

"Nectar? What does that mean?"

Lucky's face shivered. "You remember the day we met?"

"Yeah, by the lake. It was nice."

"You lay by the water, staring at the sky, drinking."

Max remembered the pink cocktail and how incredible it had made him feel, how young and happy. Max jerked his head toward the pods. "Oh." A wave of nausea bull-rushed his guts.

"Pink drink is children."

Max pulled him out the door and slammed both it and the door in her mind where bad things were bubbling up from the drains. I'm here to find and reprogram Heller. The reprogramming should stop this sort of atrocity. What's done is not worth worrying about. It's what we do that matters. Now say something reassuring to Lucky.

"This will all be fixed once Heller is a good guy."

Lucky nodded and stopped squeezing his hand so tightly.

Max snapped a picture and attached it to a text to Hawk and Cat. "Don't drink the nectar (pink stuff)!"

They walked around the barrels and were making their way toward the storeroom when Lucky cried out and shocked the shit out of Max's hand. Max felt a pinch in her back as Lucky fell, and every nerve in her body lit up like the console of a starship. When it stopped, she was on the floor. She felt hands on her then flickered and passed out.

✶✶✶✶✶

18 minutes earlier:

Hawk gritted her teeth as the woman's leg reared back then shot into Boomer's new junk. It hit so hard the pressure in the room dropped, sucking a gust of pain from the throat of every onlooker.

341

Boomer fell to his knees, whimpering. Tears played hopscotch in the handprints on his face.

Damn, shoulda seen this comin'. Somebody shoulda told him he can't get away with the shit he pulled when he was a girl. Too late now, and I can't help him without blowing my cover. Dumbass shoulda known better than to drop trow and slap a stranger on the ass with his flaccid cock.

Still, his innocence made the retaliations a painful and confusing thing to watch. The girl who'd kneed him looked ashamed, like she slapped a kid in public. Curious whispers blew through the room asking who he was, how he got there and whether he was mentally deficient or criminally insane.

It'd started the second they arrived in the bar. Boomer walked up to a lady in a red low-cut gown, said, "how bout dem apples", then swept her off her feet and kissed her right in front of her hubby. She'd slapped him, and the husband had made a scene before dragging her away.

That was three minutes and four sexual assaults ago.

Hawk hid behind a large Roman column and watched security drag Boomer to the elevator. Hopefully they'd just escort him off the property, but she half expected to have to rescue him on the way out.

It's probably for the best. Cat's everything you don't want in a covert operative. Crazy bitch didn't even last long enough for me to take advantage of the distraction. Probably best he's out of the way.

Hawk made her way around the bar, the balcony, and the restroom, mapping it all out in her head. She almost went in the men's' room by mistake, but a quick glance at his bazooms from an egressing male reminded him of his place.

The women's room stank worse than a fishmonger's socks. She dallied there for a few minutes, pretending to be on her phone while observing the bathroom habits of the rich and powerful. From what she could see, no amount of gilding was enough to make a toilet seat an acceptable place for a woman to park her ass. They treated the toilets like giant urinals, squatting with arms and legs jammed anywhere they could to get fifteen percent of the stream into the bowl. Hardly any of them closed the door.

She eventually pried herself away, crossed the bar, and went through the door on the far wall. It opened onto a long hall a long hall with marble floors that wore the rich red rug like a classy thong. There were doors every thirty feet. Most of the walls were covered with huge framed mirrors that made the hallway feel like a maze. He wondered what minotaurs might be hiding behind those doors.

Hawk respected Heller's mind-fucking skills. It was nice to have a worthy foe again, or any foe for that matter. She put on her reading glasses and readied her phone. Max had told her the far door was an arena, so she went to work on the others.

The first door on the right led to an empty Greek Bath. The well-worn marble was stained by centuries of feet, but the water was clear and bright. It looked nice, but for a fraction of the cost he could have had a Jacuzzi that size full of Cristal.

She shut that door and moved on. The air was getting noticeably warmer the farther she went, and there was a faint humming coming from further down. Its high, insistent tone thickened the air and tripped some ancient psychological alarm in her head.

She opened the next door anyway.

"Holy mother of Hell."

She closed the door on the puppet museum and moved on to the next.

"What's behind door number three?" She opened the door and saw another hallway and a shitload more doors. This one had portraits instead of mirrors, but was otherwise the same.

"I'll come back to you."

She skipped the arena and approached the door across from the hall. This was where the hum was coming from. She was sweating and slightly disoriented, which is probably why she turned the handle despite every inch of her gut telling her there was something incomprehensibly dangerous in there.

The hum and heat intensified as she carefully opened the door and peered into a small room filled with computers, or maybe just one big one. The hum was coming from hundreds of hard drives lining the walls, and processors laid into the racks every fifteen inches like jewels.

There were no people, so she opened the door all the way.

"The fuck is all this for?"

The machines were using so much electricity she could feel it fucking with the electromagnetic fields around the room. She was reminded of playing Pathburner as a kid when Jerry described the Pit of the Undead God. She couldn't do anything to it without attracting unwanted attention, so she moved on.

Her phone made the doink noise saying she received a text. Max had sent a picture of something she couldn't make out, and a message that didn't make sense.

Is this a code I've forgotten about, or is letting me know she's in danger? Maybe she's been drugged, or maybe it's autocorrect.

She responded, "Huh?"

She waited, but no response came.

"Shit monkeys."

She pulled up the finder app and saw Max and Lucky were 4,586 feet away and slowly getting farther.

Goddamn this place is big. No response means captured or under heavy scrutiny. Either way, I better move to intercept.

She ran down the hall, fell, cursed the inventor of high heels, got up, and checked Max's signal. She was moving away from the entrance. Hawk weighed the likelihood of her catching up with them if she went back through the party against the risk of traversing unknown territory under the assumption they would connect. She turned and clomped toward the second hall as quickly as she could without falling down.

These are about the most unfavorable conditions I can imagine; no intel, nowhere to hide, no reason to be here. Tidier's the only weapon I have, and I have to exit Finder to pull it up.

"Oh, and my battery's low. I just charged ya, ya piece of shit."

Best case scenario, they're gettin' a tour. I can say I got lost looking for the bathroom. Just about any other scenario ends with us getting caught. Great granny's folds, this was a stupid idea.

The app said she was still 2,581 feet away.

Goddamn this place is huge.

She took off her shoes and ran. There was no telling how many doors she passed, or what was behind them. A place can only have so many bathrooms and broom closets. Then it clicked that this was just one floor of a skyscraper and the skyscraper was just the part that stuck out of the ground.

She swooned, fell to her knees and vomited. The implications of that level of wealth, that level of power made her feel like a mouse with no legs trying to raid the cage of a viper. But Max needed her, maybe, and that maybe was enough to get her moving again.

Finder said Max was 436 feet ahead and a little to the left. Hawk sprinted to the next intersection, verified it was clear and snuck to the next. Max was right around the corner, so she closed Finder and opened Tidier.

Hawk's bad feeling got even worse. Why don't I hear nothing? Max ain't that stealthy. This is a goddamn trap.

She turned and ran face first into an opening door. She steadied herself and braced to dash, but the creak of opening doors was coming from all around her. She was surrounded before she could say wrinkled titties.

"Fuck."

Tasers came from all directions, clenching her into a full body Charlie horse and jerking the plug on her consciousness.

✶✶✶✶✶

Max came to, naked, in a one-man cell identical to the ones in Castle Greystoke. She sat up and glanced around. Her brain was pounding against the walls of her skull, and from the looks of things, it had a better chance of escape than she did.

"Lucy? I mean, Lucky?"

No answer came.

She stood and stared through the thick fiberglass window. The cells across from her were empty.

"Lucky!" She screamed as loud as she could, but her throat felt like it was stuffed with a crusty Shamwow.

The cells could be sound proofed.

She didn't want to think about the long list of other potential reasons for the lack of a response.

"Fuck. Fuck. Fuck. Fuck. Fuck. Fuck."

After a few minutes of pacing, she heard the whoosh of an automatic door.

Pressing herself against the left wall, she was able to see Hawk and Heller walking toward her, arm in arm.

She let out a little squeak of joy. "Fuck yeah! We win! Suck it evil."

Heller stepped in front of her cell with a big, waspy smile. He pulled Hawk's cell phone out of the pocket of his tux and wiggled it with his fingers. "Very ingenious. I must say, I'm impressed."

"I'm glad you like it. Let me out?"

Heller laughed. "It wouldn't have worked on me, of course."

Shit.

She looked at Hawk. The bitter squint of fear was gone from her eyes. She was looking around the room, her mouth hanging open in childish wonder.

Shit. Fuck. Shit. Goddamn dogfucking son of a shit-filled fish sucker.

"At least I don't think so. I don't suppose we'll ever know."

"Still evil, huh?"

Heller laughed again, this time with twenty percent more buzz. "Me? Evil? Don't be ludicrous. Evil implies the absence of good. Was it not good of me to let you walk away from our last meeting despite your being an immense pain?"

Max stuck out her tongue.

Heller smoothed his moustache with his little Tootsie Roll fingers. "I like your new look, also very clever, though I can't imagine what you thought trespassing in the orchard would accomplish."

Max gritted his teeth. She didn't know what she'd been thinking. Lucky was picking the lock and she went along with it like a fucking idiot. Maybe they'd been playing too many RPGs.

Max glanced at Hawk. "You reprogrammed my friend?"

"Yes, another example of my magnanimous nature. I cleared away all that fear and hatred, the scars of war, though I did leave the insecurity. I find that women with severe insecurity tend to be pleasers, and you always want your sex slaves to be pleasers. Her life will be much happier now that it's devoted to pleasure instead of killing."

"What about Lucky?"

Heller frowned. "Her inclusion was unfortunate. You see, I couldn't run the risk that her mental discipline would make her reprogramming fail. I couldn't put a powerful sorceress like that in a cage, and, if I let her go, she would make trouble for me one way or another."

"So she's dead?"

"Of course not. What a waste that would be. She is in the orchard, feeling no pain, I assure you. They are all dreaming sweetly."

I figured he'd be a fate-worse-than-death kind of guy.

Max ground her teeth and forced a smile. "And Cat?"

Heller smirked. "Oh, I see."

"What's that?"

"We didn't know who the fourth member of your party was. Now it all makes sense. Most of it, anyway." He paused for a moment to stare thoughtfully as his spats. "She didn't want to be left out, did she?"

Max nodded sadly. "Where is she—he?"

"He was thrown out shortly after you arrived for sexually assaulting my guests."

"Are you going to go after her?"

"No, I've always enjoyed Cat. I really am not the monster you think I am. I would have left you alone too, if you hadn't come after me. I had even considered allowing you to assume Vladimir's responsibilities in the thirteen. You would have had a short leash, of course, but as long as you were loyal you would have been very comfortable. You could have had everything, including my ear, but given this unprovoked attack..." He shook his head. "I'm forced to reconsider.

"I keep asking myself why you would do this. It's illogical, more emotional than I thought you capable of being. You didn't care for Vladimir, so this isn't revenge. You don't want anything from me. You aren't stupid enough to think getting rid of me will change anything."

Heller grinned wickedly. "You've become addicted to adventuring, haven't you? It often happens to great warriors."

Heller was acting friendly, even complimentary. He either wanted something from her, which wasn't likely since she had nothing to offer, or he knew beyond any shadow of a doubt he had won. She was his pet, and he was probably deciding whether to keep her as herself or reprogram her into a mindless fuck-tard like Hawk. She wasn't sure which would be worse.

Max sighed and went to lie down on the bed.

"I'm right, aren't I? You got bored. You wanted one more adrenaline fix."

"Yeah, maybe that had something to do with it, but all I wanted to do was make you a decent person. I don't give a shit about how much money or power you have. Go ahead, rule the world, but stop playing with it like it's a fucking board game."

Max sat up and looked him in the eyes. "You know what the really fucked up thing is? If I'd have run the program on you, you would have finally been happy. That hole you're trying to fill with power and money, marble and in-home dungeons, that thing behind your eyes that puffs up like a demon gorilla every time you feel challenged, that shit would be gone, but you'd still be you." Max waggled a finger at his cell. "I obviously lost, but so did you, because you're always going to be a twisted little shit that hates yourself more than anything else, which is saying a lot, because you hate everything."

A cruel smile twisted Heller's face. "What is the saying? Better to be Socrates dissatisfied than a pig satisfied. All the same, I hope you enjoy your stay." He turned to Hawk. "Hawk, come."

Max smiled and lay back. "See there? You're so insecure that you use brainwashing command words on your brainwashed sex slaves."

"Max, quiet."

Fuck.

They strolled languidly out of sight.

# PUFF THE MAGIC DRAGON

Boomer stood atop the McDougle's play-thing, staring over the crowd of multicolored critters who had come to help. They were *so cute!* He wanted to scoop them all up and stuff them into his mouth like Skattles. He could almost taste the furry trickle of rainbow in the back of his throat, but he made himself focus, for Max.

Cheeky fumed at his feet. He was mad because he'd wanted to rescue Max two days ago, but Boomer had got distracted when the new Unicorn Dance Party game came in the mail. Puff was antsy too, but she probably just wanted a chance to kill something.

Having so many friends made Boomer feel like the prom queen's tits. He couldn't count that high. As far as he could see, the street was a super-ultra-megapack of crayons, all for him to color justice on the faces of his enemies.

He cleared his throat and began his prepared speech. "The bad guys took our friends! It's been three days, so I don't think they're going to give them back. They're right over there in that big building." He pointed to Heller House. "Let's go get 'em!"

All her friends cheered and rushed toward their target like a splatter painting on a steep incline. Puff took flight, yowled and burst open. Nine razor-tipped tails shot out one end while nine long necks unfurled from the other. At the end of each neck was a different monstrous head, some with snapping jaws, others with mandibles or tentacles or great sucking spirals of needle-like fangs. Her middle blew up like a big scaly airbag. Puff stretched her powerful legs, roared, and took to the skies. She circled the restaurant, soaring on giant spike-tipped wings that sparkled like a virgin's fingernails in the pink light of dusk.

Boomer pumped his fist and screamed, "Hell yeah! Now, that's what I'm talkin' about. That's my dragon! Mine!" while Cheeky climbed his leg.

The diners inside the building shrank back from the windows and disappeared.

Puff circled one more time, then, with a gentleness unbecoming of a giant claw, snatched up Boomer and Cheeky and set them on her back. Boomer squealed with delight and hugged the central neck.

Cheeky's snorts of displeasure were lost to the wind. He put on a brave face and carefully transferred his suckers from skin to scale.

Puff's wings beat ever faster, bearing them toward the roof. As they soared past their motley army, Boomer wondered if it might have been better to meet a little closer to Heller House. They were running as fast as their stubby little legs would carry them, but they would have to run several blocks just to get to the park.

Oh well, too late now.

The trip barely took two minutes, and a lot of that was circling around the building gaining height. When they reached the top, Puff hovered about fifty feet above the roof while one of her heads coughed like it had a hairball. Twenty seconds later it wharfed up a melon-sized projectile, which fell onto the center of the Hellerpad and exploded, removing the top layer of tarmac and pushing the platform a few feet down. Another head let loose a focused sonic attack that pushed the platform down a little more. Then, as if Puff's patience had all been used up, the other seven heads unleashed their fury, spewing fire, lightning, acid, rays of light, and lasers, obliterating the platform and melting a hole through to the next level.

Puff dove through the hole and landed in the garage. Her heads pointed all directions looking for a victim. Boomer focused more than he ever had before and said the magic words Lucille had taught him. She'd said it worked on more than remote controls, and by golly it did.

He saw a faint glow in the distance and knew it was Heller. He pointed. "That way."

Puff roared up another bomb and wharfed a hole in the wall. They charged through the gallery and into the foyer just as the elevator opened its doors. Puff filled the little room with fire before the guards had a chance to raise their weapons. Their bullets exploded in their clips, ricocheting around them as they melted into a single glob of burnt meat.

More guards came running from the bar. The first wave dropped to their knees on the other side of the lagoon and raised their weapons. The second wave was close behind, but one glance from Puff's laser eyes and wave two crashed over wave one like a dump truck full of lunch meat overturned on the highway.

Puff hopped over the steaming mess and barreled through the bar. Boomer pointed at the door on the right wall and Puff sprayed a stream of black acid, which popped the door like a burning photograph and ate away a good bit of the wall on either side.

Heller was getting so bright it almost hurt to look at him.

"He's in that room, last one on the left."

Puff bounded down the hall. Heller's door opened, and someone stuck an assault rifle out emptying the clip without looking. Most of the bullets hit the wall to their right, but a few glanced off Puff like light rain off a bike helmet.

Puff stopped when another man pivoted around the corner with a grenade launcher.

The man smiled.

Puff jerked her central head forward.

The guard's confidence disappeared from his eyes. He looked confused, then sad. His eyes bulged with terror.

Heller screamed, "What the hell are you waiting for?"

The guard looked into the room then back at Puff.

Puff jerked her head again.

The guard stuffed his face into the barrel, pulled the trigger, and did his best impression of paint.

Boomer was drunk on destruction, yipping like a Chihuahua and grinding his erection into the meat of Puff's back.

The beast strode forward slowly, almost sadly.

A guard fell into the hall, dead from the shrapnel of his co-worker's bones. Two more emerged, firing to provide cover for Heller as he jogged through the door across the hall. Puff lurched forward and made slippers of their torsos. The rightmost head put a laser through Heller's Achilles heel. Torsion did the rest.

Heller screamed and crashed into a doorframe, splitting his forehead open. He spun, trying to sling himself into the room, but missed the handle and hit his face on the doorknob as he fell.

Boomer screamed, "Yee-fucking-haw." He planted a big kiss on the back of Puff's neck. "You are getting so many FÜD wrappers when we get home."

He and Cheeky dismounted and entered the hallway. Puff made an irritable noise similar to the one she made when she wasn't done playing, and spewed her disappointment into the computer room in the form of fire.

Boomer ran to Heller and landed with a knee to his stomach. Heller's response was colorful, chunky and deftly deflected by a well-timed punch.

"What did you do with my girlfriend?"

Heller's head lolled backward barely conscious.

"It's not naptime yet, motherfucker." He steadied Heller's head with one hand and slapped him repeatedly with the other until those weird little eyes rolled forward again.

He spoke slowly and forcefully. "Where is Max?"

Heller smirked and glanced at the pool of blood rapidly spreading around his right leg. He coughed, and his bloody front teeth flopped forward over his bottom lip. The resulting cringe snapped them the rest of the way and they tumbled down his smoking jacket like errant buttons. He tilted his head to the side and spat out a generous portion of blood. "I can't say I'm a fan of your new look." His speech was slurred by concussion and a half-severed tongue.

Boomer slapped him again. "What have you done with Max?"

"Poor girl, I'm afraid you are too late. Your friends are dead."

"Not the answer I was looking for." He punched him again.

"Your hitting me won't bring him back any more than your mercy would spare my life. Everything is quite out of order. What is that you rode in on, by the way? I must have one if I live through this."

Boomer grabbed Heller's ear, slammed his head into the doorframe, and commenced to sob.

Heller's head rested against the door. He was still conscious, but too weak to even wipe away the stream of red snot making its way over his little moustache and dripping into his mouth.

Cheeky slithered closer, removed Heller's right shoe and pulled away strip after strip of skin like he was picking bacon off a sandwich.

Heller didn't seem to notice.

Still sobbing, Boomer leaned in and bit off Heller's nose. He wasn't sure why. The nose was as unappetizing as it looked, but he chewed it up and swallowed it anyway. Heller stopped breathing.

"Fucking asshole!" He grabbed Heller's bottom jaw, ripped it loose and used it like brass knuckles. By the time he was done, everything was so mangled he could barely tell what was him and what was Heller.

He turned to find Cheeky crying as well. Tiny tears traced every fold in his face, down his chest and into the carpet. Boomer scooped him up and sobbed into his forehead. Seconds later he felt a weird pressure in his sinuses.

"We have to finish what we came to do."

Boomer looked around for the voice and noticed Cheeky's tongue was jammed up his nose. He tried to pull it out.

"Don't do that. It could kill you. This is how I communicate."

"What the hell, Cheeky? You can talk?"

"Max never mentioned that?"

"You can talk!" He gave him a big wet hug.

"As I was saying, Max wanted nothing more than to wipe away all traces of Heller from this world. I feel we should complete his mission by bringing this place to the ground as a warning to those who would seek to replace him."

Boomer glanced back at Puff, who was trying to sharpen her claws on the carpet and accidentally ripping marble tiles out of the floor. "Yeah, I think we can do that."

Cheeky removed his tongue.

Boomer picked him up and ran back to Puff.

"He killed them all. I want to break his house."

All nine heads smiled and gestured for them to climb onto her back. Once they were secure, Puff charged down the hall, through the bar and burst through the glass of the balcony. Boomer and Cheeky clung to him like frightened geckoes as they plunged straight down. The g-force threatened to rip off their arms, as well it might have if Puff hadn't leveled off to circle the building in a quick downward spiral. She landed gracefully in front of the newly arrived cavalry.

"Captain Braveheart reporting for duty, sir!"

Boomer dismounted and addressed his friends. "Hey, everybody, I have bad news. We were too late. My friends are dead."

The critters let loose a disappointed, "Awww."

"In the name of justice, we're gonna knock down this big symbol of meanie-ness, so you should all run back the way you came."

A little kid-thing asked, "But won't demolishing a building this size fill the city with harmful pollutants?"

"It'll be fine. Just get away and hold your shirt over your face."

"But—"

"Do it!"

They ran, screaming for the others to turn around.

Puff blasted the corner of the building with all of her heads. The façade dissolved quickly, but a large pillar remained. It took a while for her to blast all the way across, but eventually all that was left were four huge columns made of an extremely dense, clear material. Neither fire nor acid could melt them, and the bombs might as well have been water balloons. It wasn't until Puff focused all eighteen laser eyes on an individual pillar that progress was made. Puff rejoined Boomer and Cheeky and bade them climb onto her back.

The heads split, then split again, and seventy-two lasers slashed through the columns until the weight of greed and arrogance crushed the remaining supports. Puff took to the air as the largest building in the city, maybe the world, tipped over like a drunken toddler.

The cloud of debris washed over the city. Smoke poured from every window, as water rushed to drown the park. Boomer was sadder than he'd ever been, but he also felt like he had done something of value for the first time in his life. He had the distinct feeling that, wherever Max was, he was looking down and masturbating with pride.

# THE REINCARNATION OF MAXWELL

When the lights first went off, Max had experienced a brief hope like roman candles shooting out of her heart. When no one came, that light burned out. She assumed it had been caused by the earthquake, and that Heller would have everything up and running again soon. A few hours later she began to wonder.

Her tummy was growling, and the cold was clawing through her one thin blanket like an excited cat. In the silence and dark, her mind began to amuse itself with sounds and images, random at first, but eventually the fractals and space ships gave way to calmer, clearer images. He found himself in a field at sunup surrounded by picturesque apple trees. They fluttered their leaves in welcome.

"Hm, I'm male again." He picked an apple off the ground and took a bite. "Mmm, honeycrisp."

"That's your favorite, isn't it?" Ernie was lounging in the shade on the other side of the tree.

"You." Max ran, intending to punt his head across the field, but his foot went straight through and cracked his toes against the wood. He gasped and fell to his knees. "This is all your fault."

"You'll thank me later."

"Fuck no, I won't. What the hell is going on, anyway? Where am I?"

"You're wherever you want to be."

"The fuck does that mean? I want to be back at Castle Greystoke with a scotch in my hand and some part of Cat wrapped around my dick."

The haze of peat rose in the back of his throat, and he was back at home getting his knob slobbed in his favorite chair. Ernie sat in the chair opposite, watching intently through the fire reflected on his screen.

"Okay, thanks. We're still not cool, though."

Ernie laughed. "I didn't do that. You did."

"Am I lucid dreaming?"

"Not exactly. You are experiencing extreme hallucinations brought on by sensory deprivation."

"So you're not real?"

"Real is a made-up word that implies only shared experience has value. That word's as much of a mistake as *is*."

"God, I hate you."

"Well, it's good to be recognized, anyhow."

Dream-Cat disappeared.

Max took a sip of scotch before setting his glass on the side table. "Can you please tell me whatever it is you came to tell me without being cryptic or lapsing into pseudointellectual bullshit?"

Ernie leaned back, chuckling. "I just stopped by to say hello, drop off a casserole and such." He nodded to Greystoke's old desk. Max turned around and saw a big, clear baking dish full of cheese and something green.

His hunger outweighed his dignity. He ran over and spooned a generous portion onto a plate. It was orzo, broccoli and cheese with onion straws on top. "Goddamn, this is good. Is that honey chevre and cheddar?"

"You've served me well, so it seemed appropriate I should return the favor." The suit melted away, and in Ernie's place stood a pale vision of beauty with bright green eyes and long blue hair that curled at the tips, just above her shoulders. Her pinched, elven features were lightly freckled, and her complexion flickered between glowing and dead. She wore a tunic made of white lace embroidered in a pattern that looked like faces twisted by madness. "There's a little bit of camembert, too."

Max spoke through a mouthful of cheese. "I'm serving myself over here, and again you and me are not cool." He couldn't get the steaming mess into his mouth fast enough.

"We will be. For now, enjoy. You can be anywhere you can imagine; do anything you like."

"But in actuality I'm starving and suffocating inside a cell in the underground fortress of my enemy."

"If it makes you feel any better, Cat took revenge for you. Heller's death was humiliating and messy."

Max smiled. "Really?"

"Really."

"And why am I still down here?"

"She thinks you're dead, so she demolished Heller house as an anti-monument to your life."

"Have you corrected her yet?"

"No."

"Well, get on that."

"Nah."

"What the fuck do you mean, nah? Go tell her now!"

"It's your eternal curse to never know what's best for yourself."

"You fucking owe me. I did everything you wanted. I created a shit ton of chaos, and didn't manage to impose any order no matter how hard I tried."

"You could say the same for anybody."

"I got The Darkness out of your territory."

Ernie shrugged. "Yeh."

"You're going to leave me here to die?"

"It's that time. Death is the next phase of your evolution."

"You know what, fine. If it brings me one step closer to being able to wrap my hands around your neck and choke you like the chicken you are, bring it on."

Ernie stood, smiling. "They grow up so fast."

Max grabbed a large book off the desk and hurled it at her. It went straight through and landed in the fire.

"I'd best be off now. Know yourself, young one. Know yourself till your balls hurt." Ernie stepped into the fireplace and burned up like he was made of wadded paper.

"And you go drown in dog shit." Max was alone in the study. He took another bite of casserole on the way to his chair. When he was full, he set down his plate. "Cat! Lucille! Fuck it. Hawk! Scarlet! Addy! Thora! April!"

The room was soon full of naked women.

"I guess it could be worse. Diablo Swing Orchestra!" His favorite band appeared on the far side of the room, playing Balrog Boogie. Their drummer was missing, but Cheeky and Puff stood in for him and were doing an adequate job.

"Well, it sure beats cancer."

✶✶✶✶✶

Max and his friends had many adventures exploring alien worlds, leaving a trail of dead monsters and bodily fluids in their wake. He assumed he died at some point, since his adventures would have taken millennia, so he was a little surprised when the Grash monsters of Kuul'fhion faded, along with his friends and the ground beneath his feet.

Blackness pressed in around him, squeezing him upward until he emerged like toothpaste from the crooked bulb of a large green flower. He landed at the feet of a tall man with chiseled abs and a mighty chin.

The man offered a Lei with his robotic right hand. "Aloha! Welcome to Heaven."

Max raised an eyebrow. "Saint Peter?"

357

"No, that guy's made up. My name is Bruce."

Max accepted the loop of flowers, but didn't put it around his neck.

They stood on a hilltop covered in glowing pink grass. To his right was an ocean filled with specks of light. Looking closer, he could see individual instances washing over a shore of results. Despite his distance, he could see them all, each droplet forced forward by time to crash against each granule. He could focus on one, or comprehend the whole. The lights, ranging in size from small specks to large melons, would wash up on the shore only to be picked up and carried back by the next wave.

On his left stood a great golden city made of palaces that stretched on infinitely.

He looked at Bruce and asked. "If this is Heaven, where my bitches at?"

"Those bitches were all figments, little bits of your ego, which died along with your body. There's none of that artsy-fartsy subconscious bullshit here. Just good, old-fashioned, straightforward soul pussy."

"So you're telling me I just died?"

"Yep. But you didn't *just* die. You ascended. Welcome to godhood, Maxie."

"Godhood?"

"You are now an immortal being of pure energy, able to shape matter with your mind, create worlds, and seed them with life. But most of us like to keep to ourselves, enjoy the good life without all that responsibility."

"Okay, is this a common thing?"

"No. Only a handful of souls ascend from each creation. There are rules, complex criteria a soul has to meet. It's about the same as the way humans reproduce. Two-hundred-fifty million sperm for one egg."

"Sounds really inefficient. How did you do it?"

"Hell if I know. I got crapped out by a flower same as you, kid. Only nobody did me the favor of a welcome party." A cooler appeared at his feet. He pulled out two bombers, popped the tops and handed one to Max.

Max took a sip of the most sumptuous oatmeal stout he'd ever had. "Shit, this is good." There was no label. "What is it?"

"This is Heaven, friend. There aren't any brands. Food and drink just appear and taste amazing. Look, there's plenty of time for details later. For now, just enjoy yourself. Let's go party! What do you want to do first?"

"Any chance you know a bitch named Eris?"

"Don't tell me you're still mad about that. She's the reason you're here."

"All the same, I'm going to get her and her little roach too."

**To be continued in Chakra Kong part 3:
Death: or One Man's Epic Journey to the Center of the Peak of the Horizon of the Final Frontier**

# Appendix

# The Divine Disturbance

Also known as "the day everything happened at once", the Divine Disturbance was arguably the most significant event in the history of mankind. After countless failed attempts at comeback tours, the heavy metal band Poison Candy was tired of being underappreciated and decided to give up the charade. On April 12, 2148, in Bryant Park, they reverted to their alien form, melding into a giant glowing Heavy Metal god. The psychic energy released from their melding shot out over the world at just the right frequency to raise the consciousness of every human being to a state of enlightenment for about ten minutes. It also killed all the batteries.

Everyone experienced the entire circle of life simultaneously; giving birth, being born, dying, having sex as male and female, struggling—living every failure and achievement since the dawn of man all at once. Their perspectives were both detached and involved as though it was happening to them, but they were also seeing it happen from outside. Concepts having been freed from language were now capable of fitting together in layer after layer of dualistic truth and beauty in even the simplest of minds.

Many believe that Poison Candy is God come to Earth to free them from their muddle. Poison Candy knows better, but is happy to finally be appreciated. He sits on a giant throne in the center of Bryant Park, granting wishes to those who compliment his hair.

Of the Divine Disturbance's many bizarre side effects, perhaps the most puzzling were the sudden changes to human biology. About thirty percent of people experienced a genetic mutation that made them able to heal at an amazing rate. While studying cases where the wounds would have traditionally been fatal, doctors would occasionally find someone capable of surviving without functioning organs.

Scientists were unsure whether it was an evolutionary leap, a miracle, or a curse. People could still die, but regardless of whether they were recipients of the healing mutation, the dead would always reanimate as rotting nuisances with the IQ and personality of a Roomba. Extensive zombie studies were done, but the data stymied the world's greatest minds. All they could agree on was that these anomalies were somehow connected to the Divine Disturbance. A lot of rules changed that day, leaving mankind floundering in a spooky new reality-tunnel.

# Districts: Economy and Security

After the fall of the world's governments, all cities were divided into new economy-based corporate districts, each with its own security firm. K. Co. develops and manages middle-class areas known as K-Districts and provides security through their world famous K-Squads. Security for high-end I-Districts is seen to by I-Force (a division of IMD), and low-end S-Districts are seen to by Sav-Cops (a division of Sav-Mart).

S-Districts

Inhabitants of S-Districts are known as Savanians, taken from Sav-Mart, which manages the district. These are the poorest of America's districts and the most plentiful. They have service-based economies and provide unskilled labor to the other districts. The educational system ends at grade six, but successful Savanian families often send their children to K-Districts for further education.

Sav-Mart began as one man's vision of a friendly place to purchase almost anything at a good price and quickly grew into an untouchable financial juggernaut. By the time the major political and economic turmoil began, Sav-Mart was large enough that it not only weathered the series of global calamities, but it benefited, as sixty-seven percent of the population couldn't afford to shop anywhere else.

Crime is rampant in S-Districts because Sav-Cops are not paid enough to risk their lives in combat. Sav-Cops are more likely to run away than they are to help, but the consensus is that they are better than nothing. They are paid minimum wage, and wear basic blue uniforms. They service two-thirds of the population, but the only real perks to being a Sav-Cop are that they get to carry guns and, as long as they stay out of the way of other security firms, it is virtually impossible for them to get into trouble.

K-Districts

Inhabitants of K-Districts are known as Sonians, taken from the Soni Corporation (a subsidiary of K Co.), which is the prime manufacturer of the goods they sell. Sonians are middle class with a decent standard of living and their educational system has fourteen grades. The economy is based in research and development, but it also provides middle management to other districts.

Crime is rare in K-Districts. K-Squad offers dependable security at affordable prices to roughly twenty-five percent of the population. They have access to most modern weapons and surveillance equipment. Perks of belonging to K-Squad include above average pay, full benefits, the respect of the general populace and the potential to be purchased by I-Force.

At one time, K Co. was roughly on par with Sav-Mart in regards to prices, quality of service and products, but they were only a fraction of the size. A decade before the collapse of the government, K Co. was bought by a large Japanese conglomerate, which had recently been taken over by Kenji Sono, a notorious samurai enthusiast.

When the unemployment rate reached twenty-five percent, Mr. Sono used the desperation of the masses to leverage several unreasonable stipulations in K Co.'s employment contracts. One of these was the seppuku clause, an agreement that a member of K-Squad who failed to protect a client would have to commit ritualistic suicide to atone. Every new hire had to accept this condition to get the job. The seppuku clause encouraged faith in his product, which made him able to charge more and in turn pay more to the employees who could handle the job. Sono trademarked all reasonable variations of the seppuku clause. One year later he received a Nobel Peace Prize.

I-Districts

Inhabitants of I-Districts are generally referred to as Klipsch and have the highest standard of living in the country. Their name comes from the high-end electronics company Klipsch, because they are the only people who can afford their products. Unlike Savanians and Sonians, their name was foisted upon them by the lower classes. They refer to themselves simply as People.

People *are* the economy. They own and or run all the businesses and make all the decisions on how the other classes live. Their extravagant displays of wealth determine their place in the Klipsch hierarchy. Rather than an educational institution, every child is brought up with a small army of tutors who groom them for their roles as world leaders.

I-Districts are hardly managed, but what little management is needed is provided by IMD (a.k.a. International Monetary Divestures a.k.a. the Bank), a division of Macrosoft. In the early 2000s, IMD was the first bank declared too big to prosecute. Despite stealing, insider trading, money laundering, collusion with terrorists, and a long list of other major offenses, they were publicly acknowledged by several governments as being above the law. With their new power, IMD executed a series of schemes that ultimately led to their checkmate and acquisition of all the other banks. Ironically, several years later their software/communications provider, Macrosoft, shut down IMD's systems and transferred all its employees' funds into their own accounts. Macrosoft, now too big to prosecute, liquidated the bankers and replaced them with their own people. Business continued as usual.

I-Force offers air-tight security to the five percent of the population that can afford them. I-Districts have an average of two and a half officers per block. Their clients, tiny pockets of gated communities and high-end shops, are guarded by highly trained police equipped with body armor, machine guns, tanks, helicopters and every other state-of-the-art gadget money can buy. I-Force boasts five million officers worldwide (half as many as K-Squad).

Once purchased, an officer becomes the property of I-Force. Most live on-site in emergency facilities or surveillance plazas. Though technically slaves, desertion is nonexistent due to the work-hard-play-hard lifestyle. Officers have the option to retire after age sixty, but it rarely happens as the retirement package (a house in K-District with utilities paid and a monthly stipend of $2000) is unthinkable after prolonged exposure to Klipsch decadence. To keep their elite forces young and fit, I-Force officers are frequently ordered to take part in bare-handed death matches for the amusement of their owners. To decline an invitation to participate is grounds for immediate retirement, or worse, but most consider it an honor.

# Iiites

The Iiites (pronounced E-Ites) are a violent race of sewer-dwelling mutants who are notorious for committing random attacks of brutality on surface institutions. Many call them lobsters because of their disproportionately massive right arms. They are deeply entrenched in a long-term war with their nemesis the Riot Nrrds.

Many years ago, before the release of the Blacktooth chip, people played video games on what were known as consoles. These consoles were primitive computers, with which the player could communicate through use of a variety of handheld controllers. In the beginning these controllers were connected to the consoles by long cords, but over time they progressed to using lasers and eventually PANs.

One of the first groups to utilize this new technology was a Japanese gaming company by the name of Genki-Suki. In the early part of this century, Genki-Suki came out with a new platform called the Ii (pronounced E), which revolutionized the gaming industry. Despite the pronounced lack of quality games, it met with immediate success because of its unique controller system, consisting of two sticks, one for each hand. These sticks were covered in buttons and connected to the console by way of a primitive PAN. Unlike previous controllers, players now had to move their limbs while playing. The movements were more natural and easier for the elderly to learn than the previous button-only configuration, and within a year there was an Ii in one of every three homes in the world.

Not long after the system became successful, doctors discovered a new disease. Iiitis (pronounced E-I-tis) was caused by the jerking motions necessary to do well at the games. The symptoms were inflamed joints, carpal tunnel syndrome, and decimated cartilaginous tissue in the right arm followed by a sudden mutation of the muscle tissue, resulting in a disproportionately massive appendage. The number of reported cases increased dramatically as the systems began to break. Grandmothers frequently crushed their grandchildren to death while hugging or cradling them with their new gargantuan appendages. The children adapted much more easily, excelling in sports and other physical activities. Pets suffered enormous casualties.

What no one knew at the time was that the CIA had signed a contract with Genki-Suki's mother company, the Bakemono Corporation, to dispose of toxic waste left over from American nuclear power plants. When the shareholders' union got wind of the deal, they sent a representative to the C.E.O. with a note explaining their dissatisfaction and threatening him with removal should he not immediately find a way to sell the waste back at a considerable mark-up.

The Ii was the solution. They mass produced two-inch by four-inch canisters of toxic sludge for use as power supplies in the Ii and its controllers. After a while the lead electroplating came off the cartridges and they began to leak free radicals directly into the bloodstreams of the players. One third of Ii users died of an aggressive form of cancer. Another third were either immune or lucky enough to ditch their systems before they leaked. The last third adapted. Their bodies used the radiation as an evolutionary catalyst, metamorphosing frayed ligaments and torn muscle tissue into meaty hydraulic presses.

Those who proved to be immune quickly became envious of their handy-capable brothers. They were fine when the mutants were only flooding the hard labor market as ditch diggers and factory workers, but when they found a home in professional sports it had gone too far. They were sick and tired of watching their favorite teams taken over by mutants. It got to a point where a regular Joe with a fanny-pack full of steroids couldn't even join a junior-high Frisbee team.

"Lobster" became a common slur. Complaints were screamed, bills were passed, and segregation became the norm. Iiites lost their jobs. They were denied business loans, and what businesses they already had were boycotted. "Lobsters" were systematically ostracized as the racism grew successively more overt. Anyone who had a problem with that was dealt with swiftly and brutally.

Iiites were forced to band together in order to survive. Regular folks would never consider dating—much less fucking—a lobster, so Iiites were forced to interbreed. Iiitis was transferred to their offspring and soon the shadows were teeming with loblets. This new generation grew up seeing nothing but hatred and abuse from normals. Reverse racism turned militant when the new generation reached adolescence. Teen angst became guerilla warfare on normal society, and violence became commonplace.

With every generation the Iiites became stronger and more organized. Computers were stolen and used to host a multitude of blogs, anti-establishment forums, and chat rooms. They moved into the sewers and sucked bandwidth from the homes above. They popped out of manholes and dragged unsuspecting joggers underground for breakfast.

The Iiites were forced to educate themselves, which allowed them to disseminate large quantities of information without the hindrance of the public education system. Before long, Project

Prometheus* was put into action. This led to a much more intelligent race than their surface-dwelling counterparts, who were only taught enough to make them smart shoppers and good workers. Individualism and imagination flourished, creating a cultural renaissance from which developed a multitude of scientific advances and subsequently a higher standard of living.

The Iiite government consisted of two branches. Felix Mitton presided over the Iron Fist, which existed to spread disinformation and fear through terrorism. Xavier Mitton presided over the Meta-Intellectual Liberty Foundation, or M.I.L.F., which focuses on the advancement of the race. The Mitton's were genetically engineered to increase the qualities the Iiites found amiable. Hyper-intelligent, super-strong, and notoriously ugly, the Mitton brothers ruled from the shadows, hidden even from the Iiites by a veil of secrecy and misdirection. Using manipulation and underground explosives, they toppled the infrastructure of the world's governments, allowing hand-picked corporations to step in and supply relief while restructuring civilization to fit a more profitable and efficient paradigm.

Before the war these two agencies controlled every aspect of government above and below ground. Now, the Fist consists of a few dozen guards, and their only job is to protect Xavier and the high council. The Nrrds have been reduced to a single unit. Their leader, Maxwell Quick, has proven to be resourceful and merciless in battle. No one believes that he will stop at the Fist. The sewers are filed with the sounds of gnashing teeth as the Iiites wait to see how the final round is played and whether Xavier's secret weapon is everything it is rumored to be.

# Riot Nrrds

The Riot Nrrds, are a train wreck of punk ideology and classical nerdiness. In the 1980s the powers that be decided to lower the overall IQ of the masses. American pop culture presented stupidity as the new cool, and the youths of that time were grateful for an excuse to tune out, drop out of society, and spend their time getting turned on by an overdose of sex and drugs. Those who didn't buy in to the decline of western civilization were wedgied, swirlied, mocked, and beaten. Dubbed nerds, loonies, paranoids, radicals, revolutionaries, extremists, terrorists, conspiracy theorists, kooks, weirdos, fanatics, and a plethora of other hateful monikers, disenfranchised thinkers the world over grew tired of watching mankind dig its own grave.

Robert Schneider, an independent scientist, discovered the radioactive vials in the Ii while playing with his Geiger counter app at home. He blogged, posted on social networks, and sent messages to news outlets, but no one was listening. If they had, the systems could have been recalled long before the first mutation. But the masses were neither interested nor willing to admit how out-of-control governmental corruption had gotten. Even after the effects of the radiation became overwhelmingly obvious, people were commonly more focused on the negative ways Iiites were impacting their lives than making sure it never happened again.

While the Iiites were being persecuted for their differences in physiology, nerds were being persecuted for their differences in lifestyle and social awareness. Their calls to action were seen as pretentious, obnoxious and melodramatic. The combination of propaganda with the systematic eradication of free thought resulted in an environment where any logical discussion would inspire hatred and potentially violence in otherwise decent people.

The Nrrd revolution was born in a Starbucks on September 21st, 2128 when a political joke turned into a semantic argument between Laslow Huggins and an unknown normal (Normal is the term both Riot Nrrds and Iiites used to describe the sedated masses). The argument escalated into a full scale riot when several strangers chimed in with their opinions and the normal threw his tablet at one of them. Laslow was martyred in the riots, but remains today an icon of intellectualism and conviction.

Starbucks was selling WWLD memorabilia within the week. The following week WWLD was in all the stores, stamped on everything from coffee mugs to tramps. The coopting of the symbol of the downtrodden intellectual was the final straw. Some nerds took their rage to the streets, others to the web. Copycat riots sprang up all over the world as Nrrds stood up for the truth and demanded change. Formerly isolated intellectuals organized, forming a loose confederation of cabals united under a common symbol, the pilcrow. Soon a pilcrow tattoo was the only way to gain access to their meetings.

Using the recently formed mythology of Laslow as a prototype, Hubert Selby V created an ideological platform that united all the smaller groups under a single agenda; the overthrowing of the global elite and deprogramming of the masses. Despite their best efforts at waging an information war, the Iiites maintained the lead in the race for power. It was much easier to subjugate the masses than it was to free them, and the Iiites were no longer interested in playing fair.

After years of failing to reform the M.I.L.F. or prevent them from doing damage to Normals, the Riot Nrrds declared war. They enlisted Maxwell Quick, a man with no military experience or interest in anything but survival, to lead their militia into battle. Why they picked him is still unclear, but his victory stands as a testament to their intelligence.

After a brutal war resulting in the decimation of both sides Maxwell and a handful of shell-shocked geniuses eradicated The Fist and backed the M.I.L.F. into a corner. Their leader, Xavier Mitton, is rumored to have gone insane, and the Iiite high council is in chaos, but rumors of a secret weapon in the bowels of the Earth give the Iiites hope that they may still come out on top.

# The Order of the Owl

The Order of the Owl is a secret society masquerading as a publicity firm that's masquerading as a secret society. On the surface they are a group of silly men who enjoy representing their positions of power using camp. Their ridiculous appearance and the fact that their agendas come across as the sort of cheesy sleight of hand you would expect from a magician at a child's birthday party blinds people to the fact that their agendas are always accomplished.

"The Order was founded in 2084 by a group of prop comics, musicians, magicians, actors, and ventriloquists who all worked in the seedy underbelly of New York's entertainment industry. It started out as an idea that The Great Martini had one night when he was sucking down free drinks after a show with an improv group called Blackout. They were lamenting their bad luck and how it wasn't fair that they had been performing for so long without achieving success while others would do a couple of shows and suddenly be on the Late Show. He postulated that people in their position would be much more successful if they were to become organized. The news spread and soon every talentless hack in New York was working together to suppress the quality acts and promote the crap. They succeeded.

Members swore an oath to help their lodge brothers when and if they became successful. Eventually the entertainment community was so flooded with hacks that people started to think bad performances were a bold new style of comedy. People started laughing at jokes because they weren't funny and gauging a magician's abilities by how cliché his tricks were. People assumed the Owls were good since they were getting so many gigs. Eventually everyone forgot what good entertainment was and now anyone with real talent is considered a hack.

The Order made a deal with the thirteen families to forward their agenda of commercializing art completely. Everyone started writing jingles instead of songs and incorporating commercial art into their comedy. Now no one wants anything else.

# The Neo-Catholistic Church

Formerly a Christian religious sect known as Catholicism, the Neo-Catholistic Church is one of the largest and most powerful corporations in the world. The Catholic Church grew from a monotheistic religion based around the teachings of Jesus Christ, who they believed to be the son of God. Jesus preformed magic and taught his followers to reach their spiritual potential through love, forgiveness, experience of the divine, and the control of base instincts. One of the core beliefs was that humans have an energy body which is consigned to one of two places after death. Good Christians would go to a paradise called Heaven, and everyone else went to a very unpleasant place called Hell.

Those in power did not like Jesus' message of personal liberation, so they executed him. He could have used his magic to escape, but as a sacrifice to his father, he allowed himself to be nailed to a T-shaped piece of wood and put on display. In return, his father broke down the barrier between God and man, granting the repentant forgiveness for their sins without further sacrifice. Three days later Jesus rose from the dead, reassured his followers, and passed into the afterlife of his own volition.

After his departure, his disciples converted as many people as they could. Those followers would meet to talk about Jesus and his teachings. As their numbers grew, a complex hierarchy emerged to protect them and keep them organized. Their strategy of evangelism and adaptivity helped their religion to become one of the most widely practiced in the world.

As their power grew, so did their ambition. The Church launched a series of holy wars against Muslims, Pagans, Slavs, Orthodox Christians, Mongols, Hussites, Cathars and political enemies of the popes. Crusaders took vows and were granted all-inclusive spiritual pardons, allowing them to rape and murder the unfaithful as well as plunder their possessions.

In an effort to drive Muslims out of Europe, the Church launched Inquisitions, in which a government would prosecute Christians who publicly dissented from key doctrines of the Catholic Faith. Believing that the souls of those deemed to be heretics were in danger of being consigned to hell, the authorities used whatever means they considered necessary to make the sinner recant. Although the Church originally condoned these proceedings, abuses eventually forced the Pope to withdraw support.

In 2002, papal pedophilia got so out of hand that it was impossible to conceal. Officials of various Catholic dioceses were aware of some of the abusive priests, and shuffled them from parish to parish (sometimes after psychotherapy), sometimes allowing contact with children. A survey of the 10 largest U.S. dioceses found that 234 priests out of 25,616 had allegations of sexual abuse made against them in their careers.

In response, the United States Conference of Catholic Bishops initiated strict new guidelines for the protection of children in Catholic institutions. However, by this time the Catholic Church was associated with so many atrocities that it did little to stop their numbers from dwindling.

After many unsuccessful attempts to repair the Church's public image, Pope John Paul III looked objectively at the Church saw a massive not-for-profit organization made up mostly of homosexual atheists. The Church owned more than half of the world's land, art and wealth. They no longer needed a God to frighten the people into submission.

Two percent of the Church's wealth was spent on the largest ad campaign in history. They wanted to distance themselves from the Church that was known for torture, manipulation, hypocrisy, etc... Trillions went into market research. Among other things, they found that people are most likely to have positive associations with words ending in the letters 'ic'. After testing over five-thousand variations they settled on the name Catholistic.

Soon after the initial changes, they removed themselves one step further by staging another schism, in which the most respected clergy members split off in protest of the Catholistics' use of funds donated by their followers to improve their image. Neo-Catholisticism was so popular that no one noticed when regular Catholistics disappeared completely.

The Neo-Catholistics framed themselves as the world's biggest charity. Rather than alienating their followers who believed in a God, the shift of focus was sly and gradual. Severe dogma softened into cheery slogans. "God wants you to do good works" became "why should we need a God to make us help each other" and then simply "people helping people." "Birth control is against the will of God" became "the more people there are, the more helpers we have" and finally "the more the merrier." Perhaps their most inspired action was to make the Church "Cool" by coming out against chastity, and even going so far as to claim that it was a satanic conspiracy meant to limit the numbers of the papacy and drive them mad. Virtually the only thing that stayed the same was the Catholic tradition of ornate regalia and over-the-top showmanship.

Without the judgmental airs and religious dogma, the Church was free to accept tithes from atheists and members of other religions. Membership quadrupled in the first year. There were so many grand gestures of charity and good-will that no one noticed they were only using three percent of their income. Today, Pope Benny II is the best-loved TV personality in the world.

# The Baptastic Party

The Baptastic Party formed when the Republican political party officially merged with the Southern Baptist sect of Christianity. Originally, the American government feigned separation of church and state, making it necessary for politicians to pretend that their religious views were separate from their political views. No one believed them, but without laws limiting religious rights, it was impossible to keep them from manipulating politics to coincide with their religious beliefs. After the government fell there was no longer any reason to pretend they were separate.

Membership fell off steeply during the period of adjustment. They now function as a secret society, using the you-scratch-my-back-and-I'll-scratch-yours method of back-room manipulation to encourage laissez-faire consumerism, hinder other ideologies, and wage their war on abortion, gambling, gay marriage, and recreational drugs. Though they discuss morality ad nauseam, very little of it can be observed in their actions.

Inspired by the success of the Catholistic Church, they changed their name to the Baptastic Party. The name change was the final nail in their public image's coffin. At best the Baptastic Party was seen as an amusing anachronism, at worst a bunch of rich crackpots who hate everything enjoyable. Still, they strive to impose their religious beliefs on as many people as possible, in any way possible. Mostly they fund radical terrorist sects, but they have had some success in convincing a few prominent physicians to come out with an official stance that drugs, abortion, gambling, homosexuality and sex in general are all unhealthy practices.

# Jengists

Jengism is a construction-based religion focusing on the purification of the soul through the act of creation. In his book, *The Holy Manual of Structure,* Jim Jenga outlined the cycles of creation and destruction as apparent in nature and societies since the dawn of time, saying that anything that has structure must be built in some way and everything that has been built will someday collapse. Focusing on the beauty of the cycle rather than individual creations, it teaches that destruction and creation are the same holy act, because nothing can be created in a world that is already full.

Jengists believe that, since God is timeless, the amount of time any given thing exists is inconsequential. It is more important to create a wide variety of things than it is to keep them in working order. Life and death are inconsequential, because people are part of the natural cycle and therefore bound by its rules. Death is seen as a transformative gift from God, and an honor since that is God's way of saying you have achieved perfection. Jengists live for the day they will be transformed into something new.

People flocked to Jenga's new religion, happy to finally have a simple explanation for the meaning of life that could be observed in concrete terms. Blind faith was not required since the application of the scientific method could prove the principles of Jengism conclusively. Thousands of Jengist churches sprang up all over the world in parks, sports fields, and anywhere else with enough room.

Whereas most religions see church as a place to pray, sleep, and listen to their leader speak, Jengists show their devotion in a more corporeal fashion. Rather than choosing one or two times a week to meet, Jengist churches are open twenty-four hours a day seven days a week. To join a church, one must donate two thousand dollars to the building fund, which is used to buy large metal and wooden beams and pay for the construction equipment needed to put them in place.

Most churches begin as a four-level structure consisting of thirty-two beams stacked on top of each other to form an octagonal base. Once the base in completed, the congregation is free to add beams to the structure using any resource necessary. Since the structures are not meant to last, the builders do not bother with blueprints or nails. In fact, the only thing a Jengist is encouraged to do is stack the beams symmetrically so the balance can be maintained a little longer and provide more geometric possibilities. Once the building materials have all been used, they begin to create variations on their church by pulling beams out and inserting them or stacking them somewhere else in or on the structure. As building progresses, the structure becomes more unstable and eventually collapses, sending the builders on to glory. Those who are chosen by the structure are recorded in the Jengist Book of Saints.

# NAADP

The National Association for the Advancement of Dead People was founded almost immediately upon the appearance of the first zombie. Hipster activism had been growing in popularity ever since the collapse of the world government, but of all the mini-movements, the NAADP was the most prolific. This was probably due to the fact that so many people had seen their friends and family mistreated at the hands of fearful mobs during the initial confusion.

Since it was more or less a humanitarian effort, neo-hippie founder Teddy Ruxpin decided to take a less violent approach than most other special interest groups and teamed up with the budding Order of the Owl to create a fecund Media© campaign to manipulate the masses into acceptance of the deceased up-and-comers. No art-form was forsaken as the growing bohemian horde sank their tendrils into the minds of the public. In everything from prop comedy to major motion pictures, zombies were portrayed as innocent, harmless, and even friendly. Before long it was more common for a person to tell a cute story about a zombie than a scary one.

The efforts of the NAADP did little to reduce the instances of violence from or against zombies, but they were largely successful in creating an equilibrium in which zombies were allowed to mind their own business. Zombie legislation flip-flopped more frequently than abortion had in the past, but people's attention to the matter as well as anti-zombie violence began to dwindle on its own once people got used to them. Today the NAADP is unnecessary, but they continue to function due to generous donations from the grieving whose heart strings are easily plucked by their propaganda.

# The Cult of Abel

Many years ago a conceptual artist named Alan Abel formed a fake activist group and tried to convince the population that, "A nude horse is a rude horse." This group, The Society for Indecency to Naked Animals or SINA, strove to clothe every animal in the world. Despite the initial support of the religious right, SINA quickly died out when it was exposed as a hoax.

Many years later Bob Crane, the Pastor of a small church in Athens, ran across an old pamphlet and heard the call of the lord. He quickly introduced his new philosophy to his parishioners and stoked the fires of controversy with weekly protests in dog parks, pet shops, and outside theaters, which were currently showing children's films featuring exhibitionist animals. As of March 5, 2125, eight states have adopted ordinances regarding nude animals. The Cult of Abel continues to harass, lobby, and threaten any and all supporters of animal nudity.

# PITA-4



The second most radical PITA organization, PITA-4 defends their furry brethren by promoting cannibalism among humans. Their logic is that there are too many people already, and the ones who victimize the helpless creatures of the world deserve to be shown how it feels to be rationalized onto a plate. Oddly enough, none of their members have ever been arrested. The police turn a blind eye and the rest of society tolerates them because of their remarkably ingenuitive ad campaigns. On average, four of the top ten hits at any given time are written by PITA-4, and their contributions to film and art are only rivaled by the NAADP.

# Igor Stanislavski Commemorative Park

Founded in 2016 to honor the sole survivor of a survivalist cult who had lived for a year and a half trapped underground after an earthquake had crushed the exits of his subterranean compound, the Igor Stanislavski Commemorative Park has retained its name despite a multitude of bizarre events. The controversy started when it came to light that Stanislavski had not only survived by cannibalizing his followers, but he had actually planned on doing so from the beginning. Mayor Earnest "Stay the Course" Pickle, who had confused Stanislavski's name with his lover's favorite composer when shown a list of park-sounding names, refused to admit his mistake even when it threatened to end his career. Luckily, this was the kind of move that had endeared him to the public to begin with. He kept his job and the park kept its name, but it soon lost funding.

A sympathetic Japanese suicide cult stepped in and turned it into a kaiyū-shiki homage to Stanislavski where bonsai trees were shaped into artistic representations of major events from his life. After the cult committed suicide there by impaling themselves on long spikes that lined the sidewalk, the Park was once again without funding. With no one to maintain it for over a year, its beauty gave way to vagrancy and violence.

It was unexpectedly snatched from the jaws of urban sprawl by PITA-4, which was only recently coming into its own thanks to donations from the eccentric heir to the Hershey fortune. Ironically, PITA-4 was unaware of the park's historical link to cannibalism. They bought it at a pittance to use for promotional barbeques and yearly muzik festivals.

When not in use by PITA-4, ISCP became a prominent dog park. When the Cult of Abel heard about the takeover, they decided it would be highly effective to establish a permanent presence and spread their message in what they considered the most belligerent and vital public sector. Soon after they put their plan into action PITA-4 heard of their animal oppressive proselytizing and decided to put a stop to it.

Push came to shove and soon the Pet Wars* were under way. After the war, repairs were made and people returned, but most left their pets at home. Today, the Igor Stanislavski Commemorative Park is considered a national treasure and a symbol of human perseverance in the face of unimaginable circumstances.

# The Pet Wars

Though little known outside of Southern California, hundreds died on either side as PITA-4 faced off against the Cult of Abel in one of the most brutal conflicts in recent history. PITA-4, a cannibalistic sect of fanatical animal rights activists, had purchased and restored the Igor Stanislavski Commemorative Park only a few months prior to the invasion by the Cult of Abel. The Cult had chosen the newly founded dog park as their base of operations in the war to ban animal nudity. PITA-4 considered the clothing of animals to be cruel and ridiculous, so they barred the Cult from the premises.

In the beginning, fighting was primitive, with rocks and sticks as the primary weapons, but both sides adopted progressively more effective tactics as the battles escalated into war. PITA members were trained to conceal themselves in the trees and drop like silent tornados of steel at the first sign of Cultist presence. As a warning, the skins of fallen Cultists were fashioned into ornate clothing and placed on animal statues throughout the garden. Cultists then brought in heavy artillery, which damaged the park to the extent that no one wanted to go there anymore.

Since the fighting never spilled over into the surrounding area, no one paid much attention. Those who did viewed it as a good thing since two groups of fanatics were killing each other off. Eventually the war ended the same way as any other; both sides were losing too much money and too many converts to make it worth their while. A truce was established, and the Cult was allowed on the premises three times a week with no repercussions. The public has learned not to go on a Monday, Wednesday, or Friday.

# Cheekworm

A cheekworm is about as long as a grown man's arm and a little thicker. Their name comes from the fatty lumps which cover their bodies, which resemble the ruddy cheeks of babies. A new cheekworm can grow from even a tiny sliver cut from another. They are very sweet to their masters, but are extremely jealous and fiercely territorial. A mad cheekworm is very dangerous. Although soft to the touch, the two-inch layer of fat is just enough to conceal the four inches of muscle underneath. They have strong suckers running along the bottom of their bodies which are roughly ten times as powerful as any other cephalopod. A mad cheekworm can tear an alligator's hide like tissue paper. The only way to calm a pissed-off cheekworm is to gently hum polka music while blinking repeatedly to communicate your submission. Even then, the cheekworm may only pause before rending you asunder, depending on how mad it is.

# Bio-Bed

The Bio-Bed is one of Bio-Corp's greatest achievements. When Dr. Gus Mengela was a child, he observed that there was nothing softer than a big fat cat. As an adult working for Bio-Corp., he tinkered with feline DNA in his spare time and eventually perfected the Bio-Bed. He started by combining the DNA of housecats and kangaroos and expanding the marsupial pouch all the way to the creature's sides to make a natural hcatcd blanket. He then removed the genetic codes for limbs and bones so they would be born quadriplegic and unable to roll over onto their owners. Next he adjusted the metabolic rate so they would grow to be ten feet long and eight feet wide with a sleep radius of seven by eight feet. They were made hypoallergenic, and shedding was reduced to ten hairs per day. They were given an array of modified dopamine glands to keep them in a state of perpetual bliss. The end result was a huge lump of furry fat, which purrs its owner to sleep.

Bio-Beds are cheap to grow and easy to maintain. They rarely have to be replaced, and upkeep is as simple as changing out the convenient IN and OUT bags once a week. The IN bag is an IV filled with nutrients and sedatives. The OUT bag collects the waste. Best of all, they grow at the perfect rate to complement the growth of a human. A child can be given a Baby-Bio and it will grow along with them. Mattresses or dead beds are obsolete and rarely seen outside of low-income guest rooms and prisons.

# Project Prometheus

Citing the high probability of a group of children being forced to live underground devolving into a race of violent uneducated monsters, a doctor unfortunately named Hugh Gasol was able to convince Iiite parents to send their children to a separate educational facility where he promised to use any means at his disposal to save them from their hopeless future. Rather than hiring teachers, he recruited specialists in every available field and allowed the students to choose the courses that most appealed to them. He designed a tiered reward system in which good test scores earned prizes.

Grade 1:
A- candy bag – big plush
B- choco-pop – medium plush
C- starlight mint – small plush
D- nothing

Grade 2:
A- candy bag deluxe – big toy
B- candy bag –medium toy
C- piece of candy – small toy
D- nothing

Grade 3:
A- slice of cake - board game
B- snack cake – large toy
C- piece of candy – medium toy
D- nothing

Grade 4:
A- favorite dessert - computer game C
B-slice of cake or pie – board game
C-snack cake – large toy
D- nothing

Grade 5:
A- favorite meal- accessory D - computer game B
B- favorite dessert – computer game A
C-slice of cake or pie – board game
D- nothing

Grade 6:

A- favorite meal – accessory C– computer game A - lingerie catalogue

B- favorite dessert- computer game B

C- slice of cake or pie – board game

D- nothing


Grade 7:

A- favorite meal –accessory B– computer game A - or pornographic magazine C

B- favorite dessert – game time- accessory C

C- slice of cake or pie – board game time

D- Lose a class


Grade 8:

A- favorite meal – new accessory B – computer game A – pornographic magazine A

B- favorite dessert – accessory C – game time – lingerie catalogue

C- slice of cake or pie – board game time

D- Lose a class


Grade 9:

A - favorite meal – new accessory A – computer game A – pornographic video B

B - favorite dessert – new accessory B – game time – pornographic magazine A

C - dessert

D – Lose a class


Grade 10:

A- favorite meal – new accessory A – computer game A – Pornographic video A

B- favorite dessert – new accessory B – game time – pornographic magazine A

C- dessert

D- lose a class


Grade 10:

A- favorite meal – new accessory A – computer game A– stripper

B- favorite dessert – new accessory B – game time B – pornographic magazine A

C- dessert

D- lose a class

Grade 11:
A- favorite meal – new accessory A– game time A– sexual encounter B
B- favorite dessert – new accessory B – game time B– pornographic video B
C- dessert
D- lose a class

Grade 12:
A- favorite meal – new accessory A– game time A– sexual encounter A
B- favorite dessert – new accessory B– game time A– pornographic video A
C- dessert
D- lose a class

Students who worked the hardest also played the hardest, which conditioned them to associate being cool with doing well in class. Since more courses meant more rewards, students wanted to take as many courses as possible.

The children's knowledge grew at a remarkable rate. By the time the second generation was graduating the first had developed better ways of teaching. Inventions became more common than acne. Breakthroughs in genetic engineering yielded smarter and smarter children who went on to learn more, faster. IQ and information transfer methods doubled with every subsequent generation. Classes evolved from time with a teacher to subconscious info-dumps. Instead of standardized tests, students were given actual real-world problems to solve and graded on the ingenuity, effectiveness, and efficiency of their solution.

Though hugely successful, the program didn't work for everyone. In utero modifications did not always take. Occasionally children would be born with normal levels of intelligence and heightened Endocrine production, making it extremely difficult for them to function in the educational system. Typically, by third grade these unfortunates had become so violent and distracting to their fellow students that they had to be removed to a special ROTC class where they learned to defend their homes and acquire the things they needed from the surface. The ROTC class eventually grew into the

Iron Fist and the rest formed the Meta-Intellectual Liberty Foundation.

# Victory

Developed by Adhra Duke, Victory is a designer mind-control drug which combines the worst elements of cocaine, crystal meth, heroin, PCP and pure adrenaline to create a highly addictive, high-biological impact drug that is indistinguishable from regular ecstasy. A sort of conditioner catalyst, Victory tunes the decision-making parts of the brain to be ultra-susceptible to suggestion. The speaker's voice, entering the brain at a time of such extreme pleasure, will destroy associations that contradict it by hardwiring whatever is said to be associated with pleasure. It wrings out the dopamine gland so that the user won't notice the damage being done to their basal ganglia.

# Füd

Just before the collapse of the world's governments, The U.N. passed a law that required all non-nutritional foodstuffs to be labeled as FÜD. This was part of a health initiative to point out the amount of high-fat-low-nutrition garbage that the masses were consuming. Overall, it was considered a joke. The masses didn't care what they were eating as long as it tasted good. A hand gesture denoting the umlaut became a popular pop-culture joke, making the term so popular that it stuck around even after the law was defunct.

# Scrap Cookers

Designed by Bio-Corp, the Scrap Cooker (better known as the crap cooker) was the perfect solution to the problem of waste disposal in a post-governmental society. The landfills were getting full. Recycling was time consuming and frequently created more pollution than it prevented, so Dr. Gustav Mulagatani designed a machine that would solve all the waste issues.

How they work: A person with items they would like to get rid of will open the door and place the objects on the disposal platform. With the door closed and fee paid, the objects are incinerated by jets of compressed gas. The smoke and ash are then sucked through a series of liquid filters which reclaim useful substances and compress the rest into sheets of light non-toxic waste which is spooled and resold as packing material.

Coin operated waste disposal units are cheap to franchise and easy to transport, which is why they are considered the greatest hope for Savanians who want to move up in the world. They are available in a range of shapes and sizes. The most popular are about the size of a vending machine and dispose of objects up to 25" square. They cost around $20.00 a day to rent and $1.00 to use.

# Fnordian Necklace

A Fnordian Wave transmitter invented by Dr. Emma Pond, the Fnordian Necklace cloaks the wearer by creating an EM field around them that emits an ultra-low frequency the human brain is incapable of interpreting. The brain immediately tries to regain its bearings by focusing on something that it can understand, so onlookers are overtaken by the urge to look at anything else.

The Fnordian Necklace works at any distance. From far away the wearer is simply camouflaged as the viewer's brain edits the wearer out of the picture. Up close, it inspires a strong urge to look away and nausea in those who don't. The wearer is protected from its effects because they are within the electromagnetic bubble.

# Super House

In 2118, medicine and the human libido finally managed to bring the human population to critical mass. People continued being born, but there was simply nowhere to put them. Human rights groups kept euthanasia and eugenics at bay at the expense of the majority of the forests. With 21 billion people and only 10 billion jobs, something had to be done.

Heinrich Pooperhaus was a McDougles fry cook living in a three-bedroom house with his wife and 56 of his relatives when he came up with the Super House. The idea came to him as he was stocking dry storage. "Why not apply the same principal to people?"

Heinrich took his idea to the Mayor, and the Super House was born. The Super House occupies one city block and houses up to 10,000 people. The building is supported by its many columns of bunk beds. Each floor has a 75' square common area in the center surrounded by public restrooms. The rest is sleeping quarters, enclosed 4 X 5 X 9 bunks stacked six high per floor. Each bunk has its own tab-dock, electric blanket, and cooling mattress. Walls can be easily added or taken away to offer varying levels of privacy.

Soon after Super Houses sprang up all across the planet, the roach-flu wiped out half the world's population. Real Estate prices plummeted, and there was wiggle-room once again. Super Houses are still in use today, but only by the extremely poor.

# McRoads

When the U.S. government collapsed, and many of the services Americans had taken for granted were no longer being seen to, it became apparent that they weren't as useless as everyone thought. The McDougles Corp. stepped in to maintain the roadways, hence the term McRoad.

Whenever a road was in need of serious repair, McDougles would build a restaurant on it with drive-thru as a toll station. These stations offered items spanning the entire Associated Foods family of restaurants: readymade pizza, burgers, tacos, and everything man has ever thought to fry. The public loved the convenience.

There were a few hiccups in the beginning that might have lost them their support if there had been another option. Over time, roads were rerouted and obstructed to route as many drivers as possible through the toll stations, which led to problems in areas with heavy traffic flow. The best example of this was McHwy 42, where the toll station was built two blocks after four lanes narrowed to two. The resulting bottleneck became known as McDonner Pass, because even if you weren't hungry when you entered the line you'd be ready to eat the drivers in front of you by the time you got out. Today, great care is taken to keep drive times from getting out of hand.

Rather than paying a regular toll, drivers could order anything on the menu, just so long as they bought something. Seven out of ten drivers opted to purchase their next meal, doubling McDougles' net worth in the first six months.

# New York City

New York City is the only sovereign nation within the borders of the former U.S. The syndicate was regulating everything there without the government's help, so while society was collapsing everywhere else it was just an average day for New Yorkers. They formed trade agreements with the Iiites and corporations coming to power, but took every precaution to ensure their independence.

This all changed after the Divine Disturbance.* New York City was ground zero for POISON CANDY's, reformation. The effects lasted longer and their proximity to "God" made it harder to forget. The syndicate couldn't compete with the developing theocracy, as most of their soldiers converted into Metists. The heretics who wanted to maintain their positions worked with the Metists to make New York City a holy utopia for the devout. Bryant Park is designated a permanent party zone, recreational drugs are free to citizens, and the only law is "to rock."

NYC quickly became the number one exporter of leather clothing, spandex clothing, glitter, glam metal, pyrotechnic displays, electric guitars, demon-porn, and hairspray, but the majority of their GDP is spent importing cocaine. Work is being done on a massive greenhouse called the coca dome, but progress is slow due to the number of on-the-job accidents. There is a hole in the ozone layer directly above NYC that grows at twice the rate of any other, making it warm there year round. Projections say that in a few more years it will be hot enough they won't need the greenhouse anymore.

If the ozone continues to deplete at the current rate, the earth will be completely underwater within a decade and a burnt-out husk in fifty years. New Yorkers are having too much fun to care, but the rest of the world is teeming with conspiracy theories. Some say that "God" is actually an alien who is terraforming earth for his kind. Savmart, being a "green" company, has threatened them with war, but nobody thinks they will act on it, because S-districts are the number one importer of New York goods.

# ABOUT THE AUTHOR

S.T. Gulik is a magical cockroach.

He started his life as a common wood roach in 1681, living in a small castle outside of Dublin. One day, a human alchemist blew himself up while trying to brew the elixir of life. S.T. survived the blast, but the fumes cursed him with self-awareness and immortality. A lot has happened in three-hundred-thirty-five years. Everyone he knew and loved has died. Vampire movies make him cry.

On the up side, he's had countless adventures and learned many things. He worked for the goddess of chaos for one-hundred-twenty-three years. About thirty years ago she turned him human and disappeared, which is fine because humans are smart and likable.

Oh, and he writes absurdist fiction. That's important. Gotta mention that.

Discover more at Sausage-Press.com.

Read more S.T. Gulik:
Muffy or a Transmigration of Selves
Dead Bait 3
Killpoet Issue 9
Pussy
Dolphin Cock Massacre
The Final Draft
Birth or The Exquisite Sound of One Hand Falling Off a Turnip Truck

Stalk me:
Facebook (Stephen Gulik)
Google+ (S.T. Gulik)
Twitter (@stgulik)

Need some Karma? Paypal fnord33@sausage-press.com literally any amount of money. This is a great option for people who read this book for free, but don't want the author to starve.

www.ingramcontent.com/pod-product-compliance
Lightning Source LLC
Chambersburg PA
CBHW070744120726
47910CB00001B/161